Alexandra Raife has lived abroad in many countries and worked at a variety of jobs, including a six-year commission in the RAF and many years co-running a Highland hotel. She lives in Perthshire. She is the author of four previous novels, *Drumveyn*, *The Larach*, *Grianan* and *Belonging* all of which have been richly praised:

Praise for Alexandra Raife:

'[*Belonging*] has all the emotions … we have come to expect from Alexandra Raife's characters'
Woman's Weekly

'An absorbing story with a perfectly painted background' *Financial Times*

'A love story with an unconventional twist and a very readable novel' *The Times*

'The power of a natural-born storyteller' *The Lady*

'A welcome new storyteller' Rosamunde Pilcher

'A real find … the genuine storyteller's flair'
Mary Stewart

'*Drumveyn* had me hooked from the first page. A delightful book which I enjoyed enormously'
Barbara Erskine

'Warm, friendly, involving … lovely' Reay Tannahill

Also by Alexandra Raife

Drumveyn
The Larach
Grianan
Belonging

Sun on Snow

Alexandra Raife

CORONET BOOKS

Hodder & Stoughton

Copyright © 1999 Alexandra Raife

The right of Alexandra Raife to be identified as the Author of
the Work has been asserted by her in accordance with the
Copyright, Designs and Patents Act 1988.

First published in Great Britain in 1999
by Hodder and Stoughton
First published in paperback in 2000
by Hodder and Stoughton
A division of Hodder Headline

A Coronet Paperback

10 9 8 7 6 5 4 3 2

A CIP catalogue record for this title is available
from the British Library.

ISBN 0 340 73832 4

Printed and bound in Great Britain by
Mackays of Chatham PLC, Chatham, Kent

Hodder and Stoughton
A division of Hodder Headline
338 Euston Road
London NW1 3BH

For Hannah

Chapter One

Max replaced the receiver and with a small explosive sound of defeated irritation swivelled his chair away from the laden desk. He ran his fingers through his hair and linked his hands behind his head, leaning back against the worn curve of leather to stare unseeingly across the cluttered estate room. The light of the single lamp angled onto the desk caught only the lean jaw, the slight hook of the nose, the high forehead where the light hair had fallen forward again. The rest of his face, lined and tired, looking older than his thirty-four years, was in shadow.

He had said he would let Jeremy know the answer when he had talked to the family, but he knew there was no decision to make, no choice. Jeremy would know that too. Or at least he would assume, as he had assumed for the last seven years, that Allt Farr and everyone and everything in it were at his disposal, no matter what difficulties he had been dragged into by his own fecklessness.

Max cursed with exasperation in the quiet dimly-lit room, the silence of the big house stretching beyond it, and beyond that the frost-stilled silence of the glen on a bitter January night. His mother, whatever tart opinions she might express about Jeremy, however forcefully she might protest about this invasion into their lives, would accept the obligation without question for reasons only she and Max understood. His sisters would between them range through dismay, concern, dutiful acceptance and a genuine willingness to help. Neither of them, however, would seriously condemn Jeremy, who to give him his due hadn't ever asked them to take in one of his cast-off girlfriends before.

Oh, God, do I have to go through all this tonight, Max thought wearily, swinging back to the desk to slam shut drawers and leave in some order the returns he had been slogging through when the phone rang. Harriet would make such a meal of it and ask so many inane questions, and though Joanna would be anxious to help her vague sweetness could be as annoying as her elder sister's fussing. His mother's comments would probably be rewarding though. A faint grin lightened his grim expression at the prospect.

It was all arranged with great speed. For the household at Allt Farr, if they were going to have to do this, a few days either way would make no difference. For Jeremy, sweeping the uncomfortable business under the carpet and getting back to ordinary life without delay was the prime motive. While Kate herself, on whom the crisis and discussions and decisions centred, was impelled to flight by an urgency which had left no room for doubt or even ordinary speculation about what lay ahead.

Out of the climbing swaying darkness, scarcely pricked by lights, where rocky tree-hung cliffs swung perilously close and deep rushing gorges opened almost under its wheels, the train slid at last to a halt. It was fortunate that Kate was already at the door, bags in hand. She barely had time to step down, it seemed for ever, her foot skidding on frozen snow, an icy wind in one instant shredding the warmth of the train to shivering misery, before the long train was pulling away again.

No one else had got out. For a moment of pure panic she thought she had made a mistake, that this wasn't a station at all. That must be why she had had to step down so surprisingly far, why there was no one else to be seen, why, as she now realised, there were no lights of a town. What had she done? Then she pulled herself together. Dim as they were, these were platform lights. By the hazy glow of the nearest she could see the top two-thirds of the word MUIREND above plastered snow. And here hurrying towards her were two figures, slipping on the icy ruts. In thankfulness and shame she forced panic down and reached for the crammed case which contained perhaps all she would ever see again of her belongings.

'Oh, here now, lassie, leave that to me,' reproved a kindly voice, and it was twitched from her hand as though it weighed nothing.

'Kate? Hello, I'm Joanna, from Allt Farr.' A tall girl bulked out by a big jacket with its hood up, escaping trails of wavy hair amber under the snow-blurred lights, ducked her head to smile at Kate. 'Poor you, have you had an awful journey?'

Kate shook an offered hand, her feet nearly going from under her as she did so. Awful? No, it had been warm, enclosed, un-invaded by speech, eye contact or awareness. Her brain had been numb, unable to grapple with the fact of being carried mile upon mile from all she knew and cared about, to which there could be no return.

'No, it was fine, thank you,' she said. 'I'm sorry you've had such a wait though.' The train was half an hour behind time; just one more factor which she could not control, must un-protestingly accept.

'Don't be silly, it's not your fault.'

Kate liked her voice, warm and friendly, and did not guess the relief her own voice had been to Joanna.

Kate's high-heeled ankle boots gave no grip on the icy surface of the apparently endless platform where the wind from the north pushed against them like a hand, and a wild swing of her arm to balance herself caught Joanna with her big satchel laden with make-up.

Joanna gasped and floundered. 'Would it be better if I took that?' she suggested.

'Sorry, but really, I can manage it,' Kate said breathlessly, steadying herself. Unexpectedly laughter seized her. It seemed bizarre that walking the length of a station platform could be such a trial of endurance, scrabbling feet with no feeling in them, cheekbones and ears burning with cold, fingers in unlined gloves numb, shoulder aching from that wild jerk of her arm.

The little spurt of laughter reassured Joanna even more than the surprisingly acceptable accent.

'Off to fetch Jeremy's tart?' she heard her mother's acid query. 'Dear heaven, what have we let ourselves in for?'

As they caught up with the porter, already opening the back of the Fourtrak, Joanna felt the first gritty touch scarify her cheek. Snow. Or could it just be particles of ice whipped up by the savage wind? But she knew that was a vain hope; the smell of snow had been in the air all day. Remembering it had made the half hour's wait stretch worryingly, in spite of being tucked up warm in the porter's den. There were many steep and twisting empty miles between them and home, and she was glad her passenger missed the porter's parting comment, 'Some game you're going to have getting up Glen Maraich the night.'

After a brief tussle with the door, the wind making a last mean attack on her quivering legs as she climbed in to what she supposed would be called an off-road vehicle, Kate found the sudden stillness gave a disproportionate feeling of security, a feeling instantly dispelled by a new horror. As she sagged back gratefully in her seat a large blond head appeared at her ear and a heavy chin was laid confidingly on her dark bilberry wool shoulder. A great jaw equipped with terrifying teeth opened within a couple of inches of her right eye. A gust of warm biscuity breath fanned her cheek.

'Buff's making you welcome, I see,' Joanna remarked with the chronic insensitivity of the dog lover, slamming the door behind her and leaning forward to wipe an ungloved hand across the windscreen. 'I wish he wouldn't breathe so much though.'

Kate wished he would cease to breathe altogether. She had always agreed with her mother's view that dogs were dirty, smelly, unnecessary nuisances. Also, though she wasn't aware of it, she had imbibed much of Jessie's mistrust of them which amounted to fear.

'Buffie, lie down,' Joanna ordered, pushing back her hood and releasing a rippling mass of hair. 'We're going to have to concentrate, I fear.'

The remark passed Kate by in her relief as the big head was withdrawn with a sigh.

'Is this Muirend?' she asked, as a spread of lights grew before them, some suspended surprisingly high against the blackness of the night.

'It is. Nearly a mile from the station. I suppose we're lucky anything still stops here.'

As they ran through the small town Kate had a jumbled impression of a central square dotted with frozen heaps of dirty snow, a main street of unappealing small shops, narrow empty side streets diving away, but above all of dour, forbidding, damp-streaked stone. Then the houses were thinning, gone, and the road swung up through overhanging trees which soon fell back, leaving darkness flecked here and there by the outside lights of farms, and laced by the first whip of thin snow.

'You must be exhausted. Did you have a very early start?' Joanna enquired kindly, partly to keep her mind off the hazards ahead but chiefly to encourage her silent passenger who, almost as small as Joanna's daughter Laura, tense with nerves and so absurd in those smart clothes, aroused her natural protectiveness.

'Oh, not too early really,' Kate replied, the words automatic, all she could manage as the memory came back of the silent house, the obdurately closed bedroom door, the running taxi engine summoning her, hurrying her, the pleas and apologies which could never now be voiced tumbling agonisingly in her brain. The quiet car-lined suburban road down which she had walked to school, to secretarial college, and for two years to the office, had seemed alien, a scene already lost to her.

'They'll wait dinner, anyway,' Joanna went on cheerfully. 'However long this takes us.'

'Oh, no! I mean, that's very kind . . .' Kate longed only for the oblivion of bed and dreaded causing disruption. At Lamorna, Wilton Avenue, tea, which Jessie had long ago given up trying to make Jack call dinner, was unalterably served at six. Also this waiting household seemed increasingly daunting as the reality came nearer. When Jeremy had first described it to her she had merely done her best to absorb facts and names; it was only later that she had thought it sounded odd. An elderly mother with a son and two daughters, Harriet the eldest in her forties, and all unmarried. At least Joanna had been married. Her husband had been drowned with Jeremy's parents when their yacht went down off the Azores seven years ago. She had one daughter who, Jeremy had worked out with a bit of trouble, was eleven. Kate knew that much of her dread of meeting the unknown family centred on this child.

However, in spite of apprehension and weariness, the reference to food had stirred a faint hunger. She hadn't eaten all day. She had bought sandwiches on the train, then had glimpsed the grey-green ring round the egg-yolk and had felt her stomach rebel.

'Damn,' said Joanna softly as a wild flurry of larger flakes blotted itself against the windscreen. She leaned forward to peer through the reduced arc the wipers made and dipped her lights to help visibility.

Kate abandoned her vague fears of what waited at the end of the journey and began to pay some attention to the present. The road was climbing all the time, its surface white now, and the dance of the snow in the lights was thickening by the minute to a blinding density.

'Kirkton,' Joanna announced at last. 'Nearest shop. Singular.'

A huddle of cottages, a garage forecourt, a hotel, parked cars with white roofs and bonnets and thin new snow on their windows.

They had arrived. Allt Farr, Kirkton, had been the address to which Kate had sent her shy, stilted letter of thanks when the Munros had so amazingly agreed to give her refuge. Jeremy had told her not to bother. 'They'd do anything for me, always have. Our families have been friends for about a hundred years.' But Kate had needed to make contact for herself, not be bundled off like a parcel.

But Joanna was pushing on, the road narrower, the impression of empty wilderness more intense after the brief evidence of human presence.

'Is it very far?' Kate asked, and was aware of the nervousness in her voice as Joanna turned her head.

She's terrified, poor little thing. 'Only a few more miles,' Joanna said encouragingly, and registered Kate's dismay. If we make it, she added grimly to herself. If only that wretched train had been on time.

Broken down dykes were mounds of white above high banks. An occasional bowed-down bush of broom or gorse released its soft load as the Fourtrak brushed it and Kate thought Joanna was driving rather close to the kerb, with no idea of how much trouble she was having on the steep bends with the new fall deepening by the second on the indifferently swept frozen surface of the old.

'Now *this* might be interesting,' Joanna commented, as they hauled themselves up a final corkscrew and the road levelled briefly. Glancing at her, observing her more focused concentration, then peering fearfully ahead herself, Kate saw to her horror blurred lights coming towards them, coming, it seemed to her, appallingly fast.

She gasped, then yelped aloud. Screamed, she supposed afterwards. It all happened so quickly. They seemed to have been driving through a deserted landscape, as though the treacherous road, the storm, were all they had to worry about – and were enough, surely. The possible appearance of other traffic on the road in these conditions hadn't entered Kate's mind.

Because of the dense whirl of flakes there was an illusion of seeing the oncoming lights from far away; in fact they were almost upon them. Joanna made some very explicit comments, her equivalent of Kate's yell, resisted the impulse to brake and held to the narrowing gap between wall and skidding van. It somehow crabbed and scrambled out from under their wheels, side-swiped them then skated round to burrow its nose into the deep snow which concealed a rudimentary ditch below the bank.

'That maniac Doddie,' said Joanna in a completely normal voice, switching off. 'Better go and have a look.'

'Get out?' Kate squeaked involuntarily, and hoped ever afterwards that with scarcely enough breath left to speak her protest had been too feeble for Joanna to hear.

'You all right, Buffie? Did you get a bump? All right, don't give me a hard time, I did my best. You'd better stay, though. Stay! Kate, you'll have to get out this side.'

So matter-of-fact. Kate gulped in a couple of deep breaths, got her heart beating normally again, and suppressing a base longing to stay huddled and uncaring where she was, slid towards the driver's door, having some trouble both in avoiding Buff's solicitous interest and disentangling the skirts of her coat.

It was very, very unpleasant holding the flailing door sufficiently wide to slide out after Joanna, sinking down into snow over the tops of her boots, and meeting the whining fury of the wind which beat snow blindingly against her face. She had barely had time to wonder what they could possibly do if they found some bleeding senseless figure slumped across the steering wheel of the van, when she heard a voice saying conversationally, 'My, that's some night.'

'Doddie, are you quite mad? Where on earth are you going?' Joanna demanded, sounding more resigned than angry.

'Ach, I'd these mole traps of Willie's to take down. He's been at me long enough about them.'

Mole traps? Kate thought dizzily, tottering as the wind attacked from another direction.

Doddie put out a quick obliging hand to steady her.

'Yes, and Judy's home this week,' Joanna supplemented. 'God, Doddie, you never change. This is Kate, she's at Allt Farr for the summer.'

Don't waste time introducing us, Kate screamed inwardly. Just let me get out of this howling bedlam and be an ordinary human being again.

'I'm very pleased to meet you,' Doddie said with formal courtesy, shaking hands and bending to look into her face. Kate tried to raise snow-clogged lashes to look at him but there was only an impression of a tank-like figure and a square smiling face framed by long ear flaps.

'Will we get it out, Doddie?' Joanna asked, raising her voice as the wind rose in a sudden piercing whine.

'No bother,' averred Doddie. 'One good shove'll do it. Lucky I wasna' going fast.' No self-justification, and no recriminations, Kate noted. 'Maybe the lassie'd best drive it out, she's no just dressed for the weather.' With a nod at Kate to apologise for talking about her.

'Yes, she'd better not push. Poor Kate, what an arrival. Oh – you can drive?'

Kate fell into a brief urgent dilemma. She had passed her test, driven her father's cherished Jaguar once, been forbidden to touch it ever again and had gratefully let the whole nerve-racking business go. But instinct told her that this was no time for hesitation. Quite apart from her silly clothes she wasn't pushing material.

'Yes, I can drive,' she said in a faint voice.

Doddie opened the back of the van and getting out a shovel began clearing snow from round the wheels. Joanna fetched another from the jeep to help him.

Kate found herself, with her coat rucked under her, with soaking hair and collar, icy fingers and aching feet, crammed into the oil- and cigarette-reeking van, on a seat nearly on the floor-boards which rocked under her. The passenger seat was absent altogether. Movements and snuffling behind her warned her she was not alone. Ready to leap out again she decided she just wouldn't look. She peeled off her wet gloves and wiped snow from her face with white fingertips, then searched for the ignition. Only after the engine had coughed awake did she remember with horror that the van could have been in gear. With a huge effort she made herself remember the rules. Mirror; she thought she could forget that. Signal; with giggles rising danger-ously she thought she could forget that too. Manoeuvre; she would have to await orders. Tense, determined to do her part, she stared ahead at the snow-packed windscreen.

'Right now.' Doddie was at the window. The snouts of two collies instantly interposed themselves between his face and Kate's. 'Whist now, you lads. If I come in there to you you'll know about it,' he roared. The snouts withdrew and Kate got her breath back. 'Now, just take it easy. Wee bursts as we push. We'll rock her out among the lot of us no trouble at all. When I say, now.'

Kate nodded, quite unaware of how grim she looked, found reverse and gripped the wheel, knuckles staring. An indis-tinguishable shout came in with the snow flurries at the open window. She released the clutch, accelerated hard and rammed the van solidly into the drift.

The engine cut out. The collies with startled yips cannoned into the back of her seat. A great silence fell outside. Horrified, shaken, Kate leaned her forehead on the wheel. Two huge tears, warmer than anything else about her, squeezed between her lids.

'Hey.'

She twisted her head without lifting it. Doddie's face, Joanna's at his shoulder, was at the window again. And amazingly, they were both grinning, the grins widening into laughter, spontaneous, entirely non-acrimonious laughter.

'I'm sorry,' Kate said helplessly, straightening up, tears checked by astonishment. 'I'm so sorry.'

'Was it heading for Silverstone you were?' demanded Doddie. 'I see I should have shown you the gears, though if I had I doubt you'd have the back end buried the other side of the road by now.'

'Is that how they drive in Wimbledon?' Joanna enquired. 'Come on, we'd better do some more digging.'

Why weren't they furious? Fumbling for a wet handkerchief in a wet pocket Kate wished she could wake in her own bed at home and find that nothing in the last two months had ever happened.

Chapter Two

With no fear of meeting anyone in the Allt Farr drive Joanna put her foot down and the jeep took the last sharp pull triumphantly, coming out onto a level space bright under a single light where the wind spun up delicate spirals of snow to chase each other across the unmarred expanse. Kate blinked to see a higgledy-piggledy mass of stone buttresses and towers vanish upward into the night, their bases pale gold where the light caught the snow clogging the spread arms of climbing bushes.

It's a castle, she thought blankly. Jeremy didn't say anything about a castle. Terror, a deep sense of her own inadequacy, and the new insecurity and loneliness which she had not yet had time to come to terms with, rushed overwhelmingly upon her.

Buff, eager for dinner, pushed his head over the seat and put a paw on its back.

'Don't even think of it,' Joanna warned him. 'I'll bring your bag, Kate. Most of the other stuff can wait. There's nothing freezing will hurt. You go in.'

The steps were smooth as folded sheets in a linen cupboard. Kate located a heavy iron latch and tentatively swung open a door which seemed twice as high as she was, finding herself in a stark stone porch equipped only with a huge chest, its lid propped open, piled with logs. An inner glazed door led to a dimly lit hall. She opened it and released chaos. The wind tore in, bringing a great puff of snow with it, the dog shouldered past her, the chest lid slammed down like a gun going off, a minor crash somewhere ahead followed it and an imperious voice shouted, 'Oh, *please*, one door at a time. We shall all be blown away!'

Kate grappled in feverish haste with the inner door, coat skirts whipping, happy to shut herself outside it if only she could get it closed, but made no headway till Joanna behind her thumped the outer door to and everything miraculously sank to calm.

The owner of the imperious voice surveyed Kate without favour. 'Kate? How do you do? I am Eleanor Munro.' She held out a bony hand with a gesture of authority rather than of welcome.

Breathless, Kate took it nervously. Tall, thin, with thick white hair growing vigorously upwards and dark, deep-set, assessing eyes, wearing a haphazard collection of layered clothes in vivid colours, a scarlet bird's-eye scarf twisted rakishly under one ear, the figure that confronted her was an imposing one.

'You've made good time,' Mrs Munro commented, removing her gaze from Kate as though she had learned enough and addressing Joanna. 'Did you have any trouble?'

Kate waited for the account of their dramas and struggles.

'A bit tricky on the Mennach Brae,' Joanna said, putting Kate's case on the bottom step of a dark oak staircase. 'Met that idiot Doddie flying down though.'

'Doddie? What on earth was he doing going anywhere tonight? Run out of cigarettes, I suppose.'

'Judy Mearns is at home,' Joanna said succinctly.

'Ah, well, almost as compelling a motive.'

'He clipped the back end of the jeep and went in the ditch. We had to push him out.'

'You have had adventures.' A mere polite rejoinder. 'Did he take any paint with him?'

'Haven't looked.'

Paint? Kate, testing to see if she could still move her toes in the ice forming round them, considered it would have been fair to point out that conditions weren't ideal for checking paint-work.

'Yes, well, if it needs a respray he can pay. It cost quite enough to repair the suspension on the Hilux after his last little escapade.'

I suppose this house contains food, a bed, warmth of some kind, Kate thought, suspended in a sort of inert stoicism. Certainly there was no warmth in this cavernous stone-flagged hall where two tiny wall lights bracketed a fireplace as big as a larder, empty of anything but a faded embroidered firescreen. In the shadows lurked high carved cupboards, dark chests, weapons, the heads of beasts. There was no proper furniture. If there was a ceiling it was invisible in the gloom. *Nacht und Nebel*, Kate thought frivolously.

'Poor Kate must be longing to get dry,' Joanna said. 'I'll take her up. Where's Harriet?'

'In the kitchen. Fussing. Max has gone to check on Torquil, though even he might be expected to have the sense to use his shed on a night like this.'

I won't even wonder what she's talking about, Kate decided, light-headed with emotion, starvation and weariness.

'No,' Mrs Munro went on. 'You go and fetch whatever has to come in from the jeep and I'll take Kate up.' She turned to the stairs, ignoring the suitcase.

Well, I am here to work my passage, Kate reminded herself. In fact, it's probably surprising that we're using the front stairs. It may be the last time I ever use them. I may end up polishing them though. Jessie would have had a carpet down in no time. Am I hoping it will hurt less to call her Jessie, not mother? A question it was not the moment to examine.

The slippery steps were treacherous; Kate could hardly feel her feet any more. The heavy make-up bag slipped down her arm and banged against her knee.

'Here.' A firm hand grasped the suitcase and twitched it away with impressive ease.

'Oh, no, please, I can manage.' That white hair.

'I can perfectly well carry a suitcase.' The words, 'which you clearly can't', hung on the foggy freezing air of the corridor as Kate hurried meekly in her wake. Steps up, a half flight down, abrupt turns round pillars of stone, narrow corridors repeated, indistinguishable, thinly floored with khaki whipcord, the plaster on their walls swelling ominously with damp, crooked pictures, brown identical doors.

'Now, you should be comfortable here.' It was an order.

Kate stood dwarfed, dismayed, chilled to the bone. The room was huge, with two long windows shrouded in dark curtains whose last six inches buckled on the beige carpet. It was lit solely by a bedside lamp like a silver candlestick with a frilled glass shade, whose light barely reached the foot of a very long, very high brass bed, its lace frills dipping in careless tatters to the floor. Enormous pieces of furniture loomed round the walls; the cold reached out like a tongue.

Mrs Munro tossed the suitcase down on a sagging armchair and turned to the door again. 'The reason we gave you this room –' was that amusement in her voice? Surely it couldn't be '– was this.' With her stalking stride she led Kate, past questioning anything, to the next door.

Warmth. The first real warmth Kate had felt since she launched herself into the icy blast at Muirend station, flowed out and with magical benison lapped her round. A bathroom of antique splendour, as big as her bedroom at Lamorna, lay before her, a massive bath spreading claw feet on a pink carpet, red velvet curtains faded to cream on the folds, enormous fluffy towels on a towel rail as high as her chin, welcomed her with the first uncomplicated kindness of a long, long day.

Mrs Munro made a brief sound which was almost a laugh. 'Don't be long, dinner's ready.' She was gone.

Oh, bliss. Kate shut the door, tottered forwards, laid her forehead on the soft thick folds of towel and wrapped her hands round the gleaming pipes. Blisteringly hot; all the better. She pulled a layer of towel in between. She wanted to climb all over this marvellous monster, intertwine herself in it, hang upside down like a sloth, and never go down to dinner.

'Later,' she promised the bath with yearning.

'So, not as bad as we feared?' Joanna said hopefully as her mother came into the kitchen. She liked things to be amicable.

'Humph.'

'Joanna says she's really quite civilised. That's lucky, isn't it?' Harriet, down on one knee unnecessarily stirring a casserole which had been plopping and bubbling as peacefully as a hot mud wallow, flapped the blast from the oven away from her beaky face.

Not quite in those words, Joanna thought resignedly, watching her sister haul herself to her feet with the aid of the Aga rail like a woman of eighty.

'She hardly uttered a word,' their mother said.

'Did you frighten her?' Joanna protested. 'Poor dear, she's shaking in her shoes as it is. Really, she's very sweet.'

'Sweet. And in those ridiculous clothes I might also say dainty, neither word calculated to predispose me in her favour.'

Joanna giggled. 'She was so appalled by everything, coming up. But she did get out and try to help with Doddie's van. I thought for a moment she was going to cling to her seat like a limpet. She's scared to death of Buff, though.'

'Oh, no, really, that is a complication we do *not* need,' Mrs Munro said with exasperation.

'What's that?' demanded Max, coming in with the sack of wholemeal flour Joanna had left in the jeep.

'This wretched female of Jeremy's. She won't be the slightest use to us, just as I feared. She's no bigger than Laura, terrified out of her wits and dressed in you-too-can-be-a-career-woman clothes.'

'Very promising.' If only they could banish her to her own cottage as they did the students who helped in the summer, but thanks to Jeremy this girl had to be taken into the family circle. 'I've put the jeep away, Jo. Were you planning to leave it at the front door all night?'

'Yep,' said his sister cheerfully.

'I thought I'd save myself the trouble of digging it out in the morning.'

'Good for you,' Joanna said, unmoved.

'Where is this girl?' Harriet was asking. 'The stew's drying up. Did you tell her dinner was ready, Grannie?' Since Joanna brought Laura to Allt Farr this was the form of address her children – and half the glen – had fallen into for Mrs Munro.

'I told her to waste no time.'

'Too scared to come down,' Joanna commented.

'Or lost,' her mother amended. 'Someone had better field for her. I have small hopes of her resourcefulness.'

'I'll go,' Max said shortly. It was late and he was hungry. Joanna's casual abandoning of the jeep had irritated him. A snowfall like this, coupled with a high wind, would bring all too familiar problems tomorrow, hours of shifting snow, clearing estate roads and tracks, getting feed to stock, digging out vehicles, dealing with the crises of the unwary or improvident. No one else could be trusted with the snowplough. Doddie went too fast, taking chunks out of banks and more than once gateposts with him, Jim Coupar, the grieve, was too cautious and got bogged with maddening regularity, while Willie Mearns would probably never get up from the Mennach in the first place. The dragging feeling of it all being down to him, unalterably, forever, descended on Max as he crossed the hall and took the stairs two at a time, and he pushed it away angrily. It surfaced in his mind far too often these days; it would hardly make life more rewarding if he let it take hold. And nothing was going to change.

Kate, shivering, hurrying, fumbling, dug in her case for something to wear for dinner. She had pressed down the small peardrop light switch on its brass plate at the door and a green flash had come out of it, but nothing more had followed beyond a feeble light appearing through the splits in a silk shade suspended at mid ceiling. She could still hardly see. She had equipped herself sketchily for this new environment, knowing she would soon need different things. The sum of Jeremy's advice had been to bring lots of sweaters and now she pulled out one after another the lambswool jumpers, the cashmere polo-neck, the Shetland sweater which wouldn't do for evening. Even it felt light and flimsy, unbelievably different from when she had tried it on in her cosy room at home. Oh God, don't let yourself see it, she warned, tears threatening as a swift image came of its frilled, peachy, softly lit, womb-like safety, her collections of carved animals and fans and corn dollies peopling it.

This stark dim room, the outer reaches of which she hardly dared examine, repelled and rejected her. With a little sob that was as much anger as despair she shook the melted snow – amazing that it had melted – off her coat onto the tiles of a high fireplace and went to hang it in a wardrobe with a beetling overhang like a cliff. Away above her, quite out of reach, ran a brass rail with a row of big shaped wooden hangers with cross bars.

Have I come to a land of giants? Kate thought in despair. Perhaps I'll just get in and shut the door and never be seen again.

When she pulled off her sodden boots cold air eddied round her ankles, tangible as water. All she had to put on instead were high-heeled shoes.

Outside her room she turned in the opposite direction from the bathroom. That much was clear. Then she was adrift in a maze of draught-scoured passages leading nowhere, stairs she had never seen before, finally arriving in a sort of minstrels' gallery which appeared to have no escape route. She listened. Silence. The faintest whine of wind beyond muffling stone. A stir of gelid air, a creak of wood. As the temperature changed? Idle thought.

I do not want to be here. I do not want to exist.

'Hi! Where've you got to?'

The impatient shout made Kate jump bone-shakingly.

For a second she was literally incapable of answering.

'Hello!' The voice was moving away.

'Here,' she called in panic, her voice lost in the high inimical distances. 'I'm here,' she tried again, starting back the way she had come.

Round the curve of the passage came striding one of the giants who inhabited this awful place, tall, grim-faced, in tweed breeches and a padded waistcoat over dark sweater.

Max checked as he saw her. His mother was right; she was as small and slight as a child, neat in damson-coloured jersey with crisp blouse collar over it, darker skirt. Her hair looked dark too in this light, and was very short. Her face was small and pointed, her eyes wide with unconcealed apprehension.

'Come on,' Max said, his voice less abrupt than he had expected it to sound. 'I think we're all rather in need of dinner. I'm Max.'

'Hello, I'm Kate.'

Her voice was soft, nervous. What earthly use Jeremy thought such a fragile little object would be to them in the coming season Max couldn't imagine. Except that Jeremy would not have looked that far ahead. He would feel he had met his obligations and would be happy to leave it at that.

'You were more than a little off course,' Max observed, leading Kate rapidly down a stone spiral which brought them out above the hall.

'I'm afraid I didn't pay attention,' she admitted. To her surprise, for Allt Farr was a good deal larger and grander than anything she had expected, Max led her through a swing door at the back of the hall, beyond which the panelling disappeared and the lighting improved, and into a big kitchen.

Glorious heat, light and food smells melded in dazzling welcome. Joanna was there, dropping rolls from a baking tray into a napkin-lined basket and flipping her fingers to cool them. Her mother was standing with her bottom against the Aga rail, a pair of half-moons on the end of her nose, holding a newspaper to the light. Another female who must be the elder sister was ladling soup into plates patterned with dark blue and gold. Buff, unexpectedly, bustled out of his basket to greet her, but went back to it at a word from Max, propping his head on its chewed edge to watch proceedings. The basket was by the cooker, Kate saw. That wasn't very nice.

'Ah, good, you're here. Kate, tuck yourself in there.' A highbacked settle flanked a long table. 'This is my elder daughter Harriet.'

Harriet, carrying in both hands a soup plate she had overfilled, flashed a smile on and off and concentrated till the plate was safely down. Then she reached across and shook Kate's hand, saying, 'How do you do, Kate? We're so glad you could come. What sort of journey up did you have? What a shame the weather's so ghastly for your arrival.'

She was taught to say that as a child, Kate found herself thinking. And taught to shake hands firmly.

Harriet was definitely middle-aged, much older than Max or Joanna. She looked tired and faded, her face too thin and fleshless for the large spectacles she wore, the eyes behind them light-lashed and vulnerable. She shared Joanna's colouring but in muted tones. Where Joanna had a great mass of lighttextured red-brown hair, and in the light over the table Kate could now see its beauty, Harriet's was a sandy frizz. It grew naturally forwards but she tried to make it go back, so that a limp inch or two jutted over her forehead in a little platform which she continually dabbed at. Joanna had a soft comfortably covered body; Harriet was an angular collection of bones. She was the sort of woman who had never learned to tuck in her blouse properly.

Kate, beginning her soup, some indeterminate vegetable mixture and very good, stole a look at Max. His thick hair was lighter than either sister's, and he alone had the dark eyes of their mother. He's bored with this, Kate thought unexpectedly. He was spooning in soup rapidly, breaking his roll with a decisive gesture, his face set in faintly disparaging lines which she hoped were not his usual expression.

Feeling braver, as Harriet worried aloud about what the storm would bring, dripping out thoughts one by one to be snapped up and dismissed by her mother like a dog catching peanuts, and Joanna seemed to have retired into a dream of her own, Kate dared a look around the kitchen. She had never seen anything like it. With lights on only over the Aga and the table where they sat, the rest stretched away into the remote subfusc distances she was coming to expect. Uncouth domestic objects whose purpose she could hardly guess at huddled on high shelves or shouldered each other round the floor. No one seemed to have thought of painting the tall wooden cupboards, or indeed the walls. There was nothing that could be described as a unit. Two sash windows rose to the ceiling blank and black, and Kate could see the reflection of the lighted scene moving under the attack of the wind. They could at least have had blinds, floral ones to brighten the place up a bit perhaps.

Then disaster came. Joanna took away the soup plates, Max, surprisingly, mashed a panful of potatoes with an enormous beetle, lashing in butter and cream, and Harriet bore her precious casserole to the table. The lid came off and up rose a cloud of steam and a waft of rich flavours. And what unknown objects were these in the creamy sauce on her plate? Kate could not identify them and dared not ask. She took two brave mouthfuls and the richness of the unknown meat, the heat of the room after the shivery cold, the misery and exhaustion of the day and the treacherous nausea of early pregnancy surged together in one huge curling wave of wretchedness.

'She's going!' It was Max's voice, faraway, matter-of-fact, then everything happened at once. The table was pulled away, Kate was twitched bodily to her feet, a powerful arm was half leading her, half carrying her away, cold air chilled her clammy face, there was an impression of shiny black walls spinning round her and the hysterical thought, They're putting me in a box. Then beneath her reeling eyes appeared the bowl of a shallow, odd-shaped loo, beautifully painted with flowers, and Joanna's arm was supporting her, Joanna's sympathetic voice murmuring beside her, 'You poor old thing, how absolutely miserable for you.'

Chapter Three

Kate surfaced with that luxurious feeling – rare in an ordered life where alarm clock, household noises, morning traffic generally pulled her out of sleep – of having woken naturally. It was still dark. Before anything else, for a moment of supreme peace, she was aware of the silence, then reality came leaping back.

She jerked upright, anxiety, guilt and humiliation seizing her before she had even pinpointed their source. Then memory and cold hit her together, and with a groan she flopped back and dragged the bedclothes over her face. She had been horribly sick, dragging Joanna away from dinner, causing hubbub with hot-water bottles and offers from Harriet of Disprin and hot milk which had nearly made her retreat again to that strange dark loo (had it really been painted black or had she imagined that?) then reeling dizzily through those endless corridors with Joanna supporting her. Now she knew why the pictures were crooked. She giggled, and groaned again. She hadn't even managed to get into bed under her own steam. Then the recollection of the blissful moment of finally rolling into it returned, the divine welcome of downy pillows, faintly lavender scented, the friendly warmth of a mammoth velvet-covered hot-water bottle contrasting voluptuously with the glassy smoothness of the sheets. No duvets here, but blankets of a superlative softness and a great mound of eiderdown. That suited the room, Kate thought, reaching for the lamp. Her bare arm was frozen by the time she had discovered the button on its base. She squinted down the bed; there was no evidence that she was in it, and it seemed to stretch away for ever. Tentatively she stretched her feet and met an expanse of ice. She withdrew hastily into the warm zone. The tip of her nose ached.

She studied the room. The carpet was dingy and worn, the armchairs covered in indeterminate chintzes, the wallpaper a sort of trellis with ivy leaves. Not pretty at all. (So much for William Morris.) Was this a sort of upper-grade servant's room? It was very big. Or a lowest-grade guest room? She couldn't decide.

But with the question conscience stirred. She was here to work. What time would they expect her down? What would she have to do? Cook breakfast for them all? She thought of the old-fashioned kitchen with its cumbersome equipment like some torturer's DIY kit and mewed with dismay. She hadn't even unpacked her clock. She looked on the bedside table, an eighteenth-century commode, but couldn't see her watch, then realised it was still on her wrist. She held it up to the light. Hadn't they heard of 100 watt bulbs? God, God, it couldn't be. Forgetting the temperature she sat up in horror. Her watch must have stopped; she'd hit it on something going to bed. It must have been about that time. But it hadn't stopped. Her first morning here and she had slept till eleven.

But why was it still pitch dark? Was there another storm? Oh, this nightmare, nightmare place. Bracing herself she threw back the bedclothes and went down and down to the floor. It was like getting out of the train at Muirend all over again. What a completely ridiculous bed. No slippers. She rushed across to the curtains and seized their heavy folds. They wouldn't budge. She tugged, sobbing tearlessly in frustration. Too cold to waste time on them; they were stuck. She rushed back to her still half-full case, found her dressing-gown and pulled it on, wincing as its silky coldness met unprotected flesh. Back to the curtains, craning backwards to see what was sticking. Some kind of cord. Oh, what a fool. Annoyed with herself she hauled the curtains apart, releasing a faint smell of age.

Outside a mountain reared up, so close that it reminded Kate of the gesture of putting a hand against your face to indicate a broken nose. Between the house and a hill-face composed of streaks of snow patterning wet rock, foggy air hung in the tips of dark conifers, their lower branches borne down with snow.

Kate shuddered, closing her eyes and leaning her forehead against the pane, then hastily unsticking it again. How could Jeremy have sent her to such a hideous place? 'A house in a glen,' he had said. 'Nice spot.' No, that wasn't exactly what he had said. 'Right at the top of a glen,' his words had been. They had meant nothing, unimportant in the hurt and shock and driving need to get away, far away, somewhere unknown and unconnected.

Jeremy. Of course she had expected nothing from him. At the very first moment of meeting him at that appalling party she had made a cold, deliberate decision, completely unlike her, to break out of her cage of conscience and inhibition and endless good behaviour. Reckless, keyed up for new experience, she had lied to him, determined to be free of the meek and dutiful self who endlessly did what was required of her.

But there was no time for this now. She had made the break; that much was accomplished. Jeremy, surprisingly, had done his best for her before he ran for cover; had done more, much more, than she would ever have asked, once he had accepted her refusal to consider an abortion. He had made in theory the ideal arrangement, providing her with somewhere to live till the baby was born, where she could organise doctor and hospital bed, and at the same time be useful and earn her keep.

Earn her keep. But first she had to dress in this arctic room. She remembered the bathroom and grabbing up the warmest clothes she could see fled to its haven. It didn't seem as blissfully warm as it had last night, her friend the towel rail was no longer too hot to touch and the reticent light of the dismal day revealed a decided shabbiness, but after a praying wait boiling water did finally gulp and spurt from the enormous tap – to pour down the plughole. What on earth was this tube-like contraption with a sort of cage on the bottom and a white enamel top saying 'Waste'? It was held upright between the taps by a metal clamp and didn't reach the plughole. Struggling with it with cold hands that barely went round it, Kate swore vigorously and uncharacteristically. Was there no single object here that was simple, normal, and which *worked*? At last she freed the thing entirely and with her flannel stuffed round its foot achieved a hot, deep bath. So deep in fact that when she lay down she floated away and her hair went under, but nothing much affected its short curls and the warmth was such a sybaritic delight that she didn't care anyway. The only thing was the water steadily dwindled away and she could do nothing to stop it, feeling goose-pimples come up on her stealthily exposed skin.

Heading downstairs at last, finding the route after only a couple of casts, the silence of the house struck her once more. Was it quite empty? Had those towering, peremptory, competent people of last night been characters in her dreams?

Good, she'd made it. Here was the hall. The swing door was covered in leather, she found. The kitchen door lay ahead.

The kitchen was empty, tidy, bare, Aga lids down, not even a fridge to hum. In the dog's basket were teeth-pitted log, rubber bone, grimy slipper – and a cabbage stalk, she noted with interest. Did dogs like cabbage?

What should she do? Where would she find someone? It was so awful to be late, she who was never late, who could always be relied upon.

A thud, the faint sound of a voice, then the door at the other side of the kitchen burst open and in hurried a new figure, an elderly woman in tweed coat and black wellingtons, grey hair escaping from a woollen headscarf checked in grey, maroon and mauve, her round cheeks pink and small eyes bright, a basket in one hand.

'Here's me talking to myself,' she exclaimed at once with no apparent embarrassment. 'But there's nearly all the hens off their lay together with the cold weather and I'd a time of it finding enough eggs for the table what with all this snow, and won't I be glad to see the back of it. All very well for they skiers, but they should think on that ordinary folk have to go about their business just the same, that's what I say. Now, you'll be Kate, and I was to let you have your sleep out and give you your breakfast when you came down. I've the porridge pot on the back of the stove and I'll easy whip you up your bacon and eggs, just wait while I put these past and get my coat off, then is it tea or coffee you're wanting, and it'll be brown bread for your toast, I dare say, that's what they're always mad for here, though I don't fancy it myself, or there's baps can go in the bottom oven . . . .'

She had shrugged off her coat as she talked, revealing a flowery wraparound apron over a comfortable bulk of sweaters and a shapeless skirt, and still in headscarf and boots was darting about banging pots and kettle and oven doors.

'Please, no!' Kate begged. 'I really only want coffee.' She had forgotten all about morning sickness, but the sight of an encrusted porridge pot abruptly reminded her.

'Oh, but you must have something. Harriet said most particularly you was to have your breakfast whenever you showed your face. Will I boil you a wee fresh egg?'

'No, truly. It's very kind, but I only ever have coffee.'

'Well, I'd best make you some toast just the same. Willie's pigs can get it if you don't. Now sit yourself doon and I'll have the coffee in to you in no time. No, no, not in here, I've my work to do.'

'But I can make my own –' Useless to protest. Kate was firmly directed to a pretty dining-room with silvery-striped wall coverings and a rosewood sideboard still cluttered with orange juice, cereals and hotplate. French windows filled the end wall, white tape sealing them together and a draught excluder, stained with damp, packed against the bottom. Outside hung fog.

I cannot stay here, Kate thought. This place has served its

purpose, got me away from Jessie's rages and Jack's infinitely worse hurt silence. From here I can go anywhere, back to some kind of normality. But there had been two sides to the bargain. Jeremy had said the Munros needed help. That was why she had felt it possible to accept this refuge. She couldn't let them down.

'Now, sit in about.' Mrs Grant came bustling in. 'Here's some nice hot coffee for you. That's a dreich kind o' day, right enough, though I doubt there's worse to come. February's the month for it up here. Those folk down in Muirend dinna' ken when they're well off. If there's anything else you're wanting you've only to say—'

'I'm sorry, I don't know your name.'

The easy flow of chatter broke off. The pink cheeks grew scarlet. 'Well, rightly, I'm Effie, I suppose,' was the obscure answer and she was gone in a flurry of embarrassment.

Obviously a gaffe. A pity, Kate had wanted to ask where everyone was. She helped herself to coffee from a silver pot with a dent in its flank, waited for inner objections and risked a sip. Tentatively she took a piece of toast and entered on a new experience. Wholemeal bread made by Harriet, toasted on the Aga, spread with home-made Jersey butter and dark marmalade with erratic lumps of peel cut by Mrs Munro's careless hand, was very different from anything on offer in the Lamorna dinette, with its pine table pale under six coats of varnish and its bench seats cushioned in purple mock-leather.

'Oh, good, Mrs Grant's looked after you.' Joanna came smiling in, still wearing her jacket and with her bright hair looking as though she'd forgotten to brush it. So it wasn't Effie. 'Sorry I wasn't here when you came down. I've been digging. Did you sleep well? How are you feeling today?'

It seemed a strange time of year to be gardening. 'I slept beautifully, thank you. I never reached the bottom of the bed though.'

Joanna laughed. 'No, I shouldn't think you did. It was made for one of my great-uncles who was about seven feet tall.'

'I'm sorry to be so late. I should have set my alarm clock—'

'Whatever for? Nothing much doing today. Any coffee left in that pot? Oh, great.' Joanna stuck her head into the corridor. 'Hi, Mrs Grant, could you bring another cup, please. Anyway,' she said, scrutinising Kate with benevolent concern as she sat down, 'you look a lot better than you did last night.'

Kate blushed. 'That was awful. I'm so sorry about it, I ruined everyone's dinner—'

'Don't be silly, of course you didn't. Harriet flapped a bit, but you don't think anything would put Max or Grannie off their grub, do you?'

Why did Mrs Munro's adult children call her Grannie when Laura wasn't there?

'I couldn't have sympathised more,' Joanna went on. 'I was hopeless with Laura for the first two months. Just mornings though. Everyone's different. Someone I know was sick at every meal for the whole nine months.'

'That's a comfort,' Kate said temperately, and Joanna shot her a quick look and laughed.

'You are feeling better.'

Kate laughed too, relaxing. She wanted to ask if it was all right for her to be having breakfast in here, served by Mrs Grant, but knew the question would be gauche. Only she didn't know how to frame the real question as to her role, her status. She had scarcely considered it when she had snatched at this solution which had seemed to answer all her needs.

'Want this last bit of toast?' Joanna enquired. 'I've expended far too much energy this morning. I was at the Cedar Hut making sure Grigor had logs in and so on. The snow always blows in badly down there. He's an old boy who worked on the estate all his life, starting at fourteen, and as he's on his own we keep an eye on him. Mind you, he's probably snugger than we are.'

Kate found no comment to make.

'Grannie and Harriet are painting,' Joanna went on, taking an oatcake from a cylindrical tartan tin.

A cosy picture of mother and daughter absorbed in shared creative activity. But Kate decided against the polite query, 'Do they have a studio?' Nothing here was as it seemed, she was discovering. 'What are they painting?' she asked instead.

'New cottage. Well, very old cottage we're doing up. We let them out for self-catering holidays, as Jeremy may have told you. It's one of our steadiest sources of income, so we add another here and there as funds are available. This one's booked for Easter and there's a lot to do still. We might go down and help for an hour or so before lunch. There's a floor to scrape, that's a nice peaceful job. Do you have anything to work in? I mean, you're rather on the tidy side.'

'I don't really have anything else,' Kate confessed. All her clothes were tidy. And since till now everything she earned, backed up by some hefty capital Jack had made over to her to avoid tax, had been hers to spend, they were expensive. Her everyday make-up took twenty minutes to apply. Her nails were shapely and painted. She wore gold stud earrings. She put on scent as automatically as she cleaned her teeth.

'We'll have to kit you out,' Joanna said. 'Though you're not really as small as Laura and anything of mine would swamp you. Grannie might have some ideas. I can find you a jacket someone left. Are those boots all right for the time being?'

They were still damp but were preferable to frozen ankles. 'Yes, fine thanks. I'll just go up and—'

'Oh, don't trek all the way up there. Do you remember where the loo is, just along the corridor? I was hopeless when I was pregnant, dashing off all the time.'

Kate thought the ache of her bladder might have something to do with the ambient temperature. There was a bad moment when she went into the black-painted downstairs cloakroom with its disagreeable reminders. She had never seen an uglier room.

Going through the kitchen as instructed she found Joanna in a stone-floored passage, its wall filled with pegs bulging with what looked like three generations' worth of coats, waterproofs, waxed jackets, binocular cases, mummified game bags, leads, whips, scarfs and hats of every description. A selection of boots stood below, all enormous to Kate's eyes. High in the opposite wall were set three small windows with sloping sills down which cold air poured.

'How would this do?' A stiff canvas coat with a fur lining. Kate took it gingerly.

Joanna laughed. 'Don't worry, it died before you were born. Come on, we'll take the jeep.'

She led the way into a courtyard where the air felt as though it had never known the touch of the sun. The house rose like a cliff behind them; ahead and to the right ran dour stone buildings; to the left was a high archway. Kate shivered, huddling the fur-lined jacket round her, as she followed Joanna to the jeep.

'Good thing Max has been down with the plough,' Joanna remarked, negotiating a steep slope below the shelf on which the house stood. Kate grasped the fact that he had not been ploughing the fields.

The cottage stood above a dark ice-fringed river, dotted with snow-capped rocks. Beyond it boulder-strewn banks climbed into mist. A desolate place. Going into a cement-and-paint-smelling interior Kate decided it had been warmer outside. Mrs Munro and Harriet were painting upstairs, in separate rooms. They hadn't even brought a radio with them, Kate noticed.

Downstairs the big gutted room waited for its walls to be finished, its irregular floor sanded down.

'Won't it make a mess plastering the walls after doing the floor?' Kate asked, as she turned in her fingers the piece of broken glass Joanna had given her.

'They're not going to be plastered. They've been repointed, they're ready.'

Bare stone? Kate shuddered.

'Sanding machines are very good,' she ventured, watching Joanna fold a piece of sandpaper round a block of wood in an intricate and business-like manner.

Joanna grinned. 'No power yet,' she said briefly. 'Anyway, we've only got to do these bits round the edges.'

'Not the whole floor?' Kate asked in such blatant relief that Joanna laughed aloud.

'All we're doing is getting off the last of this old varnish so the wood can be waxed. It's such a shame to cover it all.' Was it? 'Then we'll put a rug down.'

Couldn't they afford a carpet?

But as Joanna had said, it was a peaceful job. Certainly she herself took it at a gentle pace, chatting easily, enquiring after Jeremy in a casual way that wasn't hard to deal with, explaining that Laura was at a small private boarding school all week, asking about Kate's life with a courteous token interest.

Resigned to getting cement and sawdust on her skirt, to scuffing the toes of her boots which would never be the same again anyway, to the danger of splinters and the certainty of ruining her nails, Kate found the job not unpleasant, even becoming keen to achieve perfect results, impressed with the smoothness the glass could produce and unaware of Joanna's amusement at the minute patch she had done.

'By the way,' Joanna remarked, swaying back on her knees to squint admiringly at her own work, 'I meant to say, you absolutely mustn't do a thing you don't feel fit for. You've got to promise that.'

'Well, I did want to ask—' Kate seized her opportunity gratefully.

'Goodness, I've done enough!' came Mrs Munro's voice on the stairs. '*What* an indulgence to have the jeep to go home in.' The sarcasm was lost on Kate. 'Come along, Harriet, lunch.'

Kate saw to her surprise that it was ten past two.

'I've just got this last little bit to do,' Harriet's voice floated plaintively down.

'Do it later,' her mother commanded, pulling on a combat jacket over her emulsion-flecked guernsey.

'It won't be worth cleaning the brushes,' Harriet pleaded. 'It will only take five minutes.'

'We'll leave you then,' Mrs Munro said. 'Come along, you two.'

'Certainly not, we'll wait for Harrie,' Kate was glad to hear Joanna say. 'I'm going to look at what you've done. Want to see, Kate?'

'Then I shall leave you all.' Her mother sounded suddenly bad-tempered. She must be tired, Kate thought. She shouldn't have to paint walls at her age. Were they too poor to afford a decorator? Nothing seemed to add up.

'Jeep keys are in my pocket,' Joanna said, heading up the stairs. 'They aren't, of course,' she added to Kate, without lowering her voice, 'but I don't think she'll check.'

Kate felt a conspirator's satisfaction.

'Thanks, Jo,' said a rapidly painting Harriet over her shoulder. 'I'm so nearly finished.' She was wearing a blue nylon overall and had her hair tied up in a scarf like a wartime factory girl. The room was unexpectedly spacious, with wardrobes built against the gable end and cupboards into the lost spaces under the sloping ceiling.

'Hurry up!' Mrs Munro called impatiently from below.

'Nice view from here,' Joanna told Kate, crossing to the dormer window. 'If you could see it for mist, that is. People are going to love being so near the burn.'

Harriet painted faster, fretting audibly.

But when is someone going to explain to me what I'm to *do*, Kate thought, as at last they jounced and clawed their way up the track with Grannie annoyed and silent and Harriet defiant and flustered.

Chapter Four

Kate was no nearer knowing what was expected of her by the time she went to bed, late and tired, her head spinning with new scenes, new challenges, unfamiliar signals and unsolved puzzles. Lunch had been a non-event. Kate, her hands like sandpaper themselves, shoulders aching and knees stiff, had had a vision of hot food eaten at leisure in the elegant little dining-room. But the dusky kitchen, afternoon light shadowed at this time of year by the crowding hills, was barren of offerings. Mrs Grant had gone. There was no sign of Max. Grannie took a lump of Stilton and a tomato and vanished. Joanna, exclaiming, 'Oh, God, I said I'd do the school run today because of taking that roe down to the Cluny Arms,' cut herself a slab of fruit cake, pushed an apple into one pocket and a banana into the other and disappeared in her turn.

'I'll warm up some soup for us,' Harriet said cosily. 'You should have something nourishing on a day like this.' She began hurrying about, happy to have someone to look after, then checked. 'Oh, this is the soup we had last night. Would that – was that what––?'

'No, soup would be lovely, thanks.' Just get on with it. 'Can I help with anything?'

'I'll put some in this small pan. It won't take long to heat through, and then perhaps you'd like a sandwich? Something plain. I felt quite guilty for giving you that game casserole. Pigeon

34

and hare can be rather strong if you're not used to them, but it didn't occur to me there would be a problem in the evenings, it's usually mornings, isn't it?'

She was pushing her pan about on the Aga, choosing the best spot, talking more to herself than to Kate. 'Now, that should be all right, I'll just get out some bread, or perhaps rolls would be better, I could pop them into the oven while the soup's heating. I think there's some cold beef, or maybe it was lamb, and there's always ham—'

'Soup will really be enough.' Kate's appetite had faded on hearing what had been in last night's casserole. And had they never thought of getting a microwave?

'Keep an eye on this for me.' Harriet went out to the stone passage and came back carrying an ashet on which a very rare sirloin of beef sat in its congealed blood and juices. Kate turned her eyes away.

'Mrs Grant will have laid the fire in the morning-room,' Harriet said, when she had at last assembled a tray. 'We'll go up there.'

Mrs Grant hadn't laid the fire, she had merely left paper and sticks on the hearth and hadn't even cleaned out the grate. Harriet made no comment, however, but lumbered down in that elderly way of hers and, leaving the ashes where they were, started to build a careful edifice on top of them, making newspaper twists and criss-crossing sticks, adding small logs. She had forgotten to put on any coal but as a film was forming over the cooling soup Kate said nothing.

'Oh, dear, do start,' Harriet exclaimed, noticing she was waiting. 'I should have said. And are you sure you're warm enough in those thin clothes?'

Kate was sure she wasn't, but it seemed pointless to say so. She longed for the fur-lined jacket, peculiar as it had smelled.

'I know you young people like running about in next to nothing,' Harriet went on, poking in a stick, 'but you should be taking care of yourself. There, that's caught nicely.'

And indeed the fire had burst into leaping flames, though Kate didn't know how much effect it would have on the reaches of the narrow high-ceilinged room. Oblivious to the fact that almost every object it contained was a treasure in its own right she saw only its worn and faded air, the smallness of the windows high in the massive walls, the drabness of the fifty square feet of tapestry on the inner wall, the parting silk of sofas, the thread-bare needlework of chairs and stools. Loose covers might have helped. The back castors seemed to have broken off some of the chairs, she noted. It seemed a pity not to mend them. Eighteenth-century salon sets had not featured in Wilton Avenue.

It seemed a good moment to pin Harriet down about her duties, if she could break in on the suggestions to pop down and fetch cheese or fruit, or something to drink, with the afterthought that alcohol would be bad for Kate, and the offer to go and make coffee before Harriet had finished her own soup.

Kate, politely refusing everything, for the second time that day began, 'I just wanted to ask—'

'Oh, yes, you must ask anything at all. We're going to do our very best to look after you. Jeremy has been like a son of the house since that dreadful tragedy and naturally when he suggested that you come to us we were only too delighted—'

'I'm very grateful. It was really kind of you. But I'm not exactly sure what I should—'

'Oh, you mustn't worry, Joanna knows all about that. She's even talked to the doctor, the doctor we normally go to in the practice, though you may want a different one of course, but he's very good. His father used to stalk up here, and he'll advise you about the clinic and hospital and everything. He says there's plenty of time—'

Kate abandoned hope of useful discussion. 'The water runs out of my bath,' she said.

Harriet broke off. 'But where's the stopper?' She demanded. 'Could Mrs Grant have borrowed it for somewhere else? How odd. I must go and see at once.'

Leaving the remains of lunch she forged away, perturbed, all else forgotten in this emergency.

Kate followed peaceably. One thing at a time.

'Ah, it *is* still there! I couldn't imagine where it could have gone! But its little collar's undone, that's what's wrong. It would have been crooked and then the water would get away. There's this little knob at the back to hold it up. Poor Kate, what a shame, you should have called someone.'

Called someone? Kate imagined a thin voice wailing and floating along icy corridors, lost down twisting stairs of unheeding stone.

'Now, are you quite all right otherwise?' Harriet bustled officiously into Kate's room, glancing round with apparent satisfaction at frayed chair arms, worn patches in the carpet, the dust on the pelmets.

'There was one thing.' Tidy Kate felt ashamed that she hadn't unpacked yet, and that the contents of her case were still scattered on the chairs. At least she had made her bed. 'Is there something I could borrow to stand on? I can't reach to hang up my clothes.' She had found nothing in the room she could move.

'Oh, poor thing, what a bore for you. We're all so tall in this family. This was Great-Uncle George's room and he was huge. Everything was designed for him. Of course we'll get you something.'

Second problem dealt with. Now for the important one.

'I must think what would do,' Harriet was pursuing anxiously. 'There's the stool in the larder but we really need it in there. I shall go at once – no, goodness, it's nearly dark and I've the hens and geese to shut up, the poor darlings will be wondering where I am. And then I must rush on because although strictly speaking it's not my turn I ought to help Grannie with the cooking since we'll be so many for dinner—'

'For dinner?' What now?

'Oh, didn't Joanna say? Really, she never pays the slightest attention to anything going on around her. I thought she could have found you some boots this morning, I must say. Heaven knows there are enough in the house. Yes, a few friends are coming for dinner, a local couple and a friend of Grannie's, and our vet and his wife from Muirend.'

Kate could hardly believe anyone would drive those long, wild, snowy miles to dine in such a house.

'Is there anything I can do to help?' she asked. Perhaps at least that much would be made clear, though the prospect of a dinner party threw her into panic. Would it be smart, what should she wear, or indeed was she included?

'Oh, Kate, would you mind? If you're not too tired? That would be kind. Grannie does tend to leave everything to the last moment, and with ten of us . . . .'

Kate did the sum, which gave her one answer. 'What time would you like me to come down?'

'After you've had your bath and dressed would be quite time enough. It's those last minute things. It's so sweet of you.'

'What should I wear?' Kate found the courage to ask as Harriet turned to the door.

'Oh, my dear, absolutely anything,' Harriet assured her unhelpfully. 'Only something *warm*. That dining-room can be freezing.' She spoke as though it were somebody else's.

'Would this do?' In something so vital Kate was capable of sticking to her guns. She held up a wine-red high-waisted dress in crushed velvet.

'Oh, no, no, it's not a party,' Harriet exclaimed, sufficiently horrified to come back. 'Let me see, now this would be perfect.' She selected a lined dress in honey coloured bouclé with a high roll collar. 'You are tiny,' she added wistfully, draping it across her arm like a saleslady profferring her wares. 'Now, I must go, my poor lambs will have taken themselves to beddies already.'

For lambs Kate assumed she should read hens.

Alone in the silent room – a feature of the house seemed to be that sounds were instantly swallowed up by its thick walls – she began to sort out her belongings. Opening a drawer as big as a coffin in a mahogany chest she was startled to find it full. Was this someone's room? But what clothes were these? A red hunting coat, white waistcoat, white breeches. Enormously long. Great-Uncle George's, untouched for how many years? In other drawers she found stiff collars in a round leather box with G.I.M.M. stamped on the lid, a smaller box with studs, pigskin gloves, monogrammed handkerchiefs still boxed and pinned. Well, why dispose of them? Who needed the space in a place like this? And there were plenty of empty drawers. Giggling, she disposed of her things among Uncle George's.

A heavy knock on the door made her jump violently. The distances here were so great she had felt completely cut off. Harriet bringing something to stand on. Kate hurried to open the door for her.

A square figure stood there in tweed breeches and jacket, stockings and boots, beside him what looked like a heavy monster of a chair.

'You're none the worse for your journey, then, I see,' remarked a voice oddly familiar, and a grin flashed in the weathered face. The man of the storm. What had Joanna called him? Doddie.

'Hello,' Kate said, pleased. 'I didn't know you worked here.'

'You could say that. I'm the keeper.'

The Keeper of the Ravens? 'Is your van all right?'

'Once I'd cleared the bits of hillside out of its grill.' He shook his head, grinning, as Kate opened her mouth to apologise. 'I was in the larder when Harriet asked me would I take this up to you.'

Why in the larder? 'Thank you. It looks terribly heavy.' Kate said dubiously, as he manoeuvred it through the doorway. 'And what is it exactly?'

'Ach, some fancy piece of kit. Library steps, will it be they call it? See now, this is the way of it. No, hang on, no' just like that. Ah, this wee lug here, now what do you think o' that?' With ponderous precision this splendid piece of Victorian design went through its paces and Kate watched its transformation with the sense of dream returning.

'Now don't go nipping your fingers playing with that,' Doddie ordered her unnecessarily. 'Where do you want it set?' He looked round for book shelves.

'So that I can reach into the wardrobe.'

'You don't tell me?' Doddie's big rolling laugh joined her rising giggles. 'Some place,' he said, shaking his shaggy head, 'when you need a stepladder to put by your clothes. Oh, see now, the damn thing's on wheels. We can't have you gallivanting about hither and yon.' With unhurried interest in the unfamiliar mechanism he fiddled away till he found the locking device, adding the sly comment, 'Since you're no' that much of a driver when all's said and done.'

In a roasting hot bath, this time without the water sinking miserably around her, the velvet curtains closed against the night, Kate felt fortified for the trials ahead but knew she mustn't linger. She wasn't sure where time went here. So far there had been no chance to explore her surroundings, indoors or out. She had been tumbled from one thing to the next, and now must face a crowd of new faces when she had barely sorted out the family. At least there had been no time to think of home, or the shock of what Jessie had revealed to her. And, even more surprisingly, no time to dwell on the obsessive worries about the baby, not only through the next seven months but into the lifetime of the unknown being growing inside her.

'Is she going to be all right, do you think?'

'From her point of view or ours?'

'Oh, Max, don't be so unkind. From hers, of course,' Joanna protested.

Max grunted. As far as he could see Kate, with her delicate build and nervous air, was just another person for him to take care of.

'She doesn't say much,' Joanna went on. 'Only gazes, looking alarmed. She thinks we're all lunatics.'

'But she's so pretty,' Harriet cooed. 'So vivid. Like a little humming bird. A humming bird in the snow,' she repeated, pleased with this.

Max, almost supine in one of the capacious Allt Farr morning-room chairs, long legs outstretched, tumbler of malt in hand, lifted his lip. He had shifted too much snow today to have the energy to tell Harriet what he thought of her.

'She's willing to please,' Joanna said. 'I think she'll be quite helpful.'

'Till we need her most,' Harriet pointed out.

'We went into all that when we discussed her coming here,' Max said sharply. Harriet had worried then as now about the work. Joanna had said, 'She'll feel awful not being able to help when we have so much to do. And we'll hardly have time to take care of her properly.' Grannie had crushed them both. 'Don't be ridiculous. You're both old enough to know that these things work out somehow and are over and done with.' Yes, Grannie had accepted at once, as he had, that Jeremy had left them no choice.

'Max, you'd better go up and change.'

'I'm fine as I am.' He could happily have dozed off with the warmth of the fire beating in his face, the soles of his shoes warming, the whisky stealing deliciously about its work.

'You smell of diesel,' Harriet objected, taking him seriously, as she had for the thirty-two years he'd been capable of winding her up, one of his earliest objectives in life. 'And Penny and Andrew always change even if Gilbert doesn't.'

'Change into something warmer, you mean. And don't tell me Gilbert's coming again. He comes far too damn often in my opinion.'

'Max, you know we haven't seen him since that lunch at Drumveyn. And living on his own, he loves going—'

'Harriet, don't rise,' Joanna protested wearily. 'Where's Grannie, by the way? Is anything happening about dinner?'

'She's basting the pheasants,' Harriet said. 'And Kate's laying the table. Perhaps I should make sure she can find everything—'

'God, don't tell me that's a car. Gilbert making sure he gets an extra dram in, no doubt.' With a burst of energy Max emptied his glass, propelled himself from his chair and was gone.

'You look after Gilbert. I haven't fed Buff yet.' Joanna followed him and with primmed mouth Harriet plumped the cushions and put Max's glass on the drinks tray before going down to the hall.

Laying the table was a worry. Everything seemed to pose a question. Sweet spoon across the top? Small knife angled across the side-plate? How to fold the napkins? What had she learned at school? Not much, since Jessie wouldn't let her be a boarder. Kate thought rather wildly back to the sports club dinner at Christmas, but for that there had been all sorts of seasonal trappings. Then common sense steadied her. Probably nothing that was done at the Southfield Country Club would be much help here. Better think back to the way things had been done at Nicola's house on those rare weekends Jessie had reluctantly agreed to. But it was all too long ago. With a groan at the sensation of venturing perpetually onto thin ice which Allt Farr induced she hunted in sideboard and ceiling-high corner cupboard and eventually had ten places laid, mats with pictures of game birds largely rubbed away, serving spoons and another silver bird, very squat and ugly she thought, in the centre of the table. That would have to do. If anything was wrong she would be told, she was sure. She would go back to the kitchen and see what else was needed. Finding her way to the sitting-room upstairs where she and Harriet had had lunch, and walking in on some happily drinking, gossiping group was too terrifying to contemplate.

Grannie, who had forgotten that it takes a lot longer to cook frozen vegetables for ten than for four was at the sink running hot water over a colander of broccoli. She called from her blanket of steam, 'Did you switch on the hotplate?'

'I did,' Kate replied, pleased with herself for thinking of it.

'You found everything?'

'Yes, thank you.'

'And drew the curtains?'

'Done.'

'Good girl.' Grannie had turned on the heaters earlier. 'Just give the potatoes a turn, would you? Lucky thing Harriet had made a terrine for me to pinch.'

Like so many references today Kate let this pass, nearly wafted ceilingwards in the heat from the oven, battling to steady a swaying roasting pan on the same scale as everything else in this exhausting place, and searching for a basting spoon. The fat hissed and spat, the oven cloth felt greasy to her hands; how she hated being dirty.

It wasn't so hard to face the morning-room at Grannie's brisk heels, though it seemed full of people. It was easy to remember that the middle-sized man (thank goodness for a change), with the red face and white hair, who seized Grannie in a robust hug, was Admiral Rathlyn. But the two younger couples, Andrew and Penny Forsyth, and the vet Tim Bellshaw and his wife, she failed out of sheer nervousness to pair off with conviction all evening. She managed only to distinguish the striking dark-haired Ilona who, as Kate doubtfully sipped her pale sherry and wondered if it was meant to taste this sour, gave a rapid, accented and largely incomprehensible rundown of her Magyar antecedents and the loss of their ancestral home in Transylvania.

Kate, wishing she could discreetly hide her glass, couldn't have said for certain where Transylvania was or rather, she suspected, had been.

This phase passed in a blur, the heat thrown out by the now stupendous fire and the pace of Ilona's tongue nearly sending Kate to sleep where she stood, but at last a move was made.

'I'll go down and do starters,' Harriet offered, and Kate was awake enough to catch Grannie's wink at what Harriet was going to discover starters to be. Max covered the fire, Buff was ordered to stay and the rest headed, not down the main stairs but along the corridor. A short cut to the dining-room, Kate supposed, allowing Tim (or Andrew?) to usher her before him.

Grannie, talking to Penny (Forsyth or Bellshaw?) opened a door and halted abruptly. A startled silence fell as everyone bumped into each other behind her. Speechless for once she turned to gaze at them, then surveyed again the empty table of a vast blank-windowed dining-room with convector heaters pumping away at either end.

'Well, Kate,' she said in a composed voice after a moment of total blankness on everyone's part. 'I imagine you did something with the knives and forks?'

'But I laid the table,' stammered Kate. 'In the dining-room. I've never seen this room before.'

'Where you had breakfast?' Joanna said, beginning to laugh.

'Yes, the dining-room.'

'Well, that, oddly enough, we call the breakfast room,' Grannie informed her, but it was all she could manage before laughter overtook her, overtook them all, in a great delighted roar which muffled the plaintive request from the list shaft, 'I say, could someone unload the pâté, please. My pâté, I might point out . . . .'

Curling up round her hot-water bottle, Kate tried to sort out what had followed. Certainly everyone had seemed to think it a huge joke. Max had turned off the heaters, he and the Admiral had brought the wine, Grannie had led the way down to the breakfast room.

'Perhaps we should tell Harriet,' someone had suggested and gales of laughter had swept them again.

Dimly through her confusion Kate had seen Max quietly round up the glasses she had put out and replace them with stemmed ones of incredible thinness. Some other hand had added forks to the spoons when what they called pudding arrived.

Andrew (or Tim) on one side and the Admiral on the other had looked after her kindly, demanding little in the way of conversation. Talk had been general and what had been most striking was how Max had changed, his dark eyes alive, his lined scornful face amused, his mood exuberant. She had felt too shy, too mortified, to notice much more, and had not been allowed to help. Done enough harm for one day, she told herself now, recalling that moment of silence in the dining-room doorway with a groan. What on earth would Jessie have said if such a thing had happened to her? That she would never be able to lift up her head again. She wouldn't have laughed. And on the memory of that gusting, spontaneous, friendly laughter Kate fell asleep at last.

Chapter Five

Leaning forward, hands tight on the wheel, Kate steered at thirty-five miles an hour along the unfenced moorland road, through a landscape of dark sodden heather, islands of snow spiked with stiff brown grasses, black peaty pools and outcroppings of wet granite, fading on every side into the mist which had never relented since she came. Not that she spared much attention for anything beyond the strip of colourless cropped grass separating the road from the snow water shouldering down the ditch, though she wasn't as near to either as she imagined.

She would never have believed she would be here, two days after arriving, venturing alone across this scary moor in an unknown car to fetch Laura, the member of the Allt Farr family she was most reluctant to meet. To be confronted with a child would bring home inescapably what lay before her.

How could everyone so suddenly have become unavailable? Harriet had to fetch the estate children from school, which it seemed Allt Farr still did even though Laura's days at Kirkton were over. Joanna was taking the old man Grigor who lived in the Cedar Hut down to the doctor. And Max had some inspector coming to check the plumbing and wiring of the new cottage.

When, not taking much notice of the lunch-time discussion of these plans, she had realised that the job of fetching Laura was heading her way, she had almost refused, remembering the disaster with Doddie's van and nervous about handling the jeep. But objections had been swept aside. Joanna had taken the jeep to Muirend, and Max had introduced Kate – so that she had at least a chance of getting there and back with it, as he said – to the Metro she was now driving.

'Have a run first,' he had ordered, heading for the garages with the incisive Munro stride which forced Kate into a trot. 'Nursery car, you should manage that.'

It was the successor to the car driven by the nannies when Laura was a baby, used now occasionally by Grannie but chiefly by any summer students deemed competent, but to Kate the term implied some sort of idiots' vehicle and she had felt happier. She had been less happy when Max had got into the passenger seat.

'Round by the farm,' he had directed, not missing her look of horror.

Kate hadn't yet been as far as the farm, half a mile away across the river in a curve of level ground below the hill. However, as she conducted an expressionless Max at a trembling crawl along the narrow track, where heavy vehicles had churned snow and mud to mush with an underlay of ice, she had had little time to observe its round stone byres, stark new barns and huddle of cottages. His presence was unnerving. Kate had already discovered that, like his mother, he had a quick temper and a biting tongue, but far worse was the underlying impression he gave of impatience amounting to contempt for everything going on around him. With him silent and watchful beside her it was hard to perform adequately the simplest mechanics of driving. She had not, as Max later asserted, repeated the *Highway Code* to herself as she went, but certainly her mind had not been on conversation or the scenery as they re-crossed the burn by a lower bridge and returned to the house via the road and the drive.

She had set off down the glen almost with relief, not guessing that Max, shaking his head, had gone in to phone Shirragh Lodge to say she would almost certainly be late. Down the Mennach Brae she had rolled, round the hairpin bend at the collection of cottages Max had called Bridge of Riach, then had turned right to climb over the pass, the Bealach Dubh, which led to this empty moor.

It was good, in spite of her nervousness about the route and meeting Laura, to be on her own for a while, safe from the critical voices, the sweeping pace, the watching eyes. At least she had by now established more clearly what the Munros thought she was doing in their house. Yesterday morning she had been trying to help a resisting Mrs Grant, actually taking the broom from her hands to sweep the kitchen floor, when Mrs Munro had come in to catch the postman with a much-labelled jiffy bag.

She had taken one look and said summarily, 'No, Kate, we do not clean.'

Stung by the tone, and catching Mrs Grant's look of triumph as she tweaked the broom away, Kate had asked almost heatedly for her, 'Well, I'm sorry, but what am I to do? I really don't know yet.'

Grannie had raised her eyebrows, as surprised as if a day-old chick had pecked her. 'You do what we do,' she had said sweepingly. And really Kate was beginning to see that that was what it amounted to. Everyone always seemed to be occupied with something; all she had to do was meet the demands as they came.

Grannie had been too busy to fetch Laura this afternoon because she had an order to finish. Kate understood that too now. Yesterday, a day of surprises and many trials, she had been taken to see the workroom. The vivid colours which Mrs Munro wore with such apparent carelessness but such success were explained. In the long low-ceilinged room above the kitchen in the oldest part of the house, with tiny leaded windows and ruthless striplighting, and with a welcome heat level aided by the Aga below, exotic fabrics spilled and mingled in a riot of creativity and disorder. Here Grannie designed the patchwork waistcoats and evening skirts in silks, brocades and velvets for which she had established outlets in Edinburgh and London. Here she plotted the intricate quilts, traditional or flamboyantly original, for which she had also found a steady demand. The humdrum stage of tacking material to card templates, being portable, was carried on all over the house and farmed out to any hands Grannie could coerce to the work. Kate had already witnessed a scene, which Joanna had assured her loudly enough for her mother to hear was all too common, of a vital batch of prepared pieces being hunted for with bitter accusations through the house.

'I suppose I shall have to give up this rubbish soon,' Grannie had said gruffly, looking at the worktable with an expression oddly vulnerable. 'Fingers getting too stiff. Half the time it's not fit to sell as it is but people are prepared to buy things today that would have been laughed at a hundred years ago.'

It was slightly unusual, unnatural even, this arrangement the Munros had established for mutual support and survival. Harriet was credible perhaps in the role of daughter at home, but had Max never longed to get married and kick them all out? Yesterday Joanna had explained her part in it at least, as she and Kate had put up curtain rails in the Burn Cottage, a job Kate would not have envisaged tackling before. Among the estate employees was there no handyman? It appeared not.

Joanna, like Harriet, had wished to make the point that Jeremy was a member of the family, and that Kate was welcome at Allt Farr for his sake. Referring to the tragedy that had taken his parents' lives when he was sixteen, she had spoken briefly of the death of her husband, Simon, in the same accident. They had been living near Woodstock then, and she and Laura had stayed on for a few months in the cottage of honey-coloured stone Simon had loved so much.

'But really, there was nothing to keep us there,' she said, taking a screw out of her mouth and accepting the screwdriver Kate handed up. 'And it seemed silly to try and find somewhere else to live, when this huge place was half empty. Keeping it going is like running a tap into a bottomless bucket, so we decided to pool our resources, financial or otherwise, and muck in together. Hill farming's a disaster these days but shooting's a good earner, then we did up the cottages for letting and I gradually got the garden back into shape. In the summer we supply fruit and vegetables to the cottages and flowers to a shop in Muirend. We do freezer cooking too, though strictly speaking we're not supposed to sell it. We add it to the rent and hope no one's looking.'

Waiting in the Fourtrak outside the surgery, for she had no intention of letting Grigor slip and having to scour the Friday afternoon pubs of Muirend for him, Joanna found her mind, as it had done all day, returning to this same conversation.

It was disconcerting to find herself reviewing their way of life at Allt Farr with a new objectivity. Normally she never gave it a thought, letting the days pour past, eternally occupied and on the whole satisfactory. But seen through the eyes of a stranger, and a candid, naïve stranger at that, had it really been the best plan? Should she have stayed at the Woodstock cottage, made an independent life for herself, brought up Laura in the environment Simon had preferred? But even now, after seven years, she found herself wincing away at once from the memory of that immaculately restored, perfect house. And without Simon the repetitive social round had been vapid, meaningless. She had noticed for the first time that their circle consisted almost exclusively of young couples like themselves, outwardly comfortably placed, affluent even, but all under pressure to maintain their enviable lifestyle. She had also seen that a widow plus small daughter was an anomaly in such a group, an uncomfortable reminder of a disaster which could at any moment overtake another of the workaholic husbands with their business trips round the globe and their mandatory fast cars. She had felt deeply, frighteningly lonely, unable to admit to anyone that the loneliness was not for Simon, with whom an edgy courtesy had been the best she could achieve for some time, but for the glen, the hills, the ease and understanding of old friendships. The place where her heart had always been, though that she could not say to anyone, then or now.

Kate glanced at her watch and increased her speed. Narrow as the road was, or seemed to her, it was perfectly open and she hadn't seen a vehicle since leaving Bridge of Riach. How bleak and unforgiving this landscape was. How could she ever live in such a place? But she knew her sense of obligation, honed by the years of Jessie's moral domination, would not let her leave. These people had helped her, they expected her to help them. She had come here on those terms.

It didn't occur to her that they were hourly expecting her to announce other plans, or would have welcomed the news. Though she was more acceptable than they had dared to hope, for the offhand description of her Jeremy had given, already bored by the whole affair, had not been promising, and much less so his lurid picture of Lamorna and her parents, she patently did not have the stamina to carry her through an Allt Farr season.

Kate herself could see that the pitfalls would be many. Yesterday had been one long struggle to do the right thing, with disasters lurking at every turn. How could she have known that that disgusting blackened piece of towelling was some treasured cloth for rubbing up the silver – or that putting the silver in the dishwasher was taboo in the first place? And annoyed as Grannie had been, Kate didn't think it had been necessary to add so crushingly, 'Knives, however, are more generally known as flatware.'

Still, she hadn't seemed to mind when Kate had said, she hoped reasonably, 'But no one ever really says that, do they?' Max, who had overheard, had laughed.

Then that wretched fire. She had thought she had done so well, finding the ash bucket, making the long journey three times from morning-room to dustbin in the courtyard. And there had been uproar. The ash had apparently been as precious as the silver cloth. Never cleaned out all winter, retained its heat for hours, the bin must be emptied at once (and to be honest it wasn't in prime condition by the time this was dealt with).

Certainly nothing was done in the way she was accustomed to at home. And there, crashing back, came the thoughts which the strangeness and endless activity of Allt Farr had held at bay. There was nothing now to protect her – the memories hit her like a fresh blow finding a bruise.

Jessie's hysterical anger at the news of Kate's pregnancy had swept them at once into dramas of soaring blood pressure, palpitations, raucous breathlessness, fat hand pressed to fat mound of breasts. There had been no way to break the news without loosing this instant storm of anger and incoherent accusation, and the crucial point had immediately become not Kate's situation but the blow dealt to Jessie. Jack, his craggy face set and grim, had not uttered a word, and that had been worse than all Jessie's recriminations. As soon as Jessie was lying, panting theatrically, on her Everstyl recliner, he had tramped heavily off, still in silence, staying away for the rest of that day and the next. He had refused ever to speak of the baby, and had had nothing to say when Kate, in helpless distress, begged him to confirm or deny the truth of what Jessie now vengefully revealed.

Kate had discovered at the age of eight, in the most traumatic and destructive way possible, taunted by her cousins on one of their dreaded but blessedly rare visits, that she had been adopted. On that occasion, Jessie had rushed from defensive secrecy to smothering assurances of love in the form of an avalanche of extravagant presents, for that was the period when money had arrived in their lives.

It was then too that Jessie had drawn for her the cosy picture of her real parents, a doctor and his wife, young, middle-class, successful, killed in a crash on the M1. This attractive, though sad, image had been the background to Kate's awareness of herself as she grew up. She had fantasised about unknown relations, girl cousins of her own age with whom everything, especially books, could be shared, and had formed a definite picture in her mind of these parents who had brought her into the world. However, she was fundamentally an amenable child who accepted things as they were, and she unquestioningly returned the love Jessie and Jack lavished on her.

For Jack had been a doting father, petting and spoiling the happy, affectionate little girl. As his passion for buying and selling, mainly cars but he could be tempted by anything that offered a profit, took them from the bricked-up prefab at the back of a dilapidated garage in Bedford, briefly to a terraced house in Islington, and remarkably soon to the modern comforts of Lamorna, his whole object had been to give Kate, not Jessie, the best within his power. He had been, though Kate never saw it, as eager as Jessie to touch through this adopted daughter, so improbable a child for them, a civilised world forever beyond his reach no matter what wealth he amassed.

For Jessie, choosing this baby, as physically different from her lumbering, coarse-skinned self as could well be imagined, Kate represented in a more personal way what she could never be. Jessie knew in her heart, had always known but never admitted it, that the only reason she and Jack had been accepted as adoptive parents had been the true status of Kate's father.

And this was what Jessie had flung at her, in a venomous need to wound, to release all the helpless jealousy, the awareness that she had made a profound misjudgement, which had built up over the years during which she watched Kate turn effortlessly into exactly the sort of person she had intended, yet most bitterly resented.

'A navvy, that's what your dad was, a navvy off the roads, a drunken, fighting, Irish navvy. And your mother was a tart, nothing better than a tart even if she did come from some fancy family. They soon got shot of you, her rich dad saw to that, didn't he? And you're just like her, coming waltzing in here telling me you're pregnant, I should have known you'd turn out just the same. And here's us worked our fingers to the bone to give you a decent education, that posh school and everything. Well, we're not throwing good money after bad, you can get out now, my lady, you're not staying in this house to shame us . . . .'

But the wheezing and gasping had overtaken her, and all else had been forgotten in trying to make her relax, breathe slowly. Jessie's chest pains, blood pressure and high cholesterol count were the arbiters of life at Lamorna. She dieted, binged, weighed herself and had hysterics, dieted again and spent a fortune on new clothes, and every ounce up or down was exhaustively despaired over or boasted about. But until the torrent of revelations undammed by the announcement of her pregnancy poured over her, Kate had never guessed at the violent jealousy her own slight build had aroused. She had learned that and much more. Tears filled her eyes.

Remembering with a shock where she was, she brought the car to a jerky halt, and made an effort to calm down. After all, there was lots to be grateful for. She would never have expected Jeremy to help her, had not, in fact, ever expected to see him again after that awful party. How he must have regretted looking her up, when he could have walked away in happy ignorance, trusting her assurance that she was on the pill, not suspecting she had never taken a precaution in her life because she had never had sex in her life. She had made a conscious decision that night, defying the aridity of her life, dazzled by a glimpse of how a relationship could be with a person from that other world, the world of openness, confidence, laughter and good manners, which she had encountered in Nicola's home. She had wanted to follow her instincts for once, free of the stifling hold of gratitude and duty Jessie had clamped around her, the adopted daughter, who must never forget all that has been done for her.

Dabbing away her tears, preparing to go on, Kate felt her soul curl up with reluctance. Laura, the child, brought close the reality of the baby, not just for the term of her pregnancy, but for the life beyond. This baby too would one day be an eleven-year-old, all things being equal, and for her or for him, unimaginable as it seemed, there would be taking to school, collecting from school. Though perhaps not, Kate thought, managing a watery smile, a private prep school in the middle of a Scottish wilderness. But whatever the school, this was a child who would not be given away.

Chapter Six

A white painted board said in plain black letters, 'Shirragh Lodge'. A tarmac drive led away between leafless birches. There was no sign of habitation. At least no sign to Kate, to whom it did not occur that the stand of well-grown trees ahead and the conifer plantations checkering the hillsides had not got there by themselves. Nervously she rolled along, till round a bend she found the drive filled with an oncoming Range Rover. She jolted to a stop, well squeezed in; or so she thought. The Range Rover took to the verge. In a moment she met two more cars. Was she late? Her nervousness increased.

The trees came nearer, an imposing stone archway material-ising in their midst, through which the drive curved to reveal a lawn the size of a cricket pitch and a monstrous pile of sandstone turrets, crenellations, battlements, and big bay windows framed in paler stone. Before it, round a few large and mainly four-wheel-drive vehicles, gathered small girls with assorted luggage, rolled-up drawings, shaky models. Brisk mothers called to each other, quelled roaring babies in car seats, shouted at dogs lifting their legs on the berberis.

I should not be here, Kate wailed inwardly, making three separate decisions about where to park. And now running forward was the archetypal child of this confident race, with thin pale face, high forehead, fair hair scraped back into a band, a bright sweater of randomly mixed squares, in which the hand of Grannie could be seen, sagging from her narrow shoulders. Would she resent Kate's presence, or at best be disappointed that none of the family had come for her?

Kate wound down her window, filled with a hollow reluctance.

'You're hardly late at all.' The thin face was beaming. 'I'm so glad you came, I've been dying to meet you. Did you bring Buffie? Oh, well, it doesn't matter a bit really. And can we give Fanny a lift, her mother couldn't come, I'll tell you where.'

A darker, tubbier child bobbed at her shoulder, both arms wrapped round a bulging pink and yellow nylon holdall.

Relief at Laura's smile and the warmth of her greeting made Kate beam back at both children.

'I think Buff went with your mother.' The mere thought of being shut up alone with him in the car for miles made her shudder. 'But look, are you sure —?'

Drive off with some extra unknown child into these uninhabited wastes, leaving her — where?

'It's all right,' Laura assured her, reading her doubts with ease. 'Her mother knows. So does Miss Kilgour. Hang on a sec though. Don't get in, Fanny.'

She was off, to hover with importunate courtesy at the elbow of a tall girl, the only person present in a skirt, Kate noticed, who was calmly allowing a barrage of advice from a firm-looking mother to bounce off her.

Kate got out of the Metro, though she still held on to its door like a security blanket, and smiled shyly at Fanny, who was placidly awaiting Laura's further instructions. And that was how it was. Laura brought Miss Kilgour over, made the introductions, took the key from the ignition, opened the boot, packed in her belongings then Fanny's, opened the passenger door and called goodbye to Miss Kilgour before diving into the back, clicking the front seat down and ordering Fanny in.

In a very short space of time Kate found herself rolling

through the arch with a Discovery ahead of her and a Mercedes behind, with Fanny placid and smiling beside her, Laura's fingers knobbly under her left shoulder, and Laura's eager, friendly voice in her ear.

Extraordinary that the presence of one eleven-year-old could change Allt Farr so much. For the first time, with Laura at home, Kate felt herself steadying, seeing things in more normal perspective, able to take in something of her surroundings at last, instead of batting anxiously from one crisis to the next, too harried to absorb anything or orientate herself properly. Also, though she still hated them, the cold and discomfort were no longer a shock. She now had a supply of borrowed shirts and sweaters, and Joanna had bought wellingtons for her in Muirend. With the scarves, gloves, and socks on hand in abundance at Allt Farr, and the friendly fur-lined jacket in which she no longer cared how she looked, a comfortable level of protection had been achieved.

Laura simply took her over. When they reached home they got no further than the laundry, where the contents of Laura's bag were pushed into the washing machine and set in motion, and the rest of her luggage dumped. Laura's greetings to the family were confined to opening the kitchen door and giving a piercing whistle. A grinning Buff, who seemed to have shed five years, came bounding out to greet her and the door was slammed again.

'Come on,' said Laura, for the first of many times. 'We'd better feed Persie before it gets dark.'

'Percy?' Kate hurried after her. Should she insist that Laura went in?

'Persephone, really. Don't you love "dim meadows desolate"? It makes me cry – you know how you can deliberately let lovely things make you cry? Do you ever do that? Only we haven't got time just now.'

Yes, Kate thought, with a surge of amused pleasure, she sometimes did that. And she too loved those lines, and had never before had anyone with whom to share their magic.

Though she had to be instructed every step of the way, discovering such new pleasures for the senses as the chill slither of corn over her hand, the smell of a meal-coated feed bucket, the warm intimacy of a lighted loosebox with winter dusk turning to icy night outside, she was conscious of a new involvement, of acceptance. Even the presence of Buff, so obviously a vital element of the scene for Laura, seemed unthreatening in this different context.

'Come and say hello to Persie,' Laura said. 'Give her a pat on the neck. Bring your hand up from the side, not in front of her eyes.'

The brown Dartmoor pony regarded Kate with a liquid dark eye that was not entirely acquiescent, as for the first time in her life Kate touched warm equine skin.

'She can be a bit wicked,' Laura said fondly, after Kate had withdrawn her hand. 'We'd better do Torquil now, he'll be getting impatient.'

Torquil, it seemed, did not live in Persephone's luxury. Kate followed Laura across the gravel to a gate into the field which sloped to the river. How did I not even know they existed, the brown pony and this towering mass of flesh and bone with long mane and tail and hairy ankles and great swinging haunches, who came hurrying to meet them?

'He's Uncle Max's,' Laura explained, struggling to stay on her feet as the big garron nudged her in what was evident even to Kate was an entirely friendly way. 'Isn't he a darling? Look at his terrific winter coat. He stays outside all year, he likes that best. Uncle Max built him a shed but he only uses it to scratch his back on. He gets jolly cross if you shut him in.'

What did such a heavyweight do when he was cross? But Kate braved herself to run a tentative hand into the furry coat and was amazed at the warmth below. When Laura taught her, without asking if she already knew, to hold her hand flat to offer some horse-feed nuts, the gentleness and velvet softness of the questing lips which picked them delicately from her palm were a total and marvellous surprise.

There was a hint almost of adventure, certainly of unfamiliar freedom, in hurrying back up the field in the cold dusk, running through the tunnel between stable yard and courtyard where the lights made an intricate pattern of the high logpile stacked there, and gleamed back from the frill of icicles along the eaves.

Collecting Laura's belongings as they went (her logistical efficiency much impressed Kate) they burst into the blissful warmth of the kitchen to find the entire family assembled there.

Their presence flurried Kate at once. We should have come in first, we should have. . . .

'We've done Persie and Torquil,' Laura announced.

'Good girl,' Max said.

'Not too many Friday treats, I trust,' said Grannie, needle flying as she stitched patchwork blocks to a lattice strip.

'Oh, well—'

Kate was surprised to observe that among the greetings, questions about the week, teasing comments to herself about being side-tracked, it was to Max, browning chicken pieces in a furiously sizzling frying pan at least two feet across, that Laura went first for a hug, twining herself against him tightly before going to kiss her mother.

'Good, chicken, my absolute, absolute favourite. I'm going to do my bloody homework before it spoils the whole weekend. Where's warm?'

'Try the estate room. And don't show off.'

Laura winked at Kate. 'Buffie, come with me and make it all less atrociously tedious.'

'I don't think she heard you,' Joanna remarked to her mother. A laugh went round as the door shut and Kate was conscious of a distinct lightening of mood. Dinner that evening, earlier than usual, was also more relaxed, though Laura was not permitted more than her share of centre stage. As Kate observed Joanna, Max and Grannie preventing this (Harriet's similar chidings were ignored), she suspected that they would actually have been content to let Laura chatter as much as she liked.

Her own reservations about her were forgotten. Here was a character in her own right, a competent, active individual, with her niche in the odd family group, her own life to lead.

On Saturday morning Laura was up before anyone. So much for the young, Kate thought, finding her demolishing a huge bowl of cereal, who could not be dragged from their pits in the morning, clinging to airless curtained caves throbbing with pop music, walled with images of global destruction, smelling of trainers and unwashed T-shirts. This was almost Kate's only image of youth at home. Thus her 'cousins' had whiled away the time till bored, resentful, unemployment overtook them.

Laura was up early because she had a lot to do. Most importantly she had to show Kate round, and for Kate that day alien, hostile Allt Farr took on a new character. With Laura (and Buff, for he was Laura's dog, she learned) she made the rounds of every building near the house, stores and granary, gunroom and students' flat, old wash-house, mower shed, toolhouse, workshop, tackroom, and the engine room dating from the days when Allt Farr had generated its own electricity.

Kate discovered that for Doddie the larder was not the freezing pantry along the passage from the kitchen where she frequently found herself hunting miserably for items of food which never came packaged as she expected to see them. Doddie's larder was a slatted shed where the carcases of deer (hinds, Laura said) hung in a modern chill room, and a cauldron lurked which Laura explained blithely was for boiling heads.

Don't ask, Kate told herself firmly. This truly was the land of the barbarians. Yet as the morning went on and they went across to the farm and penetrated into barns and byres and dairy, as Kate drank strong tea or weak coffee in hot kitchens while Laura checked on the progress of babies, hamsters, budgies and a moribund collie, the resistance to the whole place that had made her so tense and anxious began imperceptibly to thaw.

When Laura, discovering with delight that Kate hadn't been shown over the house, brought her in for a detailed tour, Kate did take the chance to ask Joanna if there was anything else she should be doing.

'Not at all,' Joanna told her. 'I'm only thankful that someone's looking after you properly at last. We always seem to be so busy. I'd come with you only the freezer's getting rather bare and I want to do some batch cooking as it's my turn today.'

Kate had by now learned that each member of the family took a day in the kitchen – and that Grannie was a flagrant stealer of dishes someone else had prepared.

The tour of the house was an eye-opener to Kate. Each room in use, which to her had seemed vast in the first place, proved to have an abandoned and even larger counterpart, smelling of mildew and fuzzed by damp. In high towers draughts lifted heavy curtains; in one wing all the bedrooms led inconveniently out of one another; and Laura referred to rooms larger than the master bedroom at Lamorna as dressing-rooms. An impressive library offered the momentary reassurance of endless reading, till Kate realised she probably wouldn't have the endurance to stay long enough to choose a book. Their journey ended in a coke-smelling basement where a heating plant which looked capable of propelling a Cunarder across the Atlantic panted and heaved.

'That's the trouble with once being rich,' Laura remarked with a sigh. 'You get things like boilers and electricity first and then you can't improve them because you've got poor. Grandfather spent everything we had. He was a philanderer.' She made it sound a career, like a diplomatist. 'That's why Grannie learned to do her waistcoats and things. Aunt Harriet had a deprived childhood, but it was better for Uncle Max and Mummy because Grandfather had died by then and the mistresses weren't such a drain and they were able to come back here. Would you like to see my room?'

Kate, wondering if she should cut short these potted histories, accepted courteously, and was surprised to find a neat austere cell, bed made, slippers aligned, walls bare, window *open*. Well, perhaps that made sense. The only non-essentials were small bronzes of dogs and horses, and rows of books, mostly, she saw, the well-read favourites of an earlier generation *Flicka*, *Black Beauty*, *Rennie the Rescuer*, *Greyfriars Bobby*, and lots of Malcolm Saville and Pullein-Thompson. There came vividly back the avid, thrilling pleasure of Friday lunch hours at school when the junior library had been opened and certain pleasure had lain there for the taking. A pleasure never shared; how odd to feel so certain it could be shared if she wished with this child, known for less than a day. An image, startling, hardly formed, of one day sharing all this with her own child caught at her. It was the first truly positive and exciting glimpse of the future she had had, she realised.

'Should we have let Laura loose on her?' Grannie, her urgent order finished, packed up and sent off with Postie, was asking in the kitchen.

'You surely don't think there's any danger that the pleasure of Laura's company will induce her to stay?' Max had had a bad morning inspecting the damage roe deer, leaping in from a frozen drift in spite of all he'd spent on fencing last year, had wreaked on his young plantations, and he didn't conceal his irritation.

'That and her conscience,' his mother said. 'I suspect she feels committed to helping us out. Jeremy will have coloured the picture to suit his own ends.'

'Help us out? Almost anyone would be more use to us. Have you seen her trying to put her gumboots on? In her hands they have a life of their own. And she doesn't leave the Aga kettle empty out of idleness or stupidity; she can't lift the damn thing.'

'I must say when I saw the cream this morning I felt like suggesting that she packed there and then,' Harriet said, still aggrieved.

Kate had given up searching for milk in cartons and had filled a jug for breakfast not from the churn on the larder floor but from one of the flat pans on the slate slab, first making sure she thoroughly stirred the yellow cream waiting to be made into butter by Harriet.

'Do you think she'd hope to see Jeremy here?' Joanna pondered. 'I mean, we don't really know how things stand between them, do we?'

'I know how Jeremy thinks they stand,' Max snapped. 'He made a mistake and he's got us to sort it out for him. I'd be surprised if he shows his face here this side of Christmas.'

Joanna looked unconvinced. She was a romantic, and her lost love was not the husband who had died. 'And have you noticed,' she went on, willing to let the question of Jeremy go for the moment, 'Kate never phones or writes home, and hasn't had a word from anyone since she came?'

'They slung her out, we know that. It was the reason we took her in, wasn't it?'

'Don't be so sarcastic, Max. If she's come away as they wanted, and now no one will know about the baby, they could surely be in touch with her here.'

'Let them sort it out. According to Jeremy, her people are bloody awful anyway.'

'Well, she's not,' said Grannie suddenly. 'Oh, useless, I grant you, not at all what we need, but there is nothing in her one could possibly dislike, and she has a sort of desperate courage I can only admire.'

Her son and daughter received this with raised brows. An accolade indeed from their critical parent.

Chapter Seven

Sunday. Not at all like Sunday at Lamorna. First a tap on the door and Laura's head coming round it. 'Hi. Do you want to come and help me muck out Persie?'

Then, while Kate struggled awake working out what this might mean and deciding the answer was no, apart whisked the curtains under Laura's no-nonsense hand, revealing a morning of unimagined brilliance and splendour. With a gasp of delight, Kate slid out of bed and snatching the eiderdown to wrap round her joined Laura at the window. Below them, the shadow of the house stretched its fantastic blue-black shape over river and trees; above, oddly more distant in the sunshine, the hill face glowed in colour, climbing in ledges and ridges Kate had never yet seen to an amazing blue sky. Breathlessly she gazed. Five days, and she had had no idea she was surrounded by this stunning beauty.

'Come on . . . .'

It was a heady moment to come out through the courtyard arch and see for the first time, beyond the hoar-white lawn patterned by sharp tree shadows, the length of the glen stretching away, mile after mile in the sun, the dazzle of snow on a towering dramatic skyline till now shrouded in mist, the blue gleam on slate roofs at the farm, the unsuspected colour drawn forth from drab plantations.

Horse manure. She suspected Laura might use a simpler term.

It wasn't horrible, it wasn't even unpleasant. Why was that? She thought of Jessie's horror and laughed as she shovelled. And going into the kitchen she thought of her again, of Sunday frowstiness, the smell of frying and cigarettes, Jack's braces, mangled tabloids, Radio One, yawns, nagging. She had accepted the scene as inevitable, inescapable. Now it was associated with Jessie's abusive anger, Jack's unrelenting silence, and she flinched away from the thought of it, turning gratefully to a new scene.

'We'll start breakfast,' Laura said. 'I'm starving. Mrs Grant doesn't come in on Sundays. It's lovely, we have the kitchen to ourselves.'

At the sight of the basket of eggs she carried to the Aga Kate had to retreat, but returning found herself surprisingly hungry. An appetite whipped up by hard outdoor work on a frosty morning had little truck with morning sickness. Though she prudently stuck to cereal and toast she put away three times the usual quantity.

Was the relaxed mood because Mrs Grant was absent or because Laura was there, she wondered as one after another the family appeared, Max from outside where he too must have been busy. Mrs Munro was particularly acid in the mornings (watching her fumble with the lid of the coffee jar or tighten her lips as she got up from her chair Kate had decided she must be arthritic and thought the temperature of the house could do her little good) but today she made an effort to be good-humoured.

Harriet suffered from morning sniffles and from time to time sneezed shatteringly. As she took a deep breath to blow her nose the corner of the tissue was drawn into her mouth. How many times had she done that, Kate wondered, as Harriet unstuck it from her tongue. Grannie closed her eyes as though the sight was unendurable.

Max was in unusually good spirits, full of energy, cooking a huge breakfast for himself, pronouncing the coffee Laura had made hogwash and making more half as strong again. Coming from a background where criticism was automatically resented,

Kate found it agreeable to hear Laura giggle at his comments.

'What are we doing this morning, Uncle Max?' Laura asked as a move was made to clear the table.

'Pretty boring, I'm afraid. I promised Jim I'd look at the tractor. Gearbox by the sound of it, in which case I won't be able to do much, but it's worth a try.'

'Oh, no, not at the weekend! That's not fair!' For the first time Laura looked seriously upset.

'Sorry, little Lal, but it has to be done.'

Joanna pulled a sympathetic face at her daughter. She had been impressed at how much treasured weekend time with Max Laura had been ready to give up to Kate.

'You and Kate could come to Craigbeg with me,' Harriet suggested eagerly. 'I promised to take down some material for costumes for the Mother's Day play. Letitia's making them. She's brilliant at that sort of thing.' Turning to Kate she added in a curious mixture of self-consciousness and pride. 'Letitia is my friend.'

'Well, we could.' Laura didn't sound enthusiastic. Every other face, Kate observed with interest, had emptied of expression.

'You'll have to give it a bit of wellie, Aunt H,' Laura recommended, hanging onto the crammed basket.

'Oh, dear, I did prefer the old Land Rover,' Harriet wittered, over-accelerating in second and sending the Fourtrak whining up a gut of track between boulders where snow was still blown in. Kate pressed herself back in her seat, wondering who would choose to live at the top of what was more like a river bed than a road.

Harriet jerked to a stop on a wind-raked level adorned by a washing line dotted with clothes pegs, a tangle of wire netting and fence posts, and a stack of branches pushed by the wind into a rhomboid which looked ready to take off at any moment. A few draggled hens paced about. Ducks formed into a line and quacked off hurriedly towards a puddle. Buff whined to get out.

'We mustn't forget the cream and butter and – oh, you've got them, Laura, good girl. Poor Letitia can't get out to shop with the track like this.'

'Motorbike,' Laura explained to Kate. 'You'd better stay, Buffie darling, you know the cats hate you.' Hopping from one relatively dry patch to another she led the way to a wooden lean-to tacked onto the damp harling of the cottage and went in. Expecting some kind of porch Kate was surprised to find as she followed that they were in a kitchen. Later she thought she must have imagined the chinks of light visible through the walls. A low clay sink was flanked by a wooden draining-board rotted to a spongy frill. A gas ring sat on a fat-spattered tea-chest; rough shelves held rudimentary cooking utensils and a variegated collection of china.

'That you, love?' called a voice, and down two steps into the kitchen came a quaking mass of flesh clothed in shades varying from dead bark to dried earth. 'Laura too, that's nice now. And you must be Kate. Letitia Hughes.' A pronounced lilt in the syllables of her name. A podgy hand met Kate's in a surprisingly firm grip, and a smile of great warmth and sweetness shone from the pink-cheeked multi-chinned face. 'On with the kettle, then. And I made flapjacks yesterday, isn't that lucky?'

Laura's blank look seemed unpromising.

'This is this morning's cream, so it should be all right in here. I've brought lots of material so you can keep anything that won't do . . .' Harriet seemed very much at home, unpacking the basket, chattering animatedly.

'That's fine, love,' Letitia said, not listening, filling a brown enamel kettle then hefting it with an intent look and pouring some of the water away. 'Not good at four,' she said cryptically.

'Three,' said Laura.

Letitia poured some more water out and lit the gas ring which popped and roared. Draughts sliced by, head-high. Kate did up the buttons of her furry jacket.

'Shall I put the milk in a jug?' asked Harriet, surreptitiously checking the date on the carton Letitia had handed her.

'If you must. More washing up. I don't know, using up the world's resources.' Letitia winked at Laura who grinned back. 'No one take sugar?' It was barely a question.

Harriet put milk jug and mugs on a tray worn to the tin in the centre, with dim flowers discernible round the edges, then rearranged them.

'You did very well to get up here,' Letitia commented and Harriet flushed with pleasure. That's the first time I've heard anyone say anything nice to her, Kate realised. That's rather awful. Does her whole life consist of put-downs, or at best impatient tolerance? The unmarried, unvalued elder sister, unappealing, not particularly bright. What, really, was her role at Allt Farr? What contribution did she make? Keeping house? Everyone seemed to share that. Perhaps she helped Joanna with the garden. Other than that she seemed to be involved with village affairs, the Women's Institute or whatever it was called here, and – what? A children's play for Mother's Day? Yet she seemed busier than anyone, forever hurrying, forever behindhand. She did a lot of ironing. She even maddened Grannie over that.

'Can you seriously tell me it serves any purpose to iron tea towels?' Kate had heard the sharp voice demand. 'And squashing soft fluffy towels to gritty boards is intolerable. Allt Farr is not a second-rate hotel.'

Kate had been intrigued to observe that when Grannie had stalked off Harriet had ironed a bra. Reckless defiance or her normal practice?

Not that Grannie was consistent. She had rejected out of hand some monogrammed handtowels Kate had ironed to help Harriet. Only she had called them face towels.

'Well dampened, hot iron, something soft underneath them. There is no pleasure in using a crumpled rag.'

But there was no time to dwell on the anomalies of the Munro domestic regime, which were legion. Letitia, having filled the mugs and, with a small sound of irritation at herself, saved the excess hot water in a thermos flask, was at last leading her guests out of the icy box of the kitchen into the cottage proper.

'Light!' she called, as they crowded along a coat-smelling hall of varnished tongue-and-groove. Kate looked for a switch then heard a giggle beside her.

'She means put the kitchen one off,' Laura hissed as she turned back to comply. Thank goodness for Laura.

A bright fire in a Victorian tiled fireplace welcomed them in what was evidently Letitia's bedroom. There was an impression of hostile withdrawal as at least three cats whisked into defensive positions. A high mantelpiece, its paint smoke-browned, cluttered with damp-curled postcards, salt and pepper mills, wax-dribbled candlesticks, matchboxes and biscuit tin, dominated the room. The hearthrug was patterned with scorch marks. Geraniums in yoghurt tubs, flowering in a climate which never altered, cut off the light at the small window. A counterpane of shapeless knitted squares of indiscriminate colours covered the bed.

Half-finished macramé, knitting, embroidery, crochet, and a little spirit lamp and set of oddly-shaped tools for making decorations in wax, cluttered every surface. A strip of cushion piping, string protruding from its ends, snaked over a chair, every so often batted by a furtive paw. A design of some sort was pinned flat by a chair leg and a boot. A piece of kindling marked a book at the instructions for grafting knitting. The few other books were manuals ranging from bee-keeping to plumbing, from herbal remedies to the history of the pig. Nothing to read.

'Sit yourselves anywhere,' Letitia cried, sinking like a shot-down barrage balloon into a cushioned nest with draught-defying wings. Kate after a moment's hesitation cleared an upright wooden chair for herself, gingerly lifting a half-knitted sock spiked like a mine with needles, a length of material with pins in unexpected places, an egg-smeared plate.

'Let's have a look at what you've brought then.' The Welsh

voice was comfortable, easy, and Letitia's face was very kind as Harriet unfolded her offerings, in a flurry of, 'Of course, if this won't do,' and 'I thought this might work but if you don't think so I shan't mind a bit.'

With all its mess and squalor, Kate perceived that this was the room of a person at ease with who she was, content with what she had and did. And it was equally clear that Harriet, who unasked had added a log (of rolled-up newspapers) to the fire, found here an approbation and reassurance lacking at Allt Farr.

The room was multi-purpose; small television in the corner, telephone by the fire. With a pang Kate was reminded of her own room at home, so carefully planned by Jack as a surprise for her twentieth birthday. He had come to regret, she guessed, fitting up that independent unit for her, for once she was home from work in the evenings she had been reluctant to leave it. How dangerously she had allowed its cosy comfort to lull her into acceptance of her situation, initiative sapped, guilt at all she was missing suppressed by long habit. The present reasserted itself in the shape of one of Letitia's flapjacks. To bite or to bend, even in desperation to soften unobtrusively by sucking?

'We should have brought Buff in,' Laura whispered, banging hers on the edge of a table laden with tattered copies of *Motor Cycle News*, making no impression on the flapjack but leaving a sticky yellow line on the dusty varnish. Kate thought of the silent waiting cats and decided Buff was better off where he was.

'Here.' Laura had gnawed her way through the last of her flapjack like a dog getting down to a bone, and now disposed of Kate's under the chintz tatters of her chair. 'Somebody will get it.'

Kate glanced quickly at her hostess but she and Harriet were safely absorbed, discussing arrangements for the Kirkton hotel swill to go to someone called Fred. (Was Fred a person? You could never be sure here.) Then, the swill dealt with, and a shopping list made of various things Letitia needed, Harriet picked up an almost-finished sweater of beige and grey flecks and began to do intricate things to the shoulder.

Clearly in this house Harriet was an achiever, a benefactor, even an authority. But was there more to it than that, Kate wondered as the jeep skidded down the track. At Letitia's Harriet was the younger person, the thin person, the socially secure person. There it did not matter how she looked, how she dressed. She could hold her own in conversations about chickens, flowerpot holders, turning a heel. She could give and receive affection.

It was not the only surprising visit of the day.

Lunch, like breakfast, was eaten in the kitchen. Not that anyone went in for the red-faced struggles with a roast and gravy and apple pie and rice pudding which Jessie persisted in every Sunday.

'That's what your Dad likes and that's what he'll get,' she would pant, splatting a wodge of pallid cabbage into a vegetable dish and pushing up her spectacles with the back of a fat wrist. Kate knew that Jack, arriving late from the clubhouse, wanted nothing more than to put the paper over his face and go to sleep.

'Better go and stir James out of his sloth yet again,' said Max, discovering the coffee pot to be empty after a second brew.

'I made a chocolate cake to take with us,' Harriet said, jumping up to fetch it.

'Very original,' said Grannie, and Harriet flushed.

'We go to Riach every Sunday,' Laura told Kate. 'The Mackenzies are our nearest neighbours.'

Kate concluded that the inhabitants of the houses at Bridge of Riach, where they turned left into a long drive, didn't count. Grannie followed with Joanna and Harriet in the Metro. ('Too like a charabanc outing, don't you feel, if we all crowd into the jeep?')

'This is where they want to put a horrible new bit of road,' Laura said, 'so that coaches can come up in the summer and go on over the Bealach.'

The drive led upwards to a large white house, baldly set down on level grass, not a plant or bush breaking its severe lines, iron railings and cattle grid keeping stock at bay. As Max pulled up on the gravel Kate saw that shutters were closed over several windows.

'Uncle James's wife, Aunt Camilla, was killed three years ago falling out of the stable loft,' Laura hastily briefed her. Kate was glad someone had. 'Ow, Buff, that hurt! Hang on a minute. He goes mad because there are two bitches here. Go on, then, stupid dog.'

Grannie roared up behind them.

'Choke out all the way,' Max remarked resignedly to no one in particular. At least at Riach he could be free of these damned females of his for a while.

Silence hung in a wide empty hall. And cold. I could weep to walk into cold once more, Kate thought in despair.

'Come on, you old bastard, don't pretend you haven't heard us,' Max shouted, striding to a door on the left which led to a room almost as bare as the hall. Supine in a deep armchair, his feet on a threadbare stool, stretched a long thin man with a dark long-jowled face, his eyes closed, his hands folded across a padded gilet.

'Time to get rid of the girlie magazines,' Max warned, kicking the footstool away. 'Grannie's hard on my heels.'

'Shouldn't think they'd bother her,' muttered the inert figure. 'Have you ever considered letting me have Sunday afternoons to myself? Bridie makes some kind of effort with lunch, which is a considerable shock to the digestive system – oh, I do beg your pardon!' he exclaimed, having opened one eye a slit and found Kate standing shyly behind Max. He scrambled to his feet. 'I had no idea. For God's sake, Max, you could have said something.'

Grannie arrived. 'I see you've done nothing about those cracked panes yet, indolent James.' But surprisingly she kissed him.

Harriet followed with her cake.

'Harriet! How kind! And chocolate, my favourite.'

All part of some unshakeable ritual, Kate gathered. But there was no doubting the kindness of this stooped, bony man, with his untidy dark hair and gentle eyes, as he gestured Kate to a chair by the fire.

'How very civil,' Grannie mocked. 'Kate, he'd be horrified if anyone except Max actually stayed with him. Out comes the malt whisky, off go the womenfolk. Come along. We're allowed in again at tea-time.'

'No, I assure you –' James spoke with the hesitant eagerness of the profoundly shy. 'But please do whatever you prefer – I mean, it would be rather dull here—'

'Put the man out of his misery,' Grannie said. 'Bring your cake, Harriet. Laura, I see, has already gone.'

Only Joanna hesitated, pausing to flick through a copy of *Country Life*, as yet unopened, on a table in the window. Max's movement to a well-stocked drinks tray made up her mind for her and she hurried out after the others.

Open doors showed bleak rooms with great sash windows bare of curtains, and gilded mirrors replicating ghostly versions of austere expanses. A heavily curtained archway led to a heavily padded door.

'James goes to considerable lengths not to let warmth reach him,' Grannie explained, with a glint of a smile, and opened the door onto a different world.

Chapter Eight

In the tropical heat of the huge kitchen a scene in startling contrast to the rest of the house met Kate's eyes, as two wild-eyed red setters leaped across the chewed bones and strewn toys on the floor to greet Buff. Pop posters and nursery art covered the walls, a myriad of magnets furred the fridge, never-pruned plants ramped across work surfaces or cascaded down cupboards, their leaves pale with overwatering. A television mouthed on a high shelf, a grease-and-crumb clogged radio pounded away on top of a microwave, tapes scattered the table among food of a kind Kate had never expected to see again, most of which looked as if it lived there permanently. Crisps and Ribena, processed cheese, HP sauce, a packet of sliced ham, a plastic bag of spongy rolls, a wholesale box of Mars Bars, were circled by unfinished plates of ketchup-slathered chips, steaks or chicken-burgers.

Harriet was at the sink, making space to wash a plate for her cake. Two small dark-haired girls were at the table spooning in ice cream. Two larger girls were sprawled in chairs turned away from it, cigarettes in hand, mugs of tea and overflowing ashtray within reach. Did the small girls, clearly twins, belong to one of them? All four beamed on their visitors, with great goodwill but without moving.

'Are you coming sledging, Laura?' asked a twin. 'Would you

like some ice cream first?' She spoke from behind a piled spoonful nearly obliterating her face.

Her voice revealed she was not the daughter of either of the blowsy females lolling beside her, the marginally brighter looking of whom asked, 'Are you for tea, Mrs Munro? There's plenty in the pot. Hi, Laura, hi, Joanna.' Her eyes swivelled to Kate and stayed there.

Grannie shuddered. 'Spare me, I beg. Kate, these two creatures are Bridie and Dottie, and while I have no hope of their coming to their feet to greet you, I do insist however that the Misses Mackenzie abandon their gluttony for a moment to do so. Kate, may I present Sybilla and Sasha, James's daughters, though I do not recommend that you touch either of them. This is Kate Fletcher, who will be spending the summer with us.'

With great good nature the children slipped down, stepping over the writhing dogs who snarled ferociously as they pinned each other's necks with flailing paws. Each twin smiled on Kate, offering her a sticky hand, then each folded herself in an identical manner across her chair, using a knee to heave herself back to business.

'Ach, Sunday wouldn't be Sunday without a ticking-off from Mrs Munro,' Bridie commented, beaming. 'That's no to tea, then, so how about a coffee? Kate, what are you for? Help yourself to anything you want, Laura. Gee whizz, will you flaming dogs go take a running jump.'

'I think they are,' observed Sybilla, using both hands on the table edge to twist her chair square again and holding on as the dogs blundered past.

'Corridor, I think,' said Grannie calmly, and Joanna agreed, ordering Buff out and letting the other two pursue him in crazy leaps.

'There now, I think that looks very nice, don't you?' said Harriet, admiring her cake.

Grannie lowered her eyelids in exaggerated weariness.

'Now Kate, you can sit down without getting swept away,'

Joanna said, turning a cushion over to see if the other side looked less uninviting.

It didn't, and Kate sat down with distinct reservations. She understood why Max had stayed with James, arctic conditions or not, and was surprised to see Grannie in such excellent humour, accepting a chair but holding up her hands to ward off further hospitality.

'Doddie was in a fight last night,' volunteered the twin who talked, Sybilla. Her sister nodded, reaching for the raspberry ripple again. Grannie drew the tub away and looked her in the eye. Sasha looked back, and did not insist.

'Ach, that one,' said Bridie. 'When wouldn't he be in a fight? It was Saturday, wasn't it?' She pulled herself to her feet with the aid of the table and slapped over to the sink to refill the kettle. She was wearing the kind of stretch jeans which even Kate, who did not follow the fashions of her generation, thought had been out of date for some time. They creased her flesh unattractively into folds and bulges, above which big breasts sagged in a black sweatshirt, but, like Letitia this morning, Bridie had an air of easy self-confidence which Kate wished she could match. Her colleague, who hadn't stirred herself yet, socially or physically, wore a tent-like grey shirt over equally slack-muscled, overfed, under-exercised bulk.

'Doddie fancies Judy Mearns,' Sybilla stated.

'Really, Sybilla!' Harriet cried, and Laura grinned.

'Aye, and one or two more besides,' scoffed Bridie with a coarse skirl of laughter.

'Do turn that wretched wireless down while you're on your feet, Bridie,' Grannie begged.

'How did I know that was coming?' Bridie asked, winking at Laura. 'Still, you'll all be out in the nice fresh air soon.'

'Sunday fresh air,' Sybilla sighed, and a laugh went round.

They all talked – except Sasha, who had found a cache of broken biscuit fragments under a copy of *True Romances* and was hoovering them up with one eye on Grannie – the easy talk of people who see each other often, picking any thread they fancied out of the general gabble.

Kate felt herself relaxing. She had been at Allt Farr for five days and felt as though she had been hurled down a raceway of scenes and impressions, each contradicting the last. But did it matter? These Munros might be odd, mad and arrogant, but no actual harm had come to her, and there was warmth and friendliness here. Finding the ice cream pushed towards her by good hostess Sybilla she smiled back at the bright little face and helped herself to a bowlful.

There was a thump as a setter hurled itself against the door, bursting it open.

'It always does that,' said Dottie. Door or dog?

'We've got the best place to sledge you ever saw,' Sasha announced unexpectedly, pulling up her feet to squat in her chair and turning herself round to look directly into Kate's face. Kate recognized this as her equivalent of Sybilla's offer of the raspberry ripple.

'It won't be a new place,' Laura said, not unkindly.

'It is a new place.'

'Uncle James will have sledged everywhere you could ever think of when he was little, and Mummy and Uncle Max too.'

This continuity they took for granted; how it must alter one's whole outlook, Kate reflected.

Sasha threw a plate on the floor. The dogs lunged as one.

'Uh-uh, time to go.' Bridie gulped down her tea.

'Sasha, that was very naughty,' Harriet said, stooping to retrieve the plate and finding her hand gripped politely but warningly by a long red jaw.

'Yes, definitely time for a bout of despised fresh air,' Grannie agreed. 'Twins, where are your outdoor things? Or is that a fatuous question?'

'On the corridor radiator.'

This ancient piece of equipment, though warm, had done little for the sodden objects balanced along its top, fallen in the dust round its feet or lost for ever down its back.

'These are still wet,' Harriet fussed, putting a mitten to her cheek as though she couldn't believe what her hand told her.

'Of course they are,' Sybilla said kindly. 'We were sledging all morning. Here, Sash,' choosing the wettest, 'these are yours.'

Sasha struck her hand aside and chose for herself. Over their head Grannie's eyes, alight with amusement, met Kate's.

'We'll get our sledge and meet you by the gate,' Joanna said, and she and Laura vanished through the noiseproof door.

'Well, Bridie, are you and Dot coming with us?'

'Go outside? No' me,' Dottie declared, shuddering. 'I'm for the telly and a bit o' peace and quiet.'

'Ach, I'll give it a wee go,' Bridie said easily. 'Why not?' In her shapeless flimsy high-heeled shoes on what looked like bare feet, unhooking a gaudy anorak as she passed, she went with the stream to a back door. The three dogs exploded through it, sending the twins staggering.

As in front, so behind, Riach Lodge stood bare to the elements. A couple of doors in the rear wall suggested log shed, boiler room perhaps, but no other building stood nearer than a quarter of a mile away, where Kate could see slate roofs beyond a stand of larches. Behind these the hill rose, still snow-covered, blinding in the brilliant light of this marvellous day.

Laura and Joanna appeared with the Allt Farr sledge. Smoking and chatting, feet mottling, red-veined cheeks turning maroon, fat white neck exposed to a temperature which in spite of the sun hadn't risen above zero all day, Bridie slipped and slithered along, with never a glance around her. Kate, in her motley borrowed clothes, felt comparatively well-dressed.

When they reached the lip of the flat shelf on which Riach stood she opened her mouth in protest. Surely no four- or five-year-old, which was all the twins could be, would be allowed by any responsible adult to pitch herself down that slope? Dotted with boulders and juniper bushes the ground fell steeply away, traversed halfway down by a high stone dyke.

'Our new place has got a bump,' Sasha told Laura, continuing the argument. Sledge tracks ran over a frozen drift and reappeared in softer snow below.

'Watch us, Bridie, watch us!'

'No way. That's me,' Bridie declared, and for a moment Kate thought she couldn't face watching her charges hurl themselves into peril. 'Stand out here in this cauld, do you think I'm daft?' And pausing only to light another cigarette, swearing mildly, she swayed homewards, indifferent to pleading calls.

The twins, however, seemed to feel no emotionally damaging rejection and, aiming their plastic sledges for the bump, shoved off.

'Do be careful,' called Harriet. Kate couldn't see that the warning would help now.

'Do you know from their height I believe it's only possible to see sky,' Grannie remarked, stooping to check. 'Terrifying.' She sounded almost approving.

'Great,' Laura corrected, aligning her sledge to follow the twins, who had soared off the mound with shrill screams, landed safely and were hissing towards the dyke, the dogs bounding and barking in a frenzy beside them.

'But –' cried Kate, unable to help herself.

Joanna laughed. 'Fearless and boneless,' she said. 'You'll see.'

And indeed, following the exit modes of their choice, all three children came to a halt before the barrier of stone and without delay began hauling their sledges up the hill again.

In a flash of vivid promise, Kate saw what it might be like to have a child like this, determined, laughing, reckless, an actual person. For the first time the startling thought occurred to her that she need never be alone again.

'I must try that,' Joanna said, as Laura came up for the second time.

'Keep a bit to the right,' Laura instructed. 'Snow's softer underneath.'

And to Kate's admiration, with a shriek that matched her

daughter's, Joanna propelled herself downwards.

'I really think I should see about tea,' Harriet said.

Looking at her pinched face and lilac-tinged nostrils, the flopping hair which she scraped away from her spectacles with a Fair Isle mitten, Kate supposed she had come out with them from some obscure sense of duty. Or feeling there was nowhere else to go?

'James employs people to make tea,' Grannie said impatiently.

'Bridie and Dot do need an afternoon off occasionally. James never seems to think of that.' Harriet seemed almost glad of the chance to argue on someone else's behalf.

'Their whole life is an afternoon off,' her mother retorted. 'However, go if you must.'

How different Harriet had seemed this morning, relaxed and secure with Letitia, Kate thought, watching the solitary figure trudge away. Then she forgot Harriet, her eye caught by the blue of the river reflecting the sky, the rich green of rhododendron and juniper in the sunshine. Looking northwards she picked out the turrets of Allt Farr, backed by the high rampart of hills at the head of the glen, and realised what a spectacular site had been chosen for it.

'Going to have a go?' Joanna panted, coming up the last few feet of the slope with relief and offering the cord of the sledge to Kate.

About to refuse, Kate suddenly found temptation seize her, whipped up by sun and cold air, space and light, the bright eyes and scarlet cheeks of the children, their infectious exhilaration. The dogs were safely at the bottom of the slope doing a little private digging. Grasp the moment.

'It's easiest on your front. That way you won't tip up,' Laura said helpfully.

Was that really true, Kate had time to wonder, as the air rushed by like ice water, her ears roared with the sound of plastic tearing over crystalline snow, and her watering eyes could see only whiteness and empty blue. Then came a second's silent, breath-taking magic, soaring out into the sunshine, a sensation of slowly rolling which for some reason didn't seem alarming, and an almighty thump as the side of the sledge came down into churned snow and spun in a dizzy circle. Cries from above, hot breath at her neck, the hollow disorientating shock of being winded followed by a stab of fear. The baby! She hadn't even thought of the baby.

'Come away, Buff.'

'Kate, are you all right?'

'Clear *off*, dogs!'

'Just lie still for a minute, get your breath back. Are you OK?'

'I think so,' Kate gasped. It was shame that had held her stunned; disbelief that she could have forgotten.

'Not quite the way to do it.'

Hands, voices, Buff still pushing close, concerned, the setters trying to get into the action whatever it was, the twins taking the chance of a last run, gauging correctly that a halt would be called.

'Well, the first part was fun,' Kate said, on her feet and brushing snow off her sleeve, and caught a look from Grannie she couldn't interpret.

'Tea, I think,' said Joanna.

'Tea definitely,' said Grannie.

Kate followed them, listening guiltily for private internal messages. None came.

The children had tea in the kitchen, the grown-ups in James's sitting-room. For a moment Kate didn't know which she would be, or wanted to be. Was she seen as a sort of nannie, like Bridie and Dot? Would it in fact be nicer to be part of the careless hubbub of the kitchen? Or was that an easy way out? Then obscurely, as though she had learned new things today, she felt that because she was to have a child herself she could not align herself with the children.

In the event she was given no choice. 'Can you manage the tray, Kate? I'll bring the teapot. Or no, I think we'll do that the other way round, in the light of what's just happened. And we shan't want those.' Grannie pitched off the napkins Harriet had found somewhere and went off muttering, 'How I ever brought that creature into the world will forever remain a mystery to me.'

James and Max, who had stirred themselves only to go and look at the golden eagle James's gamekeeper was licensed to keep, had had enough drams to maintain their cheerful mood in spite of the mass return of females.

'You're practically out of Earl Grey, James,' Harriet began officiously.

'Nothing to do with me. Tell Bridie.'

The fire was high now, dispelling the bleakness of the room. Had Max seen to that? But what did James find to do here alone, Kate wondered. Sleeping and drinking seemed the only options, though he was animated enough now, coming to talk to her, asking the sort of questions about home which could be answered without pain, demanding nothing difficult of her. Whether because of being out in the crisp sunny air after days of foggy gloom, or because of hot tea or whisky, the general mood had risen a couple of notches. Max in particular seemed a different person from the aloof, impatient cynic Kate found so daunting.

'I see Bridie and Dottie continue to live off the fat of the land,' Grannie commented. 'Fillet steak for lunch, if I am not mistaken.'

'They didn't give me fillet steak,' James said, without rancour.

'I really think you ought to check the housekeeping books once in a while,' Harriet persisted, encouraged by finding her mother on her side for once.

'What housekeeping books?' Max scoffed. 'That's expecting a lot from a meat turnover and a lunatic.'

James laughed uproariously, though once she had worked it out Kate decided he must surely have heard the joke before. Perhaps he liked old jokes best.

'Did you come to any conclusions about the new road?' Grannie asked, dismissing the topic of food since Harriet was being boring about it.

'Well, thanks to my intervention, since James has failed to appear at a single arbitration meeting, Riach stock will not be entirely cut off from home base by it,' Max informed her.

James laughed, refusing to be drawn. 'Why leave my chair if you can do the arguing for both of us?'

'Think of all that ghastly tourist traffic.'

'It's going to take a good ten minutes longer to get to Muirend.'

'And can't you imagine the delays while they're doing the work?'

Kate watched and listened. Could a few hundred yards of new road make so much difference? Joanna, she observed, was contributing nothing, withdrawn into thoughts of her own. Harriet had rallied and was adding her pennyworth but by the gleam in Grannie's eyes was about to be cut off at the knees again.

Max covertly watched Kate. It was almost a pity the weather had improved – and that Laura had taken to her in such an emphatic fashion. She might be tempted to stay. Not a good plan. They had helped Jeremy, provided a breathing space, a bolthole or whatever, but clearly Kate should find somewhere more suited to her needs and style. Old James seemed to like her though. So did Buff, to her unconcealed dismay. Max grinned, settling himself more comfortably. The matter would doubtless resolve itself very soon.

Chapter Nine

Decision time. Kate stitched away swiftly in the quietness of the workroom, content with the undemanding task of securing patchwork, wadding and lining together with yards of quilting, too busy with her thoughts to be aware of Grannie's occasional glances of approval for her neatness and industry.

In the dark, muddled, freezing days of last week, when she had felt thrown into an alarming country where she could barely speak the language, there had seemed to Kate little reason to stay except for her undertaking to help the Munros during the summer, and gratitude to Jeremy for enabling her to escape. There must be a hundred places where she could find a niche more acceptable than this inhospitable place. For of the adults only Joanna had welcomed her with friendliness, and even that was impersonal, more the product of good manners and a vague good nature than real liking. Joanna always seemed slightly out of touch with reality. Was that because she still missed her husband?

Don't start thinking about all that, Kate admonished herself, resettling the bulk of the quilt so that the table took most of its weight. She must make up her mind about going or staying, and there would never be a better opportunity than this for thinking the matter through quietly. Joanna was taking Laura back to Shirragh Lodge. Max, as ever, was out working somewhere. Kate had been shown the map of the estate by Laura and had been awed by the vast scope of his responsibilities. Harriet was doing the school run, going on to Muirend afterwards to shop for Letitia. She had invited Kate to go too but Grannie had claimed her help with finishing the quilt, a tedious task she disliked, by declaring not quite accurately that it should have gone off last week. Grannie herself, urgency suddenly forgotten, had been lured to start planning a new skirt, and was absorbed with graph paper, templates and heaps of plain and patterned prints sorted into colours and colour values.

This week, if Kate was going to stay, she knew she would have to commit herself to practical steps. Joanna had already made an appointment for her to see the doctor. And she must do something about clothes, for everyone warned her that the worst of the winter was still to come. She shivered at the thought. Why stay? Why not go south again, find a flat somewhere, a temporary job? Trained legal secretaries were always in demand. In her blind haste to get away the very remoteness of Allt Farr had seemed desirable, but distance made no real difference. Jessie wouldn't care where she was so long as she was away from Lamorna and out of sight. How naïve it had been to leave a note of her address and phone number on the hall table as she left that silent house, but not even the revelation which had driven her from home had prepared her for Jessie's continued obdurate silence. Needle suspended, Kate sat hunched over the quilt, her face tightly set against tears.

Poor child, thought Grannie, with a rare prick of conscience. She has problems we haven't even attempted to discuss, too exasperated with Jeremy, and his casual way of imposing on us as of right, to think of her. The irony of that obligation, reaching back through the years, the demands that love could impose . . . Her thoughts slid away from Kate's situation to the far more fascinating retrospect of her own life.

Laura would be disappointed if she left, Kate thought. But was that true? Laura took life very much as she found it. Buff would mind then. She smiled, beginning to sew again. Buff's protective attentions had been funny and even flattering. How pathetic to be pleased because a dog liked her – and what pathetic dodging to let her mind slide off the real issue yet again.

Laura. Kate's hands went down in her lap, her head lifted to look unseeingly across the room. Laura had opened doors to glimpses of normality. With her Kate had seen Allt Farr in a new perspective, not as a foreign land, inimical and barbarous. The figures who peopled it, driving enormous roaring vehicles, doing mysterious things with sheep and chainsaws and rolls of hay, had acquired names, had waved, had shouted jokes. People had said easily, 'So you're to be here for the summer then?' without requiring an answer. With Laura she had begun to look about her at last, learning the layout of the holiday cottages, the Old Byre up a mile of steep track where the cattleman lived, Doddie's house at the top of the glen road, by a trodden open space where in summer walkers parked their cars. She had reeled under a spate of information about who had children, arthritis, a prize-winning trials dog, who had just come back from Australia, was pregnant, tossed the caber.

Because of Laura she had not felt intimidated by the Mackenzie twins. Syb and Sash. Kate smiled again. How different they were in character, how positively each was herself, even at that age. Was that how it would be . . . ?

A bed-sit in an unknown city would not be the same as retreating to her flat at Lamorna, with the choice to be alone or not. Nothing would bring back that feeling of home around her, however unsatisfactory it had been. And outlandish as Allt Farr was, what better alternative was available? Certainly the few days she had spent here had been more eventful than a year in Wimbledon. And there had been a novel excitement in the feeling of space and unexplored distances on every side.

But these Munros – could she spend months in their exacting, ruthless company? And making mistakes. Those mistakes were beginning to haunt her. Last night she had served up the gravy as the first course.

'Ah, boot polish soup, haven't seen that for a while,' Max had said, and Harriet, squawking, had come to snatch it back.

'What *are* you going to do next?' Grannie had asked, but they had appeared to find it funny.

They had been less amused to find she had thrown out the olive oil. 'But it was all green and cloudy. I thought it had gone off,' she had pleaded.

'Off? How can it go off? It turns opaque in the cold of the larder. As soon as you bring it into the kitchen it's perfectly all right again.'

There had been about a gallon of it and it *was* expensive. But though Grannie had been scathing there had still been laughter, and that was something Kate, even in so short a time, had come to value.

Oddly enough, here in the workroom at this very moment, were many of the things her soul yearned for. Peace, surroundings where she could be tidy, clean and warm, and a task meticulous and precise, within her scope, a task someone was pleased to have done. But she couldn't pretend this was altogether representative of day-to-day life at Allt Farr.

Grannie came to a decision about her *Wheel of Fortune* blocks and straightened her back with a grimace. 'How quick you are,' she commented, tipping her head to find the right bit of her multi-focals through which to survey Kate's work. 'I cannot tell you how gratifying it is to have someone in the house who can hold a needle.' And motivated by this little spurt of benevolence she took the chance to add, 'By the way, Kate, I'm not sure if anyone has said this to you, but you do know, don't you, that you are free to use the telephone whenever you wish.' The observation she was about to make, that Kate didn't appear to have been in touch with home yet, was checked by the naked pain which filled Kate's face at her words.

Startled into uncharacteristic doubt about her own tact, Grannie added more gently after a fractional pause, 'We do want you to feel at home here.'

the government, the motor trade and the state of the
...my.

...n the way home Joanna headed up a different glen, east of
...Maraich, taking grouse to another friend.

...he runs a guest house in her old family home. It used to close
...e winter but a cross-country skiing centre has started up
...by so she's opening at weekends as an experiment.'

...ally Danaher welcomed them warmly. 'You've saved my life,
...here's hardly anything left in the freezers and my menus were
...ing distinctly boring. Come and say hello to Mike.'

...Her husband, a quiet, affable, slow-moving man, was at work
...verting an old laundry into a studio, to Sally's evident pride.
...also showed them his delicate watercolours of birds and
...mals. They were persuaded to stay for lunch, during which
...ke surprised Kate by wandering off without warning or
...ology. As they drove away Joanna explained that he had
...ffered brain damage a few years ago and would never be
...mpletely fit again.

There were hidden levels beneath the surface in most people's
...es, Kate reminded herself as Joanna drove over the hill, and
...own again into Kirkton. It put her own problems into perspec-
...e.

The next morning she went with Harriet on the school run,
...e moment plainly drawing closer when she would have to take
...r turn. She sat self-consciously in front, aware of eyes boring
...o her back, in a silence broken only by the crunching of
...ps, sniffs, the regular thump of swinging boots and occasional
...losive outbursts of giggles.

'Enjoy it while it lasts,' Harriet warned her, signalling as she
...ned out of an empty farm track onto the empty road. 'It's
...ally bedlam.'

...What worried Kate more was the state of the lanes they had
...n up. It was obvious this job could only be done in the jeep
...ch she hadn't yet driven.

...Other challenges awaited her. Today was her first cooking

'Thank you,' Kate managed in a stifled voice. For a wild
moment she longed to pour out her hurt and fears, but the habit
of reticence prevailed. She had grown used to living without
communication. But, as though this single gesture of kindness
from Mrs Munro had weighed the balance, she found her mind
made up.

'That's very kind of you,' she heard herself saying. 'I expect
I'll have to phone the doctor sometimes, and things like that.'

So it was decided. For the time being she would let this
bizarre world tumble her along. Joanna would be there to answer
questions. Harriet, irritating though she could be, meant well.
Laura would be home for weekends and holidays. Max she need
hardly see, and Grannie, though her moods were unpredictable,
showed signs of thawing. If it proved to be unbearable then she
would just have to start all over again somewhere else.

One more consideration nagged at her. Jeremy. Laura's
chatter had revealed that he was often at Allt Farr. Would it
be possible for them to meet casually after all that had
happened? Suddenly she longed for him, longed for the heedless,
intoxicating attraction of their first meeting, longed for him as a
partner in this huge and terrifying adventure she could not evade,
longed for him as the father of her child. But the passionate flare
of feeling died, swamped by common sense. No, Jeremy would
not come to Allt Farr as long as she was there. He had done his
best for her and further involvement would be the last thing he
would want.

It was a busy week, characterised by a different mood now that
Kate knew she would be staying. None of the Munros had
realised how close she had been to leaving, but each registered a
new determination in her.

'It looks as though we're stuck with her,' was how Max put
it, as he helped Joanna swing bulging binbags into the back of
the pick-up. In theory the council refuse men came to a central

collection point for the estate rubbish but at the faintest sniff of snow they baulked at the drive. 'Damn, another split one. Why do they want to stuff so much into them?'

'Kate's not that bad,' Joanna said in her easy way, not for the first time.

'Oh, she's perfectly agreeable as an individual, decorative even, but for usefulness let's stick to good Scots wenches reading something practical at an ex-tech-university, fat thighs and all. We need someone who can *do* things.' Drive, beat, shop, mend a fuse, haul sacks of flour, pluck a bird, remove a thorn from a paw, pick bushels of fruit, freeze pounds of vegetables, cook for an army.

'You never had much to say for the fat farm wenches in the past, as I recall. If you consider what Jeremy might have landed us with I'd say we've been lucky.'

Max grunted, knowing his disaffection went far beyond impatience with Kate's helplessness.

'Can you honestly see her and Jeremy together, though?' Joanna pursued. 'You may think her feeble, but in my opinion she's far too nice for him.'

Harriet too thought Kate was very nice. And Letitia had liked her. Harriet didn't realise that what she chiefly enjoyed was finding someone to draw her mother's fire, that constant ironic criticism which sometimes wore her down so much that she felt quite desperate. But what escape was open to her? The interest on her tiny capital, which she contributed as they all did to the household kitty, wouldn't take her very far. And she had no training, no qualifications. Besides, she thought more briskly, reaching a familiar point in these reflections, if she wasn't there who would run the glen TV scheme, chase up contributions, accept the chore of being WRI secretary, put on the pantomime, organise the carol service . . . ? She never progressed beyond these questions, allowing them to convince her that she had no choice.

*

On Wednesday Joanna took Kate to the do
Kate thought the waiting room remarkably c
empty – till she realised they were in someone'

'Don't they have a proper waiting ro
Joanna, looking at the book-filled shelves, the
S.R. Percy loch scenes, the heaped work-bask
hyacinths.

'You mean you'd prefer coughs and sniffle
magazines with bits torn out?' Joanna teased. 'No
Charlie Fleming all our lives. His father had the
him. The only difference is nasty modern surgerie
the back, ruining the garden.'

Did everything always have to be differen
wondered, but resignedly by this stage, emerging re
her session with Dr Fleming, who didn't want to b
Fleming, and had had all the time in the world to
ignorant questions. He was big and untidy, in a twe
with leather elbow patches, had shaggy brown hair and
hands, and gave the impression that he was delight
after her. He took her back into the house, gave Joann
insisted they stay for coffee. For the first time Kate's
dread about the baby receded. Moral issues, guilt, J
anger, Jeremy's stunned look when she had told him
his dutiful rallying to help her, were less importa
actual, physical fact. She would read the leaflets Char
her, find the books he had recommended. She wou
thing that should be done.

In this positive mood she went with Joanna to
a gunsmith's, household supplies by the caseful, and
of paint from a yard in a new industrial estate. Then
fully with a cappuccino and wholemeal scone i
restaurant with bare stone walls, while one friend of
another joined them for a bout of the racing, la
Kate was beginning to get used to. It was definite
ment on Jessie's endless complaints or Jack's grun

day, and of all people Max was going to teach her. One thing she now knew, every Munro had his or her own way of doing things, and it was the only right way.

Take marmalade-making, for instance, yesterday's enterprise.

'Generous pieces,' Grannie had ordained. 'None of your mincing little slivers.'

'It's a much better method to soften the fruit first,' Harriet had gone on protesting, even when it was clear that wasn't the way it was going to be done.

'A spoonful of treacle adds a lovely dark colour,' Joanna had said, dolloping it in.

'Sacrilege!' Grannie had screamed. 'That pure amber shade is the great beauty of home-made marmalade.'

Yet now that Kate had gained a little confidence she could see that in a way they were sending themselves up when they did this – always excepting Harriet. And everyone's marmalade would be good. That was the real point. Nevertheless she was ridiculously nervous when she presented herself in the kitchen that evening.

'Cook's nips,' Max, who already had most of what they would need laid out before him, greeted her bracingly. 'That's the first essential.' Then about to pour wine into the second glass he remembered. 'Ah, no, inappropriate in your case. Sorry, Kate.'

Looking at him defensively, suspecting sarcasm, Kate was surprised to see a smile of genuine apology.

'It's all right,' she said quickly, and Max, amused, could tell from her voice that this was an ordeal she wanted to get on with and get over.

She was thankful to find the rest of the family absent (not guessing Max had banished them) and that his manner was that of the professional instructor, detached and brisk, but, she became aware as she steadied a little, precisely aware of her needs.

Resolutely she set to work, not conscious of how simple Max had kept the plot: braised pork and apple, rhubarb tansy. It seemed a terrific undertaking to her, not least because of the critics who would eat it.

Max, initially bored by the whole thing, but recognising that if Kate was going to stay here it was worth teaching her a few basic principles, found himself disarmed by her wholehearted determination to get everything right. Watching her difficulties with large utensils and unfamiliar equipment, observing the narrow wrists and tiny hands, he was entertained by how small and neat her natural scale of production was. Anything she was set to chop or slice came out in dolls' size pieces; he supposed that was fair enough. It was the first time he had worked alone with her, and he could not fault her good intentions or commitment. Perhaps after all there was more to her than met the eye. He raised his glass to her in salute when the pork, garnished with golden apple slices, was borne to the table, and Kate decided the gesture was not entirely mocking.

Inevitably she had moments of doubt about her decision to stay at Allt Farr, several a day, to be exact. She seemed to be perpetually scrambling to keep up. At home there had been endless hours to herself. When she was at school, and later doing secretarial training, she had still had the reading habit, burying herself in safe, familiar favourites – the Brontës and Jane Austen over and over again, the reassuring scale of Trollope and Dickens and Hardy. Anything 'clever' alarmed her, and she had never come much closer to the contemporary novel than du Maurier or Mary Renault, but latterly, with a growing consciousness of the futility of her life, she had wasted more and more time in experiments with make-up, lazy flicking through magazines, undemanding television.

Her room here, had there been any idle moments, did not tempt her to similar frittering away of time, and until Saturday she had not even known there was a television in the house.

'Grannie can't miss her racing,' Laura had said, as Mrs Munro hurried off after lunch.

'But where is the television?'

'In her room.'

'Do you ever watch it?'

'In the winter sometimes,' Laura had said, shrugging with supreme indifference.

Surprisingly, Kate scarcely missed it. It seemed irrelevant here, incongruous, and in any case the evenings were taken up with other things. James Mackenzie had looked in for dinner one night, though from the teasing he had had to put up with Kate gathered this was a rare occurrence. And the next evening when, reduced to yawning sleepiness by a combination of pregnancy, fresh air and exercise, she was longing for an early night, she had found herself obliged to sit through a slow-moving meal at Admiral Rathlyn's modern bungalow outside Kirkton.

Could these people never stay home and do nothing, she had wondered, jerking back to wakefulness yet again as the room swayed round her, the voices faded and returned, and the hands of her watch crept past eleven, twelve, twelve thirty. But that was not the Munro way.

Chapter Ten

In spite of getting back from the dinner party at one in the morning, Kate found breakfast nearly over by the time she crept down after a more than usually severe bout of sickness. As she huddled over a glass of orange juice which she hardly dared risk, she realised a medium-brisk argument was in progress.

'You are quite mad even to think of going to Inverness today,' Max was saying categorically, folding bacon into an extra morning roll to take with him.

'But it's the area meeting. It's most important. I can't let Letitia go on her motorbike.'

'She should get a car of her own,' Joanna put in lazily.

'You know she can't possibly afford—'

'Oh, please let's not go into all that again,' Grannie begged. 'It's too boring for words.'

'We've had to postpone already because of snow—'

'And you should postpone again because of snow,' Max said. 'You must have heard the forecast.'

'It said snow from the north later in the day.'

'And you hope to be blown home in front of it?'

'I promised Letitia – ' Harriet insisted.

'No more to be said, Max,' Grannie said, her voice acid. 'If Letitia has to be taken to Inverness then we are wasting our breath.'

'Joanna's as bad. It's ridiculous to go over to Shirragh just to take Laura her skis.'

'I'm not just taking her skis. We're both staying at Morgill, as you very well know. It's ages since Laura and Fanny had a weekend together, and even longer since Elaine and I did.'

'You'll never get out from Morgill anyway to do any skiing if this blows up. The sensible thing to do would be leave Fanny and Laura at school.'

'Oh, you'd have loved that at eleven, wouldn't you?' Joanna mocked. 'I agree with Harriet.' (That must be a first, Kate thought, getting the orange juice as far as her lips and deciding against it.) 'It's worth a try.'

'Oh, leave them to their own devices,' Grannie said, her face creasing in pain as she stood up. Perhaps she should talk to Charlie about this wretched hip soon. The busy summer loomed ahead, a marathon of pain.

So Laura wouldn't be here this weekend. Kate knew it was absurd to feel so disappointed, but Laura had proved a valuable guide in this confusing new land.

They were just finishing lunch when the snow came, snow such as Kate had never seen, whining in an obliterating whirl across the windows, darkening the day as though dusk had already come.

'Ah,' Max said, 'that looks like business.' He got up and went to the phone.

'It seems Harriet miscalculated after all,' Grannie remarked, almost with satisfaction. 'Coffee, Kate?'

'But won't it die down?' Kate asked, finding it hard to believe such malignant fury could be sustained.

'Oh, eventually.' Grannie looked as if she was enjoying Kate's dismay. She cocked her head to listen for a second to the instructions Max was rapping out. 'We'd better get our boots on.'

'Boots?' Go out in that?

'The chickens may have the sense to leg it for shelter but I expect they'd like their doors closed and some supplies to keep them going.'

'Will Torquil go into his shed this time?'

'Goodness, what a lot you've learned,' Grannie teased. 'Torquil, as ever, will probably prefer to turn his tail to the wind. However, we should do some feeding and battening down.'

Max was making another call. 'Lexy, we'll have to bring her down. It'll be far easier to get her out from here if necessary. Of course you can't bring her in the tractor, have a heart. Tell her to get her things together, I'll be up later. And how about you? Do you want to come with her? I can bring someone to look after the cattle. OK, your choice. And calm down, everything will be fine.'

'We shan't see Harriet again today,' Grannie said as he turned from the phone.

'It's Joanna we need,' he snapped. 'Though even Harrie would be better than nothing. Christ knows when we'll see either of them again.'

Grannie winked at Kate. 'What first?' she asked, and from the calmness of her voice the seriousness of the situation at last reached Kate. This, it seemed, was not like the snow of her arrival last week, which everyone had disregarded. This was real snow.

'We'll have to shift the gimmers down to the Haugh. With the wind in this direction we can't leave them up by the old fank, we'd be digging for days. Thank God the hogs are safely away.'

I didn't know there were pigs, and what are gimmers and a fank and where's the Haugh, Kate thought in a brief uprush of panic that it was all too arcane and difficult, and that she was not going to measure up.

'We'll see to everything here, don't worry.'

Max nodded, his mind rapidly sifting priorities. 'I can't leave it too long before I fetch Colleen. That track fills in so fast. Everyone had better hole up. Could you make sure Grigor and Mrs Grant are safely home?'

Grannie nodded. 'And I'd better put some heating on in Ann's room ready for Colleen.'

Who was Ann? It was not the moment to enquire.

'Not that we'll reach the equatorial level she favours,' Max said, with a brief grin. 'And I'm willing to bet there won't be much heating on offer for anybody before long.'

With this cryptic comment he was gone, and Kate and Grannie looked at each other in the suddenly quiet kitchen. Then Grannie turned to the door.

'Just tell me what has to be done,' Kate said. 'I'm sure you shouldn't do any heavy jobs with your hip.'

Grannie checked in mid-stride in sheer surprise. This extraordinary child, who said so little and always seemed consumed with apprehension, had not only seen her pain but accurately pinpointed it, something none of her offspring had been observant or caring enough to do.

'That's very kind,' she said, recovering herself. 'Between us we shall manage splendidly.'

Torquil was in his open-fronted shed. 'Hm,' said Grannie. 'Mildly ominous.'

Mildly? Kate had thought the gusts of wind-driven snow which had buffeted her in the courtyard bad enough, then had found herself twice spun bodily round as they crossed the exposed ground to the field gate. The flakes were large, dizzying in their relentless dance, reducing the visible world to a small area at her feet where even in so short a time the ground was white. She and Grannie together had to struggle to shut the gate and she was startled to hear Grannie giggling beside her.

'Can't you just see us, two useless females being flapped around by a few bars of wood?'

Kate laughed too, exhilaration seizing her.

The general note in the abodes of the poultry was of indignation shading to aggrievement.

'Stupid things,' said Grannie. 'They haven't got much to worry about – unless of course their whole house blows away.

Good thing if it did. They're only here to satisfy Harriet's mothering urges.'

'They do lay eggs,' suggested Kate, trying to blink the snow off her eyelashes so that she could see how an uncouth arrangement of latch and string worked.

'How reasonable you are.' But it was said without rancour and Grannie seemed in high spirits as they put their heads down and struggled back to the courtyard. 'Perhaps we should stock up on logs before this builds up,' she suggested as they reached its comparative haven.

Kate didn't much like this insistence on worse to come, but began to load the heavy barrow.

'I'd better take it,' Grannie said. 'You should be sensible. You're so tiny I can't believe half the time that you're *enceinte* at all.'

Kate had forgotten about it herself. 'We won't put too much in,' she said, taking the handles.

Grannie following obediently, wondered if Kate was aware that it was the first time at Allt Farr she had taken the initiative.

An hour later Max came in, looking grim. 'I daren't leave it any longer to go up to the Byre. Kate, you'll have to come with me.'

Kate knew from Laura that Colleen, the wife of the young cattleman, had been due to have her baby last week. For the second time panic seized her. What would she have to do? Would she be any use? Shouldn't Grannie go? Then shame overtook alarm. Grannie, game as she was, had looked tight-lipped and weary after going back and forth with water and feed, lifting the big logs into the barrow, and helping to steady its cumbersome weight as Kate steered it erratically through the deepening snow.

'I just want you to give Colleen company and reassurance,' Max explained, keeping impatience out of his voice as he took the first rise of the track to the Byre. He had caught that fleeting look of consternation on Kate's face and, as he saw the rigid arm out to hold the dashboard and heard her gasp as they slithered wide on the nasty corner above the burn, wondered if he had been wise to bring her. Had he cut it a bit fine? This wind was no joke. It had come out of nowhere, and was strengthening by the minute. They must do some work on this track so that he could use the blade up here. One of a dozen jobs he'd like to get at if only he had the time. He cursed as the jeep met new snow over ice.

How could he see? Kate worried. And if they ever got to the Byre could it be right to jolt Colleen down this treacherous track? Wouldn't it be more sensible to let her have the baby at home? Then they'd have to help deliver it. No, no, better the original plan.

'Not a moment too soon, as they say,' Max remarked, seeing the drifts already piling up in the steading yard. He sounded almost cheerful. 'If this wind gets up we'll be in for a spot of bother.'

'I think it's got up,' Kate shouted back, drama making her bold, and Max turned his head to look at her in amusement as he swung round to the door and pulled up.

'Maybe you're right,' he yelled in her ear as he held back the door for her to get out, then kept hold of her arm as the wind funnelled between jeep and house hit her.

Kate had not imagined such conditions could exist in the British Isles. She had only ever seen this sort of thing in documentaries about caribou or polar bears; it had not appealed to her.

Max raised one hand to knock and the other to turn the doorknob, then made a quick grab at Kate as a squeak warned him she was being whisked away. At least Colleen would have a bit more ballast.

An eighty-degree fug, smelling of tea and drying socks, gloriously enveloped them as they fell into the Old Byre kitchen, pursued by a whirlwind of snowflakes. Yellow cupboards, orange floor tiles, wallpaper with huge sunflowers, plants swarming everywhere, a red-cheeked Colleen tank-like in a red shirt, battered them with colour after the screaming whiteness outside. The stillness seemed incredible, yet they had only been out of the jeep for a minute.

'You'll have time for a wee cuppie?' Colleen asked politely, as Lexy, well-fleshed as one of his own stirks, put his shoulder to the door.

'We've got time for nothing, so forget the social crap,' Max said breezily, to Kate's great surprise putting an arm round Colleen's shoulders. 'Couldn't you organise her better than this?' he demanded of Lexy.

'Ach well, right enough, she should have dropped it last week, then we'd have been down and back,' Lexy agreed. 'Damned women, never get anything right.'

'Aye, and you had nothing to do with it, I suppose,' Colleen riposted, with a burst of raucous giggles. 'Fetch me that stuff, then, and don't be leaving anything behind. I ken what you're like.'

'At least I'll get peace for a day or two.'

'You might be luckier than that,' Max observed.

'It's a wee thing coarse,' Lexy concurred with polite moderation.

'Come on then, let's get you down the road. Better kiss her goodbye in here, Lexy, conditions outside aren't too romantic.'

Kate was struck by Max's relaxed manner, quite different from the self she saw at home. Both Lexy and Colleen were evidently on easy terms with him.

'Kiss me! That'll be the day. One kiss a year I get, and that's a peck at Hogmanay,' Colleen scoffed, trying to stoop for her bag and giving up with an oath.

'Looks to me you got a bit more than that,' Lexy said, punching her on the arm but lifting the bag.

'Must have been Postie, then,' Colleen retorted, slapping him back and cackling with laughter.

But Kate saw their eyes, full of inarticulate need and anxiety, and with sharp insight understood how much they hated being dragged apart, obliged by this unlucky stroke of the weather to be separated at this great moment of their lives. And with a tiny knife-twist came the foreknowledge of her own loneliness when the same moment came for her. The thought was gone in an instant, no more than a deeper perception of Colleen's feelings, but it was enough to make Kate move closer to her, saying in her gentle voice, 'I know it seems hard, but I think we should be setting off.'

She missed the approving lift of Max's eyebrows.

'We should,' was all he said. 'Otherwise we'll have an *accouchement* to deal with halfway down the hill.'

Out into the blizzard they fought their way, even Lexy staggering, and with eyes slitted and the breath snatched out of their nostrils, words shredded and torn away, snow driving into the crevices of cuffs, collars and hoods, Kate and Colleen were packed into the back of the Fourtrak and Max swung up in front.

'I canna' even wave,' Colleen panted, struggling to heave herself round.

'I'll wave for you,' Kate said. But she turned to find the solid shapes of cottage and buildings already invisible, let alone Lexy. What must it be like for him, seeing his wife carried away down that treacherous track in these conditions, unable to take care of her, left in that howling waste where it was a battle merely to cross the twenty yards of farmyard?

'Couldn't someone else have looked after the cows?' she asked Colleen.

'Leave his beasts to someone else in this weather?' Colleen hooted. 'You must be joking. Leave his wife to someone else more like.'

'Isn't it a terribly wild place to live?'

'Up here? It's no' that bad, especially now I've got ma new kitchen. You get some peace anyway, not like doon at the farm with everyone poking their noses in.'

Kate could only remember three permanently inhabited cottages at the farm.

'How are you liking it at the big house then?' Colleen went on, with a compulsive need to talk. 'I've always thought it looks kind o' spooky.'

Had she never been inside it? 'No ghosts that I've seen,' Kate promised, sympathising with her fears as no one else could have done. 'Plenty of draughts, though.'

Colleen winced as the jeep swung, and Max released the wheel to come out of an incipient spin.

'He'll bounce the baby clean out of me if he goes on like that,' she gasped. 'No, to tell the truth, it's Mrs Munro scares me more than the ghosts. I'm thinking she'll no' be best pleased to have me landing on her this way.'

'She doesn't mind a bit,' Kate said positively. 'She's getting a room ready for you herself.'

'Herself? You don't tell me? But where's Harriet and Joanna?'

'Joanna's taking Laura to a friend's and they're staying for the weekend. Harriet went to Inverness.'

'To Inverness? In this? Well, we'll no' see *her* this side of Easter!' Colleen seemed to find this idea highly amusing. 'So it's you, me and the old lady. My God, wait till I tell Lexy.'

'And Max.'

'Och, Max, I'm no' bothered about Max.'

That was surprising. Kate looked at him, intent but relaxed as he maintained speed to prevent the jeep bogging, and played the heavy vehicle skilfully round the tight bends. He's enjoying this, she realised, then forgot him as the burn appeared directly below her window and for a long moment the jeep seemed unable to pull back to an even plane.

'Jesus,' said Colleen, then raising her voice uninhibitedly, 'Are you trying to do the hospital out of a job, Max Munro? It's puppies you're supposed to drown at birth, no' bairns!'

'You're nowhere near drowning yet,' Max shouted back, wrestling the jeep through a drift much deeper than when they came up and grinning at them in the mirror.

He had been glad to hear them talking. Kate had been a good person to bring after all, with that quick sympathy and gentleness of hers. It had been interesting to see her natural kindness overcome her shyness. The next trick would be getting Colleen off to hospital if labour started; or preferably before it started. A helicopter could land on the lawn, while it would never have found enough level ground to get down in the upper glen, but would the weather be fit for it to make the attempt?

Chapter Eleven

That evening was to be one of the oddest of Kate's life. As at last they reached the house the lights of the jeep, dimmed by a haze of dancing snow, revealed outlines and shapes already altered almost out of recognition.

'Not much point putting it in there. We'd never get it out again,' Max said, reversing away from the smooth wave which curled against the garage doors, and going on into the courtyard. Its centre was scoured bare, but drifts had formed round anything that stuck up, making a weird new picture. 'And it looks as though we'll have to dig our way into the house,' he added, seeing the steps to the back door already buried.

He sounded matter-of-fact, mildly exasperated at most. As he switched off the wipers the windscreen was instantly blanked out, as though someone had dashed a bucketful of snow at it. Kate, awed by the power of the storm (she supposed this was a storm?) shrank at the thought of getting out into that ruthless wildness, then remembered that Colleen had a great deal more to worry about than she did.

'Stay where you are till I get the door open,' Max ordered, sliding out through as small a gap as possible. But as he opened the back to get a shovel the wind shrieked in, bringing the snow with it.

'I'll help you,' Kate shouted, conscience stirring. Why should she have the luxury of sitting here idly? There was nothing wrong with her.

About to tell her he didn't think she'd achieve much Max recalled that his troops were thin on the ground. It might be short-sighted to discourage assistance at this stage. He pulled out a second shovel. 'Come on, then.' At least in the courtyard she shouldn't blow away.

Grannie and a grinning Buff gave them a warm welcome, along with the news that Harriet had phoned and she and Letitia were staying for the night in Inverness. With perceptions sharpened by unusual events Kate guessed that even Grannie must have been worried, waiting alone for them to get down that awful road. And she was oddly pleased to find that Grannie perfectly understood Colleen's nervousness to be here in the big house, in spite of her attempt at a brash offhandedness.

But Colleen didn't mind Kate knowing how daunted she felt. As they pursued Grannie's tall figure up stairs and along corridors, a slight unevenness in her gait her only concession to the ever-present pain in her hip, Colleen gasped, giggling, 'My, she can fairly shift,' and added, snatching time for an awed look around her, 'And here's me in Lexy's old jacket.'

'I don't think anyone worries about clothes here,' Kate reassured her, nodding ahead of them. Grannie was wearing a sweater with both elbows out, and a crushed-velvet skirt over boots with studded fleecy turnovers which would not have disgraced an Albanian bandit.

'You're mebbe right at that,' Colleen conceded, as this bizarre sight whisked out of sight round a corner.

She was silent, however, when she surveyed the room she had been given. It was huge and sombre, with a Raeburn of Grannie's great-great-grandfather-in-law over the fireplace dimming by contrast the Victorian watercolours round the other walls, a lot of mahogany which Colleen thought could have done with a good dust, a second room which seemed to be just for clothes, and her own bathroom. Two convector heaters pumped out hot air which was just beginning to percolate down again from an elaborately decorated ceiling.

Kate felt suddenly very fond of Grannie.

'Now, if you want to rest we shall quite understand,' Mrs Munro told Colleen briskly. 'But I wouldn't recommend it till the room's warmer. I think the best thing would be for us all to have – ah!'

Out went the lights, the purr of the heaters ceased. Kate hoped her gasp had been masked by Colleen's screech.

'Bound to happen,' Grannie's voice continued philosophically. 'The lines could never stand up to this weight of snow. Very well, Plan B.'

'We'll no' find our way very well, will we?' Colleen said, and Kate could hear her dread of the dark labyrinth of corridors in her wavering voice.

'I think Max would retrieve us before too long,' Grannie protested mildly. 'The system may work, however. Mustn't trip over this damned flex. Now where –?'

Hearing Grannie's voice moving away, Kate remembered the ornate candlestick, with matchbox in its slot among the china flowers, which stood on the mantelpiece in her own room. She started as Colleen's hand clutched her arm in a grip accustomed to tossing bales and overturning sheep, or cowping yowes as she would have put it herself.

'Here, I don't like this,' hissed a voice going slightly out of control.

'Don't be silly,' said Grannie, already several feet away. 'Though if they are there will they be damp, I ask myself.'

A match rasped and caught and both girls laughed involuntarily in its small cheerful light.

'Rather efficient for Allt Farr, I must say,' Grannie remarked, clearly pleased. 'Candle too? Yes, candle too. We're in business. I apologise about the heating, Colleen. We shall have to do something about that for you later. Come along, both of you. We must first think about food.'

Colleen held onto Kate unashamedly as they followed the candle held by Grannie more with a view to her convenience than theirs. 'I'm no' that keen on coming back up here, I don't mind telling you,' she whispered.

'Perhaps they'll have the power back on by then,' Kate comforted her.

'Are you off your heid?' Colleen demanded, pausing to stare at her in the jigging shadows. 'In this lot?'

Kate realised to her shame that she had never before considered the reality of men struggling up poles in howling blizzards, or the problem of reaching the poles in the first place. A power cut in Wimbledon, though annoying, had been a mere technical hitch.

'Do they last long, usually?' she asked humbly, as Colleen's ponderous roll went up a gear in an attempt to catch up with the all-important light.

'Och, days at a time,' said Colleen airily, though her single winter at the Byre had not produced conditions anything like these.

Kate was silent.

The beam of a big torch met them as they reached the stairs. 'You found some light. Good,' said Max's voice. 'I'd better hook up a couple of cylinders. I see you got in a good supply of logs.'

Munros never seemed to tell their elderly mother she shouldn't tackle such things, Kate noted, not for the first time. Was that because Grannie would have brushed such comments aside or because they considered her indestructible?

The kitchen was still warm, but what did the Aga run on? It had never occurred to Kate to wonder. Oil? That would be all right then. But what pumped the oil? Electricity. Not so good. But everyone obviously expected to survive; so would she.

The mood was unexpectedly light-hearted as emergency procedures swung into action. Now, as Max brought in a cylinder and attached it, Kate saw why the old-fashioned gas cooker was allowed to take up space in the corner. Max took another cylinder up to Colleen's room, returning for a cumbersome heater. Grannie marshalled an army of lamps and candles.

'Open the freezers as little as possible,' she warned. 'And as soon as dinner's over we'll fill lots of hot-water bottles. I hope you're not planning to move into the gallons of boiling water phase just yet, Colleen.'

'I hope I'm no' either, I can tell you,' Colleen agreed fervently and Grannie laughed.

The relaxed mood prevailed all evening. Max was in a better humour than Kate had ever known him, even at those dinner parties with friends when he livened up so markedly, as he filled lamps, built a huge fire in the morning-room, helped carry trays up there for supper, poured drams for his mother and himself and concocted an alcohol-free fruit punch for the two 'in-calf heifers', a joke Kate supposed was more for Colleen's benefit than hers. He treated Colleen with an easy friendliness which encouraged her to an uninhibited humour both Munros took in their stride.

They cooked sausages, tomatoes, bacon and eggs, and Grannie even opened the freezer to get out chips – a meal geared as much to Colleen's tastes as to the power cut, Kate was sure. Though, this being Allt Farr, it was put on a beautiful ironstone ashet, and protected from the cooling air on the journey upstairs by a massive silver cover belonging to something else. They made toast at the fire, and Max went down again to make the tea he knew Colleen's soul was yearning for, bringing back with it a slab of fruit cake to add the final high tea touch.

But what Kate afterwards remembered most vividly, almost with disbelief, was the scene that followed, with lamp- and fire-light glowing on Colleen's scarlet cheeks, shadowing Grannie's deep eye-sockets and hollow cheeks, accentuating arrogant Munro noses, golden on Buff's slumbering flanks, while outside the wind ceaselessly whined, the storm wreaked its damage, and they played poker into the small hours.

They had started with gin rummy. It was Colleen who asked

diffidently, 'No one'd fancy poker, no?'

'Certainly,' said Grannie instantly, shuffling the pack with new zeal and telling skill. They insisted Kate could learn, settled the stakes and were off. Kate had enough luck to make the game fun but the battle ultimately lay between Grannie and Colleen.

Curled up in bed at last round her big hot-water bottle, Kate realised how unreservedly Max and Grannie had set themselves to make their visitor feel at ease. They had not done as much for her when she came, not in the same way. She pondered this. Had they deemed her not so much in need of reassurance? She hoped it was that; but she didn't think it really could have been.

She listened to the storm. It was a new kind of cosiness to be here, warm and safe, hearing that demented wailing beyond the thick walls. More than feeling physically safe, there was the knowledge that everything had been done that could be done and that whatever morning brought these people would know what to do. She hoped Colleen was lulled by the same comforting certainty. With more anticipation than apprehension, she drifted off to sleep.

She woke to the immense silence she was beginning to love. There came first the relief that several things would be simpler which morning brings after an evening of candles and improvisation, then eagerness to see what had happened in the night.

The room was, if possible, colder than usual. Wrapping herself in the eiderdown she went to pull back the curtains. To her surprise and pleasure she found the bowl of the glen filled with pale golden light, diffused though thin cloud and ethereally lighting a scene of magical beauty. The wind had dropped before the snow had stopped. Every branch, bush and wall was piled high, against a backdrop of pure white hills and that softly glowing sky. For that moment it was hers, an enchanted landscape, the gardens of a winter palace, the approach to Camelot.

She found suddenly it was too exciting to be alone; she wanted to be doing, sharing, experiencing. The bathroom was no warmer than her room, but she dressed there from habit. The water was luke-warm, another inducement to speed, and the nausea that came on cue a time-wasting nuisance.

'Laura will break her heart, missing this,' Grannie said as Kate came into the kitchen, in a tone several degrees friendlier than her usual morning tetchiness.

'Won't they have snow where she is?' Kate asked. Anything seemed possible here.

Max, overhearing as he came in from the corridor, laughed. 'I think even at Morgill they'll have an inch or two. We're a bit higher here. What Laura will hate missing is digging out sheep and getting Colleen to hospital.'

'Aye, and in that order,' said Colleen, leaning back wide-kneed in a kitchen chair, wearing several sweaters and looking if possible even larger than yesterday.

'Do you have to go to hospital?' Kate asked, looking at her in alarm.

'Doesnae seem a good idea to hang aboot,' Colleen said with a hoot of laughter, slapping her belly in a way Kate thought the baby might not care for.

'It certainly doesn't. We don't want any homespun deliveries here,' said Grannie, trying to shake clear of her wooden spurtle porridge which didn't look at all like Mrs Grant's.

'The helicopter will get in all right this morning,' Max assured them, drawing back exaggeratedly from the porridge bowl his mother put down in front of him.

Kate decided emergencies made him almost human. 'What about the school run?' she asked.

After one surprised stare Colleen and Grannie broke into laughter.

'Have ye no' looked out of the window yet?' Colleen demanded.

'We'll probably give the school run a miss today,' Grannie said.

'No one's going anywhere,' Max told Kate, his good humour overtaken by exasperation. Kate would seem for a moment to be getting a grip on things, then could produce a remark like that. 'There's more snow to come,' he went on to Grannie. 'But the damned temperature's going up fast and that's going to be the next problem.'

Wasn't that good? Kate wasn't going to risk enquiring.

'Will you be able to get through to the farm?' Grannie asked.

'I'll have another go. The stretch before the bridge is always the problem.'

'Could they get that far with the other tractor?'

'Oh, Christ, and pack the snow down so that the blade'll never shift it. No, thanks.' He sounded as impatient with his mother as he had been with her, Kate was gratified to hear, deciding Grannie could stand it. 'Can you handle the feeding up here if I get back to clearing the track?'

'Of course we can.'

'You're sure? There's going to be a lot of shovelling to do.'

It was the first time Kate had heard anyone show the slightest concern about Grannie's fitness for a job.

'I can do that,' she offered, not sure what would be involved and prepared for another put-down.

'I can gie a hand,' Colleen put in.

'Do you mind if we keep you in reserve?' Max asked, relaxing again with her. Perhaps when my baby's due he'll be kind to me too, Kate thought. Or would I have to be married to his cattleman to qualify?

'Colleen, why don't you go and phone Lexy? Kate and I will see to the dishes. I note, by the way, that my porridge found little favour.'

Max laughed. 'I've got enough struggles on my hands today without adding to them. Now, Colleen, any twinges, say at once. You're in a queue for the helicopter at present but if things start happening you'll get priority. No heroics.'

'Heroics? Me? You've got to be joking,' Colleen assured him. 'Well, best see if Lexy's out of his pit. It'll likely be the cat answers the phone.'

There was a fundamental pleasure in that morning which Kate had never experienced before. Getting to the animals and taking care of them was the basic task for everyone on the estate and she was part of it.

'You mustn't do too much either,' Grannie warned. 'We're supposed to be looking after you, remember. Goodness, what a lot of crocks we are. Poor Max, as if he hadn't enough to worry about. We'll just take everything steadily.'

But as they shovelled away, making paths to log shed and feed store, henhouses and loosebox, as jackets and then sweaters were discarded, a vast bursting pleasure filled Kate. Though the sun gradually brightened it never fully penetrated the gauze-like layer of cloud, and the soft light added its own strangeness to the sense of enforced isolation. It was impossible to believe that not twenty-four hours ago an arctic wind had whipped at them as they struggled with these same tasks. Now on every side she discovered breath-taking beauty. Tar barrels against the garage wall had perfect cylinders of snow on them higher than themselves; the courtyard wall and arch were topped with a two-foot crest; the outer end of the log pile was coated as if by a rich velouté sauce.

Buff capered like a puppy, leaped for snowballs, lunged like a seal through the drifts. Welcomed by Persephone with nuzzlings and whickerings it was hard to believe that a week ago Kate had been afraid of her. And Torquil, who had beaten a way for himself up to the gate, seemed as pleased to see human friends as his breakfast, when they carried armfuls of hay to him through thigh-deep drifts.

The hens were less rewarding. 'Oh, you horrible, horrible birds,' Grannie cried, kicking out as they mobbed her greedily. 'Never forget it will be a pleasure to eat you if supplies run low. The ultimate power,' she added to Kate, who for a heady moment imagined that she too could kill a hen in order to survive. Then, shuddering away from the brush of their wings as they fought over their feed, she knew she couldn't.

It was odd to look along the front of the house to where smooth high ribs of snow flowed across the drive from the base of each of the big sycamores. Down there, beyond those untouched drifts, were Mrs Grant, Doddie higher up the hill, Old Grigor at the Cedar Hut. Beyond them Bridge of Riach, Kirkton, Muirend, all as inaccessible as the South Pole. Somewhere over those high ridges to the west were Joanna and Laura, skiing, sledging? Cut off to the north Harriet and Letitia.

She did as much of the heavy work as she could but Grannie was stubborn. It was a relief when she said, driving her shovel into the mound of snow they had thrown up by the back door, 'Whoof, I think that's enough for now. Let's make coffee and keep Colleen company for a while before tackling the logs.'

Then everything happened at once. Grannie turned wearily to the steps, missed her footing and fell with a sharp indrawn breath of pain. Colleen appeared wild-eyed above them clutching the doorpost and exclaiming, 'That's me, I'm starting!', and the sun was shrouded by a sudden ominous veil.

Chapter Twelve

The whirring of the helicopter, which had been so deafening as the machine crouched, it seemed for ever, on the lawn before taking off, was blotted out with surprising speed in the mirky air. It was gone, and the tension and fears about getting Colleen away before the weather closed in were gone with it. The silence seemed tangible on the strangely mild, still air. The problems of being cut off, trapped sheep, animals to be cared for, swarmed back, and with them the new problem – Grannie with her strapped ankle on the morning-room sofa.

I'm on my own with Max, Kate realised in dismay, and then decided he must be equally appalled to be left with her, and with far more justification. For what use would she be in all that had to be done? She caught a glimpse of his face as he turned towards the house and quailed at its look of grim resignation.

Grannie had gone down with such a bang on the stone step that the two girls had cried out in concern, Colleen throwing aside her own big moment to try awkwardly to help her, Kate dropping her shovel and springing forward anxiously.

'I'm all right, I'm all right!' The snapped-out words had been pure reflex, meaning only, 'I do not intend to make a fuss'. It had been obvious that Grannie was not all right. As the three women struggled together the giggles which had overtaken them had not helped. Grannie was inches taller than either girl, and Colleen, a powerful arm clamped round Grannie's scrawny frame, had taken up so much room in the narrow corridor that Kate was nearly brushed away by the coats and jackets hanging on the wall. They were almost helpless with laughter by the time they reached the kitchen and lowered Grannie onto the settle.

'Oh, what a disaster!' she exclaimed. 'Can you *believe* it? Max will be impressed. Thank you both, but please, no more lifting and hauling. You especially, Colleen. How are you feeling? It's you we should be looking after. Kate, how's your first aid?'

The baby or the ankle? Kate could cope with neither and had gazed at her mutely, eyes wretched. Never in her life had she felt so deeply useless. Never had she been so aware of time squandered, resources untapped.

'Ah,' Grannie had said, with a lift of her eyebrows. 'Then we must do our best – organise the helicopter, get Colleen ready, tell Lexy, and I think fetch Max.'

'We should look at your ankle,' Kate had protested.

'Look at it by all means if you feel that will serve any purpose. It's not broken. But from now on you will have to do any active work, I fear.'

'I'll do anything!' Passionate, pointless words, but they had not seemed absurd at the time.

Colleen had been philosophical, full of ribald jokes, cursing freely when the pains came, though grateful that they were still brief and irregular.

With tentative fingers, wincing at every touch, bombarded with instructions, Kate had put a clumsy bandage round Grannie's swelling and already violently discoloured ankle.

Grannie had not been grateful. 'Can't even feel it's there, don't know what support that's supposed to give, could have done it better myself . . . .'

'Don't take any notice,' Colleen had advised. 'Just so's she can stand on it when the fun starts.'

'Colleen, don't even think of it.'

What had worried Kate even more than the baby starting was

the prospect of launching herself alone into a landscape of buried tracks and bottomless drifts to try and find Max.

But as she set out anger had come to her aid, anger with herself. For after all the answer had been so simple. All she had to do was go where the snowplough had gone and there Max would be. Was she so lacking in ordinary intelligence, she had asked herself furiously, that she had to go through this desperate panic before such an obvious solution hit her? Would she ever match up to the casual competence of the Munros, of Colleen?

Yet it had not been entirely straightforward. The snow was so heavy the blade had not cut through to the track; the wheel ruts were deep and churned where Max had had to go back and forth battering at a big drift, and the snow itself was so soft that she sank through it at every step and it was enormously tiring to try and hurry. But she had to hurry. Grannie's foot needed attention. Colleen's pains would be getting closer.

What would it be like, she had wondered, slipping and slithering, hot and panting, a tiny futile dot in the white wastes, when her turn came? September. No snow then; at least she supposed not. Who knew, here? But would this fearsome place produce some other trial of nerve and endurance? This morning Grannie had warned her not to do too much, but she knew she had rarely made such a sustained physical effort as ploughing through these drifts demanded. Then, rounding the bend above the river, she had seen the tractor by the bridge. Thigh muscles aching, she had gathered herself for a last effort. But no one was there. Wildly she had looked about her. Then she had seen across the field dark figures digging at a cliff of snow. One had paused, was coming towards her.

Max had listened in silence to her gasped-out news, then had turned and signalled to the men. The gesture had been cryptic to Kate but a raised arm from the diggers indicated he had been understood. Then he had set the tractor at the slope, and Kate, holding on grimly in the high swaying cab, had concentrated on suppressing all sounds as it lurched alarmingly through the ruts.

Even in the silence which seemed to throb after the engine was cut, Max had made no comment on Kate's trek to fetch him. In fact he had said nothing at all, merely lifting her down impatiently as she felt for a foothold and turning at once to go in.

She hadn't cared. He was back and in charge. She hadn't even minded his expressionless look as he unwound her attempt at bandaging and with competent fingers pressed and probed his mother's foot.

'No, not broken,' he pronounced. 'This puffing looks more like a strained ligament to me. That means keeping your weight off it completely.' He had rebandaged the ankle swiftly and firmly, then carried his mother up to the morning-room where Colleen had lit the fire.

'Good girl.' He had actually given her a pat of approval. 'Though your mind's on other things, I imagine?'

'Aye, well, you could say that.'

'Don't worry, you'll be fine,' Max had said, his voice surprisingly gentle.

'I may be fine,' Colleen had retorted, with one of her squawks of laughter, 'but will I be awa' in time?'

'I'm going to phone now, but there's no wind and visibility is still adequate. There shouldn't be any problem. And as soon as the helicopter gets here the medics are here too, so you'll be in good hands.'

He had not phoned from the morning-room, Kate had noted. When he came back Colleen had swayed off to the loo. Kate had paused to put a couple of logs on the fire and had heard Max tell his mother, 'They're not too happy about the weather. This high temperature's going to cause havoc. Hope to Christ they don't change their minds.'

'You'll be in for a busy evening if they do,' Grannie had replied with a laugh.

But Colleen, flushed with relief and the attentions of the crew, had got away successfully, in her element at jokes about overload and extra passengers. Before being hoisted in she had given Kate a crushing hug, and blinking back tears had whispered fiercely, 'You've been great, thanks a million,' and Kate had ached for the loneliness of her situation, guessing how desperately she must have been missing Lexy.

What puzzled Kate most was the general concern over the rising temperature. Surely with the power still off and as far as she could gather no immediate prospect of getting it back on, they should be thankful it was no longer freezing cold. She took a last look at the lowering sky into which the helicopter had vanished and turned to find Max waiting for her.

'I'll have to get back to the sheep. You'll be all right looking after things here?'

What things? Kate's thoughts flurried anxiously. Then she remembered Colleen, whirled away through the winter sky to hospital, and was ashamed.

'I'll do everything I can,' she promised.

'God knows when I'll get back.' Kate had the feeling Max had forgotten who she was. 'You'd better organise something for dinner. And don't leave the feeding too late.' He glanced at the sky, evidently not liking what he saw.

'Is it going to snow again?' Kate asked.

He looked at her for a second without answering, then said only, 'Keep a good fire going,' and turned to the waiting tractor.

A silly question, obviously. Kate stood for a moment longer in the gathering gloom, her feet cold from the long wait for the helicopter to lift off, her ears filled with the racket of the tractor, the dark bulk of the house climbing behind her with only a faint blur of light from the three windows of the morning-room on the first floor, and every atom of her rebelled at her circumstances. Darkness, discomfort, chores and demands. What was she supposed to 'organise' for dinner? And what was going to happen? Why those glances at the sky, which looked an ordinary dull winter one to her.

Then she remembered Grannie alone upstairs, Grannie who though she would never admit it must certainly be in pain. And if the fire got low she would be hopping up to replenish it. One thing at a time. Kate hurried through the archway and into the house, pausing to put on the kettle as she went through the kitchen.

'Poor child,' she was warmed to hear Mrs Munro greet her, then realised she was referring to Colleen. 'How wretched this is for her and how well she coped. I wish one of us could have gone with her. I've let Lexy know she's safely away. The poor man was almost in tears. Now,' dismissing human weakness for more important business, 'what is our strategy?'

In memory it was a muddled and exhausting afternoon, full of difficulties and worries. Parts of it, indeed, were more disagreeable than anything Kate had ever encountered. But even at the time there was a thread of – what? – primitive satisfaction at contending with challenges, a new consciousness of herself as she overcame by her own efforts unfamiliar problems.

Leaving Grannie ignoring the basket of patchwork pieces waiting to be tacked onto templates which Kate had fetched for her and beginning instead a long telephone gabble with Joanna and Laura, Kate went down, cleared away lunch, dressed to go out then, accompanied by a helpful Buff, assessed the resources of larder and store rooms. Plenty of cream but almost no milk; carrots and potatoes by the sackful; eggs – would she have to feel for eggs under the hens as she had seen Grannie do? Cheese and cold meats holding up, fruit down to a couple of oranges and half a dozen lemons. Why didn't they have things in tins for emergencies? Of course the bulk of the food was in the freezers. If the power cut continued, would that all be lost? She looked at the list she and Grannie had made. What if she missed something and had to open a freezer *twice*? She giggled in the chilly gloom.

'Who'd know?' she demanded of Buff, who grinned back at her, tail swinging. There was a sack of biscuits in the corner and a stack of tins on the shelf. He wasn't worrying.

'Butter,' Kate's list said. 'Bacon, sausages, venison mince.' Didn't they have ordinary mince? 'Soup, any. Teal,' How am I supposed to know what teal looks like? 'Lamb for tomorrow. Bread, or rolls if none.'

'Here goes,' she said to Buff, who watched supportively. A lot of food going about here. Also Kate was in her jacket which was promising. Playing around in the snow hadn't provided much exercise.

The scrubbed table in the centre of the larder, with its baskets and trugs and ancient scales, and the stick to hold up the lid of the biggest freezer which was liable to crash down on heads, was presently laden with hoary objects. But where were the rolls? No bread, that much was evident, but how could the rolls not be visible? With a moan of pleading, Kate blew on her fingers, sniffed back the drip on the end of her nose, and longing for the loo began again to shovel through bags and tubs. No rolls of any kind.

Abandoning the search, giving histrionic 'A-agh's', since there was no one to hear them, she carried her loot to the kitchen, its comparative warmth an agreeable treat. She had done her best.

Glancing out of the window she saw that dusk was already closing down. Max had warned her not to leave the feeding too late. Violent longing for the morning-room seized her, the draught-free shelter of one of those deep chairs that made her legs stick out in front of her like a child's, hot tea, the leaping fire.

With a sob of reluctance she turned to the door. As she went along the corridor she heard a new sound, the batter of sleet against the high windows. Her soul curled in her, shivering.

Chapter Thirteen

Soaked and tired, Max swung down from the tractor for the last time, he prayed, that day, and reached for the can of milk Jim Coupar had brought over from the farm. The sleety rain battered at him and he swore in weary anger. They had dug out the last of the ewes, none the worse for a night in the snow, but it was impossible in these conditions to shift the flock to higher ground and that, he feared, was going to be tomorrow's problem. But how serious it would be was hard to gauge and no more could be done tonight, whatever was coming.

As he reached the steps to the back door he checked. Without his mother in charge would Kate have managed adequately, or would she have missed something?

He found all the livestock content however, and even Persie ready to be affectionate. They were abundantly supplied and he smiled briefly; Kate had been making sure. Good for her; it couldn't have been much fun struggling back and forth all on her own in this downpour. Right then, the next thing was to get into dry clothes (oh, for a hot bath with a dram to hand), see that Grannie was all right, and make sure something was happening about food. This damned game with candles and lamps was a pain. Good thing there were plenty of gas cylinders on hand. He wondered what progress the Hydro Electric linesmen were making, poor devils. Would Grannie have phoned to check?

In the kitchen a most unexpected scene halted him. At the big table, a lamp on either end, a cookery book as big as a family bible propped in front of her, yeast, jug, mixing bowl, scales, flour, salt crock, lard and bread tins gathered round her, stood Kate, looking behind this formidable array like a child playing kitchens. Operations had already begun; there was a ring of flour round the scales and an ambitious mound of it in the bowl.

'Hey, hang on, wait a minute,' Max exclaimed, striding forward as he saw Kate about to empty a sachet of dried yeast into the jug of water.

Her hair in wet spikes, cheeks flushed, Kate checked with a start.

'There's no bread at all,' she explained hurriedly, actually sounding guilty at being caught. 'And I can't find any rolls so I thought I'd better make some, bread I mean. It sounds quite easy, only I realise now I should have started with the yeast because it says it takes half an hour to froth up and—'

'Kate, no.' Max caught her hand, poised again over the warm water. 'It was a nice idea, but not exactly practical. You have to prove the stuff twice, somewhere warm. Hadn't you read that far? You'll be here till midnight. Anyway, that's dried yeast, as it clearly says on the packet, and all you need to do is throw it in with the flour.'

'Grannie said I could put the dough to prove on the hearth in the morning-room,' Kate said, with that courteous way of hers of offering a fact without wanting to argue. 'The mince is there now, thawing out for cottage pie. I've done the potatoes, and some carrots, and there's plenty of cheese and Grannie said not to worry about soup because it's still like a brick.' She looked doubtfully at the cluttered table. 'If I don't need to do what it says about the yeast it would speed things up, wouldn't it?'

She gazed at him, dashed but clearly reluctant to give up the project, and Max felt his impatience simmer down a little. He hadn't heard her say so much at one time since she came, and he hadn't dared to hope she would have achieved half this much by the time he got back. In truth Kate hadn't turned out at all as he had expected, or how his anger with Jeremy and his own preconceptions had led him to imagine her. She was just a young and inexperienced person, plucked roughly from her normal element, who was doing her very best, never once complaining.

'OK,' he said, 'we'll make bread.' It was the last activity he would have chosen for the evening, but then he had expected to have to cook dinner and that appeared to be well under control. 'Hold on, though, have you changed since you were out doing the feeding?' He put a hand on the sleeve of her sweater and ready irritation swept back. 'For God's sake, with no heating on it's idiotic to hang around in damp clothes. Go and put something dry on before you do another thing.'

'I just wanted to get on—'

'It's going to be very useful if we end up with you out of commission as well, isn't it? And bring your wet things down. I'll fetch the gas fire from Colleen's room and get it going in here. Have you fed Buff?'

'Oh, no, I'm sorry, there just wasn't –' Kate, dusting flour from the front of her damp sweater with a floury hand and making long streaks on it, looked at him guiltily.

Max pushed down the annoyance he so rarely these days bothered to control. 'OK, it was only a question. You've done plenty already. I'll get changed myself and then I'll feed him.'

'I heated some water,' Kate said diffidently, and he saw that the gas cooker was crowded with kettles and pans.

He smiled at her, almost, it seemed to him, seeing her properly for the first time, the small face, the beautifully shaped head under the wet hair, the gentle brown eyes looking at him so uncertainly. They had changed her already, he realised, not sure he was glad they had. The enveloping sweater, ruffled curly hair, skin cleaned of make-up by the rain, mascara smudged under the lower lids – this was not the neat little urban secretary of two weeks ago. But the character hadn't changed, he saw. Then, as now, she was eager to help, willing to please, and all too conscious of her own deficiencies. After years of argumentative assertive Munros what was he complaining about?

'Good forward planning,' he said. 'We'd better share it. I'll take some up for you.'

When the mixing-bowl, covered by a tea towel, had been set in front of the morning-room fire, and Buff informed it was nothing to do with him, when Kate was kneeling on a cushion beside it to dry her hair and Max was at last stretched out in his big chair with a hot toddy at his elbow, Grannie brought them up to date on the news of the day. She had spent most of the afternoon on the telephone, chiefly to Gilbert, with whom she talked at least once every day of her life. The basket of patchwork pieces looked much as before.

'The Hydro Board hold out no hope of any kind and the snowplough hasn't even got as far as Kirkton. They started at eight this morning, were held up for hours getting out of the woods above Muirend where it always blows in so badly, and finally had to give up two miles below the village. Drumochter's closed, and Harriet and Letitia haven't even tried to set out.'

'That shows remarkable sense,' Max grunted, eyelids drooping as the whisky reached him and the fierce warmth of the fire replaced the barbarous if stimulating shock of a hasty wash in a cold bathroom.

'Letitia's in a great state apparently about her cats and ducks and hens, which she knows perfectly well she should never have left at this time of year.'

Max ignored the sweeping criticism. His mother didn't like Letitia, though he sometimes wondered if she quite understood why. 'Did you tell her Willie Mearns had been up to see to them?'

'Of course I did.'

Max grinned. There was no of course about it where his mother was concerned.

'However, it sounds as though Joanna and Laura are better off than we are. Joanna was full of quite unnecessary glee that the Moncrieffs had held on to their solid-fuel Aga at Morgill. The

girls have made a piste behind the house, I gather, and are entertaining the very reasonable hope that they won't be able to get
back to school tomorrow evening.'

'God knows what will have happened by then,' Max said.
That drum of rain on the windows meant the wind had come
right round to the south, and he didn't like it. 'Do we know how
Colleen's getting on?'

'Still in labour, poor child. No problems on the journey,
though. Lexy said he'd let us know as soon as he heard anything
more.'

'He's getting to the cattle all right?'

On to more important matters, Kate thought, but not in any
unkind spirit.

Only when she and Max had gone down to the kitchen again,
and Kate under instruction had knocked back the bread, shaped
it and put it into tins, while Max browned the mince for the
cottage pie, was the general mood of affability threatened.

Max, arrested by a furious spatter of rain at the window,
cocked his head to listen, muttering in impotent anger, 'That
damned wind's getting up again, and the temperature still hasn't
dropped.'

'But won't that get rid of the snow?' Kate asked. It had been
puzzling her all day. Didn't they want the snow to go, the snow
which blocked roads and buried sheep and cut everyone off?

She was unprepared for the anger with which Max turned on
her. 'Are you a complete fool? I know this place is a primitive
wilderness in your eyes, but surely that doesn't prevent you from
applying ordinary common sense to what you find here?'

'But I don't – I didn't –' Kate stammered, shocked by his
sudden aggression, clutching to her the last bread tin which she
had been trying to fit onto an already full tray with the rest.

'This is not some arcane weather feature which occurs
nowhere else in Britain. It could even happen in bloody Surrey.
It snowed, right? We had a huge pile of the stuff dumped on us;
you must have noticed that. And now it's thawing. A mild wind

will strip the snow off the hill in hours. Furthermore the ground here is in general steeply inclined, so water runs down it. It doesn't require an excessive degree of intelligence to work out what will happen next.'

Max knew he was venting on her his anger not only at the mounting problems he was helpless to control, but also some of the inner frustration which ate away at him so relentlessly these days, frustration at a situation he longed to break free of but felt himself committed to for the foreseeable future. He recognised, though so remotely that it didn't check him, the unfairness of lashing out at Kate like this, but there had been disappointment mixed with his disgust at the inane question, an odd feeling of being let down after the good showing she had made today.

'Yes,' Kate said in a small voice after a moment. 'Yes, I do see.'

She would have been more than justified in protesting, answering anger with anger, and Max knew it. He drew a long breath, deliberately focused his attention on what he was doing, turned the mince in the pan in neat sections, ran the slice round the edges to make sure it wasn't catching, then left it.

'It's just that –' he began, turning to her, residual exasperation in his voice in spite of himself. Then he stopped abruptly. Her eyes were full of tears.

'Oh, Jesus.' He ran both hands back through his hair and took a step towards her.

Kate drew back instinctively. She didn't suppose he would actually harm her but his movement had appeared angry, and she felt as though she had been tossed from one disagreeable thing to the next all day. The lamplight distorted everything, throwing heavy shadows, changing the familiar room. Max, in a black high-necked sweater under tweed jacket with a padded gilet on top, looked dark and menacing, towering over her.

At her involuntary movement his expression softened into a wry, almost contrite, amusement.

'Kate, I'm sorry. Things look distinctly unpromising for tomorrow, to say the least of it, so the fuse is a big short at present.

I suppose because you've done so well today, plunging into every-thing –' he gestured with a smile at the bread tins '– it seemed like starting at the beginning all over again to hear you ask some-thing as obvious as that. I mean, sometimes it seems as though you let being here alarm you so much that you refuse to apply your mind to the most basic facts.'

Like panicking about how to find him today, Kate thought ruefully. He was absolutely right. But for her too there were private pressures, facts behind her presence here which no one knew.

'It was a silly question,' she said honestly. 'I just hadn't thought it out. And I know you have – well, everything to worry about.' That was one of the difficulties; she could hardly conceive what his worries were, knowing only that they were enormous and that as far as she could see every man, woman and beast on the place depended on him.

Max regarded her quizzically. She had spoken with a simple directness that was generous after his sour outburst. He gestured with his head around the cavernous kitchen, its accoutrements of another era thrown into outlandish relief by the light from the lamps. 'It's all a far cry from home?' he suggested, in quite a new tone.

Kate nodded, unable to speak, her mouth trembling.

'Come on,' he said. 'It's been a long day.' And she was preg-nant too, he recalled with a jolt. She was so small and trim it was easy to forget it. Slogging round with logs and feed buckets and hay might not do much harm to someone who was used to it but she came from a very different environment. And a miscarriage would be all they needed. But his tone was less cynical than the thought as he went on briskly, 'Right, let's get this supper moving, and the bread back to the fire, or we'll be getting up in the middle of the night to take it out of the oven. Besides, Grannie will be getting lonely.'

Grannie, however, had yet more news to impart. 'Phone's gone,' she announced with casual relish as they joined her. 'I was just chatting to James, who says he hasn't noticed any storm and – phut!'

'Oh, Christ, I suppose that had to come.' Max rasped a hand down the chin he hadn't bothered to shave, mentally totting up the new complications this brought.

'Thank goodness we got Colleen away in time,' Grannie commented.

Kate glanced from one to the other, doing her best to see this as they would see it, but not risking a comment after the drubbing Max had given her.

'Well, that's that,' he said, reaching for the Glen Grant. 'For the next round it looks as though we're going to be on our own.'

Chapter Fourteen

Heart racing, frightened questions whirling – Grannie? Colleen?
– Kate made her way across the room in the near-dark. That
thump on the door, although she had been awake, her mind
already turning over the problems the day might bring, had startled her nearly out of her wits.

Max stood there, a tall dim shape behind the light of the torch
beam he kept down and away from her eyes. 'Sorry to drag you
out, Kate, but I'll need your help.'

'What's happened?' she stammered, shivering uncontrollably,
more with shock than cold.

'You'll see. Here, I brought your things up, they're just
about dry. No point in getting anything else wet, and wet we're
going to be today. Take this while you light a candle.' He
pressed the torch down on the bundle of clothes so that it didn't
roll away.

Uncoordinated and fumbling, not properly awake, mind and
body resisting being so abruptly dragged into activity, Kate lit a
candle and gave back the torch.

'Be as quick as you can,' Max ordered and was off with his
long incisive stride.

Oh no, I don't like this, Kate wailed inwardly as she hurried
into the semi-dry clothes with distaste and a growing anger to
be hurried and hustled along like this without apologies or

explanations. Then she grinned; what was she talking about, this was Munroland. She reran the scene in her mind with Max being apologetic about disturbing her, elaborating it absurdly, and felt more cheerful as she raced along twists of corridors and down stairs so familiar by now that in the growing light of dawn she didn't need a candle.

'Shall I make breakfast?' she began as she saw the empty kitchen table. Max was sitting on the end of the settle pulling waterproof overtrousers over his boots.

'No time. Pity we don't have any of these in a size that's even close for you.'

'Shall I let Buff out?'

'He's been out. Leave him. Here's your coat.'

The dried canvas was harsh and unbending, the fur lining spiky and whorled with yesterday's damp.

'What about Grannie?'

'What about her?'

But can't we even have . . . ? Coffee, was the longing thought as Kate looked over her shoulder at the dead gas stove, the cold kettle. But Max turned down the wick of the lamp and blew out the last glimmer.

It was warmer outside than in. The rain had slackened and the wind was gentler, the air smelling fresh and sweet. It was the only agreeable moment there was to be for some time.

'Get in.'

Don't give me any more orders, Kate screamed silently, her whole being out of kilter and yearning for warmth, caffeine, a moment's calm. She heard a long mournful howl from Buff; he hadn't received any explanations either.

In the grey light as the jeep swung through the archway even she registered that much had changed. The snow had sunk down dramatically, sections of rain-dark gravel actually showing through; some of the branches of the trees beside the lawn had shed their loads of snow in roughheaps and sprung back, dark patches against the white, and on the lawn itself she glimpsed curious black lines snaking across bare areas of grass. She couldn't work out what they were.

Her attention was dragged away from the question by realising that Max was not going to the farm as she had expected, but had turned left and was heading down the drive, which even in such a short time she had got used to thinking of as closed. She saw that its dwindled drifts were messy with a flotsam of twigs and gravel, larch needles and small branches.

Where were they —?

'Oh, yes!' They had rounded the first corner and Max jammed on the brakes, bringing the jeep to a skidding sideways halt almost in the springy embrace of a fallen tree. 'I knew it. And how many more after that? Come on.'

Stiff and reluctant, her stomach hollow, limbs like water, oppressed by the gloom under the great firs and wellingtonias, Kate slid down, resigned to the sight of Max coming round the back of the jeep with a chainsaw. He wasn't going to turn back like any normal, sensible human being and call out the fire brigade or police or whoever one called out on such occasions. Of course not. He was going to cut his way through this towering obstacle, and she, all too evidently, was going to help him.

'Shouldn't take long,' he said. 'You drag the pieces away.'

I hate you, Kate thought with sudden calm certainty. I've done my best to like you, to adapt to this appalling place, but I hate you and furthermore I think you are all arrogant, unbelievable megalomaniacs. These vengeful syllables did her good, and as the saw gave a couple of coughs and settled into its ear-splitting whine she pulled herself together and fought her way to where Max was setting to work.

The branches were like living entities with their own views on where they wanted to go. They were bouncy, heavy and had sharp needles on every part of them, something she had not previously known.

God, I wish I had Joanna or Laura here, Max thought, holding the saw aside as he pushed away a cut bough with his foot. Even

Harriet would be more use. He let the engine die and laid down the saw. Kate abandoned her tussle with a branch which was trying to shove her off her feet and watched in surprise as he went to the jeep.

'Here,' he said, returning. 'Try with these.'

Great workworn gloves with reinforced palms. Kate put them on, holding her hands up so that they didn't fall off again at once. She wasn't sure she would be able to bend them but the thought was kind.

'Thank you. That will be—'

He cut her short.

'We'll be here all day if you pussyfoot about like that.' He gave a quick wrench at the bough that had defeated her and it was free.

Exerting all her strength Kate closed her hands round it and pulled it clear. The gloves did make a huge difference.

'Kate, for God's sake!'

'What?' Startled, she paused.

'Don't drag it *onto* the drive.'

How justified that exasperation was, she thought, cheeks burning as she altered direction. It was the same story all over again; she got into a panic and looked no further than the immediate struggle she was involved in. She could hardly believe she had been so stupid, yet that was the effect Allt Farr seemed to have on her, as though ordinary rules didn't apply here. Battling there in the resin-smelling tangle, the footing treacherous, the jeep's lights creating a distortion of shadows so that it was hard to decide where best to take a grip, harried by the consciousness that whatever she did it was probably slow, silly or wrong, she suffered one of the worst moments of emptiness of her life. What was there to long for, where did she long to be? There was nowhere, not in life till now or in life ahead. Only huge unknown complications and responsibilities she knew she wasn't ready for, could barely envisage.

The saw whined down to blissful silence. A hand appeared

beside hers and the last of the big branches was hurled aside. 'That should do. We'll be able to get round the end now.'

As far as Kate could see the drive was still blocked. She had thought they would be there for hours. The relief was dazzling. She turned with aching shoulders towards the jeep.

'Hurry up,' Max said automatically.

He had given her plenty of orders, many of them a lot more brusque than this one, but suddenly, startling even herself, revolt and anger coalesced in Kate. She grabbed his jacket sleeve and squared up to him recklessly as he turned in surprise.

'Listen,' she said furiously. 'I don't mind doing whatever's needed and helping wherever I can. That's what I'm here for. But what reason can there possibly be for not telling me what we're doing, where we're going or what's going on? You rush me out here without breakfast—'

'Is that what this is about, missing your damned breakfast?' As he said it Max knew he was snatching at anything to hand to parry this unexpected attack.

Kate's anger blazed higher, and even as Max was conscious of surprise that she was capable of it, he knew he deserved it.

'It's about everything! You come banging on my door as though there's some huge drama, you drag me out of the house and down here and start hacking your way through this horrible tree and you tell me nothing, absolutely nothing about what's happening! I know you think I'm a useless idiot, but I'm not totally incapable of understanding simple explanations—'

She was very, very angry. She barely reached his shoulder and he could have picked her up with one hand yet Max felt a total respect for her blazing indignation.

'You're right and I'm sorry,' he said. 'The reason I didn't explain is that I'm a bad-tempered bastard with a lot on my mind. This is what's happening. I've been out to check a couple of times during the night and the river's in full spate. The first thing we have to do is get old Grigor Macfarlane out of that matchbox house of his on the bank before he or it gets washed away.'

Kate gazed at him, good sense and her natural reasonableness quenching her wrath. She was about to apologise for wasting precious time when physiology took a hand. At its appointed moment, not even thought of in the pellmell hurry since Max came hammering on her door, morning sickness overtook her, washing her skin with goose-pimples after the exertions of the last twenty minutes, lacing her forehead with sweat.

'Max, sorry,' she gulped, putting out a hand half to push him aside, half in blind search for support as she turned urgently away. 'I just need a moment—'

But between her and the sheltering trees was the springy mass of cut branches, an impossible barrier. Clamping down on the infuriating nausea, desperate, ashamed, her memory of the next few seconds was for ever mercifully blurred. She remembered being whisked up by a strong arm, and the rough bark of the tree to which she clung as the humiliating sickness swept her, and she remembered, with gratitude, that she was left alone.

Emerging stumbling and dizzy, hardly able to see, she felt guiltier than ever to have caused more delay. 'I'm so sorry. I'm fine now. We ought to get on . . . .'

'Take your time.'

Max sounded very relaxed all of a sudden in view of the emergency they were rushing to deal with.

But for Max Kate's sickness too was a human need, as inescapable as the rising flood waters. The pallor of her small face in the lights smote him; he couldn't tell if sweat or rain beaded the drawn skin. He pulled out a handkerchief. 'Here, have this. Don't know what state it's in, mind you.' His handkerchiefs did duty for many jobs they weren't intended for.

'No, really, I'm all right.'

'Don't be a fool.' He spoke as he would to Joanna, to Laura, naturally, forcefully and entirely acceptably.

Gratefully Kate wiped her face; the handkerchief smelled of oil, but somehow it wasn't unpleasant.

'Do you want to go back?' Max enquired. 'You'd probably be better with something hot inside you.'

Kate felt her spirits rise at this ordinary kindness, and knew the moment of despair about where her life was heading, her resentment against Max, that flare of uncharacteristic rage, had largely stemmed from the one physical cause. And Max was sort of apologising.

If females have to giggle, hers is one of the warmest and most infectious giggles I have ever heard, Max decided, smiling in spite of himself. 'I take it you're feeling better?'

'You're being nice to me.'

He laughed aloud. 'Yes, well, we can't stand here discussing my personality. We've got things to do.'

As he negotiated the passage they had cleared for the jeep, cursing as branches scraped its sides and having trouble re-crossing the ditch, now a rushing torrent, he reflected that that was the first ordinary joke, adult to adult, Kate had ever made to him.

Though once or twice they had to clear minor obstructions they reached the bottom of the drive in ten minutes. A light was on at the Gate Lodge.

'Good,' Max said. 'I'll just nip in and have a word with Mrs Grant.' He had slammed the door behind him before he remembered a point newly made. He opened it again and said with straight-faced punctiliousness, 'I am taking this opportunity to warn Mrs Grant that, all things being equal, we shall shortly return with Grigor and she will have the pleasure of looking after him.'

Kate laughed. The colour was back in her cheeks and her face looked bright and alive.

I must remember how profitable good manners can be, Max mocked himself as he went up the path, shouting for Mrs Grant. And in spite of the trials that were assuredly ahead, the mountain of jobs waiting to be climbed once this rescue had been made, he felt a cheerfulness stir that had been absent for far too long.

He paused only once more, on the brow of the track leading down to the Cedar Hut. There was no need to say anything. In light still reluctant to brighten under a baleful sky of wind-tattered clouds, Kate saw, laid out below her like a diagram, the elements of the crisis that was swiftly developing.

From every snow-patched hillside white ribbons of burns poured down, in some cases spreading into wide sheets; the main river which, below the high ground on which Allt Farr stood, curved through a wide level stretch scoured by glaciers, was already well over its banks, and over the glen road too, a pewter-coloured spread of water moving at a relentless speed which was frightening even at this distance.

Kate shuddered, awed by the sight. Then remarked, 'I didn't know you had a lake here.'

Max jerked his head round in exasperated disbelief but caught her expression of innocent enquiry in time.

'Very funny.' But as he released the handbrake he was delighted to find she was capable of sending herself up, and teasing him.

Grigor's cottage of pale weathered shingles, built by Max's father as a private retreat principally from his wife, still stood on dry ground, relatively speaking, at the back, but water was washing in at the front door. Grigor himself was in a sorry state, half-dressed, clumsily trying to carry random objects upstairs, more concerned about the telephone being dead than having to leave his home.

'There's naebody taking any notice,' he kept saying. 'They're a' too busy to listen to me. Oot and aboot, oot and aboot, just when a body needs them.'

'I'll help him to dress,' Max said quietly to Kate. 'Collect up anything you think he'll need. Use a binbag or something. We'll get him out to the jeep then you keep him company while I turf as much stuff as I can out of harm's way. Though it'll be a while before he can move back here, by the look of what's coming.'

Hurriedly and gratefully gulping down strong hot tea – she

never drank tea in the morning – by Mrs Grant's old-fashioned range, with Grigor happily esconced in an armchair pulled close to the warmth and relishing the prospect of a better breakfast than he ever had at home, Kate found there was more to her feeling of wellbeing than immediate physical comfort. There was a sense of sharing, of playing her part in events more demanding than she had ever had to face in Wilton Avenue. And in this moment of simple satisfaction, in spite of the threat of unknown exigencies ahead, for once the name brought none of the customary associations of rejection and pain.

Chapter Fifteen

Max pulled the Fourtrak up in front of the house but didn't switch off the engine.

'It might be a good plan if Grannie stayed in bed,' he said, as Kate opened her door. 'You might persuade her to if you remind her there's still no phone.'

About to say, 'But shouldn't you have some breakfast?' Kate remembered the barrage of such remarks which Jessie directed endlessly at Jack, and his mulish expression when she persisted.

'I'll take breakfast up for her,' she said instead, though not relishing the prospect.

'Don't do any for me yet. I'll be back when I can but I must get hold of Doddie. All right?'

Kate caught the glint of a grin. It seemed her outburst, of which she was now much ashamed, had done no harm. She stood for a moment as the jeep disappeared again into the mouth of the drive. As silence overtook the noise of the engine she found it wasn't silence at all, but a liquid, rippling sound, as though the whole landscape and every object in it was thawing, melting, pouring. From eaves and ledges, from downpipes unable to contain the excess flow, from trees and bushes, down walls and into hollows already eaten into the gravel, water ran and plopped and spattered. The mysterious lines writhing across the lawn were formed by sticks and leaves, earth and stones, washed down by new streams. There was a strange exhilaration in this living sound, the gusty push of the mild wind, the very scale of it all. It was a lot more exciting than grim ice and fog had been.

Elated, eager to tackle the jobs she felt to be within her compass, she hurried through the arch. Buff would want to go out, Grannie must be wondering where they were, the ponies would be looking for her . . . .

Grannie's lamp was lit and she was reading Evelyn Waugh's diaries. 'Goodness, he makes me cross,' she cried when Kate and Buff appeared, threading a way through the scatter of objects trailed across the carpet. 'But diaries do roll you along. You always have to read the next bit. Kate my dear, how delightful! I cannot think when I last had breakfast in bed. And proper coffee, how excessively obliging of you.'

If this was sarcasm Kate didn't mind. 'I hope it's strong enough,' she said, having heard Harriet's efforts roundly castigated. 'I'm only used to instant.'

Grannie darted at her a sharp look of interest and amusement. No apology there. The child was improving.

'Now, what new disasters are we facing today? Don't fuss with the pillows, they are perfectly comfortable as they are.'

'We've just been to fetch Grigor and take him to Mrs Grant's. The river's over its banks and across the road and the farm track.'

'Already? *Not* good news. Now listen, Kate, don't worry about me. I can't be much use to anyone with this wretched ankle, and the only cure for that is to keep it up. I'm warm here and out of the way. I think you should run down and see to the animals as quickly as possible, so that you're ready to help Max if he needs you. Have you had anything to eat yet? No? Then do.'

'If you're sure you'll be all right?' Once more large vague catastrophes loomed.

'I'm fine. Off you go. And bless you for bringing this up for me,' Grannie called as Kate reached the door, and Kate smiled, knowing the words were intended as a message of encouragement.

Do things in sensible order, she warned herself as she hurried down the dark stairs, Buff keeping close because strange things were afoot. If Grannie was staying in bed the fire didn't matter yet. Buff had milk and cereal at breakfast-time. Had Max given him that already? Well, it wouldn't matter if he had a double ration. Tiny though the decision was, it took her into new territory and was curiously steadying. Kettle on, animals. Should the hens be let out? Doubt returned as she went across the courtyard. They'd been shut up during the storm, so probably should be out, but with all this water about what feeding could they find, and might they somehow get washed away? And how furious Max would be if after all the other things he had to deal with he found himself rounding up Harriet's despised poultry. Then Kate remembered the draggled fowl wandering about in the mud at Letitia's cottage. She would leave the door open and the hens could decide for themselves. Simple.

Like an old hand she slipped some of Torquil's horse nuts into her pocket before filling her arms with hay. She felt suddenly happy as she hopped across puddles to the gate where he was already whickering to her, and the wind released some lingering sweetness from the hay and creamed across her face with a soft pure touch. She found pleasure in the feel of his nuzzling lips, liked being close enough to see his hairy chin, the soft nostrils, the beautiful dark eyes, liked running her hand up under the thick coat to warm it on his powerful body heat.

She had barely taken two gulps of coffee, which tasted better than any she had ever drunk in her life after the long wait and the exertion and fresh air, when she heard Max's quick step on the stone flags of the corridor, signalling more urgency, another crisis. Buff knew too, coming to his feet in one movement, head cocked.

'Kate, I need you.' Max was soaked, his clothes plastered with mud. 'Get your things on. I'll tell Grannie.'

Kate had come to her feet too. 'The kettle's just boiled. Do you have time –?'

'I don't have time for anything.' He was already through the kitchen without even bothering to kick off his filthy boots.

What would be required of her? Kate's hands were trembling as she pulled on her own boots again and reached down the damp canvas coat. What else could she do to get ready? Nothing. But Grannie had told her to eat something. She hastily swigged down her coffee, then slapped together the toast she had just made with butter and marmalade and pushed it into a freezer bag.

Max was back, his face set. 'No gas left on or anything silly? You stay, Buff. Come on.'

As Kate climbed up into the Fourtrak she heard him slinging things into the back and then he was in, door slamming, and they were off at high speed in the direction of the farm.

'That field by the river where the gimmers are,' Max filled her in rapidly, 'the one we call the Haugh. There's a little knowe in it, a hump, and some of them have moved onto it away from the floods. Trouble is, it looks as though the water's going to go right over it. We've got to get them off.'

He hauled the jeep out of a slide which had nearly taken them into the dyke, and slowed down slightly. 'No one can get over from the farm, there's a big hole torn out of the track. Doddie's away after some ewes stranded near the road, so this is down to us.'

About to ask, scarcely able to picture what they would have to do, 'But can we get to them in the jeep?' Kate was thankful she hadn't as they took the last curve and she gasped to see what lay before them. The swollen river was now half a mile wide, reaching from the steep bank where the bulk of the sheep huddled almost to the farm. She could see a tossing torrent, where she had not even realised a burn existed, cutting across below the farm buildings, and the dark crater gouged out of the track. Nearer at hand she gasped again to see the newly decorated Burn Cottage with water three feet up its walls, but as though all this was recorded in one comprehensive glance and put aside, her attention focused on a small grassy hillock, crested by small birches, dotted with sheep, and surrounded by a wide expanse of swiftly moving water.

'But how on earth –?' she asked involuntarily.

'Get the gate, will you?'

She couldn't shift the hook, discovered the catch which had to be pressed back to free it, and still couldn't move it.

'Lift!' Max bawled out of his window.

Kate had not been trained from birth in the knack of using one hand to raise the gate, one hand to unhook it. At its weight she tottered forward on her toes.

'Dear God.' Max was beside her, the gate was heaved aside like a matchstick toy. 'Can you manage to shut it, do you think?'

'I'll try.' She realised with shame as she waited for him to drive through that she would have left it open. Floundering, she dragged it shut, and with one determined heave got it high enough for the hook to connect.

'If the bloody boat's not sunk,' Max muttered, as they bucketed along the level above the flood, sheep scattering before them.

Kate held on, apprehensive, mute. If only Joanna had been here to cope with this, Laura even.

The sturdy flat-bottomed boat, used for taking sheep across to graze on the island where the burn divided, was tied up on the far bank of a tributary burn now in tumbling spate, its blunt bow almost under. A few yards above it a water gate, clogged with the debris of the storm, water foaming to its lip, looked ready to burst at any moment and release this mass upon it.

'Not too good,' Max remarked, swiftly sizing up his options. 'But that's the only way across with the water coming down like this.'

He crouched, and stretching out an arm leaned his weight on the flimsy looking barrier. It gave ominously, and he swore, pulling himself back. He glanced up the hill where the burn hurtled down a narrow corrie.

'We're not going to get across there, are we?' he remarked conversationally.

'Can we get round some other way, in the jeep?' She regretted the words as soon as they were out, natural though the impulse had been to share the problem. But Max seemed to understand that.

'Gate at the other end will be under water too,' he said briefly. 'No, I'll have to get across here. If the boat goes nose under, which it's about to do at any second, we can say goodbye to those sheep.'

'I'll go,' Kate heard herself say.

'Yes?' Max swung to look at her, not sounding incredulous or contemptuous, but alert and assessing.

'I'm half your weight.' He didn't take her up on that for the moment. 'It would probably bear me.'

Max studied the barrier for an intent moment. 'I think it would,' he agreed finally. 'But you'd have to put a rope on. If your weight makes it sink down much further the water will come over the top and take you with it.' Along with a pile of large unwieldy objects to bruise and stun; but he could pull her out of danger in time.

Water was one thing Kate had no fear of. Swimming had always been her favourite exercise. So long as Max saw to it that she didn't end up like Maggie Tulliver. But the sea was quite a long way from Allt Farr, indeed she couldn't think for the moment where the nearest sea might be. She shoved these rather wild thoughts aside and looked up at Max resolutely.

'I'll try,' she said.

'Good, but in your excitement don't let go of the wrong bit of rope and set the boat adrift, will you?' There was a new companionable note in his teasing.

He gave her a knife and explained carefully what she had to do. Seeing her tense nervousness he wasn't altogether hopeful of success, wasn't even sure she was listening to him, but it was the only chance they had.

'You'd better shed that coat, too heavy and awkward.' He had noticed more than once with amusement that it tended to walk her about, not the other way round. 'You are going to get very, very wet, even if you don't fall in.'

'At least it's not freezing.' But Max felt her whole frame shivering as he tied the rope round her, and wished from the bottom of his heart he didn't have to ask her to do this. It was one of the great surprises of his life to see how she went out unhesitatingly onto that sagging water gate with its dangerous accumulation of branches and rubbish, the force of the current driving its bars out horizontally, the wind buffeting and plucking at her. She went across like a monkey, apparently quite unafraid. The frail barrier didn't give an inch under her light, swift passage, and Max found himself laughing aloud at the sheer unexpected simplicity of it.

'What were we hanging about for?' he yelled at her. 'Piece of cake.'

She laughed back at him, drenched, triumphant, and raised a gleeful fist.

'Don't get too carried away. Tie on with the long line first.' What means she would use to secure the rope was another matter, he thought resignedly, as he took a couple of turns with it round the strainer. He looked back to see Kate flat on her face on the bank, struggling to undo the painter.

'Kate, get in and cut the fucking thing! Use the knife!' Harriet would have done just the same. Women had the most extraordinary approach to things. And Kate had probably planned to return by her previous route even though he could now pull her across in the boat.

The next trick would be to steer it clear of the tug of the water where the burn joined the flood. Then there was the small matter of rounding up half a dozen ewes, manhandling them aboard, and rowing the laden boat back, though it wouldn't matter where he brought them ashore. Perhaps a couple of trips would be wiser, without a dog to keep the stupid creatures in order. And spectacularly as Kate had performed so far she wouldn't be much use in any of that.

He was wrong. Flown by success and the discovery of a physical courage she hadn't known she possessed, even by being filthy and soaked which gave a new and exhilarating sense of liberation, Kate plunged into the chase, cornering racing ewes who preferred drowning to boating, grabbing handfuls of sodden fleece, feeling for the first time the nubbly roughness of the curly horns and their sharpness against her palms as the heads jerked and writhed, eye-balling mad yellow-circled orbs, yelling uninhibitedly as a narrow hoof bored into her foot. It was a hectic, wet, lively business, and entirely successful.

'You've provided some first-class entertainment,' Max observed, deadpan but delighted with her, as he edged the boat, half aided by the current, into the bank.

Only then did Kate notice that on the farm side of the flood a tractor was parked, a couple of figures comfortably propped against its wheel. She laughed and waved. Two arms were raised in response.

Max laughed as well. 'Well, you played a blinder there. I think you've earned your breakfast today.'

'Oh, the toast!' Flattened, bent and oozing, the contents of the poly bag did not look pretty.

'Nice thought,' Max said. 'Mind if I pass?'

They were both laughing as a new sound filled the sky. A helicopter was circling down towards them.

Colleen coming back? Surely it was too soon? Kate had trouble working out when she had gone.

'Hydro Board,' Max said, arm up to shade his eyes against the increasingly silvery light.

The helicopter came lower. A figure at its open hatch waved.

'Never mind waving, get the power on,' Max shouted, waving back. 'Still, they've remembered we're here.'

And as Kate climbed wearily down from the Fourtrak, painfully aware of bruises she hadn't known she'd collected, she saw lights on in the house. It seemed the ultimate in luxury to walk into the bright kitchen, to be met by Buff carrying a piece of patchwork about because he was so pleased to see them, Max striding in on her heels rubbing his hands together and saying with relish, 'Now for the biggest breakfast you ever saw.'

Chapter Sixteen

The train, rocketing southwards, slowed to take the long curve above the river. Looking down at the sunlight flashing on white water and huge rock slabs far below, and the tree-hung cliff on the other side of the narrow pass, it seemed impossible to Kate that only six weeks ago she had been travelling along here in the opposite direction, numb, hurt and frightened.

She welcomed this time alone. At Allt Farr being alone was a luxury no one seemed to care about much. Her eyes on the spring-like scene which spread before her as the train roared out of the gorge, she noted that there were lambs down here, and that a faint green, still far off in the glen, hazed the trees along the river bank. With the sun beating agreeably through the window, she let her thoughts flow.

So much had altered since the day of the floods. In itself that had been an amazing day. Prepared for a long and uncomfortable siege, first the return of electricity had removed all kinds of problems which had already become almost accepted, then the reconnected telephone had put the outer world back in touch. Grannie had resumed her endless talks with Gilbert Rathlyn, Harriet had phoned to say she was at Letitia's and one of the cats had given birth in the knitting basket, and word had come from Morgill that Joanna was on her way back and would get as far as she could. Fanny and Laura, the latter bitterly bewailing missing the excitement, had gone back to school. News had come from Bridge of Riach about the furious digging and sand-bagging which had successfully kept most of the water out of the houses, and from up and down the length of Glen Maraich accounts had filtered in of trees down, stock drowned, dykes burst through, fences torn away and large quantities of people's drives washed out of their gates.

Remembering Max's call to check on how Riach Lodge had fared, Kate laughed aloud, then looked round to see if she could have been heard.

'James is still in bed,' Max had reported. 'Can you believe it? Says it seems the best place to be and as far as he knows everything's fine.'

But best of all had been the message from Lexy, though he could hardly get the words out for excitement. Colleen had had a son, weighing nearly ten pounds, which hadn't come altogether as a surprise.

The most astonishing thing of all had been that a few hours after the rescue of the sheep, hours during which the water had washed clean over the hummock in the Haugh field, the floods had gone. The river still shouldered along to the top of its banks, its greedy hurrying voice loud even at the house, but apart from a few isolated stretches of water below the farm the drama was over.

'How can it disappear like that?' Kate had asked in bewilderment, outside to see Lexy off to the hospital in the estate pick-up, a Lexy anxious and proud in equal degrees, wearing nailed boots, the flattened cap he used for milking and a blue suit straining across his shoulders.

'Kate, please,' Max had protested.

She had gazed round her. There was more to scenery than scenery, she was being obliged to learn.

'Yes,' Max said. 'Steep hills, a glen that falls five hundred feet between here and Kirkton. Got it?'

Even so, it had seemed magical. Almost as magical had been

her new lack of concern at his sarcasm. That was how he spoke to everyone and she could survive it, just as they did. Almost she felt a new sympathy for him, though she would never have dared to express it. He had so much to look after, so many people hanging round his neck, that it was hardly surprising his temper was somewhat short.

With the disappearance of the floods and the return of Harriet and Joanna normality had returned, yet there had been a subtle difference which even now Kate could not precisely define. Besides the mammoth task of putting everything to rights – and Max swore that quite apart from the ravages to the landscape there wasn't a building on the place with its guttering intact – the atmosphere of the house had changed. Had she imagined it? But no, certainly with Grannie a closer relationship had been established. They had shared a challenge; and Kate had not been found wanting. She smiled briefly at the phrase, but it suited thoughts of Grannie.

The tale of the rescue of the sheep had passed into Allt Farr legend, and though Max recounted it in teasing terms – 'You should have seen the way she shot across the water gate, so terrified she didn't give herself time to fall in. She'd have untied the boat with her teeth if necessary. Then taking off like a lunatic after the ewes, who needed a dog?' – none of it was said in a hostile spirit.

She had received less approbation last week in the unfortunate matter of the turnips. Remembering it, Kate groaned, but couldn't resist laughing again. She still thought she had made a reasonable decision. She had been walking with Buff and had spotted some sheep who seemed to have strayed into a field where they were busily eating their way through the crop growing there. Although not long before she had been in trouble over shutting a gate which had been left open so that something or other could get to water, this patently hadn't been right. The sheep had already worked their way through quite a lot of the green vege-tables, which she didn't recognise. Buff, when bidden to help drive them into the next field, had been doubtful. Much as he loathed sheep they were forbidden prey. However, Kate had insisted, so he had thrown away the rule book and entered into the sport joyfully.

They had just got the last ewe headed for the top gate when they had been halted in their tracks by a terrific bellow from the track below, where neither of them had noticed the jeep pull up.

'What in Christ's name do you think you're doing?' Max looked angrier than Kate had ever seen him as he vaulted the dry-stone dyke and came ramping up the field, but she had still been confident that he would be pleased when he knew what had happened.

But no. 'Kate, they're supposed to eat the bloody neeps! They're food, extra nutrition – these ewes are lambing early. God almighty. Buff, you should know better at least.'

Buff had withdrawn strategically and was peeping round the gatepost. He decided he could manage without a lift home.

But in spite of his rage Max had enjoyed telling that story against her too, and she had seen the funny side of it.

There had been a different feeling with Colleen as well since she came back from hospital, an unspoken feeling of mutual support. Kate had gone several times up to the Old Byre, which now seemed an easy walk away, the hair-raising track a harmless lane, twisting beside a burn spilling meekly down between dry-topped boulders.

It had been marvellous to have the chance to handle and get to know a newborn baby, though Colleen tossed Robson round with a casualness Kate would have thought more appropriate for one of the bull calves across the steading yard. Robson, built on the same sturdy lines as his mother, accepted this treatment with stoicism, conserving his vocal forces for demands for food.

At last, as the train neared Perth, there was no snow to be seen. In the entire time she had been at Allt Farr, it occurred to Kate, snow had been visible somewhere, though by now she had grown accustomed to the marked difference in climate to be found by merely driving down to Muirend. The weather had never curtailed the social activities of the Munros, however, the weekly visit to Riach the fixture round which the rest revolved. Kate had come to look forward to it, liking James's gentleness and quietness, his refusal to be drawn into arguments, his calm blocking of any attempts to improve his domestic arrangements. And he had been, for all his shyness, very kind to her, drawing her into conversations where she felt confident and unthreatened, and always ready to protect her from Munro attacks. For acceptance into the family had come at a price; they treated her now as they treated each other, and criticism could be open and blistering.

It had not only been James's company which she had enjoyed at Riach. The lively tempo of kitchen life was always fun. More observant as her confidence grew, she had seen with interest that Max, in spite of his assertions that he went to Riach to escape female kind, nevertheless relished the rollicking spirits of the twins and Bridie's slapdash methods, which however unpredictable created a warmer atmosphere than that which maintained in his own household.

James had appeared quite often at Allt Farr, without warning and at odd times, though he never seemed quite sure why he had come, accepting whisky but refusing food, contributing little to the conversation, taking himself off again abruptly. It was small wonder that he felt awkward, Kate thought, since he was greeted with such relentless teasing about his initiative in undertaking such an arduous journey, or in getting himself out of bed in the first place.

Joanna alone never teased him, though she didn't seem particularly pleased to see him and usually found some excuse to slip away. Joanna on the whole was rather a disappointment, Kate decided. She had been at first so warm and easy-going and kind. Well, she was kind, she would do anything for anyone – if they were prepared to wait till she got round to it, Kate amended with a wry smile – but somehow she eluded contact, and no real friendship with her had developed. Kate, at first rebuffed, had come to see that it was the same with everyone. Even with Laura Joanna held back, preferring a joking, understated style to anything emotional or demonstrative. It was Max, surprisingly, who provided the cuddles and physical closeness which Laura sometimes needed. There would be a quick passing hug, an arm round her as she stood beside his chair, and always the big whirling embrace when she arrived home each weekend.

Had Joanna not shaken off her grief for her husband? She never referred to him. Yet there was something, some barrier interposed between her and everyday life. It was a shame; she was still attractive and thirty-four wasn't that old.

In Harriet's case it had been Kate who had resisted a 'let's-be-chums' approach which had slightly alarmed her. As she had earlier suspected, Harriet drew comfort from Kate's status as new girl, blunderer, ignorant innocent, seeing a chance to be expert and mentor herself for once. But there had been an undertone of, 'Isn't everyone horrid, we'll be nice to each other,' which Kate hadn't cared for.

Anyway, Harriet had Letitia, and further visits to Craigbeg had given Kate a clearer insight into how strong the latter's influence was, and what she provided in Harriet's life. She was calm waters after storm. She supported Harriet in all her glen affairs, encouraged and praised her. Unhurried, unchanging, she swayed smiling through her days, living in her own chosen way, always occupied, always content. The only thing that roused her to indignation was waste. It was obvious that saving and contriving had become more than a habit, they were now her favourite hobby. Watching her fold paper into spills, turn old socks into kettle holders, use the contents of her hot-water bottle for washing the dishes, and hoard the crumbs off the breadboard in a jar for cooking, Kate had understood the source of the economies Harriet vainly tried to impose at Allt Farr. The one that caused most irritation was switching off the kitchen corridor light. Since the switch was midway between the doors other people found this maddening, particularly if they were cooking and needed to go back and forth to the larder, or were accompanied by Buff who took his own route.

Not that the Munros were huge spenders. They were all prepared to wear any garment to hand, regardless of age, previous ownership or state of dilapidation. Parsimony over heating Kate now took for granted. Yet on the other hand for things they considered essential, alcohol, good food, entertaining friends, a fortnight's skiing in the Dolomites for Max, cars — she had recently discovered that when conditions didn't require the use of the jeep he drove an Audi estate — funds seemed unlimited.

Jessie had hated entertaining. Hated, to be honest, anyone coming to the house. She spent a fortune on it, decorating and redecorating, throwing out carpets after a couple of years, adding a conservatory, endlessly revamping the kitchen, but no one ever saw it except very occasionally her sister and family. Was it done chiefly for Jessie's own reassurance? Yet she was never satisfied with it. Perhaps bottomless resources brought their own problems. Everything you had revealed the choices you had made, without constraints, and Jessie was terrified of having chosen the 'wrong' things. But deeper than that, Kate could see from her new perspective, she had difficulty in achieving ordinary contact with people, didn't understand friendship.

Kate caught herself up. This was ridiculous. She had pushed memories of home to the back of her mind during these busy weeks, drilling herself to accept that Jessie had meant what she said, and that Jack would support her. They would never forgive her for what she had done.

She turned her mind back to Allt Farr, picking out deliberately from the images the thought of Laura, and the magic she could unfailingly work on the atmosphere of the gloomy house. She had brought Fanny home with her for the first weekend after the storm, and they had done their share of the strenuous filthy salvage work everyone on the estate was engaged in. James had brought the twins over, 'To see what all the fuss was about,' as he put it, and the whole thing had turned into a party.

Two weekends later Kate had gone with Laura to Morgill – Fanny's parents were skiing with Max so she was theoretically in charge – and had been amused to find herself stifled by the powerful central heating of an immensely comfortable and draught-proof house.

Now Easter was approaching and the cottages were all booked, though entirely by friends and relatives by the sound of it. Kate had wondered, with mixed feelings, whether Jeremy would appear, but his name hadn't been mentioned. She had found herself half hoping he would come, and then had been angry with herself, trying to keep firmly in mind the Jeremy she had last seen, doing his best to sound affectionate but with a hunted, almost furtive air, any attraction he had once felt towards her obliterated by its inconvenient consequences. But it was hard not to dream a little about him as he had been at their first meeting, good-looking, confident, and so kind to her, so teasingly protective, reassuring, tender. But Kate was well aware of the danger of using Jeremy as a peg on which to hang romantic fantasies – the father of her child, belonging to her new world. He wouldn't come to Allt Farr while she was there, and all the dreams in the world wouldn't alter that.

But these were not thoughts for this expedition, she reminded herself. This was a holiday. Summoning up enthusiasm, she reviewed the prospect of the next two days. Two days to dissipate on the forgotten pleasures of the city, wearing nice clothes, free of mud, snow, wind and manual labour, with whole nails and tidy hair, pampering herself, spending money, breathing in the almost forgotten air of expensive shops, laden with the mingled scents of newness. She would get up late and have long leisurely baths and spend hours in the beauty parlour, and tonight she would go to the theatre. Though she hadn't admitted the extent of her tiredness when this 'little break', as Harriet called it, had first been suggested, she would be glad of a rest. Morning sickness, blessedly, had stopped, but instead she had been dogged for the last few days by an aching back and a heavy dragging lethargy which was new and disagreeable.

The city was reaching out, housing estates, supermarkets with vast carparks. Kate didn't mind the ugly sprawl. This had been her territory.

She reached up for her bag. It was jammed and she took hold of it with both hands and gave it a sharp tug. A double-pronged spear of pain stabbed down her lower back, making her gasp aloud.

Chapter Seventeen

The ward was light, spacious, with shining reaches of floor and a pastel-coloured floaty peacefulness about it. Kate felt safe there, drifting in and out of half-sleep. Her body, which seemed oddly detached, felt weightless, bereft. Memories slid about in her brain, pooling and separating like spilled mercury, spreading and fragmenting, beyond her grasp.

A vivid one was of the great sheets of crocuses, white, yellow, mauve and purple, brilliant in the sun in the park across the road from the Forbes House Hotel. It belonged to a friend of Penny Forsyth's. Her mind jibbed at the name, reluctant to let it grasp the hovering glen associations. Had she left the hotel? Had she paid? An image of tall windows with white-and-black frames elongated and blurred in her mind, a pretty room.

Sinking into sleep again it was her own voice which jarred her awake, her voice crying out in anguish, 'My baby! I want my baby!'

But she had not cried out, that too was a memory. No one was looking towards her from the other beds, no nurse came hurrying across to quieten a wild protest ill-suited to this place of quiet, gleaming order. How kind the nurses had been, with a natural, unpatronising kindness. Weak tears of gratitude filled Kate's eyes.

She remembered asking, 'Are you putting me in the maternity

ward?' and remembered too the fear and confusion which had made her ask.

'No, no, the women's ward,' a soothing voice had said. The answer had satisfied her, though now she saw it meant little.

Last night the other patients had brought her small offerings, fruit, a packet of biscuits, because no one had come to see her. The treacherous easy tears started again. Last night. Was it only one night? She struggled to piece yesterday together.

She had decided to walk from the hotel to the centre of the town. It had been further than she had expected, through sunny half-empty streets past what had looked like the blank walls of warehouses, though all impressions were distorted now. The town had been hot, sunlight bouncing off plate glass, off pavements, off the bonnets of cars, and she had been glad to reach the shopping precinct. But somehow the anticipated pleasure of fun-shopping, of treats and indulgences, had hovered out of reach. Where were the enticing shops; where could she find some promising place for lunch? Smells of cheap cooking gusted out of dim restaurant doorways, pub blackboards had no ambitions beyond a ploughman's, steak pie or haddock and chips. She had felt tired, muddled, at odds with her surroundings, and told herself she had been too long in the emptiness and beauty of Glen Maraich, had grown too used to silence and clean air.

The stabbing pain had leapt without warning. How had she got back to the hotel? She couldn't work it out. She remembered thinking she must get a taxi, then realising in despair that no taxis would come cruising through the pedestrian area. Then concerned voices, helping hands. After that nothing, until she had found herself in the grip of the agonising pain, doubled forward on the loo in her bathroom at the hotel, with a tearing sensation deep inside her, a dark terrifying tide of blood.

Someone had come to help her. She could remember no more than that, only the relief of everything being looked after. The ambulance. Then questions – name, address, doctor's name. Where had those questions been battered at her? In the hospital, but not here in the ward, she was sure. No, she had been lying on a trolley, somewhere small and confined.

'I don't have anything with me, I don't have a nightie,' she heard herself saying in panic. It had been the most worrying thing.

'Don't worry, your things are all here, we'll get you changed in a moment. First of all . . . .'

The relief had been huge, out of all proportion. She must have answered the questions automatically – till they asked, 'Father's name?'

Jack Fletcher, she had almost answered, then had realised what they meant and had felt her whole being close up in mute refusal to tell, no matter how often they asked.

'Father unknown?' a voice had suggested, helpfully, briskly, wanting to get on, and Kate had felt the tears squeeze past her tightly closed lids as she nodded.

A scrape. Who had used the term, patient or nurse? It made her shudder with its brutal plainness, but when she tried to remember the correct term, the normal initials, they resisted her. CD, DC, those meant other things. Her brain rebelled at working it out.

But what did it matter what it was called, or what they had done to her? She mulled over it without distress, accepting the astonishing oblivion of anaesthesia. Whatever ignominy her body had undergone, whatever intrusion, whatever pain, it had had nothing to do with her. Those minutes – how many, how few? She had no idea how long such an operation took – had been sliced out of her life. She had not been there. There had only been the jangled return to consciousness, to that immediate, instinctive knowledge of loss, and her voice crying out, 'I want my baby!'

There had been screens round the bed, voices beyond it, movements, the presence of people. A nurse had appeared swiftly to hush her; raw need and desolation must not intrude on the ritual giving of flowers, fruit, magazines, the searching for shreds of news to exchange, the whining of bored children, the dread or longing for the moment of escape.

'There'll be other babies,' the nurse had comforted her glibly, and Kate had turned on her side, curled into a tight ball round the appalling emptiness, and wept and wept.

There had been a bad moment when she had realised she was in the hospital where Charlie Fleming had booked a bed for her in September. Perhaps in the very ward . . . ? But no, there were no mothers and babies here; that she did not have to face. There had been a message from Charlie, though. Did she want him to come down? She had cried out instantly that he mustn't, in confused dread of 'everyone' knowing, by which of course she had meant the Munros. It seemed vital they shouldn't hear that she had lost the baby. She couldn't have said why this was so important, except for an incoherent instinct that she was responsible for all that had happened and therefore must go through this nightmare alone. Also huge decisions would now have to be made and she knew she couldn't face them yet. But now she saw how good of Charlie it had been to offer to come, and also was capable of realising that of course he would tell no one anything.

As the taxi carried her back to the hotel the next morning the town looked as unfamiliar as if she had been living for months in a foreign country. It seemed impossible that people should be going in and out of shops, chatting on pavements, or that the sun should be shining exactly as it had two days ago.

At Forbes House Hotel she was met with the greatest possible concern and kindness, and taken at once into the family's private sitting-room. She was given coffee, and settled in a comfortable chair in the pleasant room with a door opening onto a garden bright with forsythia and pink frothy blossom.

'Are you quite sure you feel well enough to travel back today? There's a room free if you'd like it. And do you want us to telephone anyone? What about being met at the other end?'

But Kate wanted only to be at Muirend at the agreed time, wanted everything to appear absolutely normal, in the grip of an irrational fear that once it was known the baby was gone she would not be able to stay another moment at Allt Farr. It seemed she must keep hold of time, just a little time, in which to think, adjust, decide what she must do.

'You won't tell Penny, will you?' she asked almost wildly, nervous about the links of friends of friends, cutting across courteous nothings about the weather rushing from winter to summer overnight.

'Of course we won't. No one will say a word.'

Soothed, able to take a firmer grip on ordinary reality, Kate drank her coffee, handed over her Visa card and while her bill was being dealt with went to the window to look at the bright garden. At the edge of a small paved terrace stood a red child's tricycle. Anguish seized her, immediate and engulfing. She had no defences against such an onslaught. No rules of ordinary behaviour, no customary reticence or discipline of her own were any help. She simply disintegrated, clutching the curtain for support, bowed, shaken with sobs. It was as though her body, not her brain, had reacted to that sight, and simply could not bear it.

She was calmed and comforted at last, left in peace until it was time to leave, driven to the station, put on the train, though all the time she barely spoke. She sat hunched in her seat, blind and oblivious as the train carried her north again, and at Muirend was weakly thankful that it was Harriet who met her, Harriet who would accept a simple statement that she had had a marvellous time and was exhausted.

'Something awful's happened,' Joanna said. 'It's so odd of her to drift off like that and sit about all morning doing nothing. And she looks like a ghost.'

'Hungover probably,' Max said. 'She went off to let her hair down, didn't she?' He had come in to look for the leather punch in the estate room and had made the mistake of glancing at his mail which had been left on the desk. The letter from the Council, refusing to give an inch about plans for the Bridge of Riach bypass had made him so angry that he had brought it up to the morning-room to explode to someone about it. But though unusually enough his mother and sisters were all gathered there no one was paying the slightest attention to him. All they could think of was the small huddled figure on the elmwood seat halfway down the lawn, a figure which hadn't moved for hours.

'She may have caught a virus,' Harriet suggested. 'There are so many about these days.' She had gone to join Grannie and Joanna at the window but they hadn't made room for her and she had had to go to another one.

'Harriet, you wouldn't know a virus if you fell over one,' Max said angrily, but knew his anger went far beyond annoyance at Harriet's absurdity. What after all did they know of Kate, of what she would choose to do when away from here and on her own? He had been forced to realise, seeing the silent exhausted creature who sat through dinner last night eating nothing, and had gone dazedly off to bed immediately afterwards, that they knew her only in the context of Allt Farr. And he had remembered, with a fresh and much stronger distaste, the circumstances which had originally brought her here.

'She looks so sad,' Joanna observed. 'As though she'd had some kind of shock. Goodness, you don't think she went off to meet Jeremy, do you?'

'For God's sake –' Max began, angrier than ever.

'She's had an abortion,' Grannie stated flatly. The conviction had been growing in her all day that this could be the only expla-nation for Kate's pallor, her lost, vulnerable look, her silence. And Grannie found she hated the thought, not only for the way it touched so strangely on her own life, but fiercely disappointed that Kate might have resorted to this solution – and had talked to no one about it, had not turned to them for help.

'Oh, no, how awful! Do you really think so? But we must look after her, she'll be feeling dreadful. We can't just leave her out there,' Joanna exclaimed in concern.

Max, who had also thought of abortion, liked the idea even less than his mother, for reasons he had barely let himself examine.

'An abortion! Oh, surely not!' Press-button horror from Harriet.

Max swore under his breath. Then he realised his own recoil when the thought occurred to him had been equally instinctive.

'But that's terrible,' Joanna was protesting. 'Poor little thing, why on earth would she decide to do that all of a sudden? And why didn't she talk to us, or to Charlie?'

'And she shouldn't be sitting out there like that,' Harriet said, leaping from appalled rejection of the idea to anxious acceptance of it as fact. 'She should be in bed, or at least properly wrapped up. That sun's not nearly as warm as you'd think, it's still only March. I'd better go down and—'

'You're not going anywhere.' Max caught the quick turn of his mother's head and knew he had revealed more than he had intended.

'But Max, we should take care of her—'

'Not you, anyway,' he said brusquely. 'She's fine where she is. She can hardly be said to have exerted herself today. Anyway, we're only guessing, we don't know what's wrong with her.' Then in spite of himself, anger taking over, as though he wanted to rush headlong to confront the worst scenario, he went on, 'And if she has got rid of the baby then the arrangement's off, isn't it? We don't have to keep her here any longer.'

'But we couldn't send her away,' Harriet cried. 'I mean, without making sure she's all right.'

Grannie's eyes met Max's. Their obligation to Jeremy had been met. Kate could indeed go out of their lives if the baby no longer existed. Yet in her weeks at Allt Farr she had become not a duty to be accepted, a boring imposition, but a real and engaging person who had tackled all kinds of challenges with a goodwill and hardihood they had not expected.

'We can manage with students to help as usual,' Max

persisted, not fully understanding why he felt compelled to act as devil's advocate. 'With the additional bonus that they live in the courtyard flat and we'd have the house to ourselves again.'

'There is that,' Grannie said, and Max felt a flicker of chagrin that she had agreed with him. 'But personally I should like Kate to stay. From unpromising material I think you would agree she has turned out rather well.' Bald as the words were, in Grannie's mind there was almost a dread of losing Kate, in whom she had found a sympathy, a comprehension of her pain, absent in her own children. Through her own fault, she knew. She had distanced them, Harriet through sheer dislike of a plain, fretful child who so faithfully replicated her father in looks and character, Joanna because by the time she arrived the need to escape, coupled with the inbred sense of duty which made it impossible, had bitten deep. With Max had come guilt, and fear of revealing what she truly felt. To lose Kate now, with her gentleness and warmth, would be very sad.

Joanna's concern was overtaken by a more selfish thought. If Kate left then everything would go back to normal, and briefly Joanna longed for that. But dreary good sense warned, even as the thought tempted her, that things would never be quite the same again. Forget that, forget yourself, just think of Kate.

'I don't see why she should go,' Joanna said. 'After all, if the baby really has gone, which we don't know for sure yet, she'll be fit right through the season and able to help during the busy time.'

'She doesn't look as though she'll be much use at present,' Harriet said, seizing on a new worry. 'Just when we're busy for Easter. There are all the cottages to make up and—'

This was too boring. 'Don't you think someone should talk to Kate and establish what has in fact happened?' Grannie interposed sharply. 'And perhaps ask what she herself wants to do. If the baby no longer exists I cannot imagine why she should choose to stay, can you?'

'Jo, you talk to her.' Max longed to cut through the speculation and have some answers. Why had Kate said nothing to them?

Surely she didn't intend to stay on pretending nothing had changed? But had anything changed? And another unwelcome question could not be ignored – if there was no baby how would Jeremy react? Would he come cheerfully back to Allt Farr as though nothing had happened, problem neatly solved?

But Max could not go on evading what really hurt him. When the idea of Kate getting rid of the baby had first entered his mind every instinct had rejected it. He had intensely disliked the thought of her destroying the life she had seemed determined to bear, negating the courage and resolution with which she had faced her pregnancy. Even more fundamentally, he had not wanted her to tamper with her neat, elegant little body, just as he hated imagining Jeremy's intimate knowledge of it.

'Yes, Max is right. You're the one to talk to her, Joanna. If you will?' The little tacked-on question made Max and Joanna glance at Grannie in surprise, and her lips twisted. 'I feel ashamed that we have discussed her like this. It's quite outrageous to have made so many assumptions without even talking to the poor child.' As she turned from the window she gave a last compassionate look at the unaware figure in the curve of the big seat in the spring sunshine.

Chapter Eighteen

Kate sat with her face turned up to the sun, eyes closed, the battered fur-lined coat loosely round her shoulders, body and mind on hold, husbanding resources, terrified that one tentative move beyond the moment would bring fresh pain. She absorbed the miraculous warmth and calm of the day with weary relief. It seemed extraordinary, after the harsh extremes of weather which she had come to expect here, that she could sit outside like this, with a thin thread of birdsong patterning the sunlight, the snow reduced to mere strips and patches on the flanks of the highest peaks. A white frill of snowdrops ran below the stone wall and round the fringes of the lawn, the lawn where once a helicopter had whirred and lifted, climbing into cloud to take Colleen to—

Stab. Wince away, close off the thought.

At least the crocuses, silver-green sheathed spears clustered on either side of the wrought-iron gate to the walled garden, were not open. The vision returned, with all its associations, of reaches of their vivid colour. Where was there escape?

She must tell the family what had happened, should have done so at once, last night when she came back. Not to explain immediately was a sort of deception, for she no longer had any right to be here. The plan was in pieces. She was rootless, objectless, free to go, and that was not the relief it would once have been, but profoundly frightening. Go where, do what? Who was she?

Her mind struggled to take in the fact that she was a person alone, that the hidden accompanying being she had never known or seen, but whose presence had begun so much to thrill her and on whom her life had centred, was gone, torn apart from her. Residual traces scraped away. She shuddered; she would never get that word out of her mind.

She found it almost impossible to focus on any plan which involved herself alone. Finding somewhere to live, and an ordinary job with no arbitrary term to it seemed unreal. In fact, that removal of the huge event blocking the horizon a few months hence was the hardest thing of all to take in. She did not see that it was far too soon to try, her body's balance overthrown, its primary duty of nurturing the developing foetus made redundant without warning.

Should she have taken more care? The thought nagged at her relentlessly. Had there been signs that all was not well? She remembered the sudden cessation of morning sickness which she had greeted with pleasure. There had been that persistent ache in her back, the listlessness which had overtaken her. Had the baby – had something happened to the baby? She had asked no questions at the hospital, numb, shocked, all her energies focused on doing the next thing required, getting back to the hotel, back home. She had thought of this as home, now, when there was no longer any justification to be here. In her weakened state the irony seemed unbearable.

What were the family thinking of her, sitting out here for hours doing nothing? She tried to see it in the perspective of everyday life and knew it was bizarre. She must give them some explanation. More than that, must leave. She couldn't accept their hospitality any longer when she was contributing nothing. They would do as they had always done, arrange for student help in the summer, and then put the whole episode out of their minds. They had played their part, helped Jeremy when he needed them, and it was over. Then something struck her which she hadn't thought of before. They hadn't needed her at all. She knew by now that the students didn't arrive till June but she had rushed straight past the implications. She had actually been surplus to requirements, her presence at Allt Farr in the empty winter months nothing more than a favour to Jeremy.

Then an even more disturbing realisation came. In hospital images of Jeremy the lover, Jeremy the concerned father suddenly, magically, appearing at her side to share her ordeal, had tormented her. Now, breath-taking in its possibilities, the fact hit her that without the baby everything had altered. Jeremy might want to see her. Free of problems and responsibility, he might be attracted to her again.

In fact – her brain struggled with the concept – the whole of life might go back to what it had been. Jessie . . . Without the baby to be angry about could they re-establish some work-able relationship once more? Had all the other things Jessie had said, the things she had revealed, been born of her rage and disillusionment?

Kate shook herself angrily, opening her eyes and pushing herself upright. What lunacy to let such thoughts enter her mind. Jeremy had made his feelings clear. He had made a mistake and regretted it. He had done his duty and must have breathed a huge sigh of relief to be clear of a troublesome entanglement. And Jessie? She had thrown so many cruel words at Kate, tearing apart the whole fabric of their life. But each should be told what had happened. And longing, almost too vivid to bear, painfully mingled with dread, shook Kate in spite of all her attempts to hold on to cold facts.

A little sob of misery escaped her, and afraid of sinking back into despair she came to her feet, meaning to face her first obligation of telling the family what had happened, and assuring them she wouldn't presume on their hospitality a moment longer than necessary. Then she saw Joanna coming down the lawn towards her, the sun bright on her floating mass of amber hair, her freckled face smiling to hide her anxiety.

Joanna had not argued about doing this job. She knew she

wasn't very bright, for Simon had daily pointed out the fact to her, but she thought she was probably a bit kinder than the others. Admittedly, she didn't always show it these days, a deep-rooted fear of not being loved in return inhibiting her, but she knew that if anyone was to approach Kate it had better be her. And out of her natural warmth, combined with her share of Munro bluntness, she was able to ask, drawing Kate down again to sit with her, 'Poor little Kate, are you feeling awful? Is it the baby?'

She would never forget the look of anguish in Kate's brown eyes, which fixed on hers with an urgent, desperate need for help, or the naked pain in her voice as she said, choking on the words, 'It's gone. My baby's gone.'

'Oh, Kate.' Almost in tears herself, Joanna wrapped her arms round her and held her tightly. 'You poor, poor darling. But why did you decide to do it? We'd have helped you, it would have been all right.'

'Decide?' Kate struggled free, her face, wet with tears, startled and uncomprehending. 'You mean, I could have stopped it? But no one said anything about that. No one asked me. What do you mean? I don't know what you mean!'

She sounded quite frantic and Joanna was much shocked to see equable Kate in this state. Was she regretting what she had done? What must it feel like to know that she had destroyed that helpless dependent life? Sympathetic as she was, Joanna felt a frisson of repulsion at the decision.

'Did you think it would be too difficult to keep the baby?' she asked gently, doing her best.

Kate stared at her, frozen, the sense of this penetrating at last. 'Joanna –' She found her mouth dry, swallowed, tried again, though the words hurt. 'I lost the baby. I miscarried. In Perth. In the hospital where I should have –' This relatively unimportant detail surfaced again unexpectedly.

'Oh, Kate, whatever happened?' Horror, mixed with shame that this had occurred to none of them, filled Joanna. But they would have expected Kate to call on them in such an emergency, at least to tell them as soon as she came home what she had gone through. 'Why didn't you phone? We would have come down at once. You were all on your own – that's truly terrible. And we'd have brought you home, you should never have come by yourself on the train.' These practical considerations swarmed up, since for the moment it was impossible to measure the colossal difference, in mental and emotional as well as physical terms, between an abortion consciously planned and the agony of miscarriage.

Numbly, Kate shook her head. It had not occurred to her once that she could phone Allt Farr. The whole episode had seemed as unsharable as a nightmare, in an unfamiliar place, cut off from everyone and everything she knew. The heat, the dusty pavements, the traffic, the crowded shops, the pain – none of that had had anything to do with this place, these people. It had been like some dreadful punishment which no one could help her through.

Some of this she began to try falteringly to explain, and in seconds the words were pouring out, in a jumbled torrent of released feeling.

'But of course I know I can't stay now,' she wound up, for it seemed essential to make this clear without delay.

'Kate, no! That's ridiculous. We want you to stay, all of us.' Well, Max had had reservations but even he hadn't disputed it. 'In any case, it's far too soon to discuss anything of the sort. You must recover properly first. A miscarriage can pull you down horribly. We can talk it over when you've had time to think. But you mustn't imagine there's any question of your going, unless that's what you want yourself. Or perhaps there's somewhere you'd like to stay for a week or two, with friends – or at home?' She asked this tentatively, but with the baby lost the reason for leaving home had vanished too.

She was quite unprepared for Kate's response, a rejection so instant and emphatic that it brought her to her feet. 'No!' she cried. 'Not home! They hate me, don't you understand that?'

'Hate you?' Startled, Joanna rose too, putting an arm round

the slight figure, taut and quivering. 'Of course you don't have to go home if you don't want to, but I'm sure no one hates you. Here, come and sit down again. Tell me what you mean, if you feel it would help to talk about it.'

If more lay behind Kate's departure from home than her parents' anger at her pregnancy, this might be a good moment to exorcise any festering pain.

'They have always hated me.' It was out, the wound dealt her so viciously by Jessie when she had learned about the baby.

'Oh, no, that can't be true,' Joanna protested, horrified but keeping her voice as neutral as she could, the encouragement to talk all that mattered.

'Shall I call them in for lunch?' Harriet asked. 'It's all ready.'

'Leave them,' said Grannie tersely.

'But Kate hardly ate a thing for breakfast, in fact I think she only had—'

'Harriet!' Grannie's exasperation was mixed with a strange unease. She had seen Joanna hug Kate, and the two girls sitting down again, heads close. She wanted very badly to know what was being said, conscious that change threatened and that she did not welcome it. She would miss this willing, well-intentioned child, who watched the doings of Allt Farr with such candid eyes. They needed someone with her clear vision to infuse some fresh – what? – innocence into their lives. Snorting slightly at the word, Grannie stumped down to lunch.

'I was adopted, so probably she never truly loved me. I didn't guess that of course. They were so good to me, giving me everything I could possibly ask for, sending me to a private school ... .' This wasn't what she wanted to convey. Material things were not at the heart of this. 'Only perhaps with adopted children there's always some – I don't know – some difference. A need to state something. I mean, perhaps all the giving was to show I was wanted. The other side of it was that they were terribly over-protective. I wasn't allowed to have friends, and they wouldn't let me board at school, though I absolutely longed to. I can see now that Jessie was desperately insecure about everything, and must have been insecure about me too . . .' Recently Kate had begun to comprehend the depths of Jessie's social fears, her crippling lack of self-confidence.

Joanna waited, only half understanding but glad Kate was talking at last. 'Go on,' she said very gently, when Kate had been silent for some moments, her eyes on the shining curve of the river round the Haugh field.

'For the adopted child, on the other hand,' Kate resumed obediently, but in a tone which suggested she was hardly aware of speaking aloud, 'there is gratitude.' She paused on the word, but Joanna did not risk prompting her again. 'There is a huge obligation to do and be what is required. I don't think natural children feel that. When I wanted to go to university, they wouldn't hear of it. They, Jessie anyway, held on to me as fiercely as if I was some possession she couldn't risk losing. I had to be part of their lives; I couldn't make one of my own. Holidays with them, awful, awful holidays, Jack silent and resentful from the moment we shut the front door behind us till the moment we got back. I did my best, I really did.' Joanna could imagine it, but resisted a consoling pat, not wishing to check the flow. 'I went underground, I think,' Kate said, though it sounded exaggerated and incredible at this distance. 'I created a life that was bearable — comfortable and contained and undemanding and safe. Whenever possible I disappeared into books. I just let it roll me along.'

'Tell me what happened,' Joanna said. She had no opinion of herself as a psychologist, and was daily aware of having wrecked her own life, but she was sure anything Kate could be persuaded to put into words would help, and that Kate needed help.

'When I told them I was pregnant —' Kate was so locked into

the images of the past she actually saw this as an issue separate from her present loss, and though Joanna held her breath she went on obliviously, '– the anger was terrible. Jessie was beside herself. She just couldn't handle it. I suppose I can see why now. She flung all sorts of things at me – told me, for one thing, who my real parents had actually been.' The tense told her she still hadn't absorbed the fact that they were alive, leading complete lives of their own, perhaps with partners, children . . . .

Giving her time, trying to imagine how all this must have felt, Joanna was aware of peripheral things. The others would be starting lunch; it didn't matter. And as a clear sweet call cut across the mingled sounds of the birds in the garden she thought, that's the peesies back, and was glad of this sign of spring.

'She wanted me to be everything she wasn't,' Kate said abruptly. 'She more or less said so. She chose me because I was tiny and she's huge, always dieting but putting weight back on right away. And she chose me because my mother belonged to some family she thought was rather grand. I think at first she was proud of me.' Was that true, or just a belief she could not dispense with? But surely Jack had been proud; she could not have invented the memories of praise and petting, or mistaken that loving approbation. 'But later, only I didn't realise it, she grew to hate me, for being all the things she had made me. She envied me, but despised me too. She couldn't bear the way I spoke, dressed, behaved. She even hated me reading or watching things on television that bored her.'

'Are you certain your mother wasn't saying these things out of anger about the baby?' Joanna asked.

'No, I don't think so.' Kate shook her head. 'It was as though that just gave her the chance to spill all the hatred out. It had been there for years. That was the frightful thing, to know my whole life had been based on a pretence.'

'But what about your father?'

Kate's face pinched. 'He was tremendously hurt, I do understand that. He just turned his back on me. He'd given me everything and I'd let him down. But he did say one thing.' She drew a harsh breath to help her to get it out. 'He told me he'd always thought, from the very beginning, that it had been a mistake to choose me.'

Joanna, a huge lump in her throat, took Kate's hand and folded it between her own garden-roughened ones. What on earth could anyone say to that?

Chapter Nineteen

When later Joanna passed on the bare bones of this conversation to the rest of the family they left it to Harriet to make the conventional noises — how dreadful, Kate should have told them, they must look after her, she shouldn't do too much, she must go down to see Charlie, and just think of her all by herself having to cope . . . .

Jeremy's baby, Grannie thought, with a little shaft of sadness that belonged far in the past and could never be shared. What strange things time, like the slow heavings of an ocean, could toss up. Then she was deeply, warmly pleased that it had not been lost by any deliberate act on Kate's part, and knew it would have been hard to forgive her if it had. She was conscious too of deep relief that Kate didn't want to go.

'So we're stuck with her,' Max grunted, his own feelings well concealed. 'She does realise she's under no obligation to stay?'

'I can't see why you're so negative about her,' Joanna protested. 'I know she's done lots of idiotic things but you couldn't say enough about her when she rescued those damned sheep of yours last month.'

'That doesn't mean she's more use than anyone else we could get. What we need is brawn and common sense, neither an area where Kate shines,' Max retorted, taking the balloon whisk ferociously to an Hollandaise sauce that was threatening to break.

'Well, I for one consider her a great deal more agreeable than anyone we've found before,' Grannie said. 'I think it's excellent news that she's willing to put up with us when she no longer has to.'

This was partisanship indeed from Grannie, and all three of her offspring paused in what they were doing to regard her in surprise.

'We'd better sort out some new arrangement with her then,' Max said, sticking to the practical to fudge over the disconcerting degree of satisfaction he felt. 'She should be given the chance of moving into separate accommodation for a start, and her role established on a more formal basis.'

'Then you must talk to her yourself. I shall have nothing to do with it,' Grannie said. 'And take care. Remember she's going through a very vulnerable time.'

Max found it oddly difficult to approach Kate. She was such a sad defenceless wisp, creeping about the house looking if possible even smaller than before, though the presence of the baby had never been visible. She insisted on being busy, and as everyone was united in dismay that she should try to work, sedentary jobs were in demand, since she had protested in her courteous way she didn't think she wanted to do patchwork *all* the time. Joanna was hectically busy in the garden, locked in the perennial problem of winter weather, which made any preparation impossible and unimaginable, giving way to spring with great abruptness, rushing everything, particularly weeds, into mad growth. Kate was content to sit for hours in the warm greenhouse, among the smells of compost, bonemeal and drying wood, pricking out trays of seedlings. She drew the line when Joanna, doing her best, gave her a tangled mass of raffia to sort out.

'Joanna, are you absolutely certain you need this stuff? It doesn't look as though it's been touched for years.'

'Of course I need it. All gardeners do.'

'Honestly, how long has this been in this state?'

Joanna gave in. 'God knows. I just thought it was the kind of finicky job you like.'

Kate put down the bundle with dignity. 'I'm not in need of therapy for the mentally impaired, thank you.'

It's the first time she's joked since she lost the baby, Joanna thought. How good it is to see her face bright again. She does have guts.

'Have to be laying out seed potatoes then. Can you handle that?'

'Possibly, if you explain very carefully.'

'Well, to start with, you don't cook them.'

This time Kate laughed. A few days ago she had been narrowly prevented from removing the healthy shoots of some early earlies left to sprout in the larder, and serving them up for dinner.

So there Max found her, absorbed in arranging the neat rows, her fingers dusted with pale dry earth, her face abstracted.

'What do I do with all these greeny ones? Are they still all right to use?' she asked, hearing his step and thinking it was Joanna coming back.

Max looked down on her for the second before she turned, pierced by the narrowness of her shoulders, the neck slender as Laura's where the dark brown hair curled so neatly, her air of willing industry already back in place after the wholly adult tragedy she had faced. She had resources of her own, this girl, and he admired her for them.

'Kate, I'm glad I've run into you.' Catching himself out in this rare prevarication, he knew he was more reluctant to do this than he had acknowledged.

Kate was startled to find him at her shoulder. Had he too, at Grannie's behest, cooked up some harmless job for her? She looked up at him questioningly.

'Look, Kate, I just felt, now that –' It was a week since she had come back from Perth, but facing her like this Max knew his planned opening was impossible. How could he say, 'now that you've lost the baby,' with those unhappy eyes gazing at him?

'I thought it might be a good idea to have a chat about your position here, sort out a few details, that kind of thing.'

God, he sounded pompous. Kate was looking alarmed, and this way she had of waiting in silence for people to go on was a lot harder to deal with than the Munro habit of leaping in. He perched sideways on the couple of inches of staging left free by the potato boxes and tried to look relaxed. One of them had to.

'It's just that with changed circumstances we felt,' (you coward) 'that we should offer you more realistic conditions here. We wondered for instance if you might prefer to have more privacy, live in the courtyard flat as the summer students do. Even though you're staying we'll need extra help for the shooting weeks and you might enjoy company nearer your own age. Then there's the question of pay. I don't feel we should allow you to go on working for nothing, although I know that was what you originally wanted. And you should have time off, definite hours—'

He broke off abruptly, cursing his ineptness. Kate had never taken her eyes off him, never moved, her hands still holding two of the suspect green-ended potatoes. But her eyes had brimmed with tears, her whole face disintegrating in a look of stricken dismay.

'For God's sake, Kate, don't look at me like that,' Max exclaimed, sliding off the shelf and bending towards her. 'Nothing will basically change. You can choose whatever you want. I just don't like exploiting you, that's all. We can talk about—'

'No,' Kate interrupted, and he saw her visibly summon good sense, her pale face colouring as she considered new implications. 'It's all right. Of course I see things aren't the same now. I just hadn't thought about it properly. I'll fit in with whatever you normally do. I'm sorry, I'd only been thinking of—'

'Hang on!' Max cut in in his turn, his voice a lot more brusque than hers had been. 'That's not what we're talking about.' Face to face with her, he had had a sudden glimpse, which even Joanna's account of her situation had not brought home to him, of what it must be like to be alone and rootless. Much as he kicked against the obligations which technically he had every right to walk away from, and latterly his sense of entrapment had begun almost to obsess him, this extreme alternative, to be wanted nowhere, struck him as immensely pitiable. Cursing himself for his insensitive approach he said quietly, 'There's absolutely no need for anything to change unless that is what you choose. Don't try to work out what you think we want. It's just that the previous arrangement was based on — a need that no longer exists.' There was no way to put it which wouldn't hurt her. 'Different options are open now. I only want to establish what *you* want.'

Kate stared at him, mouth trembling. Since the days of the storm her awe of him had gone. Mostly with Laura but sometimes alone she had often helped him with jobs, and had learned to accept with equanimity both his dour silences and his impatient frustration with setbacks. More than that, she had come to accept him very definitely as the head of the household, arbiter and authority, but also the protector. That seemed to her his chief role, and she had registered with interest the gap she had been conscious of when he was away skiing. There had been a feeling of everything being makeshift and incomplete. But he looked very daunting looming over her now, frowning, his eyes probing.

If only Joanna had asked her about this, or even Grannie. But there was no doubt about what she wanted. Nothing in her life had been as rewarding and enjoyable as the busy, varied, unstructured days here, the sense of involvement and acceptance. To be paid would alter the whole feeling of it. Anyway, she had ample funds, Jack had seen to that. Like a swift double blow she had no time to guard against, the image of his obdurate face came to her, along with the recollection that now there would be no extra financial demands to meet.

Her thoughts swerved away. The way of life here had been so different from the compartmentalised existence of office and home, eight-hour day, five-day week, pounding on through the years. But to live alone in the flat, with two days off a week, two days without occupation, to do what, go where?

She took a deep breath. The potatoes she was clutching would never produce much now, Max thought with passing humour, seeing her knuckles whiten round them.

'I don't want anything to change,' she said in a rush, watching him apprehensively. 'If no one minds.'

Max waited a moment, but saw only appeal in her eyes. She clearly wasn't going to enlarge on this.

'Right, then nothing need change,' he told her after a brief charged pause, and was surprised to find his own voice husky.

It had not been the lengthiest of discussions, he reflected as he went back through the garden, summoning amusement as an antidote to that unexpected moment of emotion, but taking the route furthest from where Joanna was working, not ready to discuss Kate's decision yet. Why that reluctance, he wondered, letting himself out of the wrought-iron gate to the lawn with a sense of escape. Because he was pleased, and wished to savour his pleasure, was the answer to that.

With perfect timing Laura came home for the Easter holidays. Told at once about the baby, in the straightforward Munro fashion Kate was coming increasingly to value, she was subdued and solicitous for the space of a day, then joy to be back took over, and she was soon drawing Kate into her activities once more. Though Harriet continued to trot out ill-founded warnings about things being 'too much' for Kate, Grannie and Joanna knew Laura's company was the best therapy that could have been devised.

Phrases like, 'before Easter hits us', and 'there'll be no time for that once Easter's here', were on everyone's lips, and began mildly to worry Kate. The Burn Cottage had been dried out and where necessary redecorated, its furniture replaced or cleaned up. (The Cedar Hut had also been made fit for habitation again, though Grigor had not been in any hurry to leave the comfort of Mrs Grant's fireside.) The other cottages, the pair beside Doddie's, and a row of three in a converted ex-sawmill beyond the farm, were spruce, equipped and functioning. All that remained to be done was making beds and last minute dusting. So once people were in them what had to be done, Kate wondered, puzzled. Guests catered for themselves, cleaned for themselves; what else was there?

At least she had a clear picture in her mind of the names, layout, and even booking plot of the six cottages. Max, searching in his turn for quiet occupation for her, had suggested she might like to help with the pile of correspondence staring accusingly at him every time he went into the estate room.

'Use the computer?' Joanna had seized on this with gleeful mockery. 'He's actually going to let you touch his precious computer? You have to be most favoured of the favoured.'

'It's just to do a few letters,' Kate had said, beginning to look worried.

'More than he'd ever let the rest of us do,' Joanna assured her. 'What if you lose an entire year's accounts, or crash, or whatever it's called? That's what he said when Harriet wanted to put out a flyer for the Guild.'

Max had begun to look worried himself, but when with elaborate step-by-step instructions he had explained to Kate how to get into the programme, he had laughed as her accustomed fingers began to fly.

'I'd never known the keys could flash like that,' he confessed at lunch, openly jubilant for once, a huge boring load lifted from him with sweet unlooked-for simplicity.

Kate too felt satisfied. Here at last was something she could offer, an area where she could shine. She said nothing, but there was a glow to that day, and the summer stretched even more promisingly ahead, grief over the baby fading in step with her body's adjustment to its loss. Also, as daily life began to occupy her attention again, there came relief, guilty at first, that almost unimaginable responsibilities had been lifted from her.

She soon discovered what consumed everyone's time at Easter – not work but socialising. It wasn't an aspect she had even thought of. From Thursday lunch-time when the first Range Rover pulled up at the front door, its occupants, human and canine, pouring exuberantly as of right into the kitchen, there was hardly a second of solitude or silence, apart from the brief hours in bed, for the next two weeks. That first afternoon, except for a young splinter group playing croquet on the lawn, then rampaging in to ask if Doddie could help them put up the tennis net, a job Max had been trying to get to for days, everyone settled round the kitchen table and ate, drank and gossiped the hours away.

It set the fashion for the whole holiday period, when whole-sale moves to other kitchens, other firesides, regardless of scarcity of chairs, plates, or appropriate food, seemed to Kate as magically sudden and coordinated as the wheeling of a flock of birds. Orders for basic supplies had been put in the fridges by Harriet and herself. Some families had arrived efficiently provisioned, others relied on the Allt Farr freezers, a chancy matter at this time of year, while others again said airily, 'There wasn't time to bring a thing. Someone can nip down to Kirton in the morning. No one will want breakfast before twelve anyway.'

Alcohol, however, was in plentiful supply and much serious attention was given to comparing the quality of everyone's home-made sloe gin, apparently a tradition of the festival and one Kate rather took to.

Another tradition she enjoyed, on a day of erratic wind and sunshine that was very hot when it was there, was the Opening Picnic. This was held on Laura's island, attended not only by every cottage dweller and the Munros, but by an almost equal number of glen friends.

Grannie's chum Gilbert Rathlyn was well to the fore since he operated, and had apparently had a hand in devising and constructing, an extraordinary contraption of pipes, grids and funnels which acted as a barbecue. Forsyths from Alltmore and Napiers from Drumveyn appeared in force. Charlie Fleming came with Tim Bellshaw, the vet, and his intense wife Ilona, flamboyant in a scarlet jumpsuit. Even Sally and Mike Danaher, busy though they were with their own hotel guests at Grianan, snatched a couple of hours off, bringing Mike's two teenagers by a previous marriage. Meeting the usual barrage of friendly teasing, James Mackenzie came over from Riach with the twins, whom he handed over to Laura with the comment that he didn't much mind if he never saw them again.

'Will Letitia come?' Kate asked Harriet, as they wrapped in foil the contents of a panful of potatoes which Grannie had sensibly part-cooked beforehand then forgotten to bring. They had been delivered by a pair of staggering boatmen scarcely bigger than the pot.

'She never wastes time on this sort of thing,' Harriet said defensively, then added with an unexpected giggle, 'Grannie can't stand her.' Harriet too had been adding her vote to the sloe gin contest.

'I don't suppose it matters that your semi-derelict vessel is floating away,' a lazy voice remarked, 'but I believe there's a child in it.'

This was received with uproarious laughter, and no parental panic that Kate could discover. Glasses were raised in salute, orders were shouted at larger children to do something, and only when the boat began to spin faster in the current did Max get grumbling to his feet, setting his glass down carefully, and go after it. A father, sighing, 'I'm told it's mine,' went to help.

Reactions would have been different in Wilton Avenue, Kate could not help reflecting, as she watched Max come back, affecting boredom but grinning in spite of himself. In gatherings like this his dourness vanished so magically that it was hard to credit how much it could affect the atmosphere of the house in normal times.

Vast quantities of food were cooked, with varying success,

and willingly consumed. Layers of clothing were shed, in spite of Harriet's twitterings that there was still snow on the hills, runners were despatched to fetch swimming things Kate thought it an act of faith to have packed in the first place, and winter-white skin turned gradually pink. Ilona was faced with the problem of removing all or nothing. The boat plied back and forth, putting ashore and bringing off messengers in quest of further stocks of gin, and dogs, children and adults splashed in and out of the water working under the expert leadership of Mike Danaher on another Easter ritual, the rebuilding of the dam which created a rudimentary swimming pool below the island.

I'm here, Kate thought muzzily, part of this. It's all settled, this is how it will be for weeks and months to come. There is nothing to long for, nothing to dread. Calling voices broke across her drowsing thoughts.

'It's Ann! Wait there, we'll fetch you.'

'I have every intention of waiting.'

'Hi, Ann, you took your time.'

'In my annual endeavour to avoid this barbaric rite.' The new arrival on the bank was a tall woman, angular but stylish in khaki drill skirt and jacket, her dark hair tied severely back with a khaki and lime green scarf to reveal heavy gold earrings. Her tone did not sound entirely humorous.

'Who's Ann?' Kate enquired of James, who had come to prop his indolent length beside her. Then she remembered that Colleen had been given 'Ann's room'.

It was Laura, coming to peel off her soaking jeans and throw them down with her already discarded socks and sneakers, who answered.

'Don't you know Ann yet? No, I suppose she hasn't been since you came. That's Ann Logan, Uncle Max's girlfriend.'

Chapter Twenty

Ann was definitely one of the grown-ups. It was hard to define exactly why, Kate thought, once more in the role of observer, subtly separated from the group by the presence of a newcomer known to everyone but her. For it was clear that Ann was firmly at the centre of the clan. Also, after the noisy wave of greetings when the boat (which she complained smelled of sheep) had delivered her, the group had reformed. Before her arrival there had been a casual mingling of age groups. Now the younger element distanced itself, whether consciously or not, and their seniors gathered in a gossiping knot out of the reach of the fumes from the barbecue, brought to white heat by the Admiral's endeavours. A natural regrouping, surely? Glasses had been replenished, people were eager to welcome the newcomer, catch up on news. Yet it was more than that.

Kate, tucked quietly into her rocky niche, still technically within the group but feeling on its fringe, even James's attention drawn to a new focus, came to the conclusion that people had abandoned their holiday selves. Ann brought with her the breath of a more serious world.

'Nothing much to offer you here, Ann, I'm afraid. Underdone chop? Couple of burned sausages? There's sure to be a potato somewhere.'

'I think not, if you'll forgive me.' Not precisely a put-down, yet not precisely a joke. It raised a laugh, but Kate thought the tone at least two shades too cool.

'We'll find you something more civilised at the house,' Grannie promised, glancing at her watch.

Civilised. Exactly. Drifting almost into sleep, the brush of warm wind delicious across her face and bare arms, for she still tired quickly and had perhaps done more than a sensible share of dam-building, Kate was aware that extraneous topics had been introduced, the latest London bomb, the Middle East, a cease-fire here, a conference there.

'Old Henry said the roads campaign debate was a complete farce . . . .'

'England all out for two hundred and seven, can you bear it . . . ?'

People sat differently. No, she must be imagining that, Kate amended, surveying the group under lowered lids. But it was true; there was less lolling, less feckless indifference to appearance. Perhaps one couldn't discuss the Middle East peace process flat on one's back. Ann herself did not loll, looked indeed scarcely capable of lolling. How did she look so smart without being in any way incongruous? That khaki suit could not be called over-dressed for a picnic, yet achieved a look of sophistication which set her apart. Her coarse-textured hair, springing back from a high bony forehead, was cleverly shaped to balance the strong jawline. Her big hands, linked round her knees, were well-kept, something Kate was conscious of after weeks at Allt Farr. On her equally big feet she wore expensive loafers in a beige suede that was asking for trouble here.

The biggest effect she had had, Kate finally allowed herself to admit, was on Max. He, too, was undeniably one of the grown-ups again. In a recent conversation with Laura Kate had been surprised to discover that he was the youngest of the Munros. She had mentally placed him with Harriet, who at over forty had always felt, indeed almost was, a generation away.

Ann's arrival seemed to have made Harriet more nervous than

ever, Kate observed with a protective indignation reluctantly mixed with amusement, as she watched Harriet clean her spectacles with a tissue then put them back on her nose with it caught in the hinge of the sidepiece. She sat for an appreciable moment in puzzlement at the white veil which had appeared beside her eye.

Max could be Harriet's age right now, Kate decided, with a resentment she put down to tiredness. This rock was getting pretty uncomfortable and her back was aching as it still occasionally did, though there was no other physical reminder of her miscarriage, which her body seemed to have taken in its stride. That was silly, it was her body which had rejected the growing embryo, so presumably it was natural that her mind should accept its loss with similar speed. An inbuilt protective system? She felt sad when she thought about it but the sadness itself was growing elusive, the image of an actual baby somehow beyond her reach.

'Don't you feel you've done your bit?' Ann was asking. 'Can't we abandon this pile of stones to the young? Anyway, no matter what anyone else wants to do, I'd like to tidy up. It was a ghastly drive, roads swarming with idiots.'

'All driving at half your speed, no doubt.'

'You didn't think of stopping somewhere between Oxford and Glen Maraich?'

Nevertheless the group began good-naturedly to stir itself, fathers gathering up leftover alcohol, mothers cutting out selected offspring for instructions.

'*All* clothes back please, not one boot and someone else's sweater.'

'None of the tiddlers pushed off to sea alone, remember.'

'And don't go anywhere near Gilbert's barbecue. It has every appearance of imminently blowing up.'

A chorus of, 'OK, Mum,' in tones varying from cheerful through tolerant to deeply bored, was tossed over shoulders in response.

'And somebody make sure the boat's tied up.'

'*OK.*'

'Food for you lot will be at about six.'

'Mum, you know it won't be ready anywhere near six.' This was said quite kindly.

'Six at the latest. Good God, it's after four now. Can that be right?'

Crowing laughter.

'Come on, they'll be fine.'

Could she stay too, Kate wondered, with a strong disinclination to be dragged away from the idyllic scene. Or was she more accurately reluctant to go back to the house, knowing with certainty that this newcomer would alter its atmosphere? Would anyone notice if she stayed? But Grannie was saying Ann must have something to eat, and Kate thought she should help.

Excitement seemed to be building over some new enterprise. A bottle race? What did they mean? Empty wine bottles were being eagerly sought, James and one of the cottage guests (the wall-planner in the estate room flashed up on command – Colin Devereaux, 3 The Sawmill) had evidently decided to stay and run it.

'No broken glass in the burn,' Max shouted to them as he hopped long-legged across the river by a route no one else would contemplate.

'You're as bad as the mothers,' James shouted back, waving him away.

Would Max have preferred to stay, with the sun and the scented breeze and the eager children? No, to judge by his dour expression he would not have enjoyed it in the least.

'Ann always has this room. She comes for everything,' Laura said. 'Christmas, shooting, stalking. It's funny you haven't met her, it feels as though you've been here for ages. You wouldn't have seen her when they went skiing, of course.'

So Ann had been part of that trip to the Dolomites. 'Where does she live?' Kate asked. 'In Oxford?'

'She has a little house there, absolutely stacked with books, you can't move for them. But her real house is in Scotland. It's called Talla and it has one of the best fishing beats in the country.' This was delivered in the offhand tone in which children repeat adult phrases. 'We often go there. Well, Uncle Max does mostly, for the fishing. It's a gorgeous house but it's often shut up because Ann's got no family, she's an only child like me. She can't live there all the time, she has to go on digs, and write articles and things. Anyway, come on, Grannie said we could make ice cream to take to Burn Cottage this afternoon for Chloe's birthday party.'

Ice cream made of cream from the farm and the last of the fruit in the freezer was one of the discoveries of Allt Farr for Kate. She wasn't sorry to follow the racing figure of Laura out of Ann's room, where they had been putting flowers.

'I should have done it yesterday, Ann likes all that stuff, but there were so many things happening,' Laura had admitted. 'Have to be snowdrops and catkins and those blue things round the front door. The silly daffodils are never out in time for Easter.'

Kate guessed why Laura wanted to stay close to her today. Practically every adult including Joanna, persuaded to abandon her garden yet again, had left early for a day's golf at Pitlochry. Had Ann instigated it? Certainly it was the first time anyone had shown any wish to leave the estate, every trip to Kirkton or Muirend being a source of heated arguments about whose turn it was to go.

And from Laura's angle, as Kate could understand, Max had been removed by a force which could not be contested. Laura was clearly accustomed to it, and didn't protest, but she minded, and temporarily needed the comfort of company beyond that of friends and cousins.

At first Kate wondered why Ann's presence had to remove Max completely from Laura, who after all was used to a good deal of his company, but during the next few days it became clear there could be no halfway house, simply because of the person Ann was.

She reminded Kate of the deputy headmistress at school, an energetic, positive person with an unsettling habit of receiving with a cool stare any comment she found tedious or superfluous. Ann had that same air of sifting, assessing and finding unworthy the idle comments of less intellectual companions. No one else, to give Ann her due, seemed bothered by this abrasive approach, even relishing it in the same way that Grannie's barbs were relished. Was it because she knew Grannie better now, even felt affection for her, that Kate found more humour behind her pungent comments than behind Ann's?

There was no doubt that whenever Max and Ann appeared they were immediately the dominant element in a group. Both tall, both good-looking, though Ann had an angularity, even a masculinity, about her which did not appeal to Kate, both determined, decisive and articulate, there was no denying the power they generated. Max drew his authority partly from his role as laird, ruling on such matters as when and where clays could be shot, and whether the children could ride, go out with Doddie after rabbits or drive a tractor. Ann relied on her natural forcefulness, and the fact that she was well-read, well-travelled and well-informed. Sickening really, Kate thought in Laura's language, giggling to herself.

Certainly the lazy, heedless mood had altered. For the few days of the Easter weekend itself the house filled up, mainly with Munros of a collateral branch though there was never time to work out the intricate relationships. A large dinner party was organised and Kate couldn't help feeling, as she cleaned piles of silver with Mrs Grant, who refused to take the task outside on an enticing spring morning in spite of all cajoling, that Ann was at the root of it. Preparations took up most of the day, not helped by the fact that the dining-room only appeared splendid if you didn't look too closely — or touch anything. Kate made the mistake of trying to rearrange the curtains, thinking they would look better if their surplus nine inches of dust-pale tatters were tucked out of sight. As soon as she laid hands on the first curtain a shower of dust, dead flies and fragments of butterflies fell on her head, and worse, a large portion of the curtain came clean away. Horrified, she went with it still clutched in her hand to Grannie.

'Look! Just look what I've done!'

'Oh, my dear, who'll notice or care? The only possible thing to do with those curtains is to walk carefully round them. But maybe I should warn you not to attempt to open a window. The results in that case might be life-threatening.'

It was a hectic time, punctuated by crises such as Max having to deal with the results of excess demand on the sewage system in one cottage, and a water supply failing in another, neither problem surprising in view of the number of extra bodies sleeping on sofas or floors. A hoover, not used for months, went on fire, and a mouse's nest was found in the hose. Mice had also gone in one end and out the other of a leather suitcase left in a loft to save the rags of clothing considered suitable for Allt Farr being lugged home after every holiday. A child broke its wrist playing the summer game of jumping off bales in the barn, ignoring the fact that the hay had been mostly eaten by this time of year.

The finale, on the evening before the main exodus began, was a football match on the lawn, played first by the light of a moon which withdrew as the first goal was scored, engendering furious controversy, and afterwards in the dazzle of vehicle headlights. Ann and Harriet didn't play. Grannie did, and so did Buff and all the other dogs.

Then it was over. There was a quieter day when the stragglers, subdued after post-match celebrations, were volunteered to mend grouse butts, and attempted a picnic on an exposed moor with the rain driving horizontally in front of their faces and the temperature dropping back hour by hour to winter levels.

Then the scrunching of gravel, last-minute shouts, waves, each of the family briefly releasing one of the arms folded across their shivering chests to wave back, and they were turning to go in with nothing to say to each other in the anticlimax of an ordinary day.

Except for Max. He had followed Ann as she accelerated away in her gleaming Mercedes E-class, off for a fortnight's golf together at Newcastle, Co. Down and points west. And except for Laura, going to spend a few days with the Devereaux family, a departure which Kate minded more.

'She always feels so bereft when everyone vanishes,' Grannie said, sounding rather bleak herself.

When Max goes off in her precious longed-for holidays, Kate thought would be nearer the truth.

Chapter Twenty-One

Although the house seemed eerily quiet with the throng of cheerful callers and chatterers gone, it was good to have some stretches of empty time. Not unoccupied time – for weeks to come Joanna would be begging and coercing help in garden and greenhouses – but regrouping time.

Joanna herself, though she hated Laura going away in the holidays and wished she could have gone too, was glad of the long monotonous hours out of doors, mostly alone. She had known if Kate stayed she would have to come to terms with some hard facts, but that didn't make it any easier when they were thrust under her nose. The state of suspended feeling she had lived in since she brought Laura back here had been bearable; the rules as it were laid down, the format by no means ideal but acceptable. Now the pattern had been broken. But could she grudge a new chance for happiness for someone she cared about so much? That would be selfish indeed.

Harriet was glad to be able to resume her visits to Craigbeg. If anyone had ever been cruel enough to explain to her the true nature of her dependence on Letitia she would have been too shocked ever to see her again, but the mere fact of turning off the glen road and heading up towards the scruffy little cottage filled her with deep soothing happiness. Though she had lived all her life at the very heart of the network of Munro friendships and relationships, she never felt at ease in it, and times like Easter were a trial to her. She was wretchedly conscious of her failure to strike the right note with her comments, forever struggling to keep up with the racing conversation. Her happiest moments came when she was feeding her chickens. That was awful; she could just hear her mother's cutting comments. Thank goodness Kate was staying. She was never unkind, and when she was there even Grannie's tongue was gentler. And look at the effect she had had on James. She was just what he needed to draw him out of his solitude. It was three years since that dreadful business about Camilla, more than time he pulled himself together.

There was Letitia, trying to prop up two wooden frames covered with wire netting. Making a new run? Old silly, she couldn't possibly manage that on her own.

For Kate there had been little chance between the confused events of Perth and the influx of Easter guests to sort out her thoughts, and with time to herself at last she was almost ashamed to find that grief over the baby had lost its immediacy. Perhaps this was because the pregnancy was something that should never have happened, she mused, something to which she had been obliged to adapt. Now it was possible to regard it separately, as the crisis which had brought her here, breaking apart the unsatisfactory structure of a life based on deception and dislike. That still hurt, would always hurt, but at least now she need not feel adrift and alone. She knew she should write to Jessie but couldn't face it yet. She could and would tell Jeremy, though.

Kate wrote that letter in her head a hundred times, and though she managed in the end to make it brisk and factual, all hints that she would like to see him again faithfully pruned away, she could not suppress all hope. The original image of Jeremy was back in place in spite of herself, as he had been at that awful party. Well, the party itself had not been awful, but the evening up to the point when she met Jeremy had. There had been a dinner-dance at the sports club, and when she arrived with Jack and Jessie to join a party of Jack's dubious business cronies, she found separate tables had been organised for parents and offspring. Dinner had been bad enough in this rowdy company, but afterwards, when the young decided to go in search of more lively entertainment, they had agreed to take Kate home, had driven down Wilton Avenue and slowed in front of Lamorna – then yelling with laughter had accelerated past, carrying her on towards Kingston in spite of all her protests and pleading.

Loud, brash, drunk enough to be delighted with their enterprise, they had gate-crashed a party which Kate had seen, when her shyness and confusion allowed her to examine her surroundings, was not a casual young people's gathering but a rather smart affair where their unwanted entry was being treated with frosty courtesy. The house had been elegant, the atmosphere so different from the striving vulgarity of the dinner she had just attended that she could have wept. In fact, when Jeremy found her, shrinking into the lost space between a doorway and the corner of the room, she had been crying. Panic had filled her about how she could escape, how she could get home, how she could apologise to these civilised people.

Jeremy had danced with her, looked after her, promised to take her home. That was all it had taken. She couldn't remember what had happened to the people she had come with, but the ice-cold moment of decision was still vivid – to grasp this chance, see where it would lead her, do what all her generation did with such ease and familiarity, be reckless, free. So she had lied, baldly and without a qualm, telling the single huge lie of her life, assuring Jeremy when the moment came that she was 'all right'.

It was wonderful. Remembering, she straightened from the seed-bed she was raking smooth, carried far away from the quiet walled garden. It truly was wonderful. Later it had grown muddled and shadowy with guilt and fear and remorse. Later Jeremy had been conscientious but appalled, barely touching her except for the occasional hurried kiss as he headed thankfully back to his own carefree world. But those few days when they had first made love, when every moment had been filled with longing for him, dazzling with a new awareness of everything around her, a new awareness of herself – that brief time had been good. And now, perhaps, she might see Jeremy again. Of course there could be no return to that first heady mood, she knew that, but with no baby to make him feel trapped into something he had never wanted or intended . . . .

No baby. The words seemed scarcely to hurt any more. There had been bad moments of course. The one which had brought the most rending sense of loss had come when, going into the Burn Cottage for the children's party, she had heard a high fluting burble and had swung round to see a baby rocker on the kist in the corner, its occupant, a few weeks old, waving tiny fists and blinking at the firelight. Tears had come then, in a shaming, drenching torrent, but Grannie had been there to draw her away, with a few quick words of explanation, and to walk her quietly up the hill to the house, letting her pour out jumbled hysterical words, letting her pause to lean sobbing against the rough stones of the dyke. She had never seen the baby again, no one had ever mentioned it, and she knew that particular, knife-like grief would not return, not in that way. She also knew there was something else she must do, and believed she now could do. She must go and see Colleen.

There was no sign of Robson when she walked into the kitchen at the Old Byre, though there was plenty of evidence of him strewn around.

'Hi, stranger, it's good to see you,' Colleen greeted her, folding her in a hot hug which, though the friendship between them forged in the melodrama of the storm had not vanished afterwards, was still unusual.

Colleen's face was flushed, her small round eyes uncertain. Robson was asleep next door, but she was expecting him to wake at any moment. 'You surely didn't walk – oh, here,' catching back what might seem tactless concern, 'hark at me blethering when all you'll be wanting is a cuppie. Wait while I get the kettle on.'

'Are there lambs already?' Kate asked, going to look at the two in a makeshift pen beside the hearth. 'I thought lambing didn't start for another two weeks.' Down near Muirend lambs were everywhere, charging around visibly greener fields where pussy willow edged the river with gold and gardens were bright with daffodils and flowering currant. But here, as she knew, everything was at least three weeks later.

'That damned Riach shepherd, he's a lazy sod,' Colleen said with easy indignation. 'He should keep his tups where they belong. And Lexy says Riach cattle had more feeding out of the Red Corrie last summer than ever an Allt Farr beast did.'

Kate decided it was too political for her, and accepted a mug of Colleen's weak tea gratefully. The day had seemed cool when she set out, but in a way she was becoming familiar with the sun had broken through with sudden warmth, burning down uncomfortably onto the stony track through clean air, and she had regretted her thick socks and gumboots.

'Anyway, you knew there'd be early lambs,' Colleen said slyly, relaxing a little. 'Wasn't there something about running the yowes off the neeps?'

'Their mothers?' Kate began to laugh too.

A high wail arose from next door; Colleen's eyes swivelled to Kate's in quick anxiety.

'Shouldn't you – ?' Kate had trouble making her voice sound natural.

'Ach, let him cry. He'll be fine,' Colleen said, but uncomfortably for that was far from being her normal practice. Robson's voice rose in vigorous complaint. He had had his sleep; he wanted company, food, attention, and he expected to get them without delay.

'I don't know what's got into him,' Colleen said, her face even redder, crossly slapping the biscuit tin down on the table. 'Take no notice.'

'Colleen, it's all right. Really.'

'He's just trying it on—'

'I mean it. I'll be all right. Do fetch him.'

Colleen blinked back ready tears. 'When I saw you coming across the yard I didn't know where to put myself. If I could I'd have grabbed Robson and gone fleeing away up the hill.'

'Very friendly,' Kate commented, determined to be calm since Colleen was obviously going to have both of them deep in weeping and anguish in another two seconds. Colleen managed a strangled gulp of a laugh.

'Look, I wanted to come,' Kate assured her. 'I've left it far too long as it is. I knew Robson would be here. I can handle it. I've got to, Colleen, don't you see?' In spite of herself her voice grew a little ragged. 'I can't duck it for ever; there are babies everywhere.'

Robson's roars went into phase two. This hanging about was not acceptable. 'If you're sure?' Colleen looked and sounded harried, and this time it was Kate who got up to hug her.

'You're good to be so worried about it. The thing is, I know I can do it here, with you. It will really help me – I'm not sure I can explain.'

Colleen looked at her, gave one brusque comprehensive nod, and went to fetch her son.

With Max away an incohesive, almost feckless, mood seemed to creep over the house. Was it the absence of his forceful person-ality, or merely that females without a male slipped naturally into an easier style of living, Kate wondered. Or perhaps it was some-thing to do with the weather, for she had found Munros were in the garden at every blink of sun, in conditions Kate wouldn't have considered sitting out in at home, with brisk winds tugging at hair and sewing and papers, blowing lettuce off a roll or salt anywhere but on the plate. At first she found it maddening to have to trek such distances to make it work, away up to her room to dress or undress to an appropriate level (she usually got it wrong anyway), then back and forth to kitchen, estate room, workroom. The favourite place was the seat down the lawn, and she felt she'd done a half mile trip by the time everything was assembled. She got used to it though – and it was worth it. These clear days of spring, lengthening at astonishing speed, were magical, though at this height not a leaf was out, the daffodils were only just beginning to swell, and the nights were still sharp and frosty. She specially loved evening walks with Buff along the Haugh, listening to the hurrying voice of the river, the calls of hunting owls, the fluting voices of oystercatchers and curlews – she wasn't absolutely certain she knew which was which yet – and able by this time to recognise the distinctive wingbeat of peewits in the chilly dusk.

But no, the sense of incompleteness stemmed from more than the hand-to-mouth existence they had fallen into without Max. As she had found when he was away skiing, there was a feeling of everything being in suspension, waiting for his authoritative grip to make the wheels turn smoothly again. He was the source of decisions, solutions, orders. It had surprised Kate at the beginning that when a machine broke down or there was some drama with sick animals, bogged tractors, flooding washing machines, blocked chimneys, a terrier down a foxhole, Max was the one who dealt with it. She had thought with a farm manager – whom she had learned to call a grieve – shepherd, cattleman, gamekeeper, he was well supplied with help, but he was always summoned just the same. But Kate knew that for her his absence went deeper than this general sense of marking time. Without him she felt insecure, as though unguessed-at dangers might threaten.

Of the family Harriet was the one who positively enjoyed him being away, happy to be free of the teasing she had never learned not to mind. In this liberated mood she was more confident about inviting Kate to do things with her, instead of always with the others, and Kate thought she must have visited every inhabited house in the glen as they pursued contributions for new windows for the Kirkton hall, or subscriptions for the Games in August, took a hen to sit on duck eggs there, or eggs to be sat upon by quite another hen somewhere else.

Kate always enjoyed her visits to Letitia's cottage, a much less

Chapter Twenty-Two

Even without Laura, back at school for the summer term, Kate's range was extending beyond the immediate surroundings of house, garden and Old Byre. She took her turn at the school run, finding the jeep alarmingly large but not difficult to drive, went down to check on old Grigor Macfarlane, supposedly looked after by a flighty granddaughter but mostly left on his own, shopped in Muirend and even Perth, finding that driving down to the latter oddly separated it from the place she had gone to by train, on that journey which now seemed a feverish dream.

She felt more at home on Allt Farr, given confidence by Colleen's friendship, and was gradually piecing together its hierarchy, relationships and feuds. She knew Doddie best, as his province of game larder and gunroom were close to the house, and though all the men came freely in and out of the estate room, or the kitchen if Max couldn't be found anywhere else, Doddie appeared most frequently and seemed to have more time than anyone to spare for fly cuppies with Mrs Grant.

He was an engaging layabout. Where everyone else was paid on a Thursday, as glen wives clung to Friday as their traditional shopping day, Doddie's pay was held back a day, Max having grown tired of never getting more than four days' work out of him. Also Doddie liked cash, so somebody had to remember each week to have it available for him. Few weekends went by without

spartan place now doors and windows stood open, and as at Allt Farr as much domestic activity as possible was carried on outside, on a patch of rough grass with views as breathtaking as any found by the skilled builders of the big houses. Though some of Letitia's winter habits had repelled Kate, such as drying her vests and knickers along the hearth, these uncouth garments seemed less offensive flapping over their heads as they sat outside drinking (twice brewed?) coffee and eating fusty digestive biscuits. Kate had acquired the Scottish pronunciation 'foosty' and thought it far more descriptive.

'I don't have meals,' Letitia would boom, handing round the breadboard with loaf, knife and lump of cheese. 'Just food.' If she did cook anything, and even Harriet was not besotted enough to consume willingly her strange combinations of any odds and ends to hand, she ate from the dish, scorning the convention of transferring hot food from one receptacle to another of a different shape. She cut her own hair, dressed from the jumble she collected, though always scrupulously paying whatever she estimated the garment would have fetched, ate nuts, mushrooms, sorrel, dandelions, nettles, horseradish, herbs and fruit garnered from the landscape, and used its resources for medicinal purposes as well. Kate was part of a damp expedition to dig comfrey roots from the slippery sides of a well-filled ditch. Letitia also collected tufts of sheep's wool and the combings of dogs and ponies, spinning and knitting them into surprisingly soft pretty scarves which she sold at the Kirkton craft shop. She despised housework, liked the patterns smoke made on wallpaper and ceilings and from choice had baths by the light of a candle or the battered brass lamp which had been tossed out of one of the glen cottages.

Kate enjoyed Letitia's pragmatic eccentricity, her good nature and serenity. It seemed to her sad that she and Mrs Munro had never established contact. Did Grannie guess at Harriet's true feelings, and find herself unable to accept them? Impossible ever to raise the subject, in spite of Kate's growing ease with Grannie, and the hours they spent talking, either well wrapped up and stitching away in fitful sunshine till their fingers got too cold to hold their needles, or in the luxury of the workroom when they gave up and dived for cover. Not that the sewing was always creative. For a delicately-built female child Laura was unbelievably hard on her clothes.

'We might as well be mending for a rugby side,' Grannie complained, holding up a shirt with its armhole gaping wide and its collar half off. 'Ah, well, the penalty for growing up in a place like this, which was more than I was able to offer her mother.'

'Where were you living then? In London?'

'In London.' Grannie's voice was brusque, and for once her busy hands stilled in her lap, the abused shirt crumpled and forgotten.

Kate was silent, afraid her question had been unwelcome, securing a button next to the jagged hole it had been torn from on the waistband, impossibly tiny even for an eleven-year-old, of a cherished pair of jeans.

'Harriet had the worst of it,' Grannie said unexpectedly. 'One can hardly blame her for being so — well, anyway, it was a difficult time. Allt Farr had to be let, though nobody took it twice,' she added with a huff of sardonic amusement. 'We lived in London, where my husband preferred to be for his own purposes and pleasure. It was all very straitened and disagreeable, and I was a cross, impatient, careless mother.'

Kate glanced at her, surprised, and saw Grannie's thoughts had taken her a long way from this room.

'I was resolved not to have more children, and Joanna was entirely unplanned. But somehow,' her voice and her deep-set dark eyes softened, 'somehow when I saw her, she enchanted me, and as she developed, with that bright hair and sweet smile, I just —' She broke off sharply. 'Kate, dear child, how thoughtless of me! Am I hurting you unbearably? I'm afraid I'd forgotten. How unforgivable—'

'No, truly, it's all right. I hadn't made any connection. In fact, though you'll think this dreadfully callous, I've almost forgotten

about the baby, or at least, not forgotten, but alre[ady] something distant, something I can't bring back or [ ] in sometimes.'

'A natural healing process,' Grannie said, laying a [ ] arm. 'Nothing to feel guilty about there. You have a g[reat] courage, Kate, and you have dealt with this whole m[ ] bravely.'

Flushing with pleasure, Kate gave her a smile of th[ ] would you go on with the story?'

'Ah, the story. Well, my husband died and witho[ut] boundless drain on our finances and, it must be said, em[ ] life, our fortunes improved.'

Kate remembered Laura's words, 'Grandfather [ ] philanderer'. Clearly his wife had not felt constrained to n[ ] him.

'So, Joanna was more fortunate than her sister. The st[ory] becomes fairly boring after that.' A snap and sparkle in Gran[nie's] eyes suggested that it did not.

'And when did you come back to Allt Farr?'

'As soon as Joanna left school and we could afford to. [ ] was fifteen. Poor boy, it was the end of youth for him, if tha[t] too exaggerated a phrase.'

Her face had become grim again in a familiar way [ ] Kate asked no further questions. The more she disc[overed] about the Munros, the more still seemed hidden behin[d] unconventional family arrangement, and the more in[ ] she became.

him being involved in some escapade, chewed over by the glen with friendly relish. Kate enjoyed his company and sitting in the gunroom on a backless chair with a once-green velvet cushion, sharing the flask which he brought down to the kitchen each day to be filled, gleaned much useful, when comprehensible, information about her new environment.

She wished Doddie had been on hand the afternoon she ventured on a new undertaking. Or indeed anyone, she amended, hot and breathless after a futile quarter of an hour spent trying to catch Persie, now out in the field with Torquil. In the precious few days that Laura had been at home between her visit to her Devereaux cousins and going back to school, she had given Kate her first riding lessons, after carefully taking the stuffing out of Persie, who could not be relied upon to treat a new rider with any kind of care. Kate had decided she was up to a small expedition of her own and today seemed an ideal opportunity.

Max was still in Ireland. Joanna had gone to help Harriet sort out the offerings for the sale in aid of the Kirkton Hall windows, and had kindly saved Kate from being dragged in too.

'Why should you waste a fabulous afternoon on a dirty, boring, depressing job you couldn't care less about anyway?' she had said cheerfully, ignoring Harriet's hurt look. 'Take some time for yourself. You've earned it, goodness knows.'

Grannie, though she pretended she was doing almost anything else, had fallen into the habit of taking a nap in the afternoons, since the days when her twisted ankle had forced her to rest. Kate was severely tempted to call her bluff as the pony eluded her yet again. Persie had acquired to perfection the timing of pretending to graze, one eye on her pursuer, with the quiet drift out of reach as soon as the halter was an inch away from her neck. Kate had seen her do it a couple of times with Laura, but somehow she had never got away with it a third time. So what had Laura done? Told her off, certainly, in the choicest of terms. Kate tried that. Persephone flicked an ear, decided there was more pleading here than authority, and took another well-judged step, showing the white of her eye. Was Laura simply quicker? Kate made a grab at the dark forelock and Persie snatched up her head and gave an indignant flourish of her heels. Such an unsubtle approach was not part of the game.

Kate gave up. She could hear Laura remonstrating, 'You must never let her think she's in charge,' but she knew that the pony was in every sense one step ahead of her, and the game could go on for ever. She wondered how many slyly amused eyes were observing her struggles, for she had learned that the landscape was never as deserted as it seemed.

Well, she would not give up. To amble along some grassy hill track on this sunny afternoon in the drifting air which still amazed her with its sweetness, with the delicate colours of spring subtly altering and softening a scene she no longer saw as stark and hostile, was too attractive to abandon. There was still Torquil. After she had learned the basics on Persie and had progressed to gentle circuits of the Haugh, Laura had accompanied her on the big garron, nimbly mounting him from the dyke and kicking him into a surprisingly stylish trot. Surely it would be possible, once on, just to sit there and let him sway along?

Could she catch him? Then there would be the matter of tacking him up. Grinning at the phrase, she nevertheless knew she was going to try.

Torquil was kinder than Persephone. He had also been trained by Max and, biggest help of all, was wearing a head collar. Perhaps, too, he didn't seriously believe he would be expected to go anywhere. He followed obediently at Kate's shoulder and stood patiently while she tied the halter to a ring outside the stable door in a knot that would have anchored a barge. He wasn't quite so helpful about the bridle. This was beginning to look like business, it was a warm afternoon and Persie was still in the field. Kate couldn't understand why she was unable to reach him with the bit. Small as she was Laura was smaller, and she had had no trouble. What Kate didn't realise was that Torquil, without any appearance of uncooperativeness, was holding his head out of reach by the finest margin. When he saw her look round for something to stand on he lowered it slightly, sighing. He was nothing if not good-natured. He took the bit in his mouth before the whole thing fell on the cobbles and waited, dozing gently, while Kate fastened the straps. She did have the sense to bring a bucket for putting on the saddle, though its weight as she tried to swing it over his back nearly toppled her backwards.

It had always seemed ruthless to drag on the girth as she had seen Laura do. 'They blow themselves out. You can see the right hole, don't let them get away with any less.' Clear, logical. But heaving that strap up notch by notch round Torquil's solid torso was like trying to compress a tank. Hot work, so hot and exhausting, in fact, that Kate felt by the time she'd finished that she had had her exercise for the afternoon. But there was her mount, saddled and bridled. It seemed a shame to waste such an achievement. She led him to the dyke and somehow scrambled on, glad Laura wasn't there to see, then found the stirrups out of reach. Max must have ridden Torquil last. It was harder to adjust them from the saddle than she had realised, each leg in turn held up awkwardly, but no way was she getting off again.

They were actually in motion. Kate blew air up over her hot face, no hand spare to wipe it, and steered for the route that would lead her furthest from human view. But what had happened to the measured, swinging gait she had expected? Torquil stumbled forward in what seemed utter weariness of spirit, grinding to a halt every few yards. What had Laura said? 'Use your knees.' What possible impression could her knees make on this heavy saddle and the barrel-like frame beneath? None that Torquil noticed anyway. She drummed with her heels and he lurched forward with a groan. Had she done something wrong, twisted something, pinched him somewhere? Surely not; he was just being obstinate. Increasingly determined not to be defied, she kicked uninhibitedly, flapped the reins, and in the privacy of the piney dappled shade of the windbreak above the house told Torquil exactly what she thought of him.

What she didn't realise was that on previous rides he had simply followed Persie, content to go wherever she went. He didn't like going out alone to be ridden, having been used originally as a hill pony, bringing down panniers of grouse or a stag across a deer saddle. It took Max's inflexible control to carry him into anything past a walk if Persephone wasn't there for company.

Kate, however, saw it as a simple battle of wills, and she had come a long way from the docile immature girl who had been content with a life ordered and restricted by the whims of others. She had planned to ride along the route the caterans had long ago taken on their raids from Glen Ellig, a high open path which ran grassy and level along the face of the hill, giving long views down to Kirkton and beyond, and requiring, she had supposed, minimum attention to her riding. Buffeting a sluggish Torquil along here, hotter and more frustrated by the minute, had not been part of the plan. Better to have been cleaning up old lawn-mowers or wiping mildew off books about goat-keeping or Christian Science in the Kirkton hall. Well, perhaps not.

She would go as far as the Riach march, no matter what Torquil thought, or how often he pulled his head free and turned it almost to her stirrup to gaze at her with exaggerated pleading. There was a gate in the high dry-stone dyke which ran clear from the ridge to the river far below, a gate which suited both estates for such purposes as gathering sheep which had strayed on higher open ground. Here Torquil showed a most unexpected willingness to go through, standing innocently in the correct position as though all his dawdling and obstruction had been entirely in Kate's imagination.

Kate frowned at his furry ears, now pricked so willingly forwards. 'And if we do go on, will you start your horrible games all over again?'

Not at all, said Torquil, model mount.

It was a glorious day, and Kate had never explored beyond this point. No one would mind, that was certain. With Torquil's thoughtful help she got the gate open and shut again, and went on. It was like riding a different pony. Head up, stride comfortably lengthened, Torquil stepped out with enthusiasm. He didn't trot; he wasn't much in favour of trotting and wasn't certain his rider would stay with him if he did, but he definitely hurried. Since they had come this far they might as well visit a friend he was even more attached to than Persie, a friend who being a garron too conformed more closely to his ideal of equine perfection.

When Kate decided it was time to turn back, not wishing to be seen by critical eyes at Riach any more than at Allt Farr, she found the matter was out of her hands. Impervious as a juggernaut without brakes or steering, Torquil hastened to his love. Across the empty expanses around the house, past the sitting-room window where a surprised James had one glimpse of Kate's helpless face and tugging arms, on towards the farm.

'Hey, Kate, where are you off to? Come and say hello at least!' James hadn't moved so fast for a long time, but by the time he reached the steps Kate was already well on her way to the steading. All she could do was to throw him one harassed backward glance, calling breathlessly, 'I can't!'

James wasn't the only person who had spotted her. Out came pell-mell Sasha and Sybilla, Bridie and Dot, with the two red setters madly bounding and barking round them. And from the farmhouse came the grieve, face puzzled as he tried to work out where this unexpected visitor was heading. James, almost as out of breath from laughter as from indolent habits, ran after her.

Torquil took no notice of any of them, merely pursued his goal at an even, resolute pace till he wound up by the gate to the field where the object of his affections dwelt, and there raised his voice in a long, ringing, impassioned neigh.

'Dear Kate, I haven't laughed so much for years,' James declared, wiping his eyes after he had lifted her down, though he thought it prudent not to say she had reminded him of nothing more than a monkey in a circus, perched on a steed which knew exactly what it was doing.

'He's after Molly,' said the grieve, allowing himself a grin. 'You daft auld thing, she'll no' be having you, don't you know that yet?'

'Had you *intended* to visit us?' James enquired, his usually lugubrious face alight with amusement. 'Not that we aren't entirely delighted, of course.'

As they turned towards the house and the little girls besieged her with questions about her ride, Bridie and Dot pausing to exchange some badinage with the grieve, their laughter floating freely across the gravel, Kate realised the story would go to join the epic of the ewes and the neeps in local lore. And she didn't care. Suddenly it seemed terribly, consumingly funny, and she began to stagger in wild circles as laughter overtook her.

'What you need is a stiff drink,' James decreed, catching her arm to steady her, and walking her towards the house with an arm round her shoulders. It was the first time Kate had appeared at Riach alone, and he was enchanted to see her there, though he would scarcely have known how to invite her. Now Torquil had delivered her to his door, or just past it, and he felt a forgotten exuberance mount inside him. Kate was so gentle and pretty, so unthreatening, and she needed looking after, a new and delightful experience for James.

'Syb, run back and stir up Bridie. Tell her we want some tea, and inside the next hour isn't good enough.'

With the topic of Kate's adventure ready to hand his besetting problem of finding things to talk about vanished, and Bridie found a very relaxed mood in the sitting-room when she eventually appeared with the twins at her heels and two mugs of tea on a tray, plus a plate of iced alphabet biscuits and some chocolate cup cakes long welded to their silver foil.

'Clear off, Bridie,' James said simply, when she folded her arms and propped herself against the door frame, ready to rehearse the whole story again. 'And take those two with you.'

'But what will happen to Torquil?' Kate at last thought of asking, when James, regretfully deciding after a pleasant hour that he couldn't inflict dinner on her, said he should take her home.

'Someone will see to him,' James assured her, knowing from experience that this approach never failed. 'And you certainly aren't going to ride him back. You'd have hard work getting him away for one thing.'

'I don't think I could ride again today,' Kate admitted, fore-warnings of the woes to come already making themselves felt. 'If you're really sure it's all right to leave him?' Max's horse. Whatever would Max have to say about all this when he heard?

'Of course it's all right.' It seemed pretty well certain dinner would be on offer at Allt Farr, so the evening with Kate need not be over yet.

Chapter Twenty-Three

Though James had phoned they were greeted with great mirth at Allt Farr and there was no question of James, in higher spirits than anyone had seen him for a long time, leaving before dinner.

Joanna knew the cause of his new mood was something she must learn to accept. She had fled from just such a situation long ago, pitching herself into a marriage that had never had a chance of working, and she would not be driven from the glen again for the same reason. It would not be fair to Laura to uproot her for one thing, and for another, where would they go? What other place could ever mean anything to them? And after all the years that had gone by, surely she could deal with this sensibly and generously? It was the second part that was the hardest. Not that she felt any resentment or antagonism towards Kate, that was not in Joanna's character, but she found it hard to be natural with her, and she knew after this evening it would be harder still.

Grannie, while much enjoying the story of Kate's escapade, read the pain behind her daughter's smiles, and her lips tightened. She had not been sure, through all the time since Joanna had returned to Allt Farr, whether the old feelings still existed, which in itself suggested a self-discipline she could only admire, but such a brave subterfuge could only work as long as James remained deep in his reclusive torpor. With James coming suddenly to life, renewing old habits, appearing at all the regular gatherings here and elsewhere in the glen, self-discipline of quite a different order would be called for.

Kate was scarcely aware of a deeper reserve in Joanna. She had been taken by surprise once or twice by an unexpected coolness, but although disappointed by it had come to accept it. Joanna was always so busy, shut away in her garden, and even when they worked there together they were usually busy with separate jobs and there was no occasion to talk. It didn't occur to Kate that it would have been more normal to share the same jobs.

But in her growing pleasure in her new world, and her relief that she need look no further for several months, Joanna's moods hardly impinged on her any more than James's attentions did. Kate saw him as a friendly neighbour, someone she could always rely on to be kind, but remote from her in age, background and outlook, while his gangling limbs and heavy-jowled face had no attraction for her. She felt sorry for him, was grateful for his company in the hurly-burly of big parties, was entertained by the style of Riach and enjoyed her glimpses of the twins, but that was it.

Also, she had other things on her mind. Unable to bring herself to telephone home, and with even greater difficulty than she had found in writing to Jeremy, she had finally told Jessie about losing the baby, trembling with doubt and the memories of angry scenes as she wrote. She wanted to go on loving Jack and Jessie; she wanted that ordinary family affection, which had been the foundation of life for twenty-two years, to be there still. Now she could only wait.

As she was waiting to hear from Jeremy. Had he received her letter? Perhaps he had been away somewhere; or worse, moved to a new address. She could check that, of course, but to do so seemed to be pushing for an answer. Better to wait a little longer . . . .

Fortunately there was plenty to keep her busy, even in this relatively quiet period with only two cottages occupied by what

Grannie referred to as 'arbitrary people', or 'arbs' (in other words neither friends nor Munro relatives), who required little attention once they had been made welcome.

Lambing proper had begun and the first lambs were in the sheltered field below the lawn, now bordered by sheets and sweeps of daffodils. Kate was often down there, fascinated by the tiny tottering creatures with the cord still attached, who so swiftly found their feet to feed with energetic butts and jigging tails. She often went to watch them before breakfast, taking Buff for an early run, intoxicated by the cool freshness of the early morning air, though startled one morning to see snow on the hills once more.

Doddie, meeting her out and about so early, took her up with him one day into the wood above the house to watch a family of fox cubs at play, concealing with difficulty the fact that his trigger finger was itching, and speculating with rich private enjoyment about what Max would have had to say if he'd known.

Working on the sound basis of 'while the cat's away' Doddie also suggested that Kate might like to help him repair one of the fords on the hill road. At this time of year Joanna was all too liable to provide tedious jobs for anyone looking as though they had nothing to do, and though Doddie was canny, holding several cards to play concerning vague, open-ended undertakings at a comfortable distance from the house, he didn't always get away with it. Away up the hill road he should be safe enough, and it was a job Max had specifically told him to do. The fact that the conversation had taken place last October only made the job more urgent, he reasoned.

Kate thought it sounded idyllic. After a morning spent making butter and rattling off some correspondence which Grannie had belatedly decided should be dealt with before Max arrived back tomorrow, followed by a rush to pack up three completed skirts in time for the post, it was bliss to head out on the rough road which wound up the backbone of the estate and out to the furthest point of its northern march, steadily climbing into a wide sunny country, the house a dark huddle of roofs among its trees below her, the farm laid out like a child's toy.

And there at last was Doddie, minus his shirt, his back very brown, up to mid-shin in the sparkling run of water. He waded to the bank as Kate came up, grinning at her with open pleasure. She saw that he was wearing ordinary hill boots and hadn't bothered to roll up his jeans, which were wet to the knee. He had recently had one of the spring haircuts the glen men favoured. Most of them hated going to town, and in any case preferred to keep a warm thatch during the winter, so at this time of year sudden transformations occurred, as one after another they appeared shorn to the bone. Even Doddie, who fancied his appearance, had had his shaggy locks clipped and looked the better for it.

'How's that for timing?' he greeted Kate. 'I was just about to have a wee break to myself.'

Kate knew him well enough by this time to realise he would have been just going to get his flask out whatever time she showed up, but after her long walk she wasn't about to argue. The brush of air while she was moving had felt deceptively cool, and only as she sank down on a rock beside Doddie did she discover how hot she really was. It was a delight to perch there, letting the breeze shiver across her hot skin, the miles of glen falling away to the haze above Muirend, and the great shapes of the hills to east and west rearing up against a blue sky. Then, revived by the bracing tea Doddie liked, it was fun to plowter about, as he put it, in water which was surprisingly warm after following a shallow stony bed for a level mile or so above the ford, with the sun hot on her back, employed in levelling stones shifted by winter spates. Well, she levelled stones; Doddie did impressive work with considerable boulders, though allowing himself a generous period of recuperation after each effort.

It was extraordinary, in that world of height and space, wind and sunlight, the only sounds beyond Doddie's grunted curses the swift flow of the burn and the thin calls of curlew and plover, how 'real life' fell away. Contentment filled Kate, the contentment of the moment, based on the deeper security of being settled for the time being at least in a place where she wanted to be.

'Oh, here, lads, best be doing something,' Doddie surprised her by exclaiming, sliding hurriedly down from a boulder where he had been perched with his arms round his knees and his eyes half closed against the cigarette smoke blowing fitfully into his face.

Following the jerk of his head Kate saw down the road the nose of the Fourtrak, pointing skywards, heading towards them. Harriet, Joanna? Some message?

'Aye, well,' Doddie was murmuring philosophically, back in the water and levering powerfully at a monster of a rock he had been planning to leave for another day, if not for ever. 'Things are going to be a bit less peaceful with yon lad back.'

'Max? But he's not due till tomorrow.' It was revealing, Kate thought, how peace fled for her too, and a whole cloud of doubts whirled up – should she be here, should she be doing something else – even, should she not be splashing about with Doddie in the burn wearing a tank top and rolled up jeans, soaked to mid-thigh? Kate was conditioned to obedience and conforming, and Max was the unquestioned seat of authority at Allt Farr. The roar of the approaching jeep sounded absurdly ominous.

Doddie seemed at once amused and resigned. 'We'll no' hear the last of this in a hurry,' he prophesied, winking at Kate as head down he strove and laboured.

The engine cut, the door slammed and Max came stalking across to them, eyes narrowed and the expression on his face unpromising to a degree. He gave Kate one curt nod and turned his attention to Doddie, who kept his hands wrapped round the crowbar, maintaining just enough pressure under the boulder to suggest he was reluctant to be interrupted in his endeavours.

'How long have you been up here?' Max asked, his unforgiving eye assessing, Kate was convinced stone by individual stone, the changes wrought since he last came this way.

'Oh, these past three hours or more, it'll be, likely,' Doddie said virtuously, expelling his breath in a slight artistic pant.

Max said nothing. His glance took in Kate's shirt and jacket draped over the tailgate of the pick-up, her socks and boots on the bank. 'I'll take you down,' he told her.

She found herself moving off-handedly towards her clothes rather as Buff did his best to efface himself when trouble seemed imminent, and stifled a giggle as she picked them up. She had expected to go down with Doddie, but knew she would do as she was told. Max had that effect, particularly in this mood.

'Jim tells me three lambs have been taken already,' he was saying to Doddie. He had clearly lost no time in acquainting himself with the state of play. 'Did you get that vixen in the Long Plantation yet? How about the game-larder drain? Have you had the ferrets down that big warren . . . ?'

Friendly as a shower of hailstones, Kate thought. Fun was definitely over for the day.

Max didn't speak as he negotiated the steep curves of the descent, his eye noting a clogged culvert entrance here, a runnel cut deep by the ravages of winter there, and lighter scars low on the trunks of trees in a plantation which showed rabbits were in, another problem Doddie might have been taking care of instead of fooling about with that damned ford.

Max checked his thoughts angrily. The ford had to be sorted too; it was just that Doddie's priorities didn't match his own and never would. No, it wasn't even that, and he might as well admit it. He had been sharply jealous of the tranquil scene he had come upon, the sunlight and bright water, Doddie stripped to the waist getting slyly back to work at his approach, and Kate, her skin already tanning against the white of an absurd top she might have borrowed from Laura, looking happy and at home in an activity and scene which two months ago would have seemed quite alien to her. Max had had no defence against the sharp pang of pleasure he had felt at the sight of her, and knew he must get such feelings into perspective without delay.

Kate was a mere child, nearer to Laura in age than she was to him. Only just, an inner voice instantly objected. Well, then, she was Jeremy's girlfriend; only just beginning to get over losing his child. She was a transient in their lives, here for a few short months, after which she would return to a world very different from this. Most crucially of all, James was showing an interest in her, and that was something that must not be jeopardised.

Then, left till last in his thoughts because it was a problem he knew he had been putting off for far too long, since before Kate ever appeared, there was the question of Ann.

'Did you enjoy your holiday in Ireland?' Kate chose this moment to ask, feeling his chilly silence was unnecessary, and not enjoying being made to feel somehow in the wrong.

There was a fractional pause, and she actually thought Max might not answer.

'Had a couple of good rounds,' he said.

This seemed to Kate a fairly minimal response, and the tone was curt. She would ask no more.

Max had not enjoyed his holiday. Any stretch of time spent with Ann left him feeling he had been through a strenuous bout in the ring, but usually he found that quite stimulating. Recently, however, he had grown used to Kate's company, coming to appreciate more and more her effortless good nature, her endearing readiness to admit her mistakes, and the contrast had made him strangely unwilling to spar and contend.

Moreover Ann had made it clear she thought it time to come to some decision about their future, and that had hardly helped. He felt driven enough as it was, torn between impatience at his endless responsibilities and the knowledge that he couldn't abandon them. Ann was inextricably tied up with all that. He had known her since childhood, they were products of the same upbringing and background, they enjoyed shared interests and friendships. Ann would accept Allt Farr as it was — except that she would make summary arrangements for rehousing his female relations — and improve the heating, he amended, trying to lighten his mood. Well, if he married her they would be able to afford both. His face darkened again at the reflection.

His mind went back over the days in Ireland. Good golf, particularly on the windswept heights of Ballybunion. Oh sure, and the rest? He knew he had been restless for the entire time, his mind elsewhere, impatient to get home. Sex with Ann could be as stringent as her conversation, familiar, usually acceptable, part of life in a take-it-or-leave-it fashion for some time now. During the past two weeks he had definitely wanted to leave it, and had been unable to conceal the fact. Ann had had some stinging comments to make as they parted, and he had come home feeling considerably the worse for wear.

His mood made a marked impact on the light-hearted air of holiday which had prevailed in his absence. In spite of it Kate found she was happy to have him back; Allt Farr was never truly itself without him. Laura would sort him out when she came home for the weekend.

This weekend Laura did more. She was responsible for a change in Kate's circumstances which did as much as anything to put behind her the dark weeks of winter.

They were hunting for a tennis skirt missed from the list when they'd packed for Laura to go back to school, and their search took them into the room above hers in the south tower where she used a big walk-in cupboard for overflow possessions. It was a small near-octagon with windows on three sides, bright and warm in the afternoon sunshine, with a delightful sense of height and space.

'How lovely to live up here,' Kate said, not thinking of it as a possibility, for the room had bare floorboards and was totally unfurnished.

'Would you like to?' Laura asked eagerly. 'Then you'd be near me.'

Kate thought of the scale and gloom she had never become reconciled to in her own room; the dark heavy curtains; climbing up the library steps every time she wanted something from the wardrobe; the hill-face looking in at the windows – though she had observed the odd fact that in fine weather it stepped back.

'But there's no furniture,' she said.

'The house is full of furniture,' Laura said, true daughter of Allt Farr. And indeed no one seemed to think anything of the move, except Doddie who had to manhandle a bed up the spiral stair.

'You can always move back when it gets cold again in the autumn,' Harriet said, forgetting that once autumn came Kate would be gone. Kate didn't remind her. Continuity nowadays had a pleasant sound.

Chapter Twenty-Four

'Why we bother to do this,' Grannie said, briskly and carelessly slapping emulsion paint onto the sitting-room walls of the students' flat across the courtyard, 'I do not know. If this young man runs true to form the first thing he will do will be to cover our efforts with posters of polluted Siberia or androgynous creatures in black leather with their thumbs hooked in their belts. Or am I out of date?'

'No good asking me,' Kate replied cheerfully, getting down to move the stepladder along. If she had felt out of touch with her generation's culture before, the months at Allt Farr had been life on another planet. Activities like ditching and draining, dumping and laying stones in field gateways, restrapping young willows to their supporting posts, checking the netting round plantations for rabbit infiltration, and clearing sticks and stones before strimming or mowing were a long way removed from pop art. Kate was convinced that the lawn had quadrupled in size since mowing began, and several extra areas of grass she had never noticed before had suddenly materialised around the house and buildings. Laura loved doing it all, especially using the sit-on mower, a mini-tractor which she handled like a take-and-drive-away, with roars from Max to slow down whenever he caught her. His temper had never fully recovered after his Irish holiday.

There had been a spell of drenching rain at the end of April, interspersed with sleet and snow on high ground, and Kate had been intrigued to see lambs sporting minute tartan mackintoshes in the fields by Alltmore loch. Fanny Moncrieff had come for a weekend during which it had rained solidly the entire time, and Max had muttered angrily about lead flashings, leaking gullies and rotting window frames, while Joanna, in a perpetual state of mud and wildly corkscrewing wet hair, had struggled to save her young seedlings in the saturated and puddled garden.

To remove them from this Cold Comfort atmosphere Kate had taken the children to the leisure centre in Muirend, and though they were rapturous about swimming and in-line rollerblading and various screaming, wailing, smashing and crashing video games, she had found herself unexpectedly hassled by the noisy artificial scene. Even swimming, her favourite exercise until she came to Glen Maraich, had seemed distasteful in the chlorine-smelling pool, thick with other bodies, resounding with shrieks and shouts.

The next day had been much more fun, when as usual they had gone to Riach and James had suggested a game of hide-and-seek into which even Harriet had been beguiled. Carelessly dust-sheeted rooms and cluttered attics had provided excellent though spooky hiding places, and the seekers had hunted with such remorselessness that in the end Bridie and Dot had become even more uncontrollably hysterical than the twins.

That was when Kate, coming hot and breathless down the stairs, had overheard Harriet's disconcerting comment to her mother.

'I do think Kate is good for James, don't you? He seems to be getting quite fond of her.'

Kate had seen Grannie's swift annoyed glance to check who was within hearing, and much embarrassed had drawn hastily back. James? Fond of her? It was absurd. She had been glad of his unvarying kindness, but though she felt safe in his company she didn't find it enlivening. The Munros, with all their faults, were undoubtedly more interesting.

She was impressed by the active social life they led in this remote place. One or all seemed to be continually off to some wedding, christening, funeral, or party. They had recently, Kate included, attended Charlie Fleming's silver wedding celebrations, and shortly afterwards many of the same faces had appeared at a lively gathering in the Kirkton hall for Gilbert Rathlyn's seventy-fifth birthday. The sale, followed by a ceilidh, in aid of the hall windows had finally taken place, Harriet and Letitia coming gloriously into their own, and last weekend had been as sociable as Easter with every cottage crammed once more for the English bank holiday.

One of the nicest things, Kate thought, painting away diligently, had been her move to the tower room. She loved its simplicity and light, and was determined never to move back to her old room, which in retrospect seemed eternally dark and cold, part of the self she had been then, pregnant, frightened and confused.

Now she felt she was moving forward, confident and hopeful, able for most of the time to keep at bay the question which never quite disappeared — should she attempt a reconciliation with Jessie and Jack? There had been no reply to her letter, but she had hardly hoped for one. Letter-writing was an alien effort Jessie rarely undertook.

Nor had Jeremy been in touch. That was another source of sadness which could catch her unawares. His silence seemed at odds with his concern when he had learned about the baby.

She was jolted from her thoughts by Grannie puffing out a long, weary sigh. 'I have to confess, I really begin to think I'm too old for this sort of thing.'

'Oh, Grannie,' Kate cried with compunction. 'Come and sit down for a moment. I shouldn't have let you go on for so long.' She drew her to a fat little sofa covered by a paint-flecked sheet, where Mrs Munro sank down with an uninhibited groan.

'Do you know, that's the first time I've ever heard you admit to being tired?' Kate said in a tone between scolding and sympathy.

'Oh, I can say it to you,' Grannie said, closing her eyes and leaning back for a moment's abandonment to exhaustion. 'Which is ironic, since you're the only person who ever notices in the first place.'

'You only get cross if anyone does notice,' Kate pointed out.

'Ah, Kate.' A faint smile crossed Grannie's fine-boned, arrogant face, though she didn't open her eyes. 'You say these things in such a spirit of courteous honesty that they are entirely acceptable.'

Kate regarded her with affection, thinking how handsome she must once have been, but moved to see, as well as the lines of tiredness and pain, a rare look of defeat.

'Does your ankle still hurt?' she asked gently. She wished they had a flask of something hot with them, for the air of the little room, unused for months, struck chill. But they were so near the house it had not occurred to her, and to fetch something now would break the mood of unexpected frankness.

'Twinges now and then,' Grannie said dismissively, and Kate thought for a moment she was going to be as cavalier over sympathy as ever. Then abruptly she went on, with an uncharacteristic explosion of frustrated confession, 'Twinges in my ankle, aches in my hips, pain almost everywhere else. I get so *tired* of it, so tired of being old.'

'Oh, Grannie.' Her face full of concern, Kate drew up a hideous little stool made from a camel's saddle pad, one of those useless bits of furniture which most unfairly find their way into staff quarters, and took her hand, expecting at the most to have hers acknowledged and put aside.

But Grannie gripped it, and opening her fine dark eyes met Kate's concerned look with a grimace of sardonic humour. 'I know I should rest more and be sensible, stop battling and struggling. No wonder my children don't spare me much sympathy. Why should they? My woes are almost entirely self-inflicted. But you can't imagine how driven I sometimes feel, how conscious of failure, as though there is some task still to complete and time is running out.'

Kate held the knobbly old hand, so competent, so used to work, gently in both her own, but did not speak. To hear such an admission from dogmatic, positive Grannie awed her, and she felt any words from her would be inappropriate.

'What a limping, unnatural little family I have bred,' Grannie went on, more energetically, but with a self-mockery too bitter to be comfortable. 'Harriet in her forties as nervous as a schoolgirl, even down to the crush on one of the big girls – and I do mean big girl – for emotional sustenance. She is, I am sorry to say, the most infuriating woman I know. And my little Jo—'

Grannie broke off, for she could hardly say to Kate that she suspected her younger daughter to be eating her heart out for a man at present increasingly drawn to Kate herself. 'At least she produced precious Laura who, it not infrequently occurs to me, is the only well-adjusted adult among us! And poor Max, what have I done to him? Obligations without rewards can be a dry diet.'

A dozen questions rose in Kate's mind but were rejected. What place could any words of hers have in this adult revelation of pain so suddenly and movingly laid bare?

'It's not a good thing, Kate, to feel that the seeds of disharmony and unhappiness lie in oneself, to be passed on to one's progeny in spite of all one can do. Does it hurt you when I speak of this, of children?' The dark eyes were alert again, pushing long-ago errors and guilt back where they belonged, in accustomed memory. 'You have been so brave, so controlled, but sometimes I've wondered whether we should have persuaded you to talk more about what happened. Our way is to bury grief, and I have come to see, too late, that it may not be the best answer.' She gave a tiny shake to their linked hands, and looked closely into Kate's face with unwonted tenderness. This gentle girl, with her naïve determination to stick through thick and thin to what she believed she ought to do, had touched tough, undemonstrative Grannie in a way almost unprecedented in her long life.

'No, it's all right,' Kate assured her quickly. 'It's been fine, just quietly going along with ordinary things, I mean –' it struck her suddenly as astonishing that that was how day-to-day life at Allt Farr could appear to her '– just being able to stay here was exactly what I needed. I've felt so – looked after.'

'That's good,' said Grannie, adding with the glint of a smile, 'Though how we selfish Munros managed that I have difficulty in comprehending.'

'It must have been Laura,' Kate said innocently, and Grannie laughed.

'Can I ask – I've always wondered – but please, Kate, *please* don't hesitate to tell me to mind my own business if the question is out of order – why you didn't originally consider abortion as an option? Oh, forgive me, how blunt that sounds, but in the world we live in today it seemed at least a possible choice in a case such as yours.'

'I know, and I was probably an idiot not to have done it at once,' Kate said, oddly relieved to be able to talk about it at last. How she had longed, passionately, desperately, to discuss it with Jessie at the time. 'It wasn't a moral decision or anything of that sort. It was just –' Her small pointed face, tanned now, only the soft brown eyes accentuated with make-up, became wistful, and her voice trailed away without, Grannie thought, her being aware of it.

'Just?' she prompted after a moment, feeling a quite unusual interest, even need, to know what had motivated Kate at this major turning-point of her life.

'I was adopted, as you know,' Kate said. 'My mother, my real mother, gave me up, and I knew I could never do it to any child of mine. That was the one thing that stood out clearly from all the weighing of alternatives, all the agonising. Now it seems so pointless, because I lost the baby anyway.'

'Oh, dear girl, I don't believe it can have been pointless, as you call it. Truly I don't. Nothing is. You acted from your own conviction, and that had a value of its own. And then it took you out of what sounds a rather unfulfilling way of life.' She could hardly refer directly to what Joanna had told them about the behaviour of Kate's adopted mother. 'Who knows now what will lie ahead? Your time here may be a stepping-stone to something new and marvellous.' Though how sad I shall be when the day comes for you to leave, she reflected with a return of melancholy. But she had learned one thing in the battling years; wishes are futile things.

'I know,' Kate was agreeing. 'That's how I see it. My life was such a dead end. I feel so grateful to Jeremy for arranging for me to come here.' Difficult though it was to refer to him, at least she could hold onto that. He had done that much for her.

How apropos, Grannie reflected ironically, not quite prepared for the opening so neatly offered. She had protested vigorously against the family decision that it should be she who faced Kate with the next question, but she understood the source of Joanna's reserve with Kate, and Harriet could not be trusted with such a sensitive subject. Max? Max was immersing himself in work and holding aloof from everyone, and Grannie's speculations about him were not reassuring these days.

'We're glad Jeremy sent you here,' she said firmly.

Kate turned to smile at her, pleased. 'In spite of all the idiot things I've done?'

'They had their amusing side. Now, Kate, there is something I want to talk over with you. Something for you to decide, and only you. Will you remember that? You are to say exactly what you want.'

'Whatever can be coming?' Kate asked in bewilderment. She had anticipated no decision-making on her part for some time. Was the idea that she moved into the student flat going to rear its head again? Possessive love for the little room in the tower filled her. She would certainly say what she felt about that.

'You know that our next great event is Laura's twelfth birthday party?' Grannie went on. 'It's a family tradition that twelfth birthdays are made much of, so as you may have gathered it's not really a children's party but a mixture of all the generations, and Munros to the nth degree of kinship will turn out.'

'Yes?' Kate was politely interested but puzzled, unable to see how this could concern her. Unless they would need her room to accommodate the influx?

'Now, you are to say exactly what you think,' Grannie warned again. 'But in the normal course of events Jeremy would be included in such a party. He hasn't been invited yet and won't be if you prefer not to see him. So how would you truly, honestly feel about his coming to Allt Farr?'

Chapter Twenty-Five

The high gloomy pile of Allt Farr dozed in the somnolence of a June afternoon, every room aired and burnished, even the year-round chill of the big hall touched by tentative fingers of summer air drifting in through the propped-back doors. Heat poured down into the deserted walled garden where the green pencil lines of carrots, broccoli and spinach were firmer, and the crumpled nubs of the first early potato shaws were through.

Knowing everything was done that could be done, luxuriating in the fact that there was no one to find some chore to fill the gap before the first guests arrived, Kate wandered down the lawn, its banks of rhododendrons just coming into bloom, breathing in the sweet air with delight, savouring the moment of sunny indolence and quiet. The glen looked marvellous just now, lilac, laburnum and chestnuts out and gardens bright, with up here hawthorn and rowan predominating, and great golden swathes of gorse and broom blazing on the flanks of the hills. Those were the scents that teased her, mingling on the light wind, almost unbearably vivid and evocative. Below her in the Haugh blue waves of speedwell spread where once the menacing waters of the flood had rolled. She was suddenly seized with an immense satisfaction to have experienced both these extremes, to have stayed to see this place in other moods.

And now Jeremy was coming. Was it the anticipation of

seeing him which gave this moment its keen edge, the fact that they could meet on the uncomplicated footing of their original encounter? Attraction on both sides had been real. She was sure of it, or why would he have made contact again after that first evening, so fraught with need, defiance, guilt and urgency?

Kate brought her thoughts back to the present. Here, on this perfect day, in this place where she had found a new tentative sense of belonging, reunion with Jeremy lay before her like a fresh page, dazzling as a book opened in the sunshine. Not a new image, she heard some dry Munro voice comment. Max or Grannie. She smiled, making an idle circuit of the lawn, catching the resinous tang of sun-warmed fir trees behind the lighter scents of blossom, twirling a daisy in her fingers. Then she heard a car. Harriet coming back with the lemonade and Pimms that had missed the mailvan? Joanna and Laura bringing Fanny from Morgill? Or the first arrivals?

A sports car, its top down, flashed out from the green tunnel of the drive. Not Ann? No, this car was not as gleaming or expensive as hers. A second car, even noisier, followed. Kate started up the slope, her heart beginning to thump uncomfortably.

Jeremy, wearing dark glasses, fair hair gleaming in the sun, was out already, stretching his arms with fingers linked above his head in a luxurious gesture, calling derisively, 'Knew you'd never do it!' to the driver of the second car as it pulled up with a swirl of gravel which would make Max swear. Jeremy's passenger was elegantly uncurling long legs, smoothing a miniscule skirt, shaking back shoulder-length black hair.

'Local knowledge. Unfair advantage.' The second driver, another streamlined young man wearing white trousers and a navy-blue shirt, grinned over his shoulder as he went to help out a tubby smiling girl with a head of mahogany red hair.

Somehow Kate had not envisaged this. She had always played the scene with Jeremy arriving alone. Though having heard all the plotting and planning that had gone on to squeeze everyone into the house and cottages, and having written out the name-cards for dinner and put them round the table not an hour ago, it was not hard to work out who the other three were.

'Hello,' Jeremy said in a general friendly tone as he turned to reach into the car and caught sight of her approaching. Then, taken aback, 'Good lord, it's Kate, isn't it?'

Hadn't he known she would be here? Kate wondered in sudden confusion. Hadn't anyone warned him? But she had said when she had written that she would be staying for the summer. Perhaps he was just shaken to see her; perhaps he had thought about this meeting as much as she had.

Jeremy, however, had been surprised because he had forgotten what she looked like, had in fact managed to put her out of his mind so effectively that he had almost forgotten she would be here. He had pushed it aside as something to be dealt with when the time came. Jeremy was a great play-it-by-ear man; he found it saved a lot of wear and tear. Now he scarcely recognised in this tanned, slender girl coming smiling shyly towards them, wearing a floaty skirt and simple top in a tan which looked good with her curly hair lightened to bronze by the sun, the tearful grateful waif he had once succoured. Or patronised and impregnated, he amended, being not entirely without honesty.

Shaken, he fell back on making introductions. Miranda and Jan. Gus Stephenson. At least the two girls could be relied upon to fill any awkward gaps with meaningless gabble. It was the only other thing they were good at. But he knew the crudeness of the thought was mere male ego-bolstering in a moment of rare discomfort.

'Kate's up here helping out for the summer,' he said, and the three nodded to her with a casual chorus of, 'Hi.' 'Where is everyone, Kate?'

Kate explained, feeling new-found confidence shred away under eyes which assessed her without interest.

Of course he couldn't kiss me. Of course he wouldn't have told them about me. Don't be such a fool, what did you expect? But she had the unpleasant premonition that she was not going to be able to obliterate from her memory the look in Jeremy's eyes in that moment when he had greeted her with the impersonal appraisal of a stranger.

'Jez, this place isn't at all bad!' Miranda was exclaiming, doing nothing about her luggage. 'Why did you feed us all those dire warnings about it being bat-haunted and gothic? I feel quite let down.'

'Wait till you're shoved into some stone-walled turret half a mile from the nearest bathroom,' Jeremy warned her, dropping a couple of cream leather bags carelessly on the gravel.

'Careful of those, you idiot. That's my face you're chucking about.'

Bat-haunted and gothic. Protective wrath rose in Kate, too fierce to leave room for objective amusement. She stepped towards one of the cases and said with careful civility, 'Shall I show you your rooms?'

'Oh, that's a bit boring,' the red-haired girl called Jan objected. 'I feel as if I've been shut up for hours like a sardine with the lid down. Not even a sun roof for us. You'll have to change your car, Gus, preferably before we leave. Could we possibly have tea outside?' she went on to Kate, dropping into the slightly fulsome tone of someone brought up to be polite to servants. 'Would that be a frightful nuisance?'

No question there; mere form of words. A tiny chill crept through Kate, in spite of the sun burning down from a cloudless sky, in spite of the heat striking up from the gravel. In a moment of swift inner protest and disbelief she saw that Jeremy had no intention of putting right the impression his careless words had given. And worse, making it impossible to correct it herself (and indeed, what could she say?) she wondered with mortification if that was indeed how Jeremy saw her, an employee.

'Good idea,' he was agreeing with Jan. 'We can sort the rooms out later. Let's go down to the big seat – that all right with you, Kate?'

It was the most perfunctory of questions, a piece of automatic courtesy, exactly as Jan's had been. They were already turning away from the cars, a little enclosed group, a unit, sharing the relief of putting behind them the heat and tedium of the journey.

Kate opened her mouth and shut it again. Tears stung her eyes. The plan, outlined by Grannie before she went up to rest, an indulgence she had been much more open about since her conversation with Kate about the pains of age, had been that everyone should help themselves from the scones and cakes put out in the breakfast room and that Kate, left by a combination of circumstances to look after everything by herself, should only have to make pots of tea and take people to their rooms.

'Though most of them are family and won't need taking anywhere or showing anything,' Grannie had added. 'I shall be down soon, and even Harriet can't take too long over going to Muirend and back.'

Jeremy, Kate knew, was definitely part of the family. He, of all people, could be expected to follow the custom of the house and come and help. But how could *she*, Kate asked herself helplessly, suggest it to *him*? Biting her lip, forcing back the maddening tears, she went quickly into the welcome cool and gloom of the hall.

It was a long trip down to the elm seat with the heavily laden tray. It was Gus who leapt up to set it on the table for her; the others had been too absorbed in their laughter and chatter to notice her coming.

'I hope I haven't forgotten anything.' Kate's soft voice was lost in the hubbub as they exclaimed in greedy pleasure at the spread before them.

'Mrs G's scones. Great, long time since I last had those. No one else's ever come near them,' Jeremy said with satisfaction, hitching himself to the edge of the seat to sort out plates and cups and saucers.

Kate hesitated a second longer. No one looked up. And she had actually wondered for a moment whether she should put five cups on the tray. Cheeks burning, she hurried away to the refuge of the house.

Beside the cars sprawled the abandoned luggage. With her status here suddenly in question, the sight of it checked Kate. Should she carry it up, at least the girls'? She would have helped with it as a matter of course when she took them to their rooms. She remembered Grannie seizing her own case on that faraway winter's night when she had been whirled in on a flurry of snowflakes. At Allt Farr guests were looked after; her own hurt vanity should not prevent her from doing whatever should be done. She picked up a bulging cream case, decided it was all she could manage at one time, and holding its handle in both hands tottered inside with it.

'What the hell do you think you're doing?'

Max's voice, snapping from the shadows of the kitchen corridor, made her jump. She couldn't face being bullied just now and was glad of Buff's friendly head coming to push against her in accustomed greeting.

'Jeremy and his friends have arrived. They're having tea in the garden. I thought I'd—'

'Leave it. Leave the whole lot. What on earth does Jeremy think he's playing at –?'

Max strode past her and Kate caught one glimpse of his face, dark with anger, as he headed for the door. Buff decided to stay where he was. What Kate didn't realise was that Max, on his way in via the kitchen to scrub up after spraying dockens, knowing he should put in an appearance since people would be arriving and she was on her own, had seen her going down the lawn bowed by that mammoth tray. Finding her left to struggle with the luggage had been enough to ignite ready anger at Jeremy, anger which had its source in a whole welter of resentful feelings, old and new.

Kate saw with horror that Max proposed to go storming down the lawn to confront Jeremy at once, on his first visit here for months and in front of his friends, on her behalf.

'Max, please don't!' She leapt after him, pushing Buff aside, too appalled to weigh her words. 'Please don't say anything. I should hate it.'

Max swung round in the doorway to find her at his elbow, her face full of appeal. His eyes narrowed. He thought he had been prepared for seeing her with Jeremy; now he knew that he had not. 'You're not here to run around after that lot. Jeremy had a cheek to ask to bring them anyway, since this is supposed to be Laura's party.' He knew he was seizing on the least important of the factors fusing together to ignite his ready rage.

Kate didn't think she could handle a row between Max and Jeremy. 'I really didn't –' But she couldn't bring herself to frame the lie; she had minded, desperately.

She was saved by Grannie's step on the stairs, Grannie's voice above them. 'No, Buff, don't come up to meet me, it really doesn't help. What a perfect fool you are.'

A car pulled up outside. The explosive moment, charged with so many emotions, had passed.

Kate had never guessed the sombre dining-room could look like this, though several dinner parties had taken place in it since that first famous occasion when she had failed to lay its table. Not having curtainless black windows looming in the background helped, for even by the time the splendid dinner wound to its end the long June evening was barely darkening to dusk. Bright with Joanna's flowers, lit by candles in the massive silver candelabra Mrs Grant luckily delighted in cleaning, damp-eaten plasterwork and dusty cornices invisible in the soft shadows, the room was filled with talk and laughter. And friendliness, thought Kate, restored by excellent food and wine and the familiar company of James on one side and Tim Bellshaw on the other. She was young enough to be reassured too by her presence at the table. Wondering how it would all work, for the whole enterprise sounded terribly ambitious to her, her assumption that she would be needed to help had been swept aside.

'Nonsense, this party is for us. We haul in people from all over the place to do the work. It's enough hard labour getting ready for it; once it begins, we forget all mundane considerations.' That was Grannie, airy and positive as ever – and to judge from her snapping eyes and pink cheeks now, her look of abandonment to pleasure, she had meant what she said. Harriet was not so relaxed, hopping up from time to time to call anxious messages down the lift shaft or, when her voice was drowned by a barrage of teasing, actually going down to the kitchen. How had she been received there? Kate speculated. Colleen, one of a bustling team raised without difficulty from Allt Farr and Riach, would give her short shrift for one and so would Bridie.

Everyone seemed to be involved, or to have involved themselves. Doddie was hanging about outside with Lexy and Jim Coupar, each with a half bottle stuck in his pocket, on the pretext of seeing to the parking when the house parties from Alltmore and Drumveyn arrived.

'Though the guests will have more intelligent ideas about where to park than Doddie will by the time they get here,' Max had observed resignedly after checking on his volunteers, but he'd dished out a dram apiece anyway.

Kate looked down the long table. Most people she knew or could place, from a crimson-faced Gilbert to Fanny Moncrieff sitting between the Forsyth brothers, as pink-cheeked and thrilled as Laura herself, at one end of the table facing Max at the other. Jeremy was next to Miranda, who looked striking but too dramatic for a family party in a sleek dress the colour of burnt orange. Kate glanced past them quickly, refusing pain a chance to sting. Soon there would be dancing. At last there would be a chance to talk to Jeremy, to dance with him, perhaps recapturing for a moment something of the remembered mood of the first time they had danced together, on that extraordinary evening which he had transformed from embarrassed misery to dazed delight. If that was too much to hope for at least there would be the opportunity to share with him what coming here had meant to her, and tell him how much she had looked forward to seeing him again. Would he mind if she referred to the loss of the baby? Surely he couldn't?

Discordant wails sounded faintly in the distance, settling into a full-toned blast which approached inexorably along the corridor.

'What a nightmare!' Grannie exclaimed cheerfully. 'I knew we'd never prevent Willie Mearns from getting in with his pipes. I fear we are being summoned.'

Chapter Twenty-Six

James stood by one of the windows, open to the June night, of the Allt Farr drawing-room, another abode of damp, cobwebs and dead air which had been brought to temporary life for the evening, its carpets lifted, most of its furniture removed and the rest pushed back around the walls. It could comfortably hold, as it just had, four sets for an eightsome, but now couples were gently gyrating in the kind of non-dance James couldn't cope with, while Laura and her contemporaries performed less tactile rites to a different tempo in the hall.

Grannie and Gilbert, though markedly brisker than those around them, knew what they were doing, James observed with affection, and looked very contented doing it. They really did depend on each other, these two, with their phone calls or visits every day of their lives. Why had Grannie not moved in years ago? But James at once dismissed the idea, unable to imagine her in a bright, warm, modern bungalow, however enticing its garden, or indeed anywhere but in this uncomfortable monster of a house, its dilapidations taxing combined Munro resources more severely with each year that passed. James sighed; he should know.

Deliberately he pretended to seek out Kate, but he knew exactly where she was, as he had known all evening. She looked very slim and neat in that tunic affair. Would you call that colour saffron? He was pleased with himself for dredging up the word. Whatever its colour, its simple style was more suitable for a child's party than the blatantly sexy affair which looked ready to slither off Jeremy's friend at any moment.

James stirred impatiently, knowing he was finding any target for his disquiet but the real one, and let his eyes remain on Kate. All evening he had watched her, glad to see her nervousness vanish, though waiting in vain for it to be replaced by the sparkle of enjoyment. He had been delighted to find himself next to her at dinner but had been obliged to recognise that he had never for one moment had her full attention. She had been as courteous and smiling as ever, not concealing her relief to be sitting beside him, and that had filled him with the protective care which was such a new and enjoyable experience for him, but she had been almost completely silent. Afterwards he had watched her dancing with Charlie, with Tim, with Andrew Forsyth and Gilbert, with a punctilious ten-year-old Hay of Sillerton and Mike Danaher's son Michael. He had danced Strip the Willow with her himself, enjoying her lightness and balance. Camilla had never felt like that. The reflection had jolted him; it was the first direct comparison he had caught himself making.

But all the time Kate's attention, in spite of her attempts to conceal the fact, had been centred on Jeremy. Now, at last, they were dancing together, and Kate's face wore a look of such open happiness that James could evade the truth no longer. The pieces slid effortlessly into place. It had not been chance that had brought Kate to Allt Farr to be looked after during her pregnancy. The child had been Jeremy's. So where had Jeremy been when Kate had miscarried, when she had needed help and support? And why, this evening, had he held aloof till now, while through the hours Kate's small face had become a smiling mask, hiding puzzled hurt? Jeremy meanwhile had been having a marvellous time, convinced that everyone was overjoyed to see him, explaining over and over again why he hadn't been up at Easter, as though anyone cared, fooling around with those silly girls he and Gus had brought, dancing every dance, showing off in the reels, finally commandeering – a trick James considered outworn – Willie Mearns' pipes to play for one of them.

Kate's eyes looked different now, unbearably different. With an angry jerk James pushed himself away from where he leaned against the curtain, and began to thread a way round the room. He had come alone – no hosts of any humanity would condemn overflow guests to a night at Riach – and who would notice if he stayed or went?

What a crass idiot he had been to hope that in Kate he had found someone who could transform his life, dragging him out of the shadowy place of silence and inertia to which Camilla's death had consigned him. Kate was twenty years younger than he was, for God's sake. She would go tripping back to her own world without a backward glance when the summer was over. What a fool he had made of himself. All the joking about old James coming out of his shell at last had been justified – blundering middle-aged man, with no interests and no conversation and no appeal, and a pair of riotous four-year-olds to boot, infatuated with a kind, pretty, gentle girl whose heart was elsewhere. It was a bad moment for James, and he could not adequately control his expression as he blindly forged a way past the swaying oblivious couples.

Joanna saw his face, read its shock and pain, and knew, with a lurch of fear and excitement, that one of the great moments of her life was at hand, a moment when passivity and hesitation would not serve. Taking a deep breath she turned and slipped into the empty corridor before James reached it.

Max, doing his best to convey to Ann that he was concentrating on her, though not prepared to talk, missed these moves, which would certainly have aroused some mixed speculations. As it was he didn't know which was worse, to have to watch Jeremy ignore Kate all evening and see her baffled unhappiness, or be forced to witness her look of glowing pleasure now that

Jeremy had at last had the decency to dance with her.

Harriet, pouncing on an empty glass with a mixture of satisfaction and disapproval, momentarily blocked his view, and Max swore impatiently. As she moved on to plump a cushion and, lips pursed, draw a chair away from the crumbling wallpaper, Max saw that Jeremy and Kate had stopped dancing and were moving towards the door. As Max watched, eyes narrowed, he caught a piece of by-play which enraged him more than anything else in the course of a long unsatisfactory evening. As Jeremy followed Kate he turned to locate Miranda, keeping him in her sights over the shoulder of a partner who had supposed he was doing rather well. With a chuck of his head and lift of his eyebrows Jeremy indicated he was being dragged off under duress. Miranda responded with a scornful twist of her mouth which Max thought exceedingly unattractive.

Anger for Kate almost drove him to interfere there and then, but what right did he have to do so? The choice to let Jeremy come tonight had been hers.

At the door Jeremy glanced back with a glance that said, 'Shan't be long,' and Miranda lifted an indifferent shoulder. Max felt as sure as she evidently did about where Jeremy would spend the night. Cursing inwardly, Max turned his attention back to Ann. Throughout the evening her casual possessiveness had increasingly annoyed him. In fairness to her, she was only assuming something which had long been tacitly accepted by their entire circle. Until recently Max had accepted it too, as part of his general feeling that his path was mapped out, offering no escape which would not be selfish and unreasonable.

Kate and Jeremy had to talk sometime, he understood that. So much had been clear when the question of inviting him arose. But to talk now, like this, so late, in the heightened atmosphere of a party during which Jeremy had been drinking steadily and with, on Kate's part certainly, emotions keyed up by the hopes and doubts and rebuffs of the evening — that seemed fraught with potential disaster. Or was his view coloured by his own feelings?

'Uncle Max, you'll let us, won't you? Everyone's starting to go home and we haven't had the galop yet. Can't we have it now? People could go on dancing afterwards.' Laura, beseeching, flushed, half a dozen eager friends at her heels, came racing across as the dance ended and caught at his doublet sleeve.

Max, dragging himself with an effort out of his thoughts, interpreted 'everyone' as her chums and 'people' as adults. 'Good idea, if it gets rid of the lot of you,' he growled. How fortunate that they would accept his surly tone as perfectly natural. 'Have a word with the band.'

'How conventional you are,' sighed Ann. 'I'm sure you'll forgive me if I don't indulge.'

'I'd be surprised if you did,' Max said sharply. At least Laura had had a happy evening, he thought as she tore off. That, after all, was what it had been about.

As the galop decorously began and everyone came hurrying to join in Max walked grimly away. He had hoped – what had he hoped? – that Kate would have got over Jeremy by now. How could he have been so simplistic? Had he believed she would see Jeremy in his true colours at Allt Farr, as though by spending a few months here she would have absorbed the disillusioned family view of him? Wasn't that a great deal to expect, Max mocked himself, when she had been naïve and blind enough to fall for him in the first place? Did she still feel Jeremy had looked after her well by sending her here? Had that blurred the fact that he had got her pregnant in the first place?

Well, it was no business of his, he reminded himself with weary anger. The pair of them practically belonged to another generation anyway; let them work it out in whatever way they liked.

Jeremy had not cut Kate out of the party (for in spite of the act for Miranda's benefit it was he who had suggested leaving) in order to have a deep soul-baring exchange. His powers of shrugging off anything difficult or disagreeable were well-developed, and by this time the disaster of Kate's pregnancy seemed far in the past. Once he had organised her flight, indeed even before the last time he had seen her, the whole episode had seemed to him dealt with, over. The reality of Kate's physical condition, the process of giving birth, the child itself, had been nothing to do with him, and he never dwelt on them. He considered in fact that he had done rather more than his duty and no lingering guilt disturbed him. Self-orientated and shallow, the news that Kate had miscarried had touched him not at all. He had read none of the pain in her careful letter, had never stretched his imagination to try to understand how a woman would feel at such a time. He had meant to reply; five minutes after putting the letter down the intention had been forgotten.

Now however, well tanked up and high on what he saw as a great welcome home, he was stirred again by the qualities which had originally drawn him to Kate, and agreeably tantalised by something new about her which appealed to him even more. He lacked the perception to recognise it as a developing confidence in herself. He saw only a more vivid look than he recalled, a gloss, a promise of something even more rewarding than their first encounter had provided. He wasn't sure it had been a good decision to bring Miranda, a last-minute ploy to deter any inconvenient clinging on Kate's part. Perhaps he had taken too negative a view. No harm in sliding off somewhere quiet and seeing what came of it. The estate room would probably be as safe as anywhere from chance interruptions, though the increasing pace and wild yells of the galop indicated that most people were well occupied for the time being.

For Kate this was the moment her hopes had been focused on ever since she had known Jeremy would be here this weekend. In her mind he was still the heroic rescuer, the tender and patient first lover (memory pleasurably exaggerating this), the person who had looked after her during those awful days when Jessie had turned her back on her with such shocking finality. Not even his offhand behaviour this afternoon had warned her. She had rationalised it because she wanted to: his friends had been there; he wouldn't want them to know what had happened. She had done the same this evening, telling herself that he had to throw himself into the party, it was expected of him.

But now the moment was here, pretence could be dropped and all she had gone through could be shared, not with strangers, however kind, but with the one person who was part of it. To have created a life, to have lost it, seemed to Kate a momentous and tragic thing.

'It's so wonderful to be with you again,' she said sincerely, as they went into the dim estate room.

It was an opening entirely to Jeremy's taste.

'We couldn't very well disappear before, could we?' he said. 'A bit obvious. And I had to do my bit.'

It was not quite what Kate had meant, but intent on the one vital issue between them she pushed it aside. 'I hope you weren't too upset when you got my letter? Perhaps I should have phoned, only I didn't quite know . . . But I do understand that you couldn't write back, you must have felt so devastated—'

'What are you talking about?' Jeremy demanded, steering her, by leaning unsteadily against her, towards the big leather armchair, a favourite of Buff's.

'I know it was your baby as well, and you must have been shattered to—'

'Oh, that. That's all over and done with, isn't it? Pretty lucky the way it worked out, though. I bet you were relieved.'

Kate froze, trying to resist his stumbling weight, needing all her concentration to take in what he had said. '*Relieved*?' It was all she could manage.

'Would have saved a lot of bother if it had happened a bit earlier, but we were lucky in the end, weren't we? Come on, Kate, forget all that. Miranda's not the easy-going type and I wouldn't put it past her to ferret us out down here, even though she's never been in the place in her life before.' He sounded as though he rather admired her for it.

'But what do you think —? What are you doing?'

'Well, be reasonable, you wanted to duck out as much as I did. Don't give me a hard time, we haven't got long.'

'But to talk,' Kate said wildly, appalled to feel his hand groping over her shoulder for her zip. 'To talk about the baby.' Even to her this sounded absurd in the circumstances, as she found the arm of the chair behind her thighs and knew she had nowhere to go but backwards and downwards.

'The baby? There's no baby, thank Christ. Come on, Kate, concentrate.'

'Get away from me, get *away*! Don't touch me!' Shocked by his words and the heedlessness of his attack, so different from all she remembered, Kate pushed at him violently.

'For God's sake, what's going on?' he demanded, aggrieved. 'You were keen enough once.'

'Let me go! How dare you touch me like that?' Or had she given him the right? The only man who had ever made love to her, the father of her child? No, no one had the right to do this to her against her will. Shaking, Kate fought free of him.

'All right, all right, don't get so het up. You should get your signals straight, you know that?'

Grumbling, petulant, but not seriously put out, Jeremy pulled his kilt straight and smoothed back his hair. 'Are you coming back or are you staying here?'

'Just go!'

He hesitated for a second as he caught the incipient sob in her voice. He was not intrinsically unkind, and she was a sweet little thing, even if she did tend to get a bit heavy. But women who cried were incredibly boring, and anyway, she lived here. He didn't have to worry about her getting home or anything. She'd sort herself out. And Miranda wouldn't wait for ever.

There was a bad moment when he met Max coming into the hall, but there were several places he could have been coming from, the Black Bog for one. 'Hi,' he said jauntily, keeping on his way.

Max seized his arm in an iron grip and swung him round. 'Where is she?'

Jeremy had the sense to see that prevarication would not serve. 'Estate room,' he said quickly. Even then he wasn't sure Max was going to let him go, realising too late that he should have remembered Kate had been accepted into the family.

Max's concern at present was not with Jeremy. He flung his arm free and was gone.

Letting out his breath in a soundless whistle of relief, but slightly surprised nevertheless at the violence of Max's reaction, Jeremy rubbed his arm and turned to take the stairs three at a time. He was well out of that.

When Max found Kate she was crying with a rough anguished sobbing quite unlike her normal restraint, her fingers driven into her hair and clutching her skull, elbows pressed together, forearms over her face.

Max, his own face tight, paused, carefully getting under control both his rage and a compassion which shook him by its intensity. Then moving quietly he crossed the room and knelt beside the chair. He didn't speak or touch Kate, waiting until some of that distraught grief had spent itself. She looked tiny. Curled up like that she took up less room than Buff. The rigid tautness slackened at last. Kate brought one hand down and pressed the back of it against her nose. With a passing smile for the cliché, Max felt in his sporran for a handkerchief.

'Kate,' he said, very gently, for he wasn't sure she knew he was there. 'Here.' He put the handkerchief against her hand and taking it fumblingly she sniffed and gulped and lifted drowned eyes to gaze at him with naked woe. He had thought she might recoil to see him, or attempt to muster some defences of apology or excuse. But she just gazed helplessly, so wounded she had no resources left for subterfuge of any kind.

'Tell me,' Max said, and his voice too was stripped of all conventional overtones. Everything else seemed so remote from this room that it no longer existed – the thronged house, the never found monotonous before. Their brief affair had meant nothing to Jeremy, his feelings had never been engaged. Yet in spite of that he had expected, taken for granted, that she would—

No! Fiercely Kate wrested her mind away from that thought, forcing herself to concentrate on what she was doing, producing fresh coffee, replenishing jugs of fruit juice, making toast, packing the dishwasher, listening to Laura and Fanny excitedly discussing the day's plans for a picnic and sailing on Alltmore loch. She was grateful for the easy friendliness of the house guests, drifting in for breakfast as and when they chose. Only Ann was unrelaxed.

She had appeared soon after Max had left, immaculate in the sort of denim shirtwaister that makes its cheaper counterparts look like rags, and seemed to be in as bad a mood as he had been, ruthlessly chivvying the Devereaux clan, four of whom were going on to Talla to fish.

'Steady on, Ann,' Colin Devereaux pleaded. 'It's less than two hours' drive, even for ordinary mortals like us. We'll come in our own time. All I want now is a lot of ice-cold orange juice, a lot of strong black coffee, and a little peace and quiet.'

'Bloody Max promised to come and now he's pretending he never said anything of the sort,' Ann complained. 'And it's not nearly as bright today, it's a pity to waste it.'

'He's not bloody Max,' Laura said. 'And he can't have promised because this whole weekend is my party and he never goes away for that.'

'Don't butt in like that, Laura,' Ann said sharply. 'Max is far too tolerant with you.'

'Do relax, Ann,' Colin Devereaux begged. 'I for one had rather a good night last night. Come on, sit down, have some more coffee.'

Kate, on her way to fetch a fresh supply of baps, saw the irritation in Ann's face and decided Max had shown good sense, both in changing his mind and temporarily vanishing. Her own tension mounted as everyone came and went, even Gus and Jan at last

departing families who should be seen off, even Jeremy who once more had taken what he wanted from life and avoided payment.

Kate's face crumpled as she attempted to speak, and she buried it in the handkerchief. Max made himself wait, not sure she would be willing to talk to him. But to Kate he seemed the natural person to tell. What had just happened was an enormity, and she needed help with it. She had come a long way from seeing Max as the arrogant, critical man of her first impressions. She had learned to accept his mood swings from tight-lipped, bad-tempered silence to riotous high spirits, knowing something of the demands placed upon him. Now she saw him in the role most fundamental to him, protector, source of strength and authority.

'He was glad,' she said blankly, her voice a wavery sound in the quiet room, and it didn't occur to her to explain who she meant. 'Glad I'd lost the baby. He couldn't see why I minded. He said, "Well, it solves everything, doesn't it?" He hadn't meant to write.'

Max, his throat hard, took her hand on his palm, and laid his other hand over it, warm and comforting. 'He's a bastard, Kate, and I'm sorry we ever gave him a second chance to hurt you. If I had my way he'd never set foot in this house again. But he's – well, it's his home, and it's not up to me to decide.' Not for the first time, he longed to be free of this link whose origins were forged in the defiance and unhappiness of another generation.

'No, of course I understand,' Kate said hurriedly. 'Anyway, he was right. It was just a shock, I suppose, to hear him –' Realising tears were threatening again, and aware of how dishevelled she must look, she made an effort to sit up. As she moved her dress slid down from her shoulder, and in embarrassment she reached for the zip.

'Kate, what the hell happened?' Max demanded, his face darkening abruptly. 'What did he do to you?'

'It was partly my own fault,' Kate confessed. 'I wanted him to come and talk, but he thought I wanted . . . Well, what I'd wanted before.'

'And you didn't?'

'No,' she said, and could not prevent the tears from rising again. 'No, I didn't.'

Chapter Twenty-Seven

Punctilious, self-contained, Kate was down early to help Mrs Grant with breakfast. No one else had surfaced yet except Max. Hearing his peremptory voice in the kitchen demanding why the porridge wasn't ready, Kate thought it a good plan to take Buff for a run, timing their return to coincide with the jeep's departure to the farm.

Looking after the guests as they straggled down she felt hollow, jittery with nerves, everything seeming just out of focus, the prospect of facing Jeremy a looming ordeal. In spite of having slept very little, she had scarcely had time to adjust to the painful difference in his view and her own of all that had taken place since they had last seen each other. During the whole time she had been at Allt Farr, there had been at the back of her mind the thought of Jeremy, idealised, a creation of her own need as she now saw but nevertheless something to hold on to. There had always been the hope of meeting him again, she could admit that now, when they met the chance of something vague and marvellous happening. Some happy ending, she ridiculed herself, tired scorn.

Jeremy had been right in a way, she had come to the conclusion in the restless hours of the short night, with dawn up before she was even in bed, the voices of the birds a perfect chorus, punctuated by the call of the cuckoo in a way

straggling down, neither very talkative, but still Jeremy didn't appear.

It was only when the breakfast room had emptied and Harriet began to clear away that Kate asked, 'What about Jeremy and Miranda?'

'Jeremy?' Harriet paused with her tray propped on the end of the sideboard, looking at Kate oddly. 'But didn't you know? Jeremy left last night, and he took Miranda with him.'

'Left?' Kate floundered, hardly able to take in the implications. 'But why?' Could it have had anything to do with her? Had she made him so angry?

'Well, I thought –' Harriet looked disconcerted and uneasy. 'Max turned him out. There was some row, wasn't there? I mean, weren't you there?'

Kate felt herself flushing hotly, wretchedly. 'Oh, Harriet, how awful. Jeremy didn't really do anything. It was my fault as much as his.'

'Well, you'll have to find out from Max. I really know nothing about it.'

Harriet didn't seem ready for her usual gossipy enjoyment of a drama and Kate felt an uncomfortable uncertainty grow in her. It was a huge relief that Jeremy had gone, and that she needn't face him again, yet there was something strange here, something she didn't like.

This conviction grew as she helped Joanna pack a basket of goodies from last night's feast to contribute to the picnic, for Joanna, pale and washed-out looking, had nothing whatsoever to say to her. Accustomed as Kate was to her reserved moods, which held her aloof from everyone, this silence had a different quality and perturbed Kate even more than Harriet's half-hints and sidelong glances. What trouble had she stirred up? Jeremy was part of this family. The last thing she had wanted was to cause friction or upheaval.

There was no opportunity to press for an explanation from Joanna now, too much was happening. Ann was crossly marshalling her party, a chaos of goodbyes was taking place in the hall as hungover people tried to get themselves together for a departure they weren't too keen on in the first place, and Buff set about a visiting labrador who had helped himself to a log from the hearth to carry about. Grannie was down, having sensibly breakfasted upstairs, and was not helping matters by saying with a hospitable zeal which Kate suspected was not as innocent as it seemed. 'Oh, don't rush off like this. It's too ridiculous, we've hardly seen you. Relax, stay for lunch . . . .'

'Tell Max I'm expecting him tomorrow,' Ann flung at Joanna as she slid into the driving seat of the Mercedes. 'And you might tell him I think he could have had the courtesy to say goodbye.'

'Tell him yourself,' Joanna retorted mutinously, in a tone so far from her usual amiability that several heads turned. Kate heard Grannie give a little snort of laughter.

'How agreeable our party has made everyone feel,' she observed wickedly. 'Now for goodness' sake let us swiftly despatch the sailors, then peace can descend.'

Once the handful of guests who had elected to do nothing at all had disposed themselves in various retreats where they hoped not to be disturbed before the next meal, Kate turned towards the kitchen. Although dinner was to be a cold buffet there were twenty people at least to cater for, depending on how many cottage dwellers tagged on, and as Joanna had gone to Alltmore with the children Harriet would need all the help she could get.

'Kate.' Grannie's hand was on her arm. 'There are plenty of people coming in to help. I wonder if you would be kind enough to spare me a few moments?'

The formality of the request, some quiet emphasis in Grannie's voice, arrested Kate.

'What is it?' she asked in quick concern. 'Aren't you well? Did you do too much last night?'

'I did,' said Grannie dryly. 'In common, it appears, with a great many other people.'

Kate felt herself blush again. Was this to be a reprimand? Was she, shock filling her at the idea, going to be asked to leave? Startled to discover how much she would mind, she stared at Grannie with troubled eyes.

'It's too cool, alas, for sitting outside, and I imagine every room in the house contains some torpid figure,' Grannie went on, so focused on what she was bracing herself to say that she was scarcely aware of Kate's anxiety. 'The workroom, I think, if you don't mind coming up there?'

'Of course not.' Automatic courtesy, but Kate's stomach was churning with apprehension as she followed Grannie's thin figure, moving more slowly since her fall this winter, up the narrow stairs.

It had given her time to think, however, and she blurted out at once as Grannie waved her to a seat across the corner of the cluttered table, 'I should have been the one to go. Jeremy's part of the family.'

'Absolutely not,' Grannie said, rather startled by this seizing of the initiative. 'Don't leap in like that. Please sit down and let me do the talking for the moment.'

Though she felt a deep and habitual reluctance to dredge up old grief and pain, and though she had slept even less than Kate as long-buried memories came flooding back, as sharp as if the stoical acceptance of the years had never been fought for and achieved, still Grannie had no difficulty in going straight to the point.

'We hold ourselves entirely to blame for your having to endure that disgraceful and distressing scene last night. We know Jeremy, and we should never have exposed you to his insensitivity and arrogance.'

'But –' Kate was dumbfounded. 'But you asked me if I minded. You gave me the choice and I thought we should meet – I wanted it.' She was ashamed to admit it, but felt it must be made clear.

'I know. And that's where we failed you. We allowed Jeremy to put pressure on us because he didn't want to miss the party –

and doubtless had in mind his usual shooting later – and then we left the decision to you. We should have discussed it properly, all of us, and at least added to the equation our knowledge of Jeremy – our bitter experience of his ways, perhaps I should more accurately say. My dear, we should have looked after you better, and I cannot tell you how remorseful I feel that we did not.'

'Oh, Grannie.' Even in her astonishment at this unexpected point of view, Kate's sympathy with another person's feelings did not desert her. 'It wasn't your fault in any way. I'm just so unused to – well, I haven't had many relationships, hardly any, in fact. I don't think I know how to behave. Apparently I send the wrong signals or something.' Jeremy's phrase, and although she tried to use it lightly, the words made her wince. 'It was all my fault.' That was the conclusion to which her sleepless night had brought her.

'No, Kate, listen to me.' Grannie's voice was definite, her eyes compelling, and her surprisingly strong old hand came out to grip Kate's firmly. 'And don't say a word. Do you promise? For I don't know how I shall manage to get through this if you interrupt me.'

Kate nodded, unable to imagine what was coming, but without her former apprehension. There seemed nothing threatening here, though she did have a feeling of being about to sail uncharted waters.

'Jeremy has always been the most worthless young man in the world,' Mrs Munro began, and now her eyes were lowered to their linked hands on the table, her keen face fallen into grim lines. 'I have been the one to refuse to admit it. His family and ours have been friends, and remotedly linked by kinship, for three generations at least. His – they owned a small estate,' (small in Allt Farr terms, Kate supposed, with a flicker of amusement) 'near Dalwhinnie, but his mother was essentially a social animal and refused to spend a moment more there than she was obliged to. She took Jeremy, whom she had produced rather late in life and who as I expect you know was the only child, to all the usual jet-set playgrounds with her, to the detriment of his character and education.' She broke off for a moment, with a sudden searching look into Kate's face. 'Selfish to the last,' she muttered, apparently to herself, with swift anger. 'Does this hurt you? Even after what he did, is there still some feeling? Of course I should have asked you that, forgive me.'

'No,' Kate said hurriedly. 'I think – well, I think I need to know this somehow. As though it will put things into perspective. Don't worry about hurting me. I feel incapable of feeling much today anyway. Please go on.'

'Therapy for whom?' Grannie enquired, again addressing herself with irony. 'Well,' she resumed, 'it's history now. Jeremy grew up to be irresponsible, spoiled, materialistic, and a good deal less charming than he believes himself to be. He is also dyslexic, which he uses as his excuse for failing at almost all he has attempted. He has sufficient private means to indulge in failure. He was sixteen when his parents were killed with Joanna's husband in that frightful tragedy, and he came to live here while Max took on the running of his estate for him – it was in trust till he was twenty-one. Jeremy will doubtless have told you most of this. It was immensely demanding for Max as his hands were pretty well full with all that needed to be done on Allt Farr, but he did it because – well, as I told you, there were many links between the families. But as soon as Jeremy owned it outright he sold the place, without a second's hesitation, and how much of his capital he has gone through by now I dread to think. But he's never worried because he has always known he'll be looked after by us and has every intention, I am convinced, of battening on us and being supported by us till the end of the chapter. *Had* every intention. For last night Max sent him packing.'

Kate made an involuntary movement of protest. Whatever had happened between her and Jeremy seemed too trivial to affect these long-established ties. She had no wish to be the reason for them being broken.

'I know what you're thinking,' Grannie said, giving her hand a little shake to still her objections. 'But this had to come. You are only the catalyst. And what rich irony, don't you think, that it should have been Jeremy who sent you here? You mustn't feel concerned, however. We have known for a long time that Jeremy was abusing his position here, only I was too obstinate to see it, too cowardly to let Max do what he so justifiably and correctly did last night. Even then he was careful to consult me. Well, I think you could call it consulting,' she amended, with her little bark of laughter. She went on briskly, 'No, Kate, don't waste your concern on Jeremy. All he'll miss here will be free holidays and somewhere to bring his friends for shooting and stalking. His affections don't come into it. Anyway, he's a self-replacing animal, very like the giant octopus, and nothing will ultimately harm him. Till his funds run out, perhaps.' She looked as though the prospect did not disturb her.

'I knew, really,' Kate said, her voice flat. 'I just didn't let myself see. I needed to hold on to — well, some belief that what had happened between us had some meaning. How many females have said that, I wonder?'

Grannie gave a little huff, eyebrows raised in cynical agreement.

'What I don't understand, though,' Kate pursued diffidently, 'is why you let him stay with you for so long, if you knew all this. Was there nowhere else he could have gone?'

It was the gentleness of the question, its naturalness and sincerity, which caught at Grannie. For so long she had lived with oppressive secrets, tangled motives, guilt, all kept in high relief by Jeremy's presence in the family. She knew in her heart she had been clinging to something which no longer existed, had never truly existed in the way she had wanted it to. She could speak of it to no one, least of all Max, the only person who knew the truth, since Max had been the one to suffer most from her insistence on this tenuous bond.

Kate would not judge her. Kate with her rare innocence would accept this old, sad story as it had truly been. Suddenly Grannie needed that, needed to unburden herself, to confess as it were while there was still time. She was so tired of never giving in.

She leaned back in her chair, head up, bony austere profile to Kate. 'They are brothers,' she said. 'Half brothers. Jeremy's father was Max's father.'

For one speechless moment as her brain scrambled to piece this together – the baby the grandchild of Grannie's lover, Max's niece or nephew – Kate sat stunned. Then with her natural instinct to give comfort she came to her feet and wrapped her arms round Grannie's stiff shoulders, pressing her cheek against the white, rough, springy hair.

'Oh, Kate,' Grannie said, her voice breaking. She closed her eyes and let the comfort of that spontaneous embrace spread through her, assuaging a culpability which already, after that simple admission, seemed outworn and strangely stripped of power.

Chapter Twenty-Eight

Kate turned off the track below the Old Byre, and crossed the slope of sheep-nibbled turf and lichened boulders to where the gable end and ruined walls of a cottage stood above the burn. Out of sight of track, steading and big house, this sunny place was a perfect refuge, with its pair of rowans thick with creamy scented blossom arching over the old gateway, grass starred with a dozen wildflowers from tormentil and alpine lady's-mantle to heartsease and spotted orchis, and a long view down the course of the burn to the hazy blue distances beyond Kirkton.

Kate followed the narrow path made by sheep down the steep bank and went to perch on her favourite rock slab above the foaming rush of water. She loved this place, and urgently needed its seclusion and peace. There was so much to assimilate and order in her mind, and till now there had been little opportunity to go over all she had learned from Grannie yesterday. As ever when a crowd of friends was filling house and cottages, the day had been taken up with people looking in for drinks before lunch, borrowing things, demanding help with a car that wouldn't start or a dog with a cut pad, carrying the family off for return entertainment, organising a knock-out tournament of tennis, croquet and putting, raiding the library, using the telephone. Everyone had gathered for the buffet in the evening, which had started late and turned into another lively feast. Scathing comments on the failure of some of the young to perform adequately in the reels the night before had resulted in a Scottish dancing lesson which had proved so popular it went on till midnight.

This morning, however, everyone had gone. That had meant three cottages to change, the job of all jobs Kate least liked, but they were done and ready for 'arbs' to arrive this afternoon. At present Kate was all in favour of arbs. At least they stayed under their own roofs and organised their own entertainment.

She grinned, propping herself on her arms and turning up her face to the sun, which felt much warmer down here than even ten feet higher on the exposed bank. She liked the hurly-burly really, she could just use a little space. Normally they would have gone to Riach as this was Sunday, but just as they were starting lunch Harriet had taken an abrupt phone call from James, saying he wouldn't welcome an invasion.

'Do you suppose he's ill?' Harriet had asked. 'Do you think one of us should go over, just in case? I mean, he's all on his own there, and what use would Dot and Bridie be?'

Kate had seen a tart, 'Quite as much as you', reluctantly suppressed by Grannie.

'Plunging into social life again evidently hasn't sweetened his character,' Max had remarked, and Kate had seen him look quickly at a silent Joanna.

'The poor man has probably been tired of the whole rigmarole for ages, and all this gadding about and socialising has made him brave enough to say so,' Grannie had added, in the tone of one closing the discussion. 'Please pass the salad.'

Joanna had still said nothing, but a quick tide of red had risen in her cheeks, and getting up abruptly she had gone to the Aga, burying her face briefly in the oven, returning with more baked potatoes to offer surprised people with full plates. But when Laura and Fanny began to wail that they had wanted to see the twins she had snapped with uncharacteristic anger,

'You heard what James said. He doesn't *want* us there,' reducing them to startled and scrupulous silence.

As Grannie had remarked yesterday, the party didn't seem to have done a great deal for people's tempers, Kate reflected. At any rate, suddenly for her the afternoon was blank, her own. The little girls were riding, Laura perched absurdly on an obliging Torquil wearing a butter-wouldn't-melt-in-the-mouth expression which in Kate's opinion one could have enough of.

Harriet had taken the chance to nip down (her words) to Letitia's, bearing half a ham and most of a salmon mousse. Max had seemed to think it was essential to Flymo the cottage lawns before he set off for Talla. Joanna had disappeared.

It was so odd, now, to look at the three of them in the light of her new knowledge. In that startling interlude snatched from the busy weekend yesterday morning, Grannie had talked in a swift releasing rush, the walls of habit, social conditioning and natural discretion tumbling down in a mixture of relief and, even now, ironic disapproval at her own weakness.

'Why should I burden you with all this?' she had broken off once to demand, with a little grimace of disgust, but it was a token question. The flood of memories, once set free, had been impossible to check.

Harriet had been born at the height of Grannie's unhappiness and despair, a year after her marriage, when she had had time to realise to the full Hector Munro's determination to lead precisely the life he had led as a bachelor, his extravagance, his unaltered need for new sexual conquests, and his complete lack of interest in the responsibilities he had inherited with Allt Farr.

'I loathed poor Harriet,' Grannie had said flatly, her hands turning and smoothing as she talked a piece of emerald velvet she had abstractedly picked up. 'It wasn't her fault, of course, but she was a most unappealing baby, puny, pale, with a beaky face and wispy ginger hair which never seemed to thicken. Always wailing, always arching herself backwards like a bow so that you couldn't hold her properly. Or certainly I never could. And there were problems with the nannies, so that around her there was an endless aura of difficulties and — yes — repulsiveness. I was repelled by her.'

As Grannie had reinforced the word, her hooded eyes remote and bleak, Kate guessed she had never before allowed herself to use it even in her mind.

'Her presence was forever tied up for me with the dreadful, helpless misery of that time. There was so little then that a young wife in such a situation could do. Go home again? My pride rose up in horror at such a solution, such an admission. I evaded another pregnancy successfully for six years, quite a feat in those days, but Hector — well, that doesn't matter. The fact was that by the time I was carrying Joanna my affair with Randolph Liddell, Jeremy's father, had begun. My solace and my sanity.'

Her voice had changed utterly, and Kate had sat very still, dreading to intrude on a memory which could bring such a note to Grannie's voice after thirty-six years, such a softened look to the autocratic old face.

'Though Joanna was Hector's daughter, just as Harriet was, I myself was a different person by the time she was born. I knew my life wouldn't alter in practical terms — Randolph and I were both married, and both had more to consider than our own wishes — but now, for me, there was love, and the world was changed. And then, Joanna was a totally different baby from Harriet. I don't pretend that it was fair, indeed I have lived with the knowledge of my unfairness ever since, but she charmed and delighted me, so good-natured and smiling, so irresistible with her shining amber curls and her dimples. And she always seemed so deliciously wholesome where poor Harrie had been — well, never a child you longed to pick up or hold. Joanna went right through all the barriers of how I felt about Hector, how I'd thought I felt about babies. I'd come to the conclusion that I was an appalling and unnatural mother, but after all I found I had a few normal instincts. Then, most luckily, I acquired a marvellous nannie so the whole nursery scene fell smoothly into place, and that counted for a great deal, you know.'

She had paused, her narrow veined hand with its swollen arthritic knuckles looking very old against the glowing colour of the velvet she still held, then had continued rapidly in a more prosaic tone. 'Things became very difficult for a time. Financially. Harriet had to go to a horrid local school, for which she has never forgiven me to this day. I had to do a great many things I had never expected to do for myself, though no one thinks twice about them nowadays. When Max was born Hector accepted him as his son – he had very much wanted a son – but his behaviour became even more outrageous. He lived abroad more and more, mostly in the West Indies. Allt Farr stood empty for most of the year. Such a sad place it became. Hector died in St Kitts, in circumstances which to this day I cannot bear to think about, and as soon as we could we came back here to try to make the estate pay its way. Randolph helped us out, just as he had been helping quietly for years, but Max accepted responsibility for Allt Farr, and for all of us, from that moment on. He went to Cirencester instead of university, and – well, you have seen for yourself how hard he works.'

Grannie sounded almost dismissive as she wound up her story abruptly, as though putting unwelcome thoughts back in a drawer and slamming it shut. 'There, not an edifying tale. I am grateful to you for listening.' Clearly she had already half regretted succumbing to the indulgence of telling it.

Understanding that, Kate had said quietly, 'I think you are very brave,' and could not know how much the simple words had meant to the sharp-tongued, embattled, independent old lady.

So much had been explained, Kate thought, watching an almost motionless kestrel hover against shapely mounds of cumulus so densely white they looked as though you could dig your hands into them and come away with whole fistfuls. Harriet's defensiveness in particular, her position eternally on the sidelines, her mother's damaging impatience with her, all fell into context. Of the three siblings Joanna had been the lucky one, achieving the best of everything, legitimacy with love, good looks with charm, marriage and a child. Though tragedy had come even to her, leaving her with that look of incompleteness, of never being quite in touch with what was going on around her.

And Max. His was undoubtedly the most intriguing part of the story. Why had she never noticed before how different he looked from the others, with his leaner, rangier lines and straight fair hair? Tall and fair like Jeremy, though with his mother's striking dark eyes. But his fairness wasn't the same as Jeremy's, Kate objected with a quick denial she didn't pause to question. Jeremy's hair was the colour of golden syrup. She shivered. How thankful she felt to be free of him, and of the pathetic fantasies she had allowed herself to build around him.

Her thoughts went back to Max. How hard on him not to know who his father was until after Randolph Liddell had drowned in that yachting accident. How he must have wished he could have thanked him, acknowledged his support. That must be something that dragged at him still. Then Max, in his turn, had done all he could to help Jeremy, his half-brother. And Mrs Munro, still loving Randolph in spite of his holding firmly to his own marriage – had she felt that taking his younger son into her family was a means of repaying him for all he had given her? Or had she done it out of simple love for him?

How incredible, really, how courageous, to have told Max all this. But they were very close, these two, in a way Mrs Munro could never be with her daughters, even with Joanna. She would have seen telling Max as an obligation of honour. He was the head of the family, but more than that, she had believed he had a right as an individual to know, and to share the decision about Jeremy. At least there had been honesty, she thought, her thoughts going inevitably to Jessie. But had there? For years Max had not known the truth of his parentage any more than she herself had done.

Whatever he had thought or felt Max had assumed responsibility for Jeremy without question, presumably accepting that for Grannie he was part of the deepest emotional area of her life. And now she, Kate, had destroyed that link. It was an awesome thought. Yet Grannie had seemed actually relieved, as though finally relinquishing something as ephemeral as Kate's own dreams of Jeremy had been.

She tried to picture, in the light of her new knowledge, the scene at Allt Farr when Jeremy had first asked if she could come here. Embarrassment filled her to imagine the sort of person they must have expected, swiftly followed by new doubt about her right to be here. Jeremy had not concealed his surprise that she had stayed when there was no longer any need to do so, obviously not attaching much importance to her fulfilling what she regarded as her part of the bargain.

One of the gleaming clouds, shredding westwards under a gathering wind, reached long fingers across the sun and even in this sheltered spot the temperature instantly dropped, the air off the tumbling water turning chill. Kate glanced at her watch. She should go back and find Laura and Fanny and get everything ready for an early start tomorrow, and make sure they'd remembered their homework. Laura usually took the view that the least painless method was to get it out of the way at once, but this Friday it would have been the last thing on her mind.

Tempted by the smooth dry slabs Kate began to rock-hop homewards down the burn, a beguiling sport to which Laura had introduced her and one which required total attention. She had reached the level where the track swung in close to the water, a place impossible now to believe had been so scary in the snow on that first trip up to the Old Byre, when with the uncomfortable sensation of exposure which being watched when unconscious of it brings, she saw the Fourtrak parked there, Max leaning against the bonnet, arms folded.

Feeling caught out, childish, Kate leapt up onto the bank and finished the last few yards on the track. Max must be checking sheep, or planning repairs to the road, certainly on some business that had nothing to do with her, but even so she found it hard to walk towards him naturally.

'I'd hoped to catch you,' he said abruptly, pushing himself upright, his face unsmiling. 'I saw you come up this way.'

Kate said nothing. She had long grown used to the astonishing ability, which everyone here seemed to share, to spot from miles away in the apparently deserted landscape a hobbling ewe, a weasel flicking into a hole in a dyke, or the most infinitesimal movements of deer against their natural camouflage.

'I think we need to talk,' Max went on, and Kate's stomach turned over. He was going to tell her she must go after all. Sending Jeremy packing had been an impulse of anger. Jeremy was one of the family and that was ultimately what counted. Kate had no way of evaluating how profoundly she had been affected by Jessie's rejection, or the shattering of the comfortable image of her real parents which had been part of her concept of herself as she grew up. The slightest tug to the fragile roots she had put down here made her feel unnervingly vulnerable again, unsure of herself, unwanted.

'Come and perch here,' Max said, then as she turned after a tiny hesitation to the lip of bank he indicated, 'Or is there something else you want to be doing?'

It was so unlike him to consider such a possibility that Kate smiled involuntarily. 'Only to round up things for school and give the children tea.'

'They're quite capable of sorting themselves out.' Max spoke dismissively, but he was glad of her smile, for he had not much enjoyed Kate's look of apprehension as she caught sight of him.

'I thought you were going to Talla,' she said, on what she hoped was a note of easy enquiry, as she took the hand he offered and jumped down the bank.

'I wanted to make sure you were all right,' he said, frowning at the reference. 'There hasn't been a chance to talk since – since the night of the party.'

Recalling the last time they had been alone, and her shocked distress and tears, Kate coloured, concentrating on choosing a place to sit, setting her feet among the water-bleached stones of heavy river gravel. A dipper darted along the further bank, flashed under water, emerging a moment later to bob at them from a rock.

'I'm fine, thank you,' she said, watching it with concentration. 'It was good of you to look after me.'

'Kate.' In the moment that she turned her head to look up at him with those candid brown eyes, he knew there were a dozen things he could have said to her there and then, without doubt or hesitation. But his feelings were not the only ones involved and, indeed, were so barely acknowledged, that he knew most of what he wanted to say must wait.

'My mother told me what you and she talked about yesterday,' he began, sticking resolutely to what he had sought Kate out to discuss.

My mother; he rarely used the phrase. In a flash of insight it occurred to Kate that with Grannie's fear of not being a 'normal' mother she might have refused the 'Mum' or 'Mummy' of childhood. Had 'Grannie', once Laura had been born, provided a convenient intimate form for them all?

'I want you to know I'm glad she did,' Max continued. 'It's right that you should know the situation, but even more importantly I want you to be sure that we're grateful for what you brought about. No, don't say anything for a minute. We've never had any illusions about Jeremy, and he's not going to change. I was willing to help him when he wanted you to come here, not because he's my brother, but because of how Grannie felt about his father. As long as she wanted to hold on to that tie, I would support her. Harriet and Joanna have never known, never need know.'

'It's really none of my —' Kate began, and he swung round on her impatiently. Close at her shoulder like that, overtopping her by inches, his face in shadow, he looked actually threatening, and she stopped hastily.

'It's your business to this extent,' Max said forcefully. 'I don't want you getting any silly ideas about being obliged to leave because Jeremy has been kicked out. He'll drift back eventually, knowing him, but not while you're here. At present we have a clean slate, all of us. Sorry if that was brutally put,' he caught himself up, remembering in what manner the slate had been wiped clean for Kate, 'but the decision to go or stay is entirely yours. Knowing,' as Kate nervously opened her mouth, 'that we want you to be here.' That much he could allow himself to say.

There was a moment's pause, during which Max found himself unable to watch Kate's face, instead letting his eyes follow the busy curve of water past his boot toes. Although he couldn't remember when he had last felt so tense, so deeply concerned about someone else's feelings, part of his brain still said, Must get a load of quarry stones in here, this bank's so undercut there'll be none of it left soon.

After a moment which seemed to him to last for ever Kate managed to say, and he had to bend his head to catch the words over the brisk voice of the water, 'I was clinging to the thought of Jeremy – of everything being all right. I do cling to things. I'm not much good at standing on my own feet. But it was only a fantasy I'd let myself build up, it was never real. He never gave me the slightest reason to expect anything. But it seems awful that what happened between Jeremy and me should affect your relationship with him, yours and Grannie's. It's so unimportant compared with—'

'Kate, what he did to you wasn't unimportant. And something had to snap eventually. There had to be some sort of catalyst and you provided it.'

Grannie had used the same word. Kate looked across the burn, up the steep slope beyond it where emerald grass now washed up to the young green of bracken and higher to the still-dark heather. There was so much to discover here, a richness she had never previously experienced and could not imagine finding again, by sheer chance, anywhere else.

'I'd hate to go,' she said quietly, and to Max, though he greedily seized upon the words, it seemed she was hardly speaking to him at all.

Chapter Twenty-Nine

Joanna lay on her back on the stripped divan in the bedroom of the students' flat. With its sloping ceiling and small closed gable window the room seemed confined, airless, resistant to invasion as unused rooms become. Flies buzzed against the panes; yesterday's flies dotted the sill. Joanna felt suspended, without direction or motivation, in the stifling air and blanketing afternoon silence, suspended in rare inactivity and hopeless concession to defeat.

James's tentative return to the ordinary friendly intercourse of glen life, his emergence from reclusive grief, would never survive his discovery that Kate still cared about Jeremy. Not once, even in the darkest times after Camilla's death, had he barred them from Riach. Today's telephone call was so unlike him, so harsh and telling, that Joanna had to accept she had not exaggerated his attraction to Kate.

This had been one of the longest weekends of her life, she decided, struggling for Laura's sake to maintain the party mood, going to Alltmore yesterday to help with the barbecue, rub down goose-pimpled sailors, act as loader at the clays, then returning to a thronged Allt Farr, helping with that huge buffet, taking part in the dancing. And all the time she had been rushing in her mind from the conviction that she should have gone after James, to help and comfort him even if she held her tongue about her own feelings, to the opposite conviction that she had been right to let him go, and must never let him guess for an instant how she felt.

For Joanna, it had always been James. Even before they had come to live permanently at Allt Farr (her childhood dream) the year for her had revolved round the visits they were able to make when the house and shooting weren't let. The vital factor had always been whether James would be at Riach, staying with the unmarried cousin from whom he eventually inherited the estate.

What bright visions there had been, hugged to herself, shared with no one, when deliverance had come and the Munros had left London for good. The naïve absurdity of those hopes, the seventeen-year-old confidence that because she so passionately wanted something it would happen, made Joanna wince now. It was hard to disentangle at this distance the dazzling upswings alternating with periods of utter hopelessness which had swept her along through the years that followed, against the unchanging background of old friendships, hard work and the almost equally energetic pursuits of leisure, golf and riding, tennis and parties.

Camilla had been there from the beginning, distantly related to James and, though Joanna could still not admit it without a jealous wrench that shamed her, perfect for him. She had had, as the twins did, a huge exuberance which was entirely good-natured. She didn't jolly James out of his shyness or the withdrawn moods that could overtake him when social demands hassled him too severely; she just accepted them, rode over them as though they were a normal part of life, like her car breaking down on the way to play in a Spring medal she had every chance of winning, or being thrown hunting on the first day out of the season and breaking both wrists. Camilla had been a lively, vivid, able person, supremely fitted to run James and run Riach. Not that she had had the slightest interest in the house; Sybilla at four would make a more competent housekeeper than her mother. In spite of her misery Joanna laughed aloud. And that, she thought, summed Camilla up. Nearly three years after her death, a death bizarre and swift, the thought of her brought laughter.

It had been a sunny afternoon like this, the twins asleep, house and farm at Riach drowsing and deserted. Camilla had been up in the loft above the old stables. No one had ever known why she had wanted it but she had been hauling a monstrous old iron griddle to the hatch and had suddenly started to cough and choke. One of the men had just driven into the open shed next door and when he turned off the tractor he had heard her. Running to see what was wrong he had been too late to prevent her falling, flailing and already semi-conscious, onto her head on the cobbles below, the griddle coming with her and completing a job already done twice over, according to the post-mortem.

Even now Joanna could not properly order her feelings about Camilla – affection certainly, even if it had been threaded with envy for her buoyant confidence, and indignation at her sweeping assertiveness. And admiration. That had been the fundamental problem. She had so admired Camilla, blessed with an ability and competence Joanna could never emulate, that she had fled, cravenly relinquishing the field. She had gone back to London, taken a job helping a friend running an agency for holiday accommodation at the dizzily priced top end of the market, and through Suzanne Liddell, Jeremy's mother, had met Simon.

Should she have given James longer? After all these years the question still beset her. He had shown no greater interest in Camilla than he had in her. But she had been so afraid of loving where love was not returned. There seemed no stable adult relationship in her world on which to draw for guidance or reassurance. But James, as dilatory and unsure of himself as ever, had not got around to proposing to Camilla, though few doubted she had taken the initiative, until two years later, by which time Joanna, already rashly married, had discovered how little she liked the lifestyle Simon preferred.

Oh, God, why am I going over all this, she thought, sitting up on the not very comfortable bed, angry at the tears which had taken her unawares. This is about now, about James. She had deliberately hidden herself away here, where no one would think of looking for her, to decide what to do about James. Had she thrown away the one precious chance she would have when she had hesitated and turned into the morning-room to avoid him as he walked away from the dancing at Laura's party? The memory of his stricken face filled her with fresh pain. But if he had just received such a blow about Kate, it was scarcely the moment to intrude her own needs and feelings. And if he cared about her he would have shown it long ago, turned to her for help.

This wasn't about her. At this moment, alone at Riach, what must James be feeling? The important thing was not to let him slide back into solitude and depression. Was that merely an excuse to go over there, alone, as she had longed to do a thousand times since she had come back to Allt Farr?

She had never had the courage to do it. Instead she had opted for being in the glen again, accepting the affection of old friendship and nothing more. She had seen James always in the safe context of the family group, setting her face against intolerable dreams. Until Kate had arrived it had been possible to live like that, for James had been so sunk in inactivity that it had been difficult to imagine a relationship ever developing. But Kate had charmed him, with her shyness deeper than his own, her quietness, her incongruity in this new scene, even her absurd mistakes and incompetence. How bitterly rebuffed he must have felt at seeing the glow of happiness Jeremy's arrival had produced in her.

Jeremy – another puzzle Joanna wanted to think over. All power to Kate if she had been the means to heave this particular cuckoo out of the nest. In Joanna's opinion, and Harriet's too as far as she could ever get one together, Max and Grannie had gone overboard in their allegiance to the Liddell family, good friends though they had been.

Joanna swung her feet to the floor, leaned her elbows on her knees and put her head in her hands, the mane of curly red-gold hair flopping forwards. Get to the bottom line, she told herself. James really fancies Kate and when he knows Jeremy is out of the picture again there's no reason to believe he won't resume his pursuit of her. Kate has been oblivious of James till now, but had probably been clinging to thoughts of Jeremy. None of this changes a thing between James and you.

Joanna knew she was not cut out to be one of those people who alter the course of events. She liked life to flow easily along. If she had learned anything from loneliness and unhappiness it was that no one can radically change what he or she is.

There was another consideration. She stirred restlessly, with a trapped feeling Max would have recognised. She owed something to the family. To enable them to live here and keep the house going they had agreed to unite their efforts and resources. It meant she could offer Laura the most important thing in the world, the opportunity to grow up at Allt Farr, as Joanna herself had longed to do. They were committed, all of them. Nothing had changed.

James, immobile in the deep chair in his sitting-room where he had spent untold hours in the past three years, let the familiar buffer, laziness, build its wall round him again. The whisky bottle was beside him, though he rarely stirred himself to fill his glass. He was adept at this, achieving the empty mind, the defence of a wounded animal turning its resources inwards. He was glad he had stopped the Munros coming. They had provided a lifeline he could not have done without after Camilla had died but he didn't need it now. This was a different pain. For he had seen himself through Kate's eyes, and the picture had been disturbing.

The twins, after raising a storm of protest on finding Laura and Fanny weren't coming, were playing with their old paddling pool, indifferent to the fact that yesterday's temperature, for which it had been dragged out, squashed, grimy and smelly, had not been repeated today. Getting bored eventually, abandoned by

Bridie who had gone in to watch the bit of *EastEnders* she had missed on Thursday (Dot liked to watch all the episodes and the repeat as well), they had dragged the pool across to the scummy pond at the back of the stable and launched it. As it had suffered on the journey it sank at once. Their screams alerted the grieve who hauled them out, swearing and cuffing them, ordered them to stand in the yard while he phoned Bridie, then hosed them down without mercy, deaf to their protests. Bridie hung at the kitchen door till the credits rolled, then took herself across to the farm.

James slept.

To Kate, unaware of these undercurrents, life seemed to have emerged onto a level shining plain, the single remaining source of pain resolutely buried. Even the question as to what she would do when the season came to an end was unalarming, not only because the date was vague and distant but because she believed her new-found confidence would not desert her. Also, from comments made by Joanna and Elaine Moncrieff, Fanny's mother, it seemed she would not have to search for a new job alone.

'Just say the word. Dozens of people will be waiting to grab you up,' was how Elaine put it, and the breezy exaggeration was very comforting.

Events, in any case, were bundling Kate along in the authentic Allt Farr manner. Max had finally departed for Talla but had returned a day later, with little to say about the fishing or anything else, and as soon as he was back a spate of minor dramas caught them up. Someone set fire to the hearthrug in the ill-fated Burn Cottage, which came in for its third round of decorating; an inept female, recently divorced and staring at the world with eyes as uncomprehending and alarmed as Kate felt her own must have been when she first arrived, blocked the sink of another cottage by emptying the chip pan down it, then stood the electric kettle on a lighted ring of the cooker; a lamb stuck itself to melted tar and had to be freed with oil, and on Riach and Allt Farr clipping began.

Another party was held on midsummer's eve, to celebrate the opening of Gilbert's pool, a major stage in the water garden he had been laying out with Grannie's help, though sadly that was restricted these days to bossing and ordaining. The following day the two of them left for the Baltic.

'My turn to choose at last,' Grannie gloated. 'How tired I am of all those earnest intellectual cruises from one fragment of ruined temple to another. Those droning interminable lectures when one is gasping for a huge gin and tonic. Everyone raving about the classic light of Greece. Blinding glare on blinding stone, I say. I'm not a cypress-and-olive enthusiast and how I detest being hot. So this time it's cool grey Stockholm and Helsinki, a little Sibelius, a few onion domes in the distance, and back in time for Wimbledon.'

'At least we can look forward to that,' grumbled Gilbert, who would have gone to the Arctic with Grannie if required. He just hoped no one would suggest it.

Kate missed Grannie enormously. She had gone away once or twice before, but only briefly. Two days for the York Spring Meeting had been more than enough, as she had freely confessed when she came wearily back. And though she talked about Wimbledon, this year for the first time she would be watching it from home.

It was while Grannie and Gilbert were away that tragedy struck Harriet's life. Kate was in the kitchen guiltily topping up the water in the stock pan which had been left in her charge on the back of the Aga and which she had allowed to get dangerously low, when Harriet came blundering along the stone passage, gulping and distraught as the tears she had held back all the way home overtook her. Ever afterwards she was glad it was Kate who was there, the one person before whom it didn't seem to matter abandoning herself to grief.

'Harriet! Oh, poor Harrie, whatever is it?'

Kate leapt to help her, actually thinking for one terrified moment, so clumsy and fumbling were Harriet's movements, that she had done something to her eyes.

'Sit down, sit here. Tell me what's wrong.'

Harriet clutched Kate's hand, sinking down obediently on the settle as though her legs would not support her a second longer. 'Letitia. It's Letitia,' she gasped out.

Kate's mind flew to the rough-and-ready little house, Letitia sawing logs, climbing on the roof to clean her chimney, knocking together runs for her endless poultry. Or the motorbike. 'Harriet, tell me, what's happened to Letitia?' Where had Max said he would be? God, he was in Perth, at the umpteenth meeting about the Bridge of Riach bypass. Joanna had taken some seedlings down to Alltmore so that Penny could plant them in the cool of the evening.

'It's nothing, nothing's happened,' Harriet said. 'Not anything that matters to anyone.'

Her panicky thoughts checked, Kate looked down at the bowed sandy head, the balled-up handkerchief Harriet was scrubbing angrily at her face, the shaking shoulders, and with a new, almost deeper concern, sat down and slipped an arm round her.

'It matters to you, whatever it is,' she said gently. 'Can't you tell me? Wouldn't it help?'

'You're the only person I could tell,' Harriet said fiercely. 'At least you won't laugh at me.'

'Of course I won't laugh,' Kate soothed. Indeed she felt closer to tears, seeing this wild disintegration.

Letitia was leaving the glen. She had learned that her brother, with whom she had fought so bitterly when he had inherited not only the family farm in Wales, but every penny of their father's money as well so that he could run it, had died and left it all to her.

'Of course, it's marvellous for her,' Harriet insisted, good behaviour outweighing selfishness as it always would. 'I'm really glad. Sorry about her brother, of course. But I don't think I can face it, going on here without her. I mean, we've been such friends, we can talk about things, it's always, well, so sort of easy being with her. I can't describe it.'

Even Kate, innocent as she was, had long ago agreed with Grannie's assessment of the true source of Harriet's ease with Letitia.

'I know I'll get over it, and it is best for her. It's wonderful for her, in fact, she's always loved that farm. I didn't let her see I minded, I just made some sort of excuse and came away. But, oh, Kate, it will be so awful.' And bowing her head on the table Harriet wept again, with a blank hopelessness that went to Kate's heart.

Chapter Thirty

No one teased Harriet. She went around red-eyed and pinch-lipped, all her hurrying officiousness muted, with a look of having been dealt a blow she had not seen coming and against which she had had no defence. She was thankful that no one but Kate had been there to see how she had gone to pieces when the blow fell, but that seemed the only good thing in the miserable days.

Joanna was too sunk in her own preoccupations to do more than say kindly, 'Oh, poor Harrie, you'll really miss Letitia, won't you?' There were always so many things going on at Allt Farr, and Harriet was involved in so many glen activities, that her life wouldn't change all that much, would it?

Max saw more, having reached the same conclusion as his mother and Kate about the relationship with Letitia. He knew the merest hint at its true nature would have deeply shocked and distressed Harriet, but he was sure that, unacknowledged as it certainly was, there was more here than simple friendship. If only Harriet would take her courage in both hands and refuse to let this source of happiness be taken from her. Or was the option not open to her? It was easy to imagine that Letitia's dependence on his sister might not be as great as Harriet's on her. And, apart from that, Harriet clung more tenaciously than any of them to the known, safe pattern of glen life, hardly ever accepting an invitation which took her away from it, secure in a round of duties and events that carried her busily through the year. It would be a huge step for her to consider cutting away these props which underpinned her existence.

He was nearly as bad himself, Max readily admitted, moodily staring at the computer on which he was bringing up the tedious inescapable weekly drudge of the wages. He was locked into a repetitive round of farming, shooting and stalking, increasingly feeling, especially where the maintenance of the house was concerned, that he was running to keep up and not always succeeding. That wet rot in the east wing should be dealt with without delay, half the roof valleys were leaking and there wasn't a window that didn't need renewing. Though it had seemed a feasible solution at the time for the family to club together to keep the place going they had created a self-perpetuating problem for themselves, and one which would get further out of control every year unless they spent a great deal more on upkeep than they could afford.

Was this really what he wanted till the end of his days? He knew it wasn't. His restlessness had been growing for some time and this summer had crystallised into a frustration he could hardly bear. Yet what alternative was there?

His thoughts turned, inevitably, to Ann. She had been part of his life for so long that she seemed inextricably linked with any decision about his commitment to Allt Farr. She was sending him clear signals – the kind you make with a cannon, not a hoist of flags, he thought with a wry grin – and he knew he should have talked to her when he was at Talla. There had been no opportunity. He had made no opportunity, he corrected himself. It was strangely difficult to end some unspecified understanding; harder than to break off a formal engagement. But recently Max had glimpsed how it might be to live with someone he loved and wanted, someone who charmed him and gave an entirely new focus to life, and he knew that whether he ever broke free of the present pattern or not he couldn't marry Ann. It was unfair to let her go on believing their relationship would develop or even continue as it was. He would be better alone than embarking on the sort of practical and convenient arrangement he had vaguely envisaged. Alone? When was he ever alone? He had this bunch of females permanently round his neck.

With an explosion of anger he drove back his chair from the desk and went across to the window, more for the release of movement than for anything he would see from it. The estate room looked out onto the unrelieved stone of the court-yard, pointing up his sense of imprisonment. Getting a bit dramatic, aren't you, he taunted himself, but this time failed to raise a smile.

He was evading the real point and he knew it. He leaned his forehead for a moment against the pane, his eyes closed, his face grim. What sort of life was this to foist on anyone? Kate was twenty-two, for Christ's sake, only just shaking off the inhibitions imposed by her odd upbringing, and still finding her balance after all the business of Jeremy and the baby. She was an ephemerid, here for the briefest season, and seen through her eyes the life they led must seem bizarre. Worse than that, he was sure she viewed him as she had viewed James, with the same blithe unawareness of his feelings, feelings deep enough to make him re-examine his life, his objectives, his entire future.

For all her shyness and gentleness Kate had made an extra-ordinary impact on their lives. She had freed them from Jeremy for one thing, and now that it had happened he and his mother had agreed they should have done it long ago. How his mother relied on her, and had softened and changed with her. 'A staunch little soul,' was how she described Kate, in the language of her generation, and Max thought the phrase served very well. Poor old Harrie, who got a pretty rough deal from all of them, trusted Kate and was more at ease with her than with anyone except Letitia. Laura had adored her from the first moment.

Max turned back to his desk. This question of James. It was unlikely, in spite of the knock he had taken over Jeremy, that he would slide back into the state he had been in before Kate arrived, but it was equally unlikely that he would find the courage to continue his tentative pursuit of her. Would he ever wake up sufficiently to see what was under his nose?

And for Max himself? He was at the stage of fascination when his days revolved round Kate, when hearing her voice, seeing her come into a room, filled him with delight. He devised ways to be with her, often needlessly creating what he called three-handed jobs, where unskilled help speeded up some task which was tedious or awkward for one person. He used to save them up for when Laura was home, but Laura would spend every minute she could with him whatever work he was engaged in.

It would be folly, he knew, to destroy Kate's happy oblivion about how he felt. He would only frighten her off and lose the thing he most valued, time spent with her. Over and over again his mind would turn to the idea of her staying indefinitely, hating the feeling that by the end of summer she would be gone, but he knew as well as anyone they had no need of extra hands except in the busiest months. Kate had come in February because Jeremy had asked that she should.

But Max needed more than this impersonal contact with her. There was one problem still unresolved in her life. Though she rarely referred to it he knew, as they all did, how much she minded being cut off from contact with home. She would never truly be at peace till this was resolved one way or the other. Could he help her over that? Would she let him? It was the only thing he could think of to offer her.

Kate got off the bus at the end of Wilton Avenue and set off at what she intended to be a brisk pace, but her knees felt oddly weak, and it was strange to be wearing high heels again. She had timed her arrival with care. If Jessie was still unrelenting at least Jack would soon be there and might, just might, be glad to see her. But Jack's comings and goings were unpredictable. All Kate could hope was that today he would come home for tea.

She was out of practice with London and that felt strange too. Joanna had driven her to Edinburgh airport, planning to treat herself to a day at Branklyn, where the blue poppies would be in their full glory, on her way home. On the brief flight Kate had felt hot and shut in and uncomfortable, and even travelling by tube again had unexpectedly harried her. Or was that merely anxiety about what lay ahead?

She took in little of her surroundings. She might as well have been walking down a blank corridor, holding expectation and fear at bay like a prisoner on the way to interrogation, as past the familiar gardens and house-fronts, Tudor gables and Queen Anne doors, shielding privet or open slopes of crazy paving. Only one detail caught her eye, a house-sign she didn't remember stuck in a border of gaudy bedding plants edging a parched lawn mown bald. It said 'Schiehallion'.

Schiehallion, that shapely mountain cone which swam into view as one took the high moorland road to Shirragh Lodge. How *dare* they?

Should she have come? But no matter how she had tried to put it out of her mind the need for reconciliation had gnawed at her. It was up to her to make the first gesture. Everything that had happened had been her fault, not Jack and Jessie's. They had reacted with shock and disgust but their outrage had been understandable and justified.

She had been taken by surprise when Max had first suggested her coming. It had seemed too soon and she had rushed into panic. He had been brisk and practical. 'I always go down for the second week of Wimbledon, play some golf, catch up on people. You're welcome to a lift either way or both, if you'd like to go home for a few days. You needn't decide now, have a think about it.'

Even more surprising had been his understanding of how she felt, when he had returned to the subject a day later. 'I know there are loose ends you need to tie up, and you won't be able to get on with your life till you have, or at least till you've tried. But bear in mind the situation has changed. Now that there's no baby your parents may feel very differently, but might be finding it hard to say so. And you're not a person who likes conflict or coldness.'

Kate recalled where they had been and what they had been doing when this conversation took place, mixing cement to repoint the back wall of the cottages beside Doddie's. The contrast between that scene and her present surroundings jolted her with unsettling nostalgia.

'If you don't want to go down this time,' Max had added, 'or if it's not convenient at the other end, you know you can go any time you like, don't you? Just say the word and we'll arrange it.'

Convenient at the other end? Kate had not asked. Was that lack of courage? Partly, but chiefly she was afraid of giving Jessie the chance to shut her out without hesitation, without listening. This was the only way. Apprehension running through her in sick waves, she hurried on, all other feeling suspended.

Pale glare of the concrete Jack had laid over the entire front garden; red brick of the low walls on either side, one topped with ragged box; a Citroën with trade plates in front of the garage. That meant nothing, there were always cars in transit outside Lamorna. Behind the bay window, frilled net drawn into little peaks at the centre of each pane, an ornament in each space, Kate could hear the faint quack of the television, one of the tea-time chat shows Jessie loved, when uninhibited people revealed the intimate secrets of their lives, wept, proposed, screamed, aired prejudices, fought – and announced pregnancies, learned hideous unknown facts about their parentage.

No, no . . . Hefting her bag in a hand strangely cold in spite of the dull heat which seemed to press down with a weight of its own, Kate stepped onto the polished red tiles of the porch. Then she checked; she had her key. But to use it was unthinkable. The realisation brought an ache to her throat which she could not afford just now. Summoning calm with an immense effort, she pressed the bell, keeping close to the door so that Jessie could not see who was there by pulling aside the curtain. As the screams of laughter from the television increased in volume, Kate realised in panic and relief that Jessie had opened the living-room door.

There was one incredible moment when, face to face, the normality of the years swept back. This was Mum, utterly familiar, and this was home. Then an ugly tide of red surged over Jessie's heavy features, and in a movement of instinctive denial she drew sharply back behind the door with its oval pane of tulip-patterned frosted glass.

'I just want to talk,' Kate exclaimed, all planned greetings discarded at the sight of that closing door. 'Please, just to—'

'If you want your things they're not here,' Jessie interrupted with shrill defensiveness, as though she was dealing with an importunate door-to-door salesman. 'If you couldn't be bothered to take them away I couldn't be bothered to keep them. I burned the lot, so it's no use you coming asking for them.'

Kate shook her head as though a wasp was buzzing round it, so irrelevant was this issue. Her fussy pink room and whatever belongings she had left in it seemed as far away, as lost and unimportant, as the room she had slept in as a small child.

'It's all right. I haven't come to fetch anything. I don't want anything. I just hoped that after all this time – now that the baby – did you get my letter telling you about the baby?' She had not expected to have to say this on the doorstep, part of her mind protested wretchedly, but it was essential to get Jessie's attention.

'That baby, shaming me in front of everyone!' An automatic clutching at the original grievance, unaltered by time or new circumstances. And shamed in front of whom? The indifferent strangers next door? The inhabitants of Schiehallion? 'You think you can just turn up again whenever you like, after what you did. After all this time with your posh friends, turning up your nose at us—'

'Can I come in and talk about it?' Kate pleaded, trembling but not prepared to give up. 'Please, so that we can try to understand each other?'

'Well, I can't stop you,' Jessie said furiously, hunching a fat shoulder as she turned back into the hall. She had caught sight of the curious face of a young woman turned towards them as she pushed a pram along the pavement. Also deep down Jessie hankered for a good screaming match, a chance to discharge some of the grievances which had milled and festered in her mind for months. Jack was no use, he would never listen, just cut her short or if she carried on walked out of the house.

Kate was barely over the doorstep before the torrent of invective, incoherent, wildly phrased and repetitive, met her like an actual battering fall of water. It was as bad as any of the attacks when she had first told Jessie about the baby. Nothing had changed; nothing had moved on. Kate gripped the edge of the spindly repro table below the mirror. It held a Benares brass salver and a lumpy cactus. She could smell new paint, and in a strange detached flash of perception understood for the first time that Jessie used decorating as a comforter.

Her light voice could do nothing to stem the flow of Jessie's strident anger. Quite soon, in any case, Kate realised the idea she was struggling to get across, that since the baby no longer existed they might find a way back to communication, even affection, meant nothing to Jessie. Her problem went deeper, the problem Kate had hoped against hope all this time had been seized on in anger. But it was real, ugly, and it wasn't going to change. Jessie hated her.

'You're just a slut like your mother. I should have known what would happen . . . .'

They had been here before. There was no way past this and Kate was not prepared to hear it again. Shaking, she turned to the door and got it open, and at that moment a black Jaguar pulled up outside.

In a second Jack was out of the car and up the steps. He took one look over Kate's head at Jessie's turgidly flushed face, heard her gasping breath, and shouted in fury at Kate, 'What the hell are you doing here? Haven't you done enough?'

Jack had been hurt to his deepest core by what Kate had done. All her life he had offered her every ounce of effort and care which was in his power to give, and she had let him down. He could never articulate or share this hurt, and since she had gone had refused to let Jessie mention her name, but the bitterness would never leave him. To see Kate back in the house, so pretty, so well-dressed in the way that had always filled him with pride, was unendurable. And to see Jessie, gasping and beside herself—

With a wordless growl of rage, Jack drove Kate aside with a back-handed sweep of his arm. It was not a blow, but as Jack weighed fifteen stone and Kate just on seven, it might as well have been. She staggered back, caught her foot on the bottom step of the stairs, and crashed down against the newel post.

Jessie screamed. 'That serves you right, walking in here as though you owned the place.'

Jack, his burly frame shaking with anger and a complexity of violent feelings which had nowhere to go, stepped towards Kate.

Max's Audi swung in to park beside the Jaguar.

Chapter Thirty-One

Kate looked so small and defenceless bowed in the seat beside him, hands up on either side of her face, an uncontrollable shuddering running through her slight body, that Max was filled with a burning longing to go back in and expend some of his anger on the stupid and brutally insensitive pair who had done this to her.

He had suspected this might happen, and had timed his arrival at Lamorna as carefully as Kate had timed hers. Now he wondered, with fresh anger, this time directed at himself, why if he had feared this he had encouraged her to come in the first place. But the long estrangement had been eating at her, he knew it, and after her initial flurry of panic when the plan had suddenly been presented to her, she had been eager to come.

'Are you sure you don't want me to sort things out for you?' he asked her, careful to keep his tone matter-of-fact. Sort out Jack, he meant.

Kate shook her head violently. 'I just want to go. Please, Max.'

It was what she had said in that startled moment after he had come bounding into the hall, arriving among them with an unhesitating authority that had at once put him in control of the scene.

'What's going on?' he had demanded, not of Kate but of Jack, still stooped over Kate. In fact Jack had been about to help her up, appalled at what he had done, but Max hadn't waited to find out, catching his shoulder and spinning him round. Jack, in spite of his heavily muscled frame and extra couple of stone, had been in no doubt that he wouldn't stand a chance if it came to a physical confrontation. He had read an unmistakable warning in Max's stance, the light in his eye.

'He never touched her!' Jessie had screamed, tottering forwards in the grubby high-heeled mules she always wore in the house. 'She tripped, I saw her.' She had appeared to be already rehearsing her evidence.

'It's all right.' Kate had struggled to her feet, in fact had almost been swept off her feet again, caught by Max's strong grasp, and she had clutched his shirt, partly to steady herself but also to prevent him going for Jack, which he had looked more than ready to do.

'Please can we just go.' She had hardly been able to get the words out, oddly breathless.

'If you hit her —' Max had warned Jack savagely.

'Listen, you —' Jack had blustered but his hectoring tone had held a defensive note.

'I stumbled,' Kate had interposed quickly. 'I tripped,' nodding at the step covered in willow green carpet as though it would corroborate her words, then putting her fingers tenderly to her aching cheekbone, weak tears overcoming her. She had known she couldn't argue, couldn't think about any of this yet. 'I just want to go. Oh, but my bag!'

Max had picked it up without letting her go and his powerful arm had scooped her towards the door.

Neither Jack nor Jessie had moved, their faces baffled and hostile, but already showing a glimmer of the defiant triumph which would soon bolster them up. Jessie, 'Walking in here like that, what did she expect? Thought she'd find all her things just where she left them, take up where she left off. Can you believe it? I soon told her . . .' And from Jack, 'Never laid a finger on her, she caught her foot . . . .'

Max looked at Kate with a frown. No use asking her where she would like to go, she had barely taken in what had happened yet. He knew what he wanted to do with her, and that was take her straight home, but he doubted if she was fit for an all-night drive. Also, he couldn't simply leave without warning, much as he would have liked to.

'Listen, Kate,' he said gently. 'I'm staying with friends not too far away and I'll have to pick up my kit and tell them what's happening. We'll head out that way and decide what we want to do as we go.'

But she scarcely seemed to hear, leaning back in her seat with a weary sigh as he turned up Wilton Avenue.

She'd had the drive down to Edinburgh, and the flight, then to be met with this. Max ached for her, anger surging up again. How he wished he'd got there a couple of seconds earlier, when no matter what they said he was convinced he'd have had an excuse to plant one on that surly bastard.

Thank God, at least, he didn't have to cross half London. What to do with Kate though? At the house in Shere where he stayed every year for golf at Worplesdon and the final days of Wimbledon, a large party was gathered which included Ann. He had hoped there would be the chance to talk to her sometime during the week, but in a mob like that and with so much going on opportunities for private conversation had been non-existent.

However, Kate's welfare was his prime concern at the moment. Could she face that chattering crowd, gathering about now for drinks before dinner, deep in what had happened at the fifteenth or on the centre court? Entertaining at Holm Hall was on the grand side, unlike Glen Maraich where everyone chose their own style and stuck to it and no one paid the slightest attention. Kate's face was swollen and discolouring fast; the sight of it would stir up exactly the sort of fuss she would most hate. And the sort of gossip he would most hate himself? No, stuff that, he didn't care. But, he found, he didn't altogether trust

Ann's reaction, and that was revealing. He didn't expect her to be exactly uncivilised, but nevertheless found himself preparing to shield Kate.

They were through Esher already. 'Listen, Kate, I want you to decide what you want to—'

'I just want to go back to Allt Farr,' Kate broke in, filled with nervous anxiety. 'I can get the train. I want to be back there, so that I can try to –' Impossible to put into words what she must try to assimilate and accept.

Max mentally recorded his glow of pleasure at her emphatic answer, but he was not putting her on any train tonight. 'No, I'm taking you home, as soon as I've collected my things. But first there are various choices. You can come to Holm Hall with me, only there's a mass of people there and we might find it hard to get away. You could come with me and wait outside in the car, but I don't much like the idea of that and we probably wouldn't be allowed to get away with it anyway. Or, which I think best if you feel up to it, I could drop you off somewhere quiet and peaceful to wait for me, then we could have a meal somewhere and gently head north.'

He knew the chance of being able to book rooms was virtually nil, but perhaps the hotel where last night's party had been held would be able to manage dinner.

'Yes, that would be best. I'll wait for you,' Kate said quickly. A crowd of Max's friends was the last thing she could face at present. She felt stunned, emotions flayed, her mind unable to grapple with what had happened, and apart from that she was unkempt, her skin tight with the dry air of the city, her eyes gritty, her bruised cheek throbbing. She hated to think what she must look like.

'Good girl,' Max said in relief, though as he tucked her into a corner of the residents' lounge at Ripley Grange, which would soon be deserted as everyone went in to dinner, and had a final word with the receptionist, he thought he had rarely disliked anything as much as leaving Kate alone at this moment, with her forlorn eyes and swollen face. She needed comfort and company, not being abandoned in a strange place. He drove far too fast through the lanes to Shere.

In fact, an hour alone was not the worst thing for Kate. At first she hardly glanced around her, unaware of covert glances, of drinks being brought, dinner orders taken, glasses gathered up after the drift to the dining-room was complete. Presently she collected herself enough to find the ladies' room, something in normal circumstances she would have done at once, and tried to repair the wreck of her face. Little could be done to camouflage the discoloration which was spreading dramatically, but splashing cool water against her skin, feeling her hands clean again, brushing her hair, redoing her make-up, were magically revivifying and she felt much better as she went back to the quiet lounge. She still could not focus her mind on the events at Lamorna, her thoughts bumping ineffectually against the memory like a moth at a window. She could not have said whether it was ten minutes or two hours before Max reappeared, only knowing that when the door swung open and he came towards her with his purposeful stride worries fell away.

He had already booked a table and ordered for them both. He seated Kate with the damaged side of her face concealed, and moved the lamp on the table so that she was in shadow, not only for her sake but because he could not bear to see what had been done to her.

At first, remorseful because he had taken such trouble, Kate said she didn't think she could eat anything, but Max took no notice, nodding to the waiter to serve her.

'No dinner, no journey,' he said, filling her glass himself. He had chosen food simple to deal with, and almost without noticing Kate had soon eaten some prawn and spinach roulade, and a small amount of risotto of chicken livers and mushrooms. More importantly, to Max's watchful eye, she was clearly taking in more of her surroundings and responding to his easy conversation less at random. Questions about their next move were not worrying her yet, and he was glad of it.

Gradually, inevitably, for apart from Grannie Max was the only person she could have brought herself to tell about such pain, the nightmare thoughts battering round Kate's mind spilled out, and with them the dredged-up misery of first telling her parents she was pregnant. Much of it Max knew, more he had deduced, but he let her talk, in a nervous ripple of words, eyes down, her fingers turning and turning a spoon which the waiter would have liked to remove.

The dining-room emptied. They were undisturbed except for the waiter refilling their coffee cups and at the same time handing Max a note. The receptionist had done her work well; rooms were booked in Huntingdon. With the problem of where to spend the night settled, and guessing how therapeutic this release into talk must be for Kate, Max made up his mind. He didn't think anything could hurt her more at this moment, and it might be a long time before the barriers came down in this way again.

'Kate, I've wondered,' he began carefully, when her voice had dwindled into silence, and he thought she had talked out most of her immediate shock and grief. 'After all that's happened with your adoptive parents, and what you told Joanna about your real father and mother, whether you have ever thought of trying to find them?'

Kate lifted her head, her face tense and white around the hectic bruising, as though preparing for another blow. She didn't speak.

Christ, I hope I haven't got this wrong, Max thought with a lurching sensation of fear which was quite new to him. 'Kate, God knows the last thing I want to do is cause you any more pain. You may have had as much as you can take for one day. I just wondered if it would help to talk it all out, but say if you'd rather not.'

Kate gazed at him, so many thoughts churning round her head

that she couldn't for the moment pin one down. 'No,' she said urgently. 'No, it's all right.' She didn't want to lose this chance, every instinct telling her that here was the one person who could help her.

Max read some of that in her face and keeping his voice as neutral as possible, went on, 'I expect you'll have thought about the possibility often, but it occurred to me that you might not be sure how to set about it, and might be glad of some help.'

The ready tears, too near the surface this evening to be controlled, welled up.

'Oh, Kate, I'm sorry.' Max cursed himself for his ineptness, reaching out a hand to disengage one of hers from the spoon she was still clutching, and folding it in his. 'This was a terrible moment to choose to bring this up. I'm a bloody fool. We'll talk about it another time, whenever you want to.'

'No,' Kate insisted again. 'No, it's not that. I'm just so grateful. And it's the right moment. It's part of all this. I think the thought has been somewhere at the back of my mind ever since – ever since I found out about it. Then it was tied up with vindictiveness. It was made to sound so vile and cheap. But gradually I've been able to think about it more sensibly, and wonder how it really was. A schoolgirl from some good family and a navvy. But those are just labels, aren't they? They were two people. Who knows what they were like, how they felt, whether they were happy, whether they loved each other? Or was it some-thing casual, uncaring, an act performed when they were drunk or on drugs? Was it rape? There are a million questions, aren't there? I've gone over them all.'

Max sat very still, not interrupting, her hand in his, his big shoulders and long back hunched forward as though he wanted to wrap his strength around her.

'But I don't have to believe it was something bad,' Kate said after a pause. 'Jessie wanted it to be, it helped her in some way. I think I can even understand that. But for myself,

I can imagine there were all kinds of possible answers.'

'Would you like to try and find out?' Max asked quietly, after another silence. 'It's not difficult, the legal process is there. And I can put any resources you like at your disposal.'

Kate sat with head bent, and he was glad she was returning the grip of his hand. 'No,' she said at last. 'I don't think I do want it. Because I've grown up knowing I was adopted I've always thought about finding my real parents one day. I suppose it would be impossible not to. Dreams. Knocking on a door, being welcomed in. But what happens next? How would these strangers feel? What crisis and disruption would that arrival create, even if it were planned and agreed on? When I was pregnant I thought about it a lot more. Why should a decision made by someone else years ago, with the sort of agony I went through deciding whether or not to keep my baby, be disregarded for someone else's selfish need? And I didn't need anything, I had a home, I was loved – I thought I was loved.' Kate's voice nearly failed her there, but she made herself continue. 'I think the decision I made then, when I believed in those imaginary parents Jessie had described, was the valid one. I reached it for the right reasons, not influenced by the emotional muddle I'm in now. I don't see how finding them could do anything but harm and it wouldn't lessen the hurt of knowing how Jessie feels – or Jack.' That had gone deeper, but she had always known Jack would support Jessie; that wouldn't change.

Max watched her, his jaw tight. For two pins he could have cried himself. 'Look,' he said, all his feelings in his voice, 'I understand how you feel, and I think you're very honest and very brave. But don't forget that we can always talk about it again if your thinking changes. Time can do strange things. When you've put today behind you, and life is more stable, you may feel differently. No doors have been closed.' He wished he had chosen a different phrase, hearing again in his mind the violent, conclusive slam of the door of Lamorna behind them.

Kate nodded gratefully, her expression lightening.

'That's true. It doesn't have to be a final decision.'

When life is more stable. The summer at Allt Farr; that was safe and certain.

Max had used the words in terms of a longer perspective, though he was scarcely aware himself of having done so.

Chapter Thirty-Two

Coming back up the glen on a cool green afternoon, with foliage still in the light freshness of early summer, in contrast with the dusty jaded look of London trees, Kate felt one of those moments when pure mental and physical satisfaction blend. She was tired, in the slightly disconnected way that comes after deep stress, and there were wounds to deal with that would take time to heal, but she felt safe and calm, as though she knew she had done all she could.

It was good to go into the kitchen and find Grannie there, making a batch of quiches for the freezer, and to disappear into a floury hug, never guessing the anxious questions Grannie telegraphed to Max over her shoulder. It was good to have Buff come bundling out off his basket grinning all over his face and push his big head against her, to feel the warm silky thickness of his coat under her hand. And it was good to sit down among the baking and have tea (though Max barely paused before taking his off to the estate room to go through his mail) and presently have Laura come whirling in from school followed by Joanna, provoking Buff to mad barks, wasting no time on greetings before tearing off to change into her oldest jeans and get outside to the ponies.

'Come on, Kate . . .' The weekend had begun.

Kate's subdued manner, as well as her bruised face, told their tale, and everyone in the close world of Allt Farr, whether they knew the facts or not, made it clear in various small ways that she was welcome back. Doddie, who had recently returned in a sorry state from a foray abroad to Oban, wanted to know if she'd been frequenting the same pub as he had, while Colleen loosed some partisan wrath at the potted version of events she received. The interlude in London soon seemed an unreal dream. The attempt at reconciliation had been made, now she could only accept the truth – Jessie's resentment of her was fundamental and entrenched and Jack, whatever his true feelings were, would endorse it.

In the big house each of the family had problems to deal with, and as normal life flowed on Kate's affairs took their turn with the rest and then were put aside. It was, she thought, almost the best feature of life here, this implacable rolling along of busy days.

On the Tuesday after she and Max returned he left again, for Talla. He came back inside a day in an even worse frame of mind than after his last visit there, vanishing for the next three days to cut and wuffle hay, shut up in the din and heat and solitude of the tractor cab. The family were relieved the weather was fine.

Ann had fought her corner in a way Max had not expected. She had presented several well-phrased and cogent arguments in favour of her putting Allt Farr, and him, in order, had by implication shown up many glaring deficiencies in his material and emotional life, and, becoming less controlled, had finally demanded who else he thought would be prepared to take on a semi-derelict castle and the group of dysfunctional hangers-on he trailed at his coat-tails. Even Ann had wondered after she cooled down whether she was ever likely to be invited to stalk on Allt Farr again.

Apart from the savage clawing, which he knew he had deserved, two points gave Max food for uncomfortable thought. He had been startled to discover how much Ann cared about him.

Her way of showing it might have been hard to take, but her feeling of betrayal had been unmistakable. Her reliance on, and wish for, a future together had gone much further than his own, and he should have seen that long ago. Even harder to take, and this he had not foreseen, was his altered position in relation to Kate. Until now she had been hedged around by factors which had protected him from facing his feelings for her – Jeremy, the baby, James's awakening interest. These had been removed. It was what he had longed for, yet now it had come about he saw that Kate, in her innocent unawareness, was as far from him as ever. He was forced to acknowledge the gulf between them, and dreaded jeopardising the peace of mind she was establishing, but nevertheless he needed to make clear to her, and to the rest of the family, that no relationship with Ann now existed.

Feeling craven, he chose Laura as the least complicated channel for announcing it.

'Well, Buff never liked her much,' was Laura's philosophical response, and the news was not received with a great deal more comment in other quarters.

Grannie accepted it as a sensible decision long overdue, and could not entirely quell beguiling hopes and speculations. Harriet briefly hoped it might mean Ann's critical eye would not be present so often to uncover Allt Farr's numerous domestic short-comings but, like Joanna, was far too preoccupied with her own troubles to give it much further consideration.

Kate was sorry for Max, and thought it no wonder his mood was black as he worked through the endless daylight hours of midsummer. Not a talker herself, she was unworried by his silences. In fact in her company he relaxed in spite of himself, finding it impossible to be brusque with her, and for Kate working with him, with or without Laura there, was companionable and comfortable, the thing she enjoyed most.

Harriet too was uncommunicative, still with that look of uncomprehending hurt a dog wears when it's booted out of the car far from home and hopes each person that appears will turn out to be its owner. The WRI end-of-session sale and ceilidh in the Kirkton Hall were also a farewell party for Letitia, and Harriet did her best to bury her grief in preparations for it. She cried uncontrollably during the speeches and had to rush choking into the whitewash-smelling kitchen behind the platform to sob in peace. Grannie looked severe at this public demonstration. Joanna and Kate went after her.

The following day was even worse, when Kate went to Craigbeg with Harriet, Max and Laura to help clear out the cottage. Letitia had hired a van to transport cats, ducks, chickens, motorbike and what remained of her meagre possessions to the Welsh border farm where she had been born. She was to spend her last night in the glen at the Mennach. Kate thought it wrong and sad that she had not been invited to Allt Farr.

She also thought Max surprisingly patient about the unattractive chore. As Letitia herself admitted, 'No one else is going to want anything I can't use. I'm definitely the end of the line.' Onto the bonfire went dingy sweatshirts and what she referred to as 'tracky-bums', capaciously stretched, along with wormy chairs, the gash planks which had held her DIY library, cracked lino, and rugs whose condition suggested the outdoor section of the household had been invited in on bad days.

Clouds of dust arose. Domestic makeshifts of an unappealing nature were laid bare. The fire made short work of rickety objects which must have endangered Letitia's lumbering bulk every day of her life. She entered into it all with her usual gusto; it was Harriet who fled inside, saying the smoke was getting in her eyes. Max's face remained expressionless as evidence of neglect was revealed, broken windows, peeling wallpaper, a basin stained blue under a dripping tap. Kate knew Craigbeg was an Allt Farr cottage which Letitia had agreed to maintain in good order, and thought his restraint showed admirable concern for Harriet's feelings.

Overt sympathy was not the Munro style and in the lonely weeks that followed Harriet did not invite it, keeping her own counsel and going on stolidly with the jobs she saw as hers. Only Kate was able to draw her out to talk, as together they tackled some peaceful job like harvesting and freezing vegetables and fruit, this year in copious supply.

On one occasion a simple query from Kate as to whether they should start another row of broad beans or have a break for lunch, triggered a rare outburst.

'Sometimes I just get so *tired!*' Harriet exclaimed, wincing and putting a hand to her back as she straightened up too quickly.

Kate guessed the sentence ended 'of it all.' She had observed the tension growing in Harriet and could imagine her sense of isolation. She knew from her own experience how wretched it was to live like that.

'Poor Harrie, it is a backbreaking job,' she said sympathetically. 'Let's stop for now. We've done heaps. Why don't we sit in the sun for a while before going up to the house?'

She was prepared for Harriet to say as she always did, 'Oh, no, we can't do that, there's no time for sitting about,' but Harriet said ungraciously, 'Oh, well, I suppose we might,' and perched on the stone coping of a raised herb bed, looking awkward and temporary.

'It's such a lovely day,' Kate said peaceably. 'But you are looking a bit tired, you know. Do you ever manage to get a holiday? I mean when the cottages are quiet again, of course. Do you ever go away anywhere?'

To her surprise Harriet didn't answer, just stared across the garden with her long Munro jaw thrust out, her beaky nose scarlet in the sun. 'I've had a letter,' she said abruptly.

'From Letitia?' There had been a regular flow of them, so why was this special? But no one else wrote to Harriet. Although in theory she looked after the cottages and worked hard to make them inviting, thank-you letters always seemed to be addressed to someone else.

'You won't tell anyone?' Harriet demanded, turning on Kate fiercely, pushing up her glasses then raking her flop of hair back from her forehead with spread fingers in a familiar double gesture.

That Letitia had written? 'Of course not,' Kate promised soothingly. Whatever it was.

'She's asked me to go and stay.'

'But Harrie, that's marvellous. You'd love that, wouldn't you, you must be—'

'Not stay exactly. Live.'

'Ah.' Kate fell silent, aware that this was a moment of deep significance.

'But you're not to tell anyone,' Harriet repeated, her voice rising. 'You did promise.'

'Of course I won't tell anyone if you don't want me to. But are you going to think about it? I mean, it would be so—'

'Don't be ridiculous!' Harriet cried, coming quickly and clumsily to her feet. 'Of course I can't think about it, it's out of the question. Oh dear, why did I ever mention it? I knew I shouldn't. Now you'll only keep saying –' Her voice broke and she searched madly for one of the tissues she kept about her person.

'Harriet, please don't get upset.' Kate was on her feet too, trying to hug the lean body which was not used to accommodating itself to such embraces. 'I won't say a word ever again if you don't want me to, but since we're talking now won't you tell me why you think it's impossible? You miss Letitia so much, and you'd be happy with her, wouldn't you?' She didn't want to distress Harriet more, but felt if this opportunity for talking was lost the subject would be difficult to reopen.

'I *can't*, Kate, don't you see. We, the family, I mean, have this arrangement, we all contribute. And if I wasn't here who would look after all the – everything, the house, the cottages, the laundry, the chickens . . . .'

Kate had heard Max's estimate of what the chickens cost them. In terms of productivity he rated their worth as roughly equal to Persephone's.

'There must be some way round that,' she objected, but very

gently. 'I'm sure it could all be worked out if this was something you really wanted to do—'

'No, no!' Harriet's voice held panic now, and Kate had an impression of doors frantically slamming on something too big and overwhelming to contemplate. 'There are all the things I look after in the glen as well. Who would take those on? No one ever wants to do their share. Who would run the television scheme, or the children's plays, or the church sales – *everything!*'

Kate recognised this for the cry of despair it was, despair at a decision already made, and she wisely said no more beyond making meaningless soothing noises as she gathered up the beans and shepherded Harriet towards the gate and lunch. As they crossed the courtyard Harriet turned to her again, her pale eyes full of tears, and blurted out, 'I had to tell someone, I don't know why. I couldn't have told anyone else.'

Harriet's plight, which no one could help her with, was gradually taken for granted and forgotten by everyone except Kate. The summer student arrived (only one this year because she was there), a cheerful stocky lad called Kevin reading computer sciences at Dundee. He was to be handyman, extra driver and ponyman during the grouse shooting. Doddie was all set to give him a hard time but Kevin had been brought up on an Angus farm and was tough, competent and good-natured, so Doddie soon decided to enjoy his company and lead him astray instead.

The cottage booking charts showed no gaps till the end of September and many of the summer lets were for people Kate knew. Laura came home for the holidays, friends came and went in the house, it poured solidly on the Twelfth and the bag was a disaster, and it also poured solidly on the Sunday after the Twelfth for the annual Alltmore barbecue. The holiday houses at Bridge of Riach, and up and down the glen, were packed, Joanna could hardly keep up with the demand for flowers from the hotels, and the days were full and busy – then James took them by surprise. Formal, separate, invitations arrived for everyone to attend a party celebrating the fifth birthdays of Miss Mackenzie and Miss Sasha Mackenzie.

'Has he finally gone over the edge?' Max demanded. 'A party for that pair of hooligans? The man's mad.'

'It can't do much harm in a house like Riach,' Grannie pointed out. 'I wouldn't miss it for the world.'

'Dinner and dancing. It doesn't sound like a children's party, does it? Anyway, James is sure to need help,' Harriet said, sounding happier than she had for weeks, her eyes abstracted as she debated which Riach rooms to wake from their dusty slumber.

Joanna said nothing, holding her invitation in both hands, crushing down giveaway reactions but failing to do the same for the rush of feelings which the sight of James's writing on the dye-stamped card brought swarming up. What had prompted this extravagant gesture?

After the blow to his newly re-arming courage inflicted by seeing Kate with Jeremy, James had resorted briefly to the defence mechanisms which had protected him for so long. But time had moved on. Kate had woken in him sexual responses he had almost forgotten and these emotions refused to be crammed back once more into their box. Under the stimulus of her company he had looked at his life objectively and been forced to realise he couldn't leave his daughters indefinitely to the unleavened company of Dot and Bridie, and a physical and cultural diet of burgers and chips, Radio One, the *Sun* and Dot's *True Crimes* magazine.

He missed the Sunday Munro invasions, though it had been accepted by both sides that their therapy was no longer needed and he had no wish to revive the routine in the same form, but he also, rather to his surprise, missed the tentative social contacts he had begun to re-establish after the long dark interval of solitude. He therefore decided to introduce his daughters to the wider world, though his plans would have been more appropriate had they been eighteen, not five. He booked a marquee ('Save the dusting,') and outside caterers ('Keep Harriet off my back,') then settled down to await events.

He didn't entirely succeed where Harriet was concerned, since she, ably assisted by Laura, organised the missing element, the party for the twins and their contemporaries, but even he saw the argument for this when it was put to him.

No one, not even an over-excited Sybilla or Sasha whom their father refused to send to bed, or a Bridie pounding her way through every dance, scarlet-cheeked and sweating, and absent from her post at breakfast because Doddie's van wouldn't start, enjoyed the legendary Riach party more than Joanna.

It was as though by waiting quietly, which it had been her natural instinct to do, things — she did not have the courage yet to search out a more specific word — were resolving themselves. Watching James fling himself in his well-remembered unco-ordinated fashion through the reels, she had felt with choking relief that the James of younger days had been restored. He made no special overtures towards her, there was no definable alteration in his words or manner, but the old ease shared between them in childhood and youth (until her courage failed her and she had fled because it all mattered too much) was somehow back in place. There was a sense, which she was absolutely certain James shared, of having emerged from some long shadowy tunnel full of false turnings. Am I fanciful on champagne? she asked herself, gazing at her reflection in the spotted antique mirror of a Riach bathroom which the sun never touched, or Bridie either by the look of it. But a marvellous sense of time being hers made her blurred reflection smile back with serene happiness.

Grannie, after a couple of waltzes with Gilbert which taxed her more than she would admit, was content to watch the dancing, yet another indication of a dread process she hated having to accept. She observed her progeny with an ironic expression which concealed interest, hope and concern, oppressed by a sense, more acute every day, of needing to act in their interests without more delay. This tying themselves to Allt Farr had served its purpose, but how to unravel it, how to free them? Then as she reached this point the scale of the unravelling which would be necessary defeated her once more, and she shook her head, her lips tightening.

Her attention turned to Max, whirling Pauly Napier, a girl as capable as any of giving as good as she got, through a wild schottishe, and she felt a rare fear of intruding, of endangering even by her thoughts the delicate balance of what she hardly dared hope might be happening.

She looked for Kate, being swung light as a leaf by Charlie Fleming with a calculated vigour that allowed her just enough contact with the floor, and involuntarily her face softened. She had done so much for them, this improbable migrant from another world, and Grannie did not intend to lose sight of her, no matter what plans might be made for the autumn.

Chapter Thirty-Three

As the busy weeks flashed by Max found his mind returning over and over again to the same question. But it was taken for granted by everyone, Kate included, that she would leave as planned and what possible excuse did he have for trying to change that? Although she had adapted to this new lifestyle with a readiness he would never have expected, accepting with unruffled good nature Grannie's tetchiness, Harriet's fussing and Joanna's detached dreaminess — and my bloody awful temper, he would amend ruefully — she would probably not mind moving on, for the associations here could not all be good ones for her. Also for Kate's sake such an informal arrangement as existed at present should not be allowed to continue. Although Max knew she had some kind of income from investments, she couldn't go on working for nothing indefinitely.

But to see her go. At the thought the years seemed to stretch before him, unchanging, profitless and empty, and he could see no way out.

More than once he tried to talk to Kate about her plans. She would agree, with a chill in her heart she carefully showed no hint of, that of course she must look for 'something sensible' but she was vague about what it might be or where she wanted to go. 'Joanna says something will be sure to turn up,' she said when pressed.

'That sounds like Joanna' Max said with asperity. 'What exactly does she have in mind?'

'Elaine Moncrieff knows someone who needs help, just general back-up for the house and children I think. Near Dunkeld.'

'You can do better than that,' Max snapped.

'Something like this, you mean?' Kate enquired, unpeeling another rotting lino tile from the floor of the Craigbeg kitchen, revealing interesting fungal growth on the unsound boards below. Max had decided another long lease would be best, as the cottage was too far from the house for convenient servicing for the more lucrative holiday lets. However, after years of tenancy by Letitia and her furred and feathered friends, it needed a radical overhaul.

Kate, in filthy denim shirt and jeans, with black grimed hands and cobwebs in her hair, looked up at Max innocently. She looked so bright and alive that he wanted to get down on his knees there and then and wrap her in his arms, cobwebs and all. Instead he muttered disgustedly at some rough shelving Letitia had put up, stuck his claw hammer behind it and yanked it away from the wall with a rending sound. 'You know what I mean,' he growled.

'I shall decide something in time,' Kate said, piling small fragments of lino onto a whole tile which she hoped would hold together when she lifted it. She would decide something, she knew, because she was a responsible and conscientious person. She would establish the date beyond which she could no longer be useful at Allt Farr, she would pack belongings most of which were rather different from those she had arrived with, and she would go quietly away. Not, she had already decided, to some 'ordinary' job, shutting the door of a neat little flat behind her as she came in to solitary evenings, or waking on Saturday mornings to great blanks of time to be filled with shopping and washing her clothes and going to the library. She would find some buffer zone, some lesser Allt Farr, and from there she would feel her way forward to a bearable way of living.

She would miss them all so much. As always, her thoughts wavered dangerously here. Especially Grannie. Apart from missing her, Kate wanted to go on looking after her. There was a vulnerability about Grannie, and lately a new touch almost of sadness, which neither her offspring nor Gilbert seemed to have the time or patience to see.

And she would miss Laura, Laura with her eager energy and competence, who had looked after her with such warm and natural friendliness in the daunting early days.

It didn't occur to Kate that they would miss her too. She saw only that there were gaps in her emotional life to be filled, while they were part of a family, which in turn was part of a wider mesh of relationships and friendships. Was it easiest to think of Grannie and Laura first, a shield between her and the pain of leaving Max? For she would miss Max, more than she had ever imagined it would be possible to miss anyone. She felt safe with him, and days when she didn't spend time with him were empty and incomplete. She understood he was probably filling the father role, a role essential to her because she had loved Jack, believing with a child's blind confidence that she was loved in return, but she could not rationalise her feelings for Max out of existence.

Max guessed she saw him in this light, and though he didn't much care for being cast so firmly in the part, he understood her need. Also he knew she should be given time to emerge from the turmoil of the last few months, time to grow up. Well, he promised himself as his mother had done, even when she went from Allt Farr that didn't have to mean she disappeared for good. He could wait.

Kate walked down from the Old Byre with her ears pinned back and an uneasy feeling that she shouldn't be on the hill track at all today. Common sense – and Colleen – insisted that she wouldn't actually be shot, but she still felt edgy. Easy-going Doddie had become a changed man since shooting started, a megalomanic tyrant whose word was law, and stalking seemed to be an even more sacrosanct and arcane pursuit. Disturbing the hill was a crime worse than all others, to which driving sheep off the neeps was a mere nursery peccadillo. There had been a shot not long ago, but it had been distant, she thought. But how distant? Had they killed something? And if they had did that mean stalking was over for the day, or was some unseen person armed with a rifle crawling at this very moment through the heather towards her?

Giggling, she hurried on. What a silly business it was, but they seemed passionately addicted to it, and from the correspondence she had dealt with for Max she knew it was a major source of income for the estate. She closed her mind to the fact of the kill.

The October afternoon was grey and blowy and the cold increased by the minute as the sun deserted the lower ground. A line of snow had appeared on the hills a week ago, and last night had crept lower. Kate drove her ungloved hands deeper into her pockets. In spite of its weight and the way it hung off her shoulders she had turned to the old fur-lined canvas jacket again, with absurd fondness. It brought back memories that were funny now, but with a nostalgia to them that made them very piercing. Her departure could not be delayed much longer, she knew, though stalking had provided a reprieve.

'We shall have people in the house off and on right through October,' Grannie had said. 'Even for the hinds this year, as there's such a demand for stalking. And the cottages go on longer every season it seems to me. Mrs Grant always needs a holiday by this time, though she can rarely be brought to admit it, so you would be doing us a great favour, Kate, if you would stay at least until she comes back.'

It had seemed a little contrived, even to Kate. Was Grannie just being kind? 'Are you sure this is all right?' she had asked Max privately, naïvely supposing she would get an unbiased opinion from him.

'Of course it's all right,' was all he had managed, rather tersely, out of the possible answers that swarmed through his mind, and his own questions. Is this the right moment, should I tell her I never want her to go away at all? She hasn't the faintest idea, she'd recoil in horror, it's too soon, too soon . . .

It was true there still seemed plenty to do. Joanna for one was busier than ever. Kate had supposed that once everything had stopped growing and been picked, eaten or sold work in the garden would slacken off, but autumn, it appeared, was when most of the hard labour was done. She shared a lot of it, happier now working with Joanna. For in the past few weeks Joanna had shed much of her reserve. The aura of sadness which had worried Kate had dropped away, and she had almost a look of happiness about her, as though she had accepted life as it was and found she could be content with it. Today she had actually agreed to take a whole day off to go with Penny Forsyth and Ilona Bellshaw on a frivolous shopping spree in Edinburgh.

Only Harriet had not recovered, and everything she did, all her cherished committees and meetings and projects, had lost their savour for her. She went on with them doggedly, pale and tight-lipped, but the zest had gone from organising and inter-fering, and she lived, as Kate knew, for the brief, crumpled, thumb-marked missives with a Hay-on-Wye postmark. Today she was on a WRI excursion to Stirling, but it had been clear from her tight-lipped concentration on a dozen pieces of trivia before leaving that her heart had not been in it.

Goodness, it was cold. Kate went into the hall from the kitchen passage and found the outer porch door open as it had stood all summer. Definitely time to close it. Perhaps it would be agreeable to spend the winter somewhere warmer, she reminded herself with an attempt at humour, as she heaved aside the cast-iron stag which held back the door.

It was strange to be on her own in the house, especially at such a gloomy time of day. Grannie had gone with Gilbert to the Kyle of Sutherland for an eightieth birthday party.

'Into the decades everyone wishes to mark,' she had said cynically. 'Not sure they'll see the next. Well, at eighty I should hope not.'

They wouldn't be back till the following evening.

Shivering, Kate said to Buff, 'Time for the fire to be lit, what do you think, Buffie?'

Buff wagged his tail. It sounded like a promising suggestion of some sort, and Kate was notoriously a soft touch.

'Then I suppose we'd better do those silly chickens before it gets dark.'

Buff's tail sank. That sounded less enthusiastic.

The hall was dark and unwelcoming. Kate thought of the stalkers on the hill, Colin Devereaux with Max, his son Peter with Doddie, worming their way through bog and wet heather. They didn't have to, of course. Still, it would be nice if everything was warm and bright when they came in. She'd light the morning-room fire, and this one as well. She had always enjoyed the times last winter when she had come in from snow and biting wind to see the flames leaping up below the high panelled chimney breast.

Busy, content, looking forward to Max coming back as she always did, she whisked through the chores, and though the hens did not profess themselves perfectly ready for bed Buff was delighted to give her a hand. Torquil was on the hill, doing a day's work for a change, as Max had said, but Persie was in, for the nights had been sharp of late. Seeing her cosy in her straw-filled box tugged at Kate once more with its reminder that winter was all but here.

The men were late but there was plenty to do. Dinner for six, as Joanna and Harriet intended to be back in time for it, was no problem to Kate now, but if she got everything as far on as possible then she could look after the frozen stalkers when they finally appeared.

'God, that looks good,' Max exclaimed gratefully, seeing the huge fire when they came wearily in, having shed their boots and outer jackets in the boiler room but still in soaked breeches and stockings. 'We had to go out almost to the march. Wounded stag. We got him in the end, but nowhere near the track. Doddie's bringing him down with Torquil. I'll take a dram out for him presently.'

'For Doddie, I assume,' said Colin Devereaux, putting his thumbs in some smart scarlet braces and thrusting his wet backside towards the fire. 'Oh, Kate, my darling, bless you. How did you know that late as it is I was yearning for tea? Whisky to follow in short order, but tea, tea, tea before anything.'

Max and Peter pulled up chairs to the hearth, stretched out steaming stockinged feet to the flames, warmed red damp swollen hands.

'How about hot toddies?' suggested Kate.

'Nothing better. Have we got any Crabbie's? I thought that wind would go straight through me when I was pinned on the open ground above the big stone.'

Kate thought 'the big stone', as a description for one square yard in several thousand acres of rocky ground, lacked definition, but the other two apparently knew precisely where Max meant. Swapping accounts of their sufferings, rehearsing the day's doubts and decisions in the minutest detail, they declined pleasurably from boisterously high spirits into eyelid-drooping lethargy.

'We're not in any mad hurry, are we, Kate?' Max asked, filling Colin's glass again.

'Except to remove the smell of peat,' Peter Devereaux suggested, lifting a ripe tweed elbow to sniff it assessingly. 'Mostly peat, anyway.'

'Joanna was to pick Harriet up at about eight in Kirkton,' Kate told Max. 'But no one was quite certain when the WRI bus would get back.'

'And with that yacking crew it will take them another half

hour at least to say goodbye,' Max yawned, settling deeper into his leather armchair.

'I'll go up and have a bath, I think,' Peter decided, a realistic seventeen-year-old who judged correctly that the whisky bottle had come his way for the last time.

'I'll go and feed Buff,' Kate said.

But nobody made the effort to move. In the brief lull as they thought about summoning the energy to get up, the only sound was the settle and stir of a log. And a strange falling, trickling sound in the cavity of the wall beside the fireplace.

Max frowned, tilting his head.

'Sounds as though you've got mice in that wall, Max,' Colin remarked idly.

'No, not mice.' Something in Max's tone arrested Kate and she turned her head to look at him, puzzled.

He was coming sharply to his feet and the colour had drained dramatically, frighteningly, from his face.

'That's not mice. Stay here, Kate,' he ordered. 'Don't go upstairs, any of you. I'm going to have a look.'

Chapter Thirty-Four

Afterwards it seemed to Kate that after the single moment of icy questioning, when she understood only that some dire emergency was at hand but had barely grasped what it could be, the time which followed was one long shapeless struggling muddle, dark, harried, and fearful. A moment that emerged clearly in later memory was Max saying briefly, 'Phone's burned out, I'll go to the farm,' and her selfish panicking wish that he had sent one of the others, or taken her with him. Need for him in that first moment of realisation overrode everything. But practical sense cut through the panic; he would get there and back faster than anyone else.

Then there was the race round the house, shutting every door and window, of which there seemed suddenly hundreds, and the moment when she heard from the foot of a flight of stairs which led to the attics a terrifying greedy crackling from above. Crystal clear too remained the second's pause below the spiral stair to her own room in the tower, decisions about what to rescue refusing to jell into sensible answers, and discovering that no one thing she owned had more importance than another. It was as though, even in her fear-driven haste, she had been given a moment's calm to say goodbye without a pang to everything which had belonged to her previous life.

Then there was vivid relief that Grannie was not here to see this, to be distressed, bundled out of the way, frustrated at her own uselessness. There was a moment of blind panic when the women asked what they should do and she couldn't force herself to work out the most useful contribution without getting in the way of the men, already manhandling heavy objects into the garden. Then as though a fog cleared from her brain she took them to start collecting the silver.

For everyone had come, the whole glen. That she confusedly knew; familiar faces were everywhere. Big brawny men accustomed to handling stags and bales and heavy machinery were tossing fragile antiques from hand to hand, and she heard Harriet admonishing them to take care, and laughter bubbled up irrepressibly. Then Joanna appeared at her side saying, 'Come on, we'll do the decent china and after that the stuff in the drawing-room cabinets. Not a hope of getting near the library.'

Penny Forsyth was there, and Kate heard her saying with quick authority to someone, 'No, stop, don't empty the stuff out, take the whole drawer and carry it in that.'

And there was James, coatless, all his indolence thrown aside, carrying the vast Lady Elizabeth Butler battle scene from the dining-room down the stairs with Andrew Forsyth. But when had they appeared? When had the fire engines come, and when had the snow started which, she learned with incredulity, had held them up on the way? How long did it all go on, snatching things up and handing them down the rough relay to the courtyard, with the wind driving the smoke and flames with roaring triumphant speed along the web of corridors and up the winding stairways?

At some point she found herself in the back of a police car, shivering so uncontrollably that a large friendly policeman put his arm round her while she gave her statement, and she cuddled up to him with unself-conscious gratitude. She scarcely understood the drift of their questioning. So she had lit the fire? And what time had that been? How did she know it was that time? And what was her position, exactly, in the household? That had been a poser.

She remembered Doddie, when the sparks began to arc an unbelievable distance from the house, putting Buff in the Fourtrak and driving it away to the furthest point of the lawn. Perhaps it was then that she understood the house could not be saved. Or did realisation come as she ran back from depositing a bundle of ivories in the safety of the garage and looked up at the high turreted jumble of roofs and saw the orange tongues licking down over the crest?

Hours and hours later, it seemed, there were shouts of, 'Everybody out, everybody out,' and a collecting up and rudimentary head-count in front of the stables, for the courtyard was by this time too hot to bear, and Max, his face grimed and looking ten years older, coming to make sure she was safely there, putting his arms round her and dropping his tired head down over hers, saying, 'Oh, my poor little Kate, everything of yours has gone.' She was surprised that he thought it mattered, in view of all that he and the family had lost, but not surprised at all that he continued to hold her close at his side. That seemed natural and good.

The firemen were trying to contain the fire; there was nothing more for amateur helpers to do. Weary, filthy and saddened, estate people, friends and the family staying in the Burn Cottage watched the big house roar like a torch against the light snowfall and the autumn night. The smell of burning, which would pervade the glen for days, prickled acridly in their nostrils. There was a great sense of shared grief, of mutual support. Words, tears, touch were easy to exchange. Kate felt that, even for her, the whole glen was there to care for her and comfort her and give whatever could be given. She found time to be glad Mrs Grant had been spared this.

Ian Murray from the Cluny Arms in Kirkton came to speak to Max. 'I've rooms for you all,' he said briefly. 'Shona's getting them ready. You're more than welcome.'

'We've room at the Mennach,' Willie Mearns put in, and behind him Jim Coupar, haggard and shaken, murmured his own offer of hospitality.

'You could come up tae us,' Colleen urged Kate, her voice rough with smoke and tears. 'You ken fine we'd be glad to have you.'

'Oh, Colleen, I know, and thank you.' Kate freed herself for a moment from Max's arm to hug her.

Andrew Forsyth signalled with a nod and raised brows that Alltmore too was ready to take them in.

'It's very good of you all and we're grateful,' Max said, 'but I think if Ian's got enough room we'd probably prefer to stay together. Unless you'd rather go with Colleen, Kate?' He could not bear the thought of being separated from her in this moment of heightened feeling and shock, but he wanted what she wanted and didn't even question this new priority.

She felt as he did, that she must be with him, and hugging Colleen again promised to go and see her tomorrow. As she said it a startled and frightening blankness yawned before her. Life suddenly had no known parameters. She had no possessions, no room, no roof – beyond that no job, no role, no function. Tomorrow – what meaning did the word have? Where would she go, what would she do? She clutched Max's hand, shivering, and his fingers closed firmly round hers.

'Come on, warmth and hot food is what we all need now,' he said. 'Colin, do you want to follow me with Peter? Kate, sweetheart, you go and get in the jeep with Harrie and Jo – and cheer up poor old Buff, he must be terrified. I'll say goodnight to people and be with you in a couple of minutes.'

It felt extraordinary to walk with Harriet and Joanna, with nothing to take or carry, conscious of emptiness behind them where for many generations had stood a secure and solid home, down the lawn to the randomly parked Fourtrak, Buff's anxious face at the steamed-up window, while Max went round every person present and thanked them with deep sincerity for their help. As he turned away, his face rigid with held-down emotion, for the responses as he went round the circle had been unashamedly frank and poignant, James caught him for a quick word.

'You could all come to Riach, you know. We'd manage something.'

Not a hot bath perhaps, Max thought with affection, the lump in his throat even harder to deal with. 'Thanks, James, but we've got Colin and Peter to look after. We'd better stick together, and it's easy for the hotel to lay it on. I'm only thankful mother hasn't had to go through all this. I'll have to catch Gilbert in the morning before they start for home.'

James nodded. 'I'll come tomorrow, and bring the men over to help.' His usually lugubrious face looked in the lurid light alert and positive.

Max looked at him, then reached both hands to shake his in a second's hard grip. 'Thanks, James,' he said. He hardly dared think of all that must be done tomorrow, and to have the support and understanding of this lifelong friend would mean a lot.

It was a strange night at the hotel, which was disconcertingly bustling and bright when they arrived, for after the wild scene of the fire it seemed impossible that ordinary things like electricity could be functioning normally. Ian Murray had laid on hot drinks and soup and sandwiches for everyone and the active scene felt oddly remote to Kate, as though it belonged to an existence she had once known but could barely recall. She couldn't have described later a single detail of the room she was given, but remembered forever the warmth and softness of the brushed cotton nightdress Shona Murray lent her, the sort of garment she would never wear but which in this moment of need could not have been more perfect.

Joanna and Harriet shared a room next to hers, leaving their door open, as Max, further down the corridor next to Colin and Peter, also did. All of them came and went freely from one room to another throughout the night, suffering an urgent shared need for company when dreams and horrors shook them awake. Worn out as they were, with bumps and bruises which they hadn't even known they'd collected beginning to throb uncomfortably, they found themselves strangely reluctant to put out the light and lie down and try to sleep. For alone in the dark there were no defences against the images of the night.

Only Harriet wept, but each one of them wanted contact and support. Kate's worst problem was that she couldn't get warm and Max went to find a couple of hot-water bottles for her, then sat for half an hour propped on the pillows beside her while she gratefully put one to her feet and hugged the other, though drawing greater comfort from his encircling arm.

It was essential therapy for them both to talk out their experiences, though even to Max Kate could not put into words the moment of pure fear when she had seen the flames come over the roof, and it would be a long time before Max would tell her of the moments of icy terror when Kate had been giving her statement in the police car and he had accounted for everyone but her, terrified she had dived back into the burning building to rescue one more useless treasure.

They even found things to laugh about, for in the down-to-earth manner of the glen humour had been there alongside muscle, determination and a matchless resourcefulness.

'That's a fine thing to do to the laird, take his shirts and leave his breeks,' a voice had called as a figure silhouetted against the glow was seen carrying out an armful of hangers with jackets and shirts. A roar of releasing laughter had gone up, and another when Doddie's voice exclaimed in disgust, 'Here, what's this you've just carried out, Lexy? A bucket of coal? Man, I'm thinking we can do without that!'

Kate came nearest to breaking down when she thought of Grannie and Laura being told the news. She began literally to shake, imagining this, but Max was firm.

'It's only things. Expendable objects. We're all safe, and that's what matters.'

She pressed close to him, nodding, dealing with the dangerous surge of emotion as best she could. Neither of them moved or minded when Joanna came in, moving like a sleepwalker, her wildly curling hair still damp from the shower, and with the same naturalness stretched herself out wearily beside them. Buff had followed her, still uneasy and restless in spite of most of the family being on hand.

'Here, Buff, you'd better get up as well,' Max said. 'You're in this too.' Buff didn't need asking twice.

'Harriet would tick you off about Shona's duvet cover,' Joanna said with a little laugh which smoothed some of her tension away, and Max and Kate laughed with her, not unkindly.

In the morning, though the Murrays and their staff collected up all they could for them, they basically had nothing of their own but the blackened stinking clothes of last night. It was a muted group who gathered, gritty-eyed and aching as though they'd run a marathon the day before, in the hotel dining-room for breakfast. Before it ended Max was summoned to the telephone, and from that moment on was sucked into a millstream of demands – insurance agent, assessors, police, press, salvage firms, fire brigade – for the house was still burning – and, as soon as he got back to Allt Farr, organising the stream of volunteers who came to help.

Joanna went to fetch Laura, for horrendous as the ruins looked, water now doing more damage than the fire itself, everyone agreed this was too important an event for her to miss. Her first questions when she was told what had happened were, 'Is Buff all right? And what about Persie and Torquil?'

Kate and Harriet went to Muirend and as though struggling through a bad dream did their best to assemble the basic necessities to see them all through the next couple of days. When they got back they found many contributions left in the empty Sawmill Cottage, where they had decided to set up base. People sent clothes and food (from Sally Danaher it was ready cooked which was truly kind) but also thoughtful extras like the giant bottle of Radox in Penny's box, cassette player and tapes from Charlie Fleming, an electric blanket for Grannie from Ilona Bellshaw. Drumveyn, like Riach, sent manpower, and the long depressing business began of cleaning and attempting to dry out any items worth salvaging. Messages and offers of help poured in and Meg Coupar at the farm had little time to do anything but answer the telephone, but made no complaints.

In the late afternoon Gilbert drove slowly up the drive and pulled up in front of the still smoking ruin of the house. Kate was in the garage with Max, where the freezers had been plugged in with their contents unharmed, looking for butter which she and Harriet had forgotten to buy.

'Ah,' Max said, as he heard the car, and Kate saw his face tighten in anticipation of what his mother would feel. But Grannie, out of the car leaning on her stick, hid whatever shock she felt under a robust stoicism. With cool eyes she surveyed the blackened towers and gables, the spaces in between.

'So that's that,' she said, turning away. 'A chapter closes. How lucky that not all the cottages are busy.'

No tears or embraces, no exclamations of horror or concern. Gilbert looked more shocked than she did, his jowls trembling as he took in the devastation.

The outside world fell away with extraordinary completeness in the days that followed. Life contained nothing but the burned, twisted, soaking remnants of familiar things. It was a shock, when someone checked the weather forecast, to hear unchanged voices, unchanged phrases, as though nothing had happened at all.

The Munros sat round the table in the living-dining-room of No.1 Sawmill Cottages, lunching off smoked salmon, home-made bread and a very good hock, since like the freezers the cellar had survived. Kate was taking Laura back to school. It had been her choice to go. In spite of the feeling of closeness and involvement of the four days since the fire had destroyed the fabric of their lives, she had felt the family should have some time alone to discuss plans for a future in which she had no part.

Also she needed to think. The enhanced emotions stirred up by drama had revealed with disturbing acuteness how focused on Max she had let herself become. It was increasingly hard not to show what she felt, particularly when he treated her with this new open affection and concern. Indeed the whole family, whether deliberately or not, had made her feel she was one of them and that her place was with them.

Grannie, looking round the silent group, each deep in his or her own thoughts, knew with a lurch of unaccustomed nervousness that she mustn't waste this opportunity. She would not have engineered Kate's absence, but these things would be better said without her. Bravely Grannie seized the moment.

'Your attention please,' she said crisply. 'Here is a maternal announcement.'

Max's eyes narrowed. This sounded serious.

'No interrupting,' Grannie warned, rounding them up with an imperative glance. How appalling Harriet looked, drained and hopeless to the point of illness, with red-rimmed eyes and the pink tip of her nose almost translucent. Would she be able to reach out and grasp what Grannie wanted so badly to offer them, the one thing she had come to see she had so indefensibly denied them.

'The house has gone,' she began. 'We have to accept that. Even with the insurance there is no possible way it could be rebuilt as it was, and I for one have no hankering to see that happen anyway.'

Max watched her and, knowing his mother as he did, a strange certainty of what was coming coiled deep inside him. As the extent of the damage had become clear he too had been seized by a vast, defiant relief.

'A long tyranny,' Grannie said softly, almost to herself, then went on, brisk again, 'We would never have had the courage to close the door and walk away. Now we have been offered a clean slate on which to draw any plan for living that we choose.' She saw the colour rise in Joanna's cheeks and knew her surmise of the past few weeks had been correct. Guilt stung her to think it had taken such drastic events to make her act. 'Once, we needed the house and the house was there. It was inconceivable to abandon it but in the end it took over our lives. Now we have the sort of chance to start again from basics which can be granted in few lives. We have been offered, each of us, liberty. No, dear Harrie,' (both Max and Joanna found themselves wondering how many times they had heard such an endearment addressed to their sister) 'don't speak yet. We are fortunate survivors, since we had a choice of houses ready to walk into. Though I have to say, Max, I never realised this fire was such a poor performer. Can nothing be done about it? We have lost many beautiful and valuable things but I for one can live without an eighteenth-century metamorphic table and sundry country house Raeburns. No.' Frowning, she concentrated her thoughts again. 'What I want you all to understand and act upon is this freedom. The monster that gobbled effort and worry and money has gone. Allt Farr could go too, if that's what you want. You may wish to continue as before, or you may not.' She held up an autocratic hand as three mouths opened. 'Please, don't say a word yet. Everything is raw and confused just now. I want each of you to give yourselves time to think, time to decide honestly.'

The whirling thoughts, released, excited, tentatively hopeful, could be felt in the room.

'I shall go and rest,' said Grannie, suddenly very tired. A decision would be required of her too, she knew, and would entail a sacrifice for which she was not sure she had the courage. 'Think,' she repeated, accepting Max's arm. '*Honestly*,' she threw back from the door, and even Harriet, her thoughts scurrying like creatures in a live-animal trap, managed to raise a wobbly smile at the austere command.

Chapter Thirty-Five

As his mother had guessed and hoped would be the case, Max was the first to act. Although in the immediate stunned aftermath of the fire there was no question of Kate leaving them, he knew she would soon feel there was no further excuse for staying, and would snatch at any half-satisfactory solution in her determination to go. That was a matter of practical urgency, but even without it he knew he could not have waited much longer to tell her how he felt about her. He had no idea how she would react, and that was rather salutory, he discovered. He was afraid she would gaze at him in disbelief if he told her he dreaded facing life without her. But it was true. Her gentleness and candour had made him look with new eyes not only at his way of life, but at his attitudes and behaviour, and it had not been a comfortable process. He felt Kate had brought him up all standing in a course he might otherwise have followed with increasing dissatisfaction for the rest of his life, but without her he did not trust himself not to revert to it.

How to embark on the subject without scaring her out of her wits was his next problem. He found his chance the next day. The matter of clothes had become pressing, and Harriet had taken a muttering Grannie down to Perth. Joanna, who had withdrawn from communication almost entirely since Grannie's bombshell, had vanished. She would have been surprised at how much fellow-feeling her brother had for her, though it did not carry him quite as far as to guess what she was doing.

Kate was busy with the job they all turned to these days, futile as it usually was – refurbishing some trophy turned up by the salvage men who now swarmed over the ruins, their hard hats bobbing about like so many Smarties. They were making what was left of the structure safe and removing skip after skip of charred and stinking rubbish. There was little the family could do and they felt oddly at a loss with the last of the cottages empty, the point of work in the garden suddenly in question, nothing required of them.

Kate was rubbing at a silver salver, twisted out of shape by the heat, carbon blackening its engraving. It would never be beautiful or even usable again, but such reclaimed items had a special value now.

I could flatten it more or less into shape, Max found himself thinking, and knew the instinct was to help Kate more than to preserve the silver for its own sake.

Kate looked up at him with a welcoming smile that made what he wanted to say easier, yet at the same time a thousand times more crucial and nerve-racking. 'Shall I make tea?' she offered. 'It's miserably cold, isn't it? I don't think I've felt properly warm for days.'

'I'll make it.' He wanted to be there beside her in the tiny kitchen. He wanted the ordinariness yet the staggering potential novelty of it.

'I'll just finish this, though I don't think all the black will ever come off.'

They never drank the tea. Suddenly a moment's more delay was unbearable to Max. 'Kate.' His voice rough, jerky, he turned to her abruptly, checking her busy hands. She turned her head, her eyes widening in question but, which Max could not know, her heart giving a great slamming thud of hope.

Slow down, slow down, Max reminded himself, and even though it was an inner voice it seemed stifled and breathless.

'Kate, look, we've been having a family discussion about the future, about all our futures – how things will be different now that the house has gone – what we want to do.' He found he'd expended all his breath already, and drew in more as though he could hardly remember how to do it. 'I just thought we could talk, you and I, about what you'd like to do.'

'Well, of course, I –' Kate began bravely. Was that all? Then what possible choice was there now?

'No, wait. God, I'm saying this so badly.' Max closed his eyes for a second, fiercely ordering his thoughts, his words, not realising how grim his face looked, lined and tired as it was after the stressful days and broken nights he'd been suffering.

Kate felt hopeless tears gather. No prospect had ever looked so bleak as being driven down that twisting, well-loved road, down from the hills and the glen, back to drab and solitary normality.

'We want you to stay,' Max said baldly, now looking intently into her anxious brown eyes. 'I want you to stay. I want you to be here, part of whatever changes come. I know you probably think I'm a foul-tempered brute, half your age again, but I think you're the best thing that ever came to Allt Farr or into my life, and I don't want to lose you. I don't want to frighten you off – we can take any amount of time to think about things, adjust to the new situation, talk, get to know each other better, but all I ask now is that you don't desert us.'

The words poured out urgently once he had begun, and Kate gazed at him incredulously, then after a moment of frozen stillness which seemed to Max to last for ever, she lifted her small hands, grey-black with silver polish, and grasped his wrist, then leaning forward laid her forehead very lightly against his upper arm.

It was a gesture of acquiescence – or perhaps appeal? Rigid with hope and doubt, Max looked down on the bowed curly head, the baggy collar of someone else's sweater sagging away from the childishly thin neck. He felt consumed by a passionate desire in general terms to protect her for ever, in immediate terms to crush the life out of her in a stupendous hug.

'Kate?' His voice sounded as though he hadn't used it for a year. 'Kate?'

She swung back her head, her eyes alight, smiling through her tears. That was all. She never did say very much. She simply smiled at him, and tension washed out of him in a great releasing wave of thankfulness and joy as he freed the arm she was clutching and wrapped it round her. He had never in his life felt such simple soaring carefree jubilation.

Joanna had not known she was going to walk to Riach. She had believed she was still screwing up her courage, still fighting off old doubts and a crippling lack of self-confidence. She had gone for a walk along the hill, she thought. But her feet had taken the route Kate had once famously ridden on Torquil, and they had simply gone on carrying her along the grassy track edged by rain-dark flattened bracken, crossed by bustling burns swollen by the rain which had so added to the problems of salvage work. After a while she stopped trying to think or decide what she was doing. Years ago she had made a decision, and it had been the wrong one. This time the decision would not be hers alone.

She felt conspicuous and vulnerable as she crossed the flat open ground where Riach stood like a house put down carelessly on a Monopoly board. But no shrieking children's voices hailed her, no window ran up — probably no Riach window could, she reminded herself, whistling in the dark.

The hall was a silent ice cavern; James had made sure no kitchen sounds could penetrate here. As Joanna opened the sitting-room door and saw him stretched out in somnolent peace doubt assailed her. She should never have come; nothing had changed. This was the precise image he had presented through the desolate years after losing Camilla. He would never truly shake off this undemanding, self-protective torpor. He hadn't moved; he'd think Bridie had come in with more logs or another bottle. She could retreat; he would never know she had come.

But James, coming out of an agreeably relaxed half-doze induced by a long successful day on the hill during which he'd got two stags, followed by a couple of generous drams, had registered there were neither children's voices nor the slap of Bridie's heavy tread followed by an avalanche of logs crashing round his ankles. With an unusually active movement, some instinct warning him, he rose quickly from the deep recesses of his lair.

He had fantasised about just such a moment but never, either during the long period underground, which was how it now felt, or during this summer when he had discovered that being rebuffed by Kate was not nearly as important as the new interest in life she had given him, had Joanna come here alone. Seeing her standing there now swept the years away, bringing back with anguish his disbelief and hurt when he heard she was married.

He hastily crammed fantasy back into place, shaking himself properly awake. 'Jo, how nice to see you. Come to the fire. Anyone else with you?'

'I walked,' she said, vaguely aware that this wasn't what he had asked. 'James.' Further than that it seemed impossible to go.

James hesitated, uncertain what was required of him. Then his heavy-featured face softened to a look only the twins had ever seen — and they took no notice. Joanna looked so uncertain and defenceless, her face, usually serenely good-natured, pinched and strained. During the unreal days since the fire concern for personal appearance had ceased to exist. The magnificent hair which he had always loved didn't look as though it had been brushed since she got out of bed this morning, if then, and she was wearing under her gardening jacket a grey sweater of Max's with streaks of creosote down the front. James wasn't used to being needed; in his life there had always been someone more competent and energetic on hand and he had allowed himself to be content with that. But this dear girl, part of his world for ever, this gentle person who never drove him or bossed him or expected more of him than he could give, had come to find him at this time when her whole existence had been thrown into chaos. He took two steps with his long gangly legs, threw his long tweed-clad arms around her, and crushed her to him in an all-consuming wordless hug.

Joanna responded by bursting into tears. For more than half her life this moment had seemed unattainable. To be in James's arms at last was so utterly, completely natural, as though she had always known exactly what it would feel like. She pressed her nose against the jacket which had belonged to his uncle and had crawled through many a bog in its time, and she inhaled its rich smell with tearful, abandoned satisfaction.

They almost forgot to talk at all. Then, realising it, they laughed at themselves, pulled up a faded velvet stool close to James's chair, added a few logs to the neglected fire, and released a spate of words which had waited a long, long time to be spoken.

It was always you. That was what the words were saying.

'But Camilla? You loved Camilla.'

'Well, you know, I did,' James said, as though it still slightly surprised him. 'But she organised the whole thing, you know.'

'How you amaze me.'

James laughed aloud, a sound this room had heard too rarely in past years. 'She had all that tremendous energy, she just bowled me along. It was marvellous when you thought you were choosing to let it happen, then it got a bit worrying when you realised you couldn't stop it. But she had a big heart, and I love to see Syb so like her, so full of zest for everything, with that same rollicking laugh. When you had gone I was so lost, Jo, you can't imagine. I really needed someone like Camilla to take me in hand. You've seen what a mess I make of things when I'm left on my own.'

'You've come out of it though. You didn't slide back when Kate wasn't interested.'

There was a wonderful simplicity in not having to choose words, not having to be tactful. Everything would be received exactly as it was meant. Always, Joanna thought, with a shaky astounded glimpse ahead into a future she had not dared to contemplate.

'Dear little Kate, what a delight she is. Thank goodness for her, or God knows when I'd have woken up. Yes, when I saw her with Jeremy and realised it would never have crossed her mind that I was fascinated by her, it was tempting to give up, but she'd done too good a job.' He smiled, leaning down to sweep aside the live, bright tangled hair and kiss her cheek. 'Then I began to dream old dreams again.'

Grannie came home in a very bad temper. Several hours of Harriet's company never did her much good, and the chore of struggling out of her clothes in over-heated shops, with the added insult of insistent music offending her ears, and trying on horrible conventional garments which were nothing like the vibrant exotica she preferred, had added up to an exhausting trial. Her hip was hurting, even her repaired ankle ached again under the strain, and dismay at what she planned invaded her in spite of all her efforts to repel it. But she had to do something about the lives of her children. The situation was absurd; worse, it had become damaging and unnatural. This dramatic, unlooked-for chance for individual freedom must not be marred by any feeling of responsibility for her.

Her temper was not improved by a call at the Gate Lodge. Mrs Grant, who needed a lot of support and reassurance, liked to dwell on the awfulness of the fire in morbid detail. 'And fancy me not being there . . . .'

How hateful Grannie found it to drive past the wreck of her home, to continue down the farm track and pull up in front of the row of barren little cottages, convenient, more than adequately furnished for holiday lets, but so miserably without soul or character. Pulling on the mask of calm indifference she had elected to wear, she limped ahead of a laden Harriet into the temporary refuge which depressed her so profoundly.

Max and Kate were standing together in front of the fire. Hah! thought Grannie, her spirits lifting at once. Why should that be the classic spot for startled lovers to stand? Was it the suggestion of leaping up from a sofa, the vain pretence of having some shared business on the hearthrug, the casual leaning against a mantelpiece? Her dark eyes and arrogant face lit up in one of the brilliant smiles which reminded people that once she had been beautiful.

'Perth was a madhouse,' Harriet complained, struggling to get her slipping carrier bags safely onto the round table. 'People are doing their Christmas shopping already, can you believe it?'

'Darling child,' said Grannie simply, taking Kate into her arms. 'You are going to stay with us.'

'Oh, it's far too soon for her to think of going,' said Harriet, her back turned, opening a bag because she couldn't remember what was in it. 'After such a shock it would be most unwise to start making plans so soon, and I always say—'

Max and Grannie pulled faces at each other, Kate's face was alight with laughter. Max stepped across the small room, took his sister by the scruff of the neck and turned her round. 'Do shut up, Harrie,' he begged her.

Chapter Thirty-Six

Grannie's news, delivered in a succinct manner which warned that overreaction would not be welcome, rocked them all. To leave Allt Farr; to live with Gilbert Rathyln, who, though she was fond of him, she mocked and taunted without mercy; to move to a neat modern bungalow, with square rooms, a fitted kitchen and no fireplaces?

'Don't be ridiculous, it will be heaven,' she said with annoyance as the chorus of remonstration rose. 'It's a perfectly practical and convenient arrangement. Gilbert has been suggesting it for some time.' (Kate thought that sounded somewhat tepid.) 'He says his sciatica gets worse every time he has dinner here. We shall have a most enjoyable time – unlimited gin, unlimited racing, and a garden to make.'

'But you do all that anyway,' Joanna objected. She wanted her mother to be happy but there was nothing here to match her own dazzling relief and certainty. But perhaps at her mother's age it wouldn't be like that.

'It's a bit extreme,' Max said, frowning. Gilbert was an affable bore. Grannie would have him for breakfast; they wouldn't last a week.

'How negative you all are,' Grannie exclaimed, angry now. 'How ungenerous. At last I'm free to abandon that wretched, wretched patchwork, enjoy some civilised leisure and a modicum of comfort, and not one of you can wish me well.'

'Oh, but we do!' Kate cried, anxious and repentant, for though she had said nothing she had shared the general consternation, not least because she hated the thought of Grannie being even five miles away.

'You don't have to live with Gilbert in order to keep warm,' Max pointed out.

Grannie snorted, for once unable to summon words. She had not prepared sufficiently for this opposition, which had taken her by surprise.

'And I shall tuck myself up in the wee Sawmill Cottage,' Harriet cried gaily, biting the bullet before anyone could turn round and say, 'What's to become of old Harrie?' The realisation that if Grannie went she would be quite alone had been almost more petrifying than hearing Letitia was leaving. 'Or Max can do up Craigbeg for me.' But that bit too deep, and she hurried blindly away to make more coffee. In the kitchen she held onto the worktop to steady herself. The safe, familiar walls of the family circle were crumbling round her, just as the actual walls of home had, unbelievably, fallen. At first, beset with the immediate problems of survival, worrying over food and clothes and basic necessities, she had assumed that one day, in time, Allt Farr would be rebuilt and all would continue as before. But as changes came like hammer blows a chill trepidation almost disabled her, so unforeseen, so impossible to take in were these new developments.

It was Kate, herself so recently facing the prospect of being adrift and alone, who realised the true source of Harriet's terror. It was not only that her role of running the house had been taken away, or the disturbing suspicion that she might not be wanted had entered her mind, but nothing protected her now from the possibility of accepting Letitia's proposal to join her.

Kate took her chance to approach the subject, very cautiously, when she found Harriet alone later that morning, standing looking out of the window of the clean and tidy room in the clean and tidy cottage.

'It's odd, isn't it, having so little to do?'

'Oh, there's always plenty to do,' Harriet responded automatically, but she didn't move, looking dragged down and exhausted.

'With everything so miserable here it might be a good chance to get away for a while,' Kate suggested casually. 'Have you thought of it at all?'

'Oh, no, I couldn't,' Harriet said at once, looking ready to push past Kate and escape.

Kate stood her ground. 'Wouldn't you like to go and see Letitia for a few days, to have a rest, and perhaps talk things over with her?'

Harriet gazed at her for a moment with anguished dead-leaf eyes, visibly teetering on some knife-edge of decision, then drew back. 'No, no,' she cried with a horrid gaiety, 'I shall be fine, perfectly all right. Nobody must worry about me.'

Kate, seeing it was useless to persist at present, patted the stiff resistant body which so little liked being embraced. 'Dear Harrie, you won't be on your own, you know that, everyone will still be close by.'

With sweeping but insensitive largesse Joanna offered to have her at Riach. 'Don't know when it would be,' she said airily. 'We'll get down to plans sometime soon. First I want to make sure Laura's happy about it all.' She didn't sound like a mother seriously contemplating stepfather problems, or even particularly conscious of the wrench it would be for Laura to be uprooted from her home. Joanna apparently regarded Riach as a convenient extension of Allt Farr.

Fortunately Laura seemed to feel the same, and Max and James were relieved at the way she took the news.

'Go and live with Syb and Sash? Oh, that'll be brilliant! But what about Persie and dear darling Torq? And I can take Buffie, can't I?'

'Buff's your dog, so he goes of course. Persie can go too, with my very best wishes. Torquil is a working pony and his job's here,' Max reminded her.

'Then I can't go! It can't happen, it will never work,' Laura protested wildly, clutching at him with desperate hands. 'Uncle Max, you know Persie and Torquil can't bear to be apart, they'd break their hearts, it would be awful for them. Buff and I will have to stay here with you and Kate.'

'Merciful heaven protect me,' said Max. 'Joanna, I withdraw my consent.'

'I feel that's excessive,' James objected lazily. 'How about trading garrons? I'd be perfectly happy to welcome Torquil to my establishment.'

'Too bloody right you would, he's the best working pony in the glen. But if it's the only way of making sure Laura goes—'

'Oh, darling, darling Uncle Max!'

'You're welcome to her,' Max told James, unwinding her skinny arms from round his neck. 'Old Torquil's going to be a bit put out though, when he gets to Riach and finds Molly's being shipped over here.'

'Oh, no, that's – !' Laura began, aghast at this new heart-rending complication.

'Forget it. Torquil will have Persie, and that's it. James, are you sure you know what you're doing? You'll have as many hinds underfoot as I did.'

Laura was pleased to hear the less important news that her uncle and Kate would be getting married.

'He was always so cross when Ann was here,' she said privately to Kate, in a grown-up manner.

Kate laughed and kissed her. She was living in a happy dream, but sometimes felt events were hurtling her along too fast. The idea of marrying Max still awed her and she was glad he felt as she did, that plans should wait till they had emerged from present upheavals.

James and Joanna, on the other hand, were not prepared to

wait five minutes. Easy-going though they were, they felt they had wasted enough time. They wanted minimum fuss, minimum planning. So long as the children were happy – and Sybilla and Sasha were ecstatic at the idea of being joined by Laura and Buff – they saw no point in delay, amusing their friends by this summary approach.

Grannie kept her own counsel. She had not yet, as she warned the family, found an appropriate moment to tell Gilbert of her decision and no one was to breathe a word of it till she did.

It was the change Kate found hardest to accept. In the months of growing attraction for Max, of realising how much she needed and depended upon him, she had not thought much beyond being able to stay at Allt Farr on the terms on which she had first come. That included the family group, the coming and going and activity which added up to something so different from her previous life. It was odd to picture a household for two. It would be wonderful, of course, but still there nagged the feeling that it was too neat, too selfish almost.

Harriet remained adamant that she would not intrude on the newly-weds, as she put it.

Her cheerfulness set Kate's teeth on edge. 'We must persuade her that we're quite happy to have her with us,' she urged Max.

'Are we?' he grunted, but actually he agreed. Delightful as it would be to live alone with Kate, he was inured to the extended household and had never truly envisaged being free of it. It amused him that Kate was so ready to take it on, and the memory of Ann's warnings on the subject produced a smile of dour satisfaction.

'Being on our own was never part of the plan,' Kate insisted to Harriet. 'You mustn't feel we don't want you.'

'I just never expected the house to burn down like that,' sniffed Harriet, having trouble with a Disprin which hadn't gone down, and gulping awkwardly and noisily. Never, thought Kate, between amusement and exasperation, had she seen anyone have so much trouble as Harriet with simple everyday actions and objects.

'It must be horrid for you, when everyone's so busy making plans,' she said, putting an arm round the stooped shoulders. 'But you must do exactly what you want to do. And don't forget Letitia's still there. When things have settled down a bit here you can go and see her whenever you feel like it.'

'That's true,' agreed Harriet, brightening. 'There's far too much to do at the moment. Joanna's so casual about everything and James is worse. Someone will have to see to the wedding for them, no matter how simple it is. I couldn't get away just now anyway, with the children's party and the carol service and all the other Christmas things coming up.'

Later Kate said to Max, 'She seemed almost relieved, as though it was easier to believe she couldn't go. I think it's just too big a step for her.'

'She doesn't understand her own feelings. They probably terrify her.'

'I think if she's determined to be on her own she'd prefer to live at Craigbeg. Happy associations.'

'She can have it if she wants it. I wouldn't have to do so much to it then. But she's no Letitia. I think she'd feel very cut off on her own up there.'

There persisted in Kate the uneasy feeling that everyone was in too great a hurry. The fire had been an unavoidable disaster, striking out of the blue. This flying apart of the family after it seemed too precipitate, a rushing to extremes. She knew she would never understand how they felt about Allt Farr, but she guessed that for each of them there had been a love-hate element mixed in their commitment to it. She was totally unprepared, however, when Max raised the question of selling up altogether.

'Sell *Allt Farr*?'

'You sound as bad as any of us twenty years ago,' he mocked, his face watchful. 'I thought we'd worked through that one. It isn't holy ground. The whole point of the new dispensation is making choices, surely. If we want to stay we stay, if we don't we quit.'

'But what would you do if—? No, that's not the question, is it?'

'No.'

Kate looked at him for a second, realising what he needed, and drew a deep breath. 'Then this is what I'd like. To live here, to learn as much as I can to help you, to make Harriet feel she's wanted, and to be near Grannie and Joanna and Laura.'

'That seems fairly clear.' Max kept his face blank but the black eyes were filled with loving pleasure.

'And you?' Kate asked.

'The same, broadly speaking. I just wanted to be sure how you felt.'

Kate released tense muscles with relief. 'Then don't scare me like that again. The only thing is, I'm not sure I know where you want to live. We've talked about the Burn Cottage though I'm not keen about the prospect of being flooded out, or staying where we are but you don't like the idea of having neighbours when the other cottages are busy, or making the Top Cottages into one, but I never feel you're truly keen about any of them.'

Max looked away, his face falling into familiar harsh lines, and Kate, realising that an instinct which had been growing to certainty had been accurate, made up her mind. 'Come up to the house with me,' she said, reaching for his hand.

Max raised his eyebrows questioningly, but she shook her head, saying nothing. So without argument he went with her, down the track and across the bridge in a stark dusk with the first stars already so bright that a hard frost was certain.

'I've been wondering, you see,' Kate said, her arm tucked in Max's as he matched his step to hers up the steep slope, 'whether another idea might be possible. Or reasonable, or affordable.'

'Go on.' They halted on the once-pale gravel, now like the churned lawn darkened with the dross of the fire, and looked up at the stark silhouettes of the gables.

'This is probably silly,' Kate said, her nerve failing her at the sight.

'Go on,' Max said again, turning to face her and looking at her closely in the half light.

Already shy about what she wanted to say, made more nervous by that intent scrutiny, Kate hurried into her proposal. 'Well, it's only that sometimes, down at the Sawmill, I've so much missed the light and height of the tower room. It's made me realise how perfectly chosen the site of the house was. And then, although everyone is being terribly sensible and making the best of things, there's such a feeling of exile, isn't there, of the focal point of home having vanished?'

She looked up at Max uncertainly, knowing this would cut close to the bone, and afraid such comments from her, not one of the family yet, might not be acceptable. She was startled when he took her shoulders in a tight grip and said sharply, 'Don't stop there.'

She gathered her courage. 'I wondered if something couldn't be resurrected from the part of the house that was least damaged, a sort of simple, open, new house, with plenty of light – and no draughts. Is it rather a cheek of me to suggest it? I know you'll know best—'

'Did you guess that's what I wanted?' Max cut across her hesitant words. 'Did you know how much it hurt to lose this place, after keeping it going for so long? Ironic, isn't it? I always thought I hated it, but somewhere deep down I always expected my son to inherit it one day, expected Munros to go on living in it through the generations. Common sense told me no one would ever be able to keep it up and that the estate could never support it, but the feeling was still there.'

'You love it,' Kate said.

He laughed, pulling her close in sudden exuberance at the simplicity of being with her. 'Could you honestly contemplate living in the place again?' he asked. 'Not because you think that's what I want?'

'We could design something to suit us,' Kate said eagerly. 'I've had some ideas. Well, more dreams, I suppose, because I didn't really imagine it would be possible. But even to be on this spot, with the garden, and that wonderful view, and – oh, I don't know – the sense of being in the right place.'

'You cannot conceive what this means to me,' Max said, quietly now, and though she could not see them his eyes were wet. 'It's perfectly possible. All the water and so on are in place, there's any amount of stone to hand, and this time we'd build so that we live in the sun and the light.'

'Perhaps we could even use the South Tower again, or part of it!'

'You and your South Tower.' He kissed her with delight, a new optimism about what lay in store surging through him. 'Come on, it's too dark to see anything now. Let's go and draw a million plans.'

It was the last straw for Grannie. She did her best, her very best, making wild suggestions for patios, cupolas, plunge pools – 'Well, that's what I call a Jacuzzi –' conservatory, foldaway walls and a tower-top revolving kitchen. But she hurried away too abruptly, to fetch a handkerchief she said in a brusque voice, and did not reappear.

Kate, awareness sharpened by the disquiet which had persisted whenever Grannie discussed her plans for revamping Gilbert's bungalow to suit her needs, for foreign travel and cruises and being taken racing on demand, slipped after her, unnoticed in a noisy argument about solar panels.

It was too tidy; it was all wrong. She tapped on the door of Grannie's room and went in without waiting for an answer. Grannie was standing beside the dressing table, against the window curtain. The very purposelessness of her position struck Kate. It was a room with nowhere to go, pretty and fresh, functional for easy cleaning. The contrast with Grannie's room in the big house, vividly evocative of her personality with its welter of treasured possessions and flamboyant colours, struck

Kate piercingly. So did the attitude of the tall bony figure, smitten at last, it seemed, by age and infirmity, defeated by events as it had never before allowed itself to be.

'No!' Kate cried in involuntary protest at all this told her. 'Something isn't right. You must *talk* to me.' Skirting the twin beds which all Grannie now owned in the world could not entirely bury, she went quickly to that still figure. 'You must stop pretending.'

'Ah, Kate, it would be you,' Grannie said with dry amusement. 'You are a good little soul, trite though the expression is.'

'Tell me,' Kate insisted gently, not deflected.

'I've been a fool.'

The keen hooded eyes looked away, the mouth folded tightly against more confessions.

'Won't you stay with us?' Kate asked softly. 'I can't bear you to go. And you don't want to go, do you? That's why you haven't talked to Gilbert.'

'How do you know these things?'

'Because I've been frightened and lonely myself.'

Grannie's face slowly broke up, her lips trembling uncontrollably. 'I have imposed such an unforgivable burden on them, on Max especially. I have distorted their lives. The only thing I can give them now is independence to make their own decisions. God knows if Harriet will ever find the courage to seek the happiness that's there for her, improbable as it may be, but Joanna has already redressed the past. And you and Max are not going to be saddled with me any longer,' she ended, rallying, summoning up a flashing smile.

'It seems rather hard on Gilbert,' Kate mused innocently.

It was the perfect line to choose. After one taken-aback moment Grannie let out a reassuring bark of laughter, quite in her normal style. 'Well, if you look at it like that . . . .'

'It would be a nightmare for you both,' Kate said. 'A bungalow? You? Oh, Grannie darling.'

Grannie gripped her hand in a fierce, quite painful, grasp. 'Did you mean what you said? But you cannot possibly want a mother-in-law, and such a mother-in-law, perpetually on hand.'

'I want you and I want Harriet. What I should truly like,' Kate said, her voice not quite steady, her eyes on Grannie's, 'would be to marry Max and be with the family, in the house, exactly as it was. I fell in love with it all. But it's lost and gone. Nothing can bring back the splendid awfulness of it –' Humour overtook the solemn tone in spite of her.

'Those icy mornings with the fog creeping up the spiral stairs.'

'The rat holes in the larder, the jackdaws in the chimneys.'

Laughing they clutched and hugged each other.

'It makes me cold to think of it. Come along, let us go back to the fire,' said Grannie, pushing Kate away and straightening her shoulders with renewed vigour.

'Let's go back and revamp the plans,' Kate amended.

Max rose to his feet as they came in, not even aware that he had done so, his whole being focused on the message he would read in their faces, a sure intuition telling him that whatever had been said it had significance for them all.

For once Grannie found emotion too much for her. Without words she simply drew Kate forward and as it were presented her to Max to do the telling, and he stepped forward, his face breaking into a huge smile, filled with a choking fierce pride in Kate and thankfulness for her.